The Power of Music

BOOK ONE

BRAEDEN PENDERGRASS

To my family and friends, who put up with my writing marathons, caffeine-fueled rants, and all the times I swore, "I'm almost finished with my book!"

THANK YOU!

Whether you actually read this or not, may this prove all those late nights were worth it. And to every hopeless romantic reading this may you always find love stories that make you swoon (or at least don't roll your eyes too hard).

-Brae

Table of Contents

1

May 7th, 2011

The alarm clock screaming, birds on the window pane chirping, and smells of spring filling the air; the start of what was supposed to be forever for Bentley and Michelle.

Bentley woke out of a cold sweat, trying to shake off the nightmare. Today was the day he was going to marry the love of his life, and he wasn't going to let some silly nightmare be a buzzkill. He dreamt that his bride-to-be, Michelle, left him standing at the altar in front of all their friends and family. Every man's worst fear. The whole morning while eating breakfast and getting ready to meet his parents, Bentley tried to shake the nightmare, but it kept getting to him. Something didn't feel right about it, and he had no idea what it was. He's had plenty of gut-wrenching feelings before, like in the State Championship game when his number was called for the final play that won the team the game, but nothing quite this strong. It felt almost like a premonition.

"Mom, Dad, where are you guys at?" Bentley shouted as he entered his parents' house. He wanted to meet up with his parents to go over the plans for the wedding and reception. Although they went over the plans during rehearsals, Bentley still felt that he would somehow mess up. So, he wanted a quick run-through to be well prepared.

"Hey, honey, we're in the kitchen," his mother shouted. Bentley followed the aroma of bacon. His dad sat at the kitchen table reading the morning paper with a cup of orange juice while his mother fried bacon on the stove.

"Mom, Dad, when you guys got married, did you have a gut feeling something was going to go wrong?" Bentley asked.

His mother chuckled a bit as she answered him. "Oh honey, yes, it's just nerves. I was a nervous wreck. I thought I didn't look pretty enough, and he would take one look at me coming down the aisle and jet out of the church, but he didn't. Look at us now, we've been happily married for twenty-one years, and God blessed us with you and your sister."

Mr. Riggs sat the morning paper down on the kitchen table as he looked up at his son with a half-smile and said, "Son, just as your mother just said, it's nothing but nerves. On our wedding day, I was just as nervous as she was, if not more nervous. I was so nervous she had found someone more rich and handsome than me and would leave me standing at the altar looking like a fool in front of all our friends and family."

Bentley looked relieved as he began to tell his parents about his dream, far from a happy ending fairytale.

"Mom, Dad, thank you; I needed that. Especially after the nightmare I had last night. I dreamt Michelle left me at the altar, and I don't know something about that dream just feels so real. It really has me stressing."

With an understanding look on her face, his mother said, "Son, just pray and trust in God that everything will work out. Cause baby, everything *will* work out, I promise you." She leaned over and gave him a kiss on the cheek. His Dad nodded in agreement.

After talking with his parents and going over the wedding plans, it was almost noon, and Bentley needed to get to the venue to begin getting ready. The wedding was set to take place in a little over two hours at The Pavilion in Downtown Raleigh.

When Bentley arrived, he was blown away at how they had made Michelle's dream wedding come to life. The place looked magical; it could have been a Disney princess's wedding. They had strings of lights throughout the venue, white flower petals all over the place, and white drapes from the ceiling. It was so perfect Bentley just knew nothing could go wrong now.

While Bentley waited in dressing room, he could hear the commotion of friends and family starting to arrive. The louder the place became, the more Bentley could practically feel his heart beating out of his chest. Nerves, excitement, and fear consumed him, but he tried to maintain composure.

There was a knock at the door, and in walked Bentley's best friend and partner in crime, Cameron Paige, also the best man. The one man Bentley picked to stand beside him on his big day. If not for Cameron, Bentley would have never met Michelle. Cameron was the popular kid in high school that always threw the best parties, and as fate would have it, freshman year, Michelle and Bentley just so happened to be at Cameron's party after the homecoming game. That night, Cameron saw Bentley staring at this five-foot-five brunette with a killer smile and decided to play Cupid.

"Hey, killer! How's it going in here? You nervous?" Cameron asked.

With a pale look on his face and sweat beading up on his forehead, Bentley looked at him and freaked out.

"Man, do I look alright? I'm sweating bullets and feel dizzy; I'm nervous as hell, man. What are we doing getting married? We're too young. We haven't lived life."

Cameron took a step back. He turned around and closed the door behind him so no one could eavesdrop, and he began to try and calm Bentley down.

"Whoa, man. Take a deep breath and relax. Everything's going to be ok. Yes, you and Michelle are young, but y'all are made for each other. Now, wipe the sweat off your brow, and let's get you out there at the altar so we can get you married." Cameron said with reassurance in his voice, as Bentley started taking slow deep breaths to try and relax.

Bentley smiled at Cameron and said, "Thanks, man. I really needed that. I freaked out with my parents this morning too. Like, I really do want this day to be perfect, but this dream I had last night about Michelle leaving me at the altar, has had me on edge all morning."

Cameron just walked over and wrapped his arms around Bentley and patted him on the back as he guided him out of the room towards the altar.

"If she leaves you at the altar, I will find her myself and hit her with a Rock Bottom, but I don't think you have anything to worry about. I think it's just the nerves driving you crazy, bro. You'll be fine. Now let's get you married." Cameron said.

Standing at the altar were Bentley, Cameron, and the pastor, patiently waiting for the start of the ceremony. Bentley hated that he had to stand at the altar in front of all those people for a long time before the wedding began. He felt as if he could feel everyone in attendance judging him. He didn't know what he was being judged for, but he felt judged. The longer he stood at the altar, the more his temperature began to rise. You could be at the very back of the venue and see clear as day his face turning beet red.

Cameron noticed it, tapped him on the shoulder, and said, "Bro, just relax. Take long, slow deep breaths. You got this." Bentley just shook his head.

The music started to play and out chimed, *"Take My Breath Away,"* a song from Michelle and Bentley's favorite movie to watch together; *"Top Gun."* The song played as the rest of the wedding party started making their way down the aisle. Bentley began to feel some relief as he knew it was almost time to see his bride-to-be so that they could exchange their vows. The music stopped when the last bridesmaid made it down the aisle to the altar, and everyone became silent. After a few seconds of silence, *"Here comes the bride,"* chimed out as everyone rose. Everyone was excited as all get out to see the bride's dress and how beautiful she looked. None of them were more excited than Bentley. He took a big sigh of relief, and the smile on his face grew more prominent. He knew his nightmare was just that, or so he thought.

Yet there was still no sign of the bride. The music continued to play, and the more it played, the more anxious Bentley became. He felt as if his nightmare was becoming a reality. You could begin to hear the congregation grow weary with chatter, making their own assumptions as to why the bride had yet to appear. Cameron's eyes grew more prominent as he feared that his best friend was about to be left standing at the altar. He began thinking of all the ways he would try and console Bentley.

"Man, Cam, what's going on? What's taking her so long?" Bentley asked with fear.

Cameron didn't know how to answer; his eyes sank low as he bowed his head and sighed. "I don't know, man… I don't know." Finally, after five minutes of "*Here Comes the Bride*" playing and no signs of the bride, they stopped the song. Everyone looked at Bentley. Bentley felt three feet tall to a grasshopper and was consumed by heartbreak, fear, and worry as he could feel everyone's beady eyes staring back at him. He knew that they were all waiting for answers. Fighting back tears, Bentley addressed the congregation. "Hey everyone, I don't know where Michelle is now. She should be here but give me about ten minutes to go and try and figure out where she's at."

On the way to Michelle's changing room, Cameron called her phone but wasn't getting through.

"It keeps going to her voicemail Ben," Cameron said as they made their way down the hall to her dressing room. Bentley and Cameron were greeted by Michelle's father, Mr. Champion, who had a confused look on his face.

"Ben, Michelle left. I met her here to walk her down the aisle, and she left. She said she couldn't marry you; she didn't say why; she just said she couldn't. She did leave you a note on the dresser." Mr. Champion said with a confused tone.

Bentley rushed through the door to find the note Michelle had been so thoughtful to leave behind. It was folded up on the vanity like a pop-up name tag addressed to him in her handwriting. He opened the letter and began to read what she had written. He was eager to understand what he had done wrong if anything. He started thinking of all the little things he could and should have done differently to have made her stay.

"Bentley, I hate that it took until our wedding day, but something hit me last night. We've been together since we were 15, and I love you more than anything. But at 20, I realized we're each other's first everything, and we need more life experiences before settling down. It hurts, but we're still so young. We should let go and explore; if it's meant to be, we'll find our way back. I couldn't bear to see the pain in your eyes to be able to say this in person; I hope you understand. I love you with all my heart and hope you forgive me someday."

By the time Bentley reached the end of the letter, his heart was already aching, and tears had begun crashing to the floor. Hopelessness overtook him. Cameron and Mr. Champion stood silently.

After a few moments of complete silence, Cameron finally walked over to Bentley, wrapped him up in the biggest bro hug, and said, "Everything's going to be ok, bro. I got you. I will always be here for you." Bentley finally felt like he didn't have to be strong by himself anymore as he just let go and cried like a baby.

After a few moments, Bentley looked at his watch and realized the ten minutes he asked the congregation to give him was almost up. He took a big breath and puffed out. "I guess it's time to let the friends and family know that there's not going to be a wedding today."

Cameron just pulled away and smiled, saying, "At least there's free booze and food; we can still party. That's one way to get over a broken heart." Bentley let a slight laugh come halfway out as he tried to cover up the aching he felt inside.

Bentley found his way back to the altar, and as he did, he felt the pressure of everyone wanting to know what was happening. Bentley took a massive breath. "Everyone, thank you all for giving me the extra time to find where Michelle was. I also want to thank you all for showing up today for what was supposed to be the best day of mine and Michelle's life. However, with that being said, today, there will not be a wedding. There will not be a future date for one either. Michelle decided to call us off." As Bentley spoke, shock rippled through the congregation.

"Oh, there's free booze and food at the reception. Please help yourselves, I know I will be because I've got sorrows to drown. Bentley continued.

At the reception, everyone was drinking and having a good ole' time while Bentley sat at the little makeshift bar downing shots like water, trying to grasp everything that had transpired. He couldn't believe that his nightmare had become a reality. He was pissed at himself for not trusting his gut. He let his parents and his best friend make him think he was going crazy when he really wasn't.

While sitting at the bar blocking everything around him out, Bentley's mom and dad walked up to him. It was the first chance that they had to speak to him since earlier that morning.

"Hey, son, me and your father just want to say we are so sorry about Michelle leaving you like this. We are so sorry that we took your feelings lightly when you felt something was wrong. Just pray and trust that God will work everything out in your favor. Please don't let this knock you down. You are stronger than you feel right now. We love you." Bentley's mother said as she leaned in to hug and kiss him.

Bentley gave a half-hearted smile, "Thank you guys." Bentley turned his beer up taking a chug before continuing, "This shit hurts so fucking bad, mom. It doesn't help everyone keeps coming up to me saying they are sorry." Faye wrapped Bentley in a huge hug and just held him, as Bentley broke down crying in her arms.

"Son, you need to just come on home with us and quit all this drinking. Especially so you don't get these bartenders in trouble for serving you underage." Steve butted in.

Faye lifted her head and cut her eyes sharply at Steve giving him *"the look"*.

"I'm sorry, I'm just saying." Steve said with a sheepish smile.

Bentley sniffled, wiping away tears, and took a deep breath, "I appreciate the concern, Dad, but we've already paid for the open bar so might as well get our money's worth, right? Besides, drinking numbs the pain, even if it's only temporary."

Faye released Bentley from the hug but kept a supportive hand on his shoulder. "Sweetheart, we understand you're hurting, but drowning your sorrows in alcohol isn't the solution. We're here for you, and we want to help you through this, but this isn't the way, Ben."

Steve nodded in agreement, his expression filled with a mix of worry and fatherly concern. "We love you, Bentley. We know this hurts son because it also hurts your mother and me that we can't stop what you're feeling right now. But your mother is right, this isn't the way, Ben. So come on home with us."

"Dad, Mom, please just leave me alone right now. I need to deal with this my way and this, this is my way." Bentley said in frustration. "Cam's still here, he'll bring me home later." Bentley continued after another swig of beer.

Faye sighed, exchanging a worried glance with Steve, but nodded in reluctant understanding. "Alright, Bentley. But remember, we're just a call away if you need anything. Please be safe son."

Steve patted Bentley on the back, offering a supportive smile. "We'll be waiting for you at home whenever you're ready, son. We love you."

As his parents headed for the venue exit, Faye stopped and looked at Cameron, who was standing close by with his eyes fixed on Bentley, "You keep an eye out on my boy now and please be safe. Both of you."

Cameron just looked at her and smiled. "Don't you worry Faye, I will keep your baby boy safe. You and Steve can go on home and not worry, I've got Ben," Cameron said with solid sincerity.

Bentley took another long sip of his beer, as he watched his parents finally disappear through the exit. The numbness from the alcohol was starting to kick in, but it was just a fleeting distraction from the overwhelming pain in his chest.

After a few moments of watching Bentley closely, Cameron finally approached him at the makeshift bar, concern etched on his face. "Hey, man, you sure you want to be doing this?" he asked, gesturing to the row of shot glasses.

Bentley chuckled bitterly. "What else is there to do? Everything's a mess." He motioned for the bartender to pour another round. Cameron let out a sigh but said nothing.

Cameron looked on attentively as Bentley downed the shot in one swift motion. "Alright. Fine. When you're ready to leave, we'll leave," Cameron said with a mix of concern and defeat in his tone.

Eventually, the alcohol took its toll, and Bentley's surroundings blurred. With a heavy sigh, he pushed himself away from the bar, steadying himself on unsteady legs. Cam, realizing Bentley had reached his limit, guided him away from the bar. "Let's get you out of here, buddy," he said, steadying Bentley.

Cameron guided Bentley towards the exit, his arm wrapped around Bentley's shoulder for support. Bentley stumbled slightly, the alcohol making his steps unsteady. Cameron led him to his truck parked just outside the venue.

"Easy there, Bentley," Cameron said, helping him into the passenger seat. Bentley slumped into the seat, letting out a weary sigh. Cameron circled around, hopping into the driver's seat.

As Cameron started the truck, Bentley mumbled, "Thanks, Cam. I appreciate it."

Cameron just nodded, as he pulled out of the parking lot.

"Cam, turn the radio on, but no sad shit. I've had my share for today," Bentley said with a slur. Despite Bentley's request, the first song that played was the melancholic "Somewhere with You" by Kenny Chesney. Cameron attempted to change it, but Bentley insisted, singing along with visible pain in his voice. Tears streamed down Bentley's face as he sang.

"Enough. I'm changing it," Cameron declared, switching to a slightly more upbeat song, "Sing" by My Chemical Romance. They sang along until reaching Bentley's driveway.

"Hey, man take care of yourself on that honeymoon trip if you decide to still go tomorrow," Cameron shouted as he backed out of the drive.

Thanks to Bentley's cousin, the two tickets were all-inclusive to Cancun, Mexico. His cousin, a vacation concierge, got him a steal. However, with the day still fresh, Bentley didn't know if he wanted to go despite his luggage already being packed.

As Bentley laid down to pass out, he kept thinking, 'I've already paid for the trip; I might as well go and not throw the money away.' Their families had already wasted money on a rehearsal dinner, a wedding, and a reception, so he knew he couldn't let the trip go to waste too.

2

Heartbreak Honeymoon

Bright and early the next day, Bentley rose with the birds chirping, calling for an Uber to the airport. After a night of contemplation, he decided to go on the honeymoon alone. Bentley knew that he needed to go because if not he would end up in a depressive state, living with the same old routines.

On his non-stop flight to Cancun, Bentley decided to close his eyes and take a nap to sleep off the hangover. Once in deep sleep, Bentley started to dream about Michelle. His dream felt real as he could feel her touch, taste her kiss on his lips, and her breath on his neck. He could hear her laugh, and her voice.

As Bentley's dream unfolded, he found himself back in the familiar streets of their hometown. The sun bathed everything in a warm, golden glow, reminiscent of happier times. Michelle stood before him, wearing the radiant smile he had fallen in love with. Her eyes sparkled with the same mischievous charm that had always made his heart race.

"Bentley, you've always been the one who could make me laugh even when I didn't want to," Michelle said, her voice a gentle breeze that carried a touch of nostalgia. They walked along the cobblestone paths, hands brushing against each other's as if the years of separation had never occurred.

"You left me standing there," Bentley finally found the courage to speak, his tone a mixture of vulnerability and longing. "Why, Michelle?"

She stopped and turned to face him, her gaze holding a mix of regret and sorrow. "I thought I was doing what was best for both of us, Bentley. I thought that by leaving, I was saving you from a lifetime of my own uncertainties."

Bentley's heart ached as he looked into her eyes, realizing that even in his dream, the pain of her departure was still very real. "But you didn't have to do it that way. We could have faced those uncertainties together."

Michelle reached out and cupped his cheek, her touch as tender as a whisper. "I know that now. And if I could go back, I would do things differently. But this dream, Bentley, it's a chance for us to find closure, to say the things we never got to say."

But as the dream began to fade, and the first rays of sunlight broke through the horizon, Bentley realized that he couldn't hold on to forever. He knew he had to face the reality of the situation. Michelle had left him, and he was on this trip alone, searching for answers and closure.

With a heavy heart, Bentley let go of the dream, waking up to the reality of the plane cabin. His eyes were moist with unshed tears, and he knew that his journey to Cancun was not just about finding closure; it was also about discovering who he was without Michelle, and whether he could find happiness again.

Bentley's time in Cancun seemed to fly by as it was suddenly his last night there. For his last night, Bentley decided to stroll down the streets and take in the beautiful scenery. While out, Bentley stumbled across a dive bar that was hosting a karaoke night for all the tourist in town. He felt it was good place to stop and just take in everything around him. Plus, he was drawn to a beautiful angelic voice he heard coming from inside. The girl singing had such a country twang in her voice as she gave every cover song a touch of her originality.

"What's your name young lady and have you ever thought about pursuing music?" Bentley heard the host ask the girl on stage as he walked in.

"My name is Raelynn Hart and to answer your question I have thought about pursuing music. I'm actually in the process of forming a band." Raelynn said with that touch of twang in her voice.

"Well, ladies and gentlemen, give it up for Miss Raelynn Hart as she is about to sing another song for you all from the famous LeAnn Rimes, *"The Right Kind of Wrong."* Take them away, Miss. Hart," the host announced.

As the song began Bentley turned and leaned his back up against the bar with his drink in hand while facing the stage. It was his first look at the face behind the voice. Raelynn was all of five foot four, platinum blonde hair, captivating deep blue eyes, and sun-kissed tanned skin. Bentley was in awe. Not only could Raelynn sing but she was beautiful too.

While the song continued, Bentley found himself tapping his fingers on his drink bottle and singing along. When the song faded out, Bentley knew he had to buy Raelynn a drink. After all she did deserve it, the way she commanded that stage like a seasoned veteran.

Bentley strolled toward the stage to exchange greetings with Raelynn. Yet, as Raelynn descended from the stage, she directed her steps toward a table near the front, where a young man in his twenties was seated. He possessed black hair styled in a jarhead cut, along with a strong, muscular physique with tattoo's going up and down both arms. Leaning down, he and Raelynn engaged in a passionate kiss.

Bentley froze in his tracks. He couldn't help but feel a pang of jealousy. He hesitated for a moment, unsure of how to proceed. He had been so drawn to Raelynn's performance, her energy on stage resonating with something deep within him, that he forgot about his own heartbreak and loneliness. The desire to meet Raelynn had grown immensely within him.

After a moment of internal struggle, Bentley decided to continue toward the stage, although with a heavy heart. He couldn't deny the intensity of his attraction to Raelynn, both for her incredible talent and her undeniable beauty. As he approached the table, he cleared his throat to get their attention.

Raelynn pulled away from the young man's kiss, her eyes meeting Bentley's. There was a moment of awkward silence, but Bentley managed a polite smile. "Hi there," he said, trying to keep his voice steady. "That was an amazing performance you just gave. I was really blown away by your voice."

Raelynn looked at Bentley, her deep blue eyes momentarily clouded with uncertainty, but she returned his smile. "Thank you," she replied, her voice warm and gracious. "I'm Raelynn, by the way."

"Bentley," he introduced himself, feeling a bit more at ease now. "I was actually on my way to buy you a drink as a token of my appreciation for your talent."

Raelynn's expression softened, and she glanced at the young man beside her, who nodded in understanding. "That's really sweet of you, Bentley. I appreciate the offer, but I'm here with my boyfriend, Chase."

Bentley nodded, his heart sinking once more. "I understand," he said, trying to hide his disappointment. "Well, it was still great to meet you, Raelynn."

Raelynn smiled warmly at him, her eyes reflecting a hint of regret. "Thank you for the kind words."

With a final nod, Bentley shifted his focus away, his mind swirling with conflicting emotions. As he made his way back to the bar, he found himself unable to shake the image of her stunning beauty. Deep down, he realized that this encounter would likely fade into the recesses of their memories, just a fleeting moment in the grand tapestry of their lives.

As the night wore on, the shots flowed as freely as water, a desperate attempt by Bentley to drown his heartbreak. He struggled to keep thoughts of Michelle and the longing for Raelynn at bay, feeling guilty even considering Raelynn when he hadn't fully moved on from Michelle.

As Bentley was on the verge of being blackout drunk, he couldn't help but to look back at Raelynn and Chase. He caught the two of them in what appeared to be a heated argument as Chase got up and stormed off aggressively. Raelynn stood there with her arms crossed looking confused. Bentley wanted to go to her aid to see if everything was okay, but he knew that he had no right as he turned back to his drink.

"I'll take two double shots of Crown and two mixed drinks of whatever he's got," came the familiar woman's voice next to Bentley. Intrigued, he shifted his gaze to his side, only to find Raelynn standing there.

Bentley blinked, momentarily surprised by Raelynn's sudden appearance. He hesitated for a moment, his emotions a tangled mess. But as he looked into Raelynn's eyes, he saw a mix of concern and vulnerability, mirroring his own turmoil.

"Hey there, party animal," Bentley said with a playful grin, motioning to the drinks she'd just ordered. "Going all out, I see."

Raelynn chuckled, her laughter tinged with a hint of sadness that Bentley couldn't quite decipher. She raised her glass and clinked it against his, the sound ringing out in the dimly lit bar. "Why drown our sorrows in moderation, right?" she quipped.

Bentley couldn't help but chuckle in response, the heaviness in his heart momentarily lightened by her presence and their shared understanding. After they'd downed their shots, Bentley cleared his throat, trying to find his words through the alcohol-induced haze. "You know," he slurred slightly, "we probably won't remember this tomorrow."

Raelynn chuckled softly, her voice carrying a tinge of sadness. "Yeah, probably not. But maybe that's a good thing, right? We can say whatever we want, let it all out, and forget about it tomorrow."

Bentley nodded, feeling a strange sense of relief at her words. He leaned in a little closer, their shoulders brushing as they sat side by side at the bar. "I'm sorry about earlier, Raelynn. I saw you and Chase arguing, and I wanted to help, but I didn't think it was my place."

Raelynn sighed, her gaze distant as she swirled the contents of her mixed drink. "Chase and I, we're going through a rough patch. I caught him cheating with a girl from his unit in Camp Lejeune at the beginning of the year. So, now every time a guy talks to me, he gets all pissed off and jealous."

Bentley understood the pain of betrayal, the deep scars that could linger from such wounds. The alcohol had loosened their inhibitions, making the connection between them feel both natural and dangerous.

He glanced at Raelynn, her eyes glistening with unshed tears, and his heart ached for her. Without thinking, he reached out and gently placed his hand on top of hers, offering a comforting squeeze. "I'm really sorry to hear that, Raelynn," he said softly. "No one deserves to be treated that way."

Raelynn looked down at their hands, her fingers interlocking with his. The touch was both intimate and comforting, and a surge of warmth spread through her chest. In that moment, it felt like Bentley understood her in a way that no one else did; not even Chase. She found herself leaning into his touch, seeking solace in his presence.

As their conversation grew deeper, Bentley could feel a gravitational pull towards Raelynn. He didn't know what it was, but he knew he wanted more. Before he could stop himself, he leaned close to Raelynn. "What do you say we get out of here and go for a walk on the beach?"

Raelynn's eyes searched his face for a moment before a small smile tugged at her lips. "A walk on the beach sounds like a good idea," she replied, her voice carrying a mix of curiosity and anticipation.

They both pushed away from the bar, leaving their half-empty glasses behind, and made their way through the crowded bar toward the exit. The salty breeze hit them as they stepped outside, the night air cool against their skin. The sound of crashing waves in the distance was a soothing backdrop to their steps.

As they walked down the path that led to the beach, their conversation flowed easily. Bentley opened up about his own heartbreak, the story of Michelle leaving him at the altar, the raw emotions that he was still grappling with. Raelynn shared more about her dreams of becoming a musician, her struggles with Chase's infidelity, and the complexities of their relationship.

With each word they exchanged, the bond between them deepened. It was as if they were two lost souls seeking solace in the presence of another who truly understood their pain. The moon cast a silvery glow over the beach, the sand cool beneath their feet as they walked along the shoreline.

At one point, Bentley's hand brushed against Raelynn's, and neither of them pulled away. Instead, their fingers intertwined naturally, a silent understanding passing between them. The tension that had existed earlier, the fleeting attraction that had sparked in the bar, seemed to have evolved into something deeper—a connection that went beyond physical desire.

They walked in comfortable silence for a while, the waves creating a soothing rhythm that seemed to match the beating of their hearts. Eventually, they found themselves stopping at a secluded spot on the beach. The moonlight illuminated the sand around them, casting a soft glow.

Bentley turned to Raelynn, his gaze searching her eyes for a moment before he took a step closer. His heart raced, a mixture of nervousness and longing flooding his senses. He lifted his free hand to gently cup her cheek, his touch tender and filled with unspoken emotions.

Raelynn's breath caught in her throat as she looked up at Bentley, her heart racing in tandem with his. The world around them seemed to fade away, leaving only the two of them in that suspended moment. She leaned into his touch, her eyes flickering between his lips and his eyes.

Their faces drew closer, the anticipation palpable in the air between them. Bentley's lips brushed against Raelynn's in a hesitant, almost reverent kiss. Time seemed to slow as their lips met, a soft sigh escaping Raelynn's lips as she melted into the kiss.

The kiss deepened, their shared pain and longing finding an outlet in each other's embrace. Bentley's hand moved from Raelynn's cheek to the small of her back, pulling her closer as the kiss grew more passionate, more urgent. The crashing waves seemed to echo the rhythm of their heartbeats, a symphony of desire and vulnerability.

As their connection deepened and the moment grew more intense, Bentley suddenly broke away. His breath was ragged, and he locked eyes with Raelynn, his thumb tenderly brushing her cheek. "Raelynn," he murmured, his voice hoarse, "We can't do this. I'm hurting from Michelle, and you're with Chase. It's not right."

Raelynn's lips tingled from the taste of Bentley's kiss, and her chest heaved as they both tried to catch their breaths. The world around them started to return, the sound of the waves crashing on the shore filling the void left by their kiss. She blinked at Bentley, her heart pounding not only from the kiss but from the intensity of his words.

His touch still lingered on her cheek, and she felt a strange mixture of desire and disappointment welling up inside her. Bentley was right; they were both lost souls seeking refuge in this impulsive connection. It wasn't fair to themselves.

With a conflicted expression, Raelynn nodded slowly. "You're right, Bentley," she admitted, her voice barely above a whisper. "We're just two drunk strangers trying to escape reality, if only for moment. But for a moment it felt right. But you're right. We can't do this. We probably won't even remember most of this come tomorrow anyways. Plus, you leave to go back to North Carolina in the morning, and when we leave, we're headed back to Nashville."

Bentley's gaze held a mixture of relief and regret as he dropped his hand from her cheek, and they both stepped back, putting a little more distance between them. The moment, however powerful, had passed.

Raelynn sighed, running a shaky hand through her hair. "I... I need to go. Chase is probably wondering where I am." She turned away and briskly walked toward the path leading back to the bar, her heart heavy with the weight of what had just transpired.

Bentley watched her as she retreated, his own emotions in turmoil. He knew he had made the right choice, but it didn't make it any easier. As Raelynn disappeared into the night, he whispered to himself, "One day, when the time is right, maybe we'll find each other again, but damn...I should have gotten her number."

3

The After Chase

The following morning, Raelynn awoke to the throbbing ache in her head, just as Chase planted a gentle kiss on her forehead. The warm Cancun sunlight streamed through the window of their hotel room. As she gazed into Chase's eyes, a wave of guilt swept over her, stemming from the events of the previous night. While not every fragment of the night's events was clear, the profound intimacy she had shared with Bentley weighed heavily on her conscience. It had felt both right and wrong, a conflicting duality.

"Good morning, my beautiful," Chase whispered as he gazed down at Raelynn. "I'm sorry for getting jealous last night. I shouldn't have gotten so upset."

Raelynn offered Chase a faint smile, touched by his apology. She reached up to trace her fingers along his jawline, a gesture that spoke volumes of her affection. "It's okay, Chase," she replied softly, her voice still carrying a hint of the guilt that lingered within her. "I just don't understand why you felt that way. Are you scared that I'm seeking revenge and going to cheat on you like you did me?"

The moment the words left Raelynn's lips, she regretted them. She had meant for her question to be more of a playful tease, a way to lighten the mood, but she saw the hurt flash across Chase's eyes. It was a raw wound that had yet to fully heal, a wound she had unintentionally ripped open again.

Chase's expression shifted, a mix of vulnerability and defensiveness. "Raelynn, you know how sorry I am about what happened. When are we going to drop it so you can trust me again?"

Raelynn felt a pang of guilt as she looked into Chase's eyes. She hadn't meant to hurt him; she had only wanted to ease the tension between them. She sighed softly, her fingers still resting on his jawline. "Chase, I'm sorry. I didn't mean to bring up the past like that. I'm trying to trust you again but it's hard. Especially, when you act like you did last night."

Chase's gaze softened, and he reached out to cup her cheek with his hand. "I know, and again I'm sorry. I want us to move forward, to build something stronger together. But sometimes, fear that you're going to get even creeps in, you know?"

Raelynn nodded, understanding all too well. It was difficult to completely erase the scars of the past, even when both parties were committed to healing. She leaned into his touch, her eyes searching his for reassurance. "I promise you, Chase, I'm here with you. I don't want anyone else; I don't need anyone else."

His thumb brushed lightly across her cheek, his touch comforting. "I believe you, Raelynn. I'm sorry for letting my insecurities get the best of me. I'll work on it, I promise."

She smiled softly, feeling a warmth spread through her chest. "And I'll work on being able to trust you more."

Chase's lips curved into a grin. "Deal."

As they shared a tender moment, Raelynn's thoughts involuntarily drifted to Bentley again. She pushed the memory aside, reminding herself that it was just a passing encounter, a brief moment in time. Bentley was a stranger, and their paths would likely never cross again. She couldn't let that fleeting connection jeopardize what she had with Chase.

With a determined resolve, she focused on the man in front of her, the one who had fought for their relationship, the one she imagined her life with, traveling the world. Chase was career driven with a promising future and despite all of their issues, Raelynn knew Chase was the one her heart truly belonged too.

"I love you, Chase," she said softly, her gaze unwavering.

Chase's smile grew, his eyes reflecting his affection. "And I love you, Raelynn."

Raelynn held Chase's gaze, the intensity of their connection momentarily easing the turmoil within her. His love was a lifeline, anchoring her to the present and reminding her of the beautiful future they were building together.

As they lay there, bathed in the golden sunlight, Chase traced his fingers lightly along Raelynn's arm, a silent gesture of comfort. "You know," he began softly, "we have the whole day ahead of us. What do you say we forget about everything else and just enjoy each other's company?"

Raelynn's heart warmed at his suggestion. She nodded, feeling a weight lift from her shoulders. "You're right. We're in this beautiful place, and I don't want to waste a single moment."

Chase's eyes lit up, and he reached over to the nightstand, retrieving a small piece of paper. "I was thinking we could make a list of all the things we want to do today. Starting fresh, you know?"

Raelynn grinned as she took the paper from him, her fingers brushing against his. The paper was blank, a canvas waiting to be filled with their shared desires. "Okay, let's do it."

Together, they began jotting down ideas, their laughter and excitement filling the room. They planned to explore the local markets, go for a swim in the turquoise waters, indulge in some authentic Mexican cuisine, and even take a salsa dancing class. As their list grew longer, Raelynn found herself immersed in the joy of the moment, the thoughts of Bentley's brief encounter gradually fading into the background.

Chase's hand brushed against hers as they both reached for the pen, and he cast her a playful grin. "You know, we could also add 'stargazing on the beach' to the list. Just in case the night turns out to be as amazing as the day."

The idea of stargazing on the beach sent a sudden shiver down Raelynn's spine. It was as if Chase had unwittingly tapped into her thoughts about the previous night's encounter with Bentley. Despite her attempts to push those memories away, they resurfaced with a vengeance. Raelynn's mind drifted, involuntarily conjuring images of Bentley's touch, the sensation of his lips against hers, and the electric connection that had sparked between them.

Raelynn blinked, trying to shake off the intrusive thoughts. Stargazing on the beach with Chase sounded wonderful, a chance to reconnect and strengthen the bond they had worked so hard to rebuild.

"Yeah, stargazing sounds perfect," Raelynn replied, her voice steady despite the whirlwind of emotions inside her. "I'm looking forward to it."

Chase's gaze held hers for a moment longer, as if he could sense the hidden turmoil beneath her surface. But he didn't press further, instead giving her a reassuring nod before they continued adding more activities to their list.

As the day unfolded, Raelynn found herself swept up in the vibrant colors of Cancun, the laughter they shared, and the small moments that reaffirmed their connection. They explored the markets, haggled with local vendors, and sampled mouthwatering dishes that left their taste buds tingling with delight. The sun-drenched beach beckoned, and they splashed in the clear waters, each wave washing away a bit of the lingering unease from the morning.

As the day transitioned into evening, Raelynn felt a mixture of excitement and trepidation about their plans for stargazing. The idea of lying on the beach with Chase, looking up at the night sky, should have been nothing but pleasant anticipation. Yet, the thought brought back memories of Bentley's intense gaze and the vulnerable connection they had shared.

When the time came, they spread out a blanket on the soft sand, the ocean waves providing a soothing backdrop. Chase had brought a telescope, and as he adjusted it to focus on the stars, Raelynn couldn't help but feel a twinge of anxiety. She glanced at Chase, who was completely engrossed in the celestial spectacle above.

"Isn't it incredible?" he marveled, his eyes lighting up with childlike wonder.

Raelynn smiled, allowing herself to get lost in the beauty of the night sky. The stars stretched out above them, a tapestry of light and mystery. She knew she needed to let go of the shadows that haunted her thoughts, to fully embrace the moment with Chase. As she looked at him, his excitement contagious, she felt a renewed determination to push the intrusive memories away.

Chase reached over and took her hand, squeezing it gently. "This is perfect, isn't it? Just us, the stars, and the sound of the waves."

Raelynn nodded, her grip on his hand firm. "Yes, it is."

The hours passed in comfortable companionship. They pointed out constellations, shared stories, and whispered dreams under the vast sky. Raelynn immersed herself in the magic of the night.

As the night grew darker, they lay side by side, their fingers intertwined. Chase's gaze held a soft intensity as he looked at her. "Raelynn, I want you to know that I'm committed to us. I'll do whatever it takes to make you feel secure and loved. The past is behind us, and the future is what matters."

Touched by his words, Raelynn felt a warmth spread through her chest. "Chase, I believe in us too. And I promise, I'm working on letting go of my doubts. It's just sometimes..."

"Sometimes the past feels like a heavy shadow," Chase finished for her, his understanding gaze unwavering. "I get it. But we can overcome that together."

As the night progressed, Raelynn and Chase laid beneath the vibrant Mexican stars, relishing each other's presence. Amidst this tranquil backdrop, Raelynn's mind began to drift once more. Despite her efforts, she grappled with persistent memories of her time with Bentley the night before. Her mind wandered into contemplation about the path not taken – the possibility of their intimacy deepening and the sensations it might have evoked. Despite her awareness of its impropriety, the allure of these thoughts was undeniable. Fantasy visions of Bentley's touch, exploring intimate places reserved for lovers, seemed unceasingly vivid, painting a picture that stirred both guilt and temptation.

The scent of the ocean hung in the air, mingling with the faint aroma of the street vendors' late-night snacks. Raelynn turned her head slightly to steal a glance at Chase, who lay beside her, his eyes fixated on the stars above. She couldn't help but feel a pang of guilt for the thoughts swirling in her mind. She hadn't shared these confusing emotions with Chase, unsure of how he would react, and worried that her wandering mind would hurt him.

Chase, sensing her restlessness, reached over and gently brushed his fingers against her hand. "You seem a little distant tonight," he said, his voice soft and full of concern. "Is something on your mind?"

Raelynn hesitated for a moment, her heart racing, then decided to be honest. "I'm sorry, Chase. It's just that... well, I've been thinking a lot about last night. Something I shouldn't be dwelling on."

Chase turned towards her, his expression a mixture of curiosity and care. "You know you can talk to me about anything, right? Whatever it is, I'm here for you."

She took a deep breath, looking up at the stars as if searching for answers. "Last night, after you stormed off, I went and sat at the bar beside that guy; Bentley, who had approached us earlier. While talking about life and our traumas, we found ourselves extremely drunk. We decided to walk down on the beach, and we almost hooked up... Chase I'm sorry."

After what felt like an eternity, Chase finally spoke, his voice tinged with a hint of hurt and frustration. "I appreciate your honesty, Raelynn, but I can't deny that this hurts to hear. I thought we were on a path of rebuilding trust, of leaving the past behind. And now, you've thrown this into the mix."

Raelynn's heart clenched at the raw emotion in Chase's voice, regret and guilt gnawing at her from within. She turned her gaze to meet his eyes, so full of vulnerability and pain. She reached for his hand, her fingers intertwining with his, seeking a connection, a lifeline to salvage the situation.

"I know, Chase," she said, her voice shaky with remorse. "I'm so sorry. I never meant for any of this to happen. It was a moment of weakness, a lapse in judgment fueled by alcohol and a flood of complicated feelings. Bentley was just there, and I felt like I needed someone to talk to, someone who wouldn't judge me."

Raelynn could feel the weight of Chase's gaze upon her, his grip on her hand tightening as if he was holding on to their fragile bond. She continued, her words spilling out like the truth she had kept bottled up for so long.

"I love you, Chase. You're the one who's always been there for me, who's seen me through thick and thin. But I let my guard down, and I let someone else in, just for a moment. I never wanted to hurt you, and I hate myself for causing you this pain."

Chase's expression softened as he listened, his eyes shimmering with unshed tears. The storm of emotions raged within him, evident in the way his shoulders slumped, and his fingers trembled slightly against hers.

Raelynn took a deep breath, her heart aching as she continued, "I understand if you can't forgive me, if you can't trust me right now. I'll do whatever it takes to make things right. Even if it means giving you space, giving us space. But please know that I want us to work through this, to find a way back to each other."

Chase's gaze didn't waver as he held her eyes, the turmoil in his expression slowly giving way to a mix of longing and uncertainty. He swallowed hard, the lump in his throat evident as he finally spoke, his voice raw but determined.

"I love you too, Raelynn. And I can't deny that what we have is worth fighting for. But this... it's shaken me to my core. I need time to process everything, to heal from this betrayal."

Raelynn nodded, her heart sinking at the thought of the distance that might grow between them. She tightened her grip on his hand, a silent promise that she would wait, that she would give him the space he needed.

Chase's thumb traced soothing circles on her hand, his gaze softening as he looked at her. "When we get back to Nashville," he said, his voice gentle yet resolute, "let's consider going to counseling. Together. I think we both need help to navigate through this mess, to rebuild the trust that's been shattered."

Relief washed over Raelynn, tears pricking at the corners of her eyes as she nodded. It wasn't a magical solution, but it was a step forward, a commitment to face their problems together. As they held each other's gaze, the weight of the past hours slowly lifting, Raelynn felt a glimmer of hope that they could find a way to mend their relationship, stronger than before.

4

Honeymoon Hangover

On his flight back home, Bentley gazed out of the window, the azure waters of the Caribbean fading away into the distance. The memories of his time in Cancun swirled in his mind like a captivating, bittersweet dream.

The week had been a much-needed escape, a respite from the heartache and confusion that had consumed him since Michelle had left him standing alone at the altar. He'd sipped exotic mixed drinks on the sun-drenched beach, feeling the warmth of the Mexican sun on his skin. He'd watched the world go by, and it was the first time in years that he'd allowed himself to appreciate the beauty of other women. It was liberating in a way, like a step toward reclaiming his own life.

Yet, amid the newfound excitement, a nagging sense of guilt lingered in Bentley's thoughts. He couldn't shake the feeling that his growing connection with Raelynn was somehow wrong. After all, he was deeply in love with Michelle, and he had thought she felt the same way until she left him in the most public and humiliating manner possible.

The guilt tugged at his heartstrings, whispering that he was betraying Michelle by allowing another woman into his thoughts. Bentley closed his eyes and leaned back in his seat, letting out a long sigh. He knew he had every right to move on, but the scars from that ill-fated day still ran deep.

Yet, despite the guilt, Bentley couldn't stop thinking about Raelynn. Her laughter, her smile, and the undeniable chemistry they shared had pulled him in like a magnetic force. The memory of their kiss played on an endless loop in his mind, each replay more vivid than the last.

As the plane soared through the clouds, Bentley couldn't deny the intensity of Raelynn's lips against his, the way her fingers had traced his skin, igniting a fire within him that he'd long thought extinguished. It was a sensation he had never experienced, and it both excited and terrified him.

As the plane touched down at RDU, Bentley couldn't wait to tell Cameron about his time in Cancun and he really couldn't wait to tell Cameron about his kiss with Raelynn. Cameron always gave the best advice.

As Bentley walked out of the airport he was greeted by his parents and Cameron. He walked up to them, grinning from ear to ear, not being able to wait to tell them about his week in Cancun and how he had finally turned a new leaf.

"Mom, Dad, Cam, nice to see you guys. Can't wait to tell y'all about this trip, man. It was great. I definitely needed it."

As Bentley greeted them with such excitement, he could immediately tell something was up by everyone's body language.

"Ok, hold on, what's wrong? Y'all acting as if someone died."

Their heads hung low. Bentley could immediately feel himself coming down from his high. Cameron, Mr. and Mrs. Riggs looked at each other to see who would tell Bentley the news.

Finally, Cameron looked at Bentley with tear-filled eyes and said, "Man, I don't know how to tell you. While you were gone, there was a bad wreck, and the doctors tried everything they could to save…"

Bentley abruptly yelled, "Just tell me who died, damnit!" That is when Mrs. Riggs finished what Cameron was trying to say.

"Honey, it was Michelle. Michelle's gone, baby." Bentley felt his heart drop to his stomach. The lump in his throat grew more prominent as he fell to his knees, crying. He didn't want to believe it as he looked up at them and asked with a crackling voice,

"No, please tell me no. Is she really dead?" His parents and Cameron dropped to their knees to wrap him in a hug, anything to comfort him. Bentley had felt like the world had just crashed on him not once but twice, all within a week. He was torn in two.

Bentley began to feel even more guilty about the bond he had built with Raelynn in Cancun. Why hadn't he chased after Michelle instead of going on their 'honeymoon' alone? He wondered if his dream about Michelle had been a premonition that something was going to go wrong. Or had it already gone wrong, and Michelle was coming to him in his dreams to give him closure?

As Bentley's world crumbled around him, he clung to his mom and dad, as well as, Cameron, he couldn't shake the overwhelming feeling of guilt that washed over him like a tidal wave. Michelle, the woman he loved dearly and wanted to spend the rest of his life with, was gone, and he was grappling with the choices he had made leading up to this tragic moment.

As rain started to fall around them Bentley wept in their embrace, the guilt gnawing at him. He thought about the days leading up to the wedding, the arguments, the doubts, and his decision to still go on his and Michelle's honeymoon, instead of chasing after her. It was a decision that now weighed on him like a lead anchor, drowning him in regret.

"I should have gone after her," Bentley whispered through his tears. "I should have fought for us."

Mrs. Riggs, her own eyes filled with tears, tightened her grip on her son. "Bentley, honey, you couldn't have prevented this from happening."

Cameron, his voice shaky, added, "And Michelle made her own choices, too. She is the one that left you standing at the altar to explain to all your family and friends that she couldn't go through with marrying you because of some breakthrough realization she had."

Bentley's shoulders trembled as he tried to make sense of the torrent of emotions crashing within him. He was torn between grief, guilt, and anger. The rain mingled with his tears, creating a chaotic symphony that mirrored the turmoil inside him.

Cameron's words offered a glimmer of reason amidst the chaos. Bentley knew he was right – Michelle's choices were hers alone. She had walked away, leaving him humiliated and heartbroken in front of everyone they cared about. The wedding that was supposed to be the beginning of their life together had turned into a public spectacle of rejection. But this was different. This was bigger than being left at the altar. Michelle was dead and there were no fixing things or making things right because she was gone.

Bentley's mind was a battlefield of conflicting thoughts. He remembered the warmth of Michelle's smile, the sound of her laughter, and the moments they had shared together. He thought about the dreams they had woven together, the plans for their future, and the love they had nurtured. And now, it was all shattered, irreversibly altered by the cruel hand of fate.

"Son, let's get you out of this rain and take you home." Mr. Riggs said as he reached down to grab Bentley's hand.

Bentley's father's words broke through the storm inside him. He nodded, allowing his father to help him up from the sidewalk where he had fallen to his knees. As they made their way to the car, Bentley couldn't help but glance back at the sidewalk where they had shared their embrace and tears just moments ago. It felt like a sacred place, a place that would forever be etched in his memory.

Inside the car, Bentley sat in the backseat, staring out the rain-streaked window. The city passed by in a blur, the buildings and streets reflecting the somber mood that had settled over him. He felt a heavy weight in his chest, a combination of sorrow and regret that threatened to suffocate him.

Cameron sat beside him, a silent but comforting presence. He reached over and placed a hand on Bentley's shoulder, offering a reassuring squeeze. Bentley managed a weak smile in response, grateful for his friend's unwavering support.

His mother, sitting in the front passenger seat, turned to look at him with a mixture of sympathy and concern. "Bentley, we're here for you, always," she said softly. "And remember, it's not your fault. You couldn't have known."

Bentley nodded, though he knew that the guilt would continue to haunt him. He had loved Michelle deeply, and her sudden death had left a void in his life that he couldn't begin to fathom. He couldn't shake the feeling that he should have done something more, said something different, to change the course of events.

As they pulled into the driveway of the family home, Bentley's father turned off the engine and turned to face him. "We're going to get through this together, son," he said with a determined look in his eyes. "And we'll find a way to honor Michelle's memory."

Bentley knew his family was his anchor in this storm of emotions, and he was grateful for their unwavering support. He stepped out of the car, the rain still falling around him, but somehow it felt less tumultuous now. The healing process would be long and arduous, but he was ready to face it, to come to terms with both his grief and his guilt.

As they pulled into the driveway, Bentley, with a sigh, unfastened his seatbelt and stepped out of the car, the raindrops continuing to fall on him, almost like a cleansing ritual. The house stood before him, a place that held countless memories of laughter, celebrations, and now, a profound sense of loss. His family followed suit, surrounding him with their support.

As Bentley entered the house, a mix of emotions enveloped him. The warmth and coziness of the familiar setting seemed to clash with the cold reality he was facing. The living room, once a hub of happiness, now felt like a sanctuary of sorrow. Bentley's mother, her eyes brimming with compassion, guided him to the couch, offering a comforting hug as they sat down.

His father joined them, his expression a blend of strength and vulnerability. "Son," he began, his voice steady, "I know this pain feels unbearable right now, but remember that you don't have to shoulder it alone." Bentley nodded, the lump in his throat making it hard to speak. He understood that his family was his lifeline, his shelter in this tempest of emotions.

Cameron took a seat nearby, his silent presence echoing the unspoken camaraderie they shared. Bentley appreciated Cameron's willingness to stand by him, to be a pillar of support even when words felt inadequate.

As the hours passed, Bentley found himself surrounded by memories of Michelle. The photographs that adorned the walls, the trinkets that held sentimental value — they were all reminders of the love they had shared. He knew that blaming himself wouldn't bring Michelle back, but the guilt weighed heavy on his heart.

5

Guilt and Grief

Two weeks after Bentley's return from Cancun, no one had seen or heard from him. He was taking Michelle's death hard; he was devastated. Everyone became weary of his mental state when he didn't show up for Michelle's wake or funeral. His parents called him daily, and he would just send them straight to voicemail. He occasionally would answer the phone and then hang up just so that his parents would know he was ok and still in the land of the living and just so they wouldn't drop by unannounced. Cameron couldn't even get through to him. To Cameron, that was very strange, but he tried to understand and give Bentley space, but after two weeks of no communication, he wasn't having it. Cameron decided to drive by Bentley's house and get him out of the house.

Cameron pulled into Bentley's drive, walked up, and knocked at the door several times. He stood there waiting for Bentley to come to the door, but Bentley wasn't coming to the door. While waiting for him, Cameron remembered where Bentley had hidden his spare key. He reached above his head on the overhead porch railing and started feeling around until he found the key. Cameron just smiled when he finally had the key in his hands. As he inserted the key into the door, Cameron had a

31

chilling sensation shoot through his body, sending chills up and down his spine as he feared what he might find on the other end of the door. The door swung open, and Cameron was immediately taken away by what he saw. The place was trashed. There were empty pizza boxes on the floor, as well as empty beer cans and liquor bottles distributed all throughout the house. It looked like a landfill had dumped its trash inside Bentley's home.

Blown away at what he saw, Cameron immediately started thinking, "Oh hell no! Bentley is getting his ass out of this house, and he's getting out of this house today."

Cameron stormed up the stairs towards Bentley's room when he saw Bentley, who hadn't even made it to his own room before passing out in the middle of the hallway.

"Bentley, wake your ass up and wake it up now!" Cameron said aggressively.

Half asleep and still drunk from the night before, Bentley looked up at Cameron with complete confusion. He was confused at just how Cameron got into his house.

"How the fuck did you get in my house?" Drunk Bentley asked.

Cameron smiled and responded, "You forgot I know exactly where you put your spare key? Now get your ass up! You are not staying in the house all day."

Cameron stopped in the middle of what he was saying and started looking around at the disaster zone he was standing in and then chimed back in "First things first, you're getting your ass up, and we're going to clean this house. Secondly, you're going to clean your damn self-up. You look disgusting and smell horrible. And what is this shit on your face? You got to shave it. You've had two weeks to wallow and we have all let you be but it's time you rejoin the world."

Bentley was surprised at Cameron's tone of voice and how stern he was being. Bentley didn't know what to say, "Ok, yeah, you're right. Just get me some ibuprofen and water and help me up."

Cameron looked at Bentley with a satisfied look as he reached his hand out to help Bentley up off the floor.

After about an hour of cleaning and showering, Bentley's house finally looked like a home instead of a landfill, and he looked like a decent human being again. He wasn't feeling any better, but he knew deep down that he couldn't hide out from the rest of the world forever. He had a best friend, parents, and a sister who cared for him. He knew he had to embrace life and just live for the moment. The death of Michelle made him realize just how quickly a life can be taken. He didn't want to continue taking life for granted. He remembered how he felt that week in Cancun, and he just wanted nothing more than to get back to that feeling, and it started now. He was so thankful that Cameron was forcing him to leave the house.

"Man, Ben, everyone has been worried sick about you, especially your mom and dad. I know losing Michelle was tough, but gosh, bro, you didn't have to deal with it on your own. That's why you have friends, but most importantly, you have family to help you through times like this." Cameron, out of breath from all the cleaning, said.

Cameron's words struck a chord with Bentley. He knew his friend was right. He had been so consumed by his grief and anger that he had shut everyone out. It was time to face reality and lean on the people who cared about him.

"You're right, Cam. I've been a mess," Bentley admitted, his voice filled with gratitude. "I didn't know how to deal with all of this, but I can't keep hiding from the world."

Cameron nodded, a relieved smile on his face. "That's what we're here for, buddy. We'll get through this together. Now, tell me. How was Cancun dude?"

Bentley laughed for the first time in what seemed like forever. "Man, Cancun was awesome considering the circumstances. Like, I don't know while I was there, I felt like I should have been dealing with the heartbreak of Michelle leaving me, but I didn't really feel any of that. I mean maybe there was a moment or two where I found myself down and out thinking about her but for the most part, I was in high spirits most of the trip enjoying my time, enjoying the view…" Bentley paused as he playful smacked at Cameron with the biggest grin on his face, "…you know what I mean."

Cameron chuckled along with Bentley, relieved to see his friend's spirits lifting even just a little bit. "I'm glad you managed to find some joy in Cancun, dude. I hate it for you that you had to come back to this tragedy though."

Bentley nodded in agreement, hearing the gratitude in Cameron's voice. As Cameron spoke, Bentley could feel an internal turmoil building inside him. He wanted to tell Cameron how he was truly feeling but he didn't want to be any more vulnerable than he already was. However, in a moment of bravery Bentley spoke up expressing his true feelings, hoping this would be the breakthrough that he needed to face everything head on.

"Cam… I'm not okay. I don't know if I ever will be either. I feel like I'm living in a constant hell, a nightmare that I can't wake up from. When I do wake up, I'm still here with the same pain. The same damn hurt. I go to sleep still missing her, I wake up still missing her every single fucking second of every single fucking day. Her absence is eating me alive as her memory burns like a wildfire in my brain. I feel guilty like it's my fault, like I did something wrong. I feel guilty because while in Cancun, I met a girl that for a second made me completely forget about Michelle. Like it felt so wrong but at the same exact time it felt so damn right but then I get back here to find out she died while I was off enjoying what was supposed to be our honeymoon and it makes that moment in Cancun feel even more wrong. I just feel so much guilt dude." Bentley expressed with tear filled eyes.

Cameron listened intently, his face filled with compassion and empathy. He reached out and placed a comforting hand on Bentley's shoulder. "Ben, I can't even imagine what you're going through right now. It's okay to feel all of this. It's okay to feel conflicted, to feel guilty. Grief is messy, man. It doesn't follow any rules or logic and there's no right or wrong way to go through it. Your emotions are valid, and you shouldn't blame yourself for anything. It's not your fault that you found a moment of happiness in Cancun, it's not your fault that Michelle made the decision to leave, and it's damn sure not your fault that she died in a car wreck."

Bentley wiped away a few tears that had escaped from his eyes and took a deep breath. "I know you're right, Cam. It's just hard to accept it all, but I appreciate you being here to listen. I need to deal with this pain and guilt, somehow."

Cameron nodded, his support unwavering. "You're not alone in this, Ben. We'll get through it together, and there's no set timeline for healing. It's okay to have moments of happiness or connection, even if it feels complicated. And it's okay to have moments of intense sadness and grief too. Just remember, it's all a part of the process."

Bentley managed a small, grateful smile. "Thanks, Cam. I don't know what I'd do without you, man."

Cameron smiled back, "You don't have to find out. We're in this together, every step of the way. And if you ever want to talk, cry, or just be, I'll be right here, okay?"

Bentley let a slight smile creep across his face as he was truly touched by Cameron's compassion. Bentley felt every word Cameron spoke was heartfelt and sincere. Bentley also felt that a weight had been lifted off him as he was able to open up and talk about his feelings with someone that truly cared for him.

After a few minutes of silence, Cameron sighed, looking at Bentley with a pensive expression. "Ben, I know the timing might not be right, but I have to ask, and I hope you won't take it the wrong way. You mentioned meeting a girl in Cancun who made you forget about Michelle." Cameron paused as he changed his tone to a more playful one. "As your best friend, you can't just leave me hanging. You've gotta give me the tea."

Bentley chuckled through his tears, appreciating Cameron's attempt to lighten the mood. It was exactly what he needed in that moment. "All right, all right. Her name was Raelynn and we met at a karaoke dive bar. I was walking down the street and was drawn to her voice, so I walked inside. She was so beautiful dude. She was pretty short, with shoulder-length platinum blonde hair and these amazing deep blue eyes. Her skin had that sun-kissed glow that made her look like she was always on vacation. The way her dress hugged her curves, I couldn't help but to stare. After she finished singing, I found the courage to walk up to her an introduce myself and as I was walking over, I saw that she had a boyfriend."

Cameron's eyebrows shot up in surprise. "And you still walked up to her with her boyfriend there? I don't know if I'd call it crazy or ballsy but wow. What happened next?"

Bentley heaved a sigh, the recollection of that evening still fresh in his thoughts. "Well, it definitely caught me off guard," he reflected, "but since I was already there, I decided to introduce myself. I offered to buy her a drink, but she turned the offer down and after that, I returned to the bar."

Cameron leaned in, eager to hear the rest of the story. "And then what happened? Did you just forget about her and enjoy the rest of your night?"

Bentley smiled, remembering the night in Cancun with a mix of emotions. "Not at all, Cam. As the night went on, I kept stealing glances at her. I caught her looking my way too. At one point, I looked over and saw her and her boyfriend arguing. Later that night, I found Raelynn standing beside me at the bar ordering drinks. So, I decided to strike up a conversation again, in which I found out that her and her boyfriend had an argument, and he stormed off leaving her at the bar alone while he went back to the hotel. Apparently, I made him jealous by approaching her and he took it out on her."

Cameron's eyes widened in surprise. "Wow, that's a lot more drama than I was expecting. What did you guys talk about?"

Bentley couldn't help but smile at the memory. "We talked about everything, really. From our favorite music to our dreams and aspirations. It was like we'd known each other for ages. We even got into this deep conversation about how music has this incredible power to heal and connect people. It was one of those moments, Cam, where you feel like the universe is trying to tell you something."

Cameron grinned. "Sounds like a movie, man. What happened next?"

Bentley's expression grew more thoughtful. "Well, we spent the rest of the night talking and laughing. It felt like we were in our own little world. We left the bar and decided to go for a stroll on the beach where we almost hooked up. Things got heated, way too heated."

Cameron let out a low whistle, clearly taken aback. "Okay, Ben, things escalated quickly. What did you do?"

Bentley chuckled, a hint of embarrassment coloring his cheeks. "Believe me, I was just as surprised as you are. In the heat of the moment, though, I pulled back. I couldn't let things go any further. It wouldn't have been fair to Raelynn, especially with her boyfriend in the picture. We talked it out, and she understood. We ended up going our separate ways. I stayed on the beach watching her as she disappeared in the moonlight."

Cameron nodded, clearly impressed by Bentley's restraint. "That's a tough call to make, man, but it sounds like you did the right thing. It's not easy to navigate those situations, especially when emotions are running high."

Bentley sighed, appreciating Cameron's understanding. "Yeah, it was a difficult decision, but it felt like the right one. I couldn't let a moment of passion cloud my judgment, especially considering the circumstances. I walked back to the hotel room alone, but that night, I couldn't stop thinking about Raelynn. I mean, we connected on such a deep level, Cam, and it got me thinking about my life."

Cameron tilted his head, curious. "What do you mean, Ben? What did meeting Raelynn make you think about?"

Bentley paused for a moment, reflecting on his recent experiences and the emotions he had been wrestling with. "It made me realize that life is unpredictable, and we have to grab onto moments of happiness when we find them. Meeting Raelynn, even in a sea of my own confusion, reminded me how much I used to love music back in high school. We talked about it, and she encouraged me to get back into it. I showed her some of my music and she said that I had a gift, and I should share it with the world."

Cameron's eyes lit up with excitement. "Dude, that's amazing! You've always been talented in music, and if this is something that brings you joy, you should absolutely pursue it. It might be a great outlet for your emotions too."

Bentley nodded, a newfound determination in his eyes. "I think you're right, Cam. It's time for me to stop hiding from my feelings and start expressing them. Music used to be my escape, and I think it's time to dive back into it. It's time to put my thoughts, my pain, and my emotions into lyrics and beats. Maybe that's the way I can heal and make something positive out of all this darkness."

Cameron clapped Bentley on the back, his support unwavering. "I'm all in, man. If you need any help, whether it's writing, producing, or just someone to bounce ideas off, I'm here. Let's make some music that speaks from the heart."

Bentley felt a renewed sense of purpose wash over him. He knew that this journey wouldn't be easy, but with Cameron by his side and the outlet of music, he felt ready to face whatever came his way. "Thanks, Cam. This means the world to me. Let's do this." They shared a determined look, ready to embark on a new chapter of healing and self-discovery through the power of music.

6

NashVegas

Back in Nashville, Raelynn was still trying to navigate the complex maze of emotions that had enveloped her since returning from Cancun. It had been a couple of weeks, and she found herself unable to shake the memory of that intimate kiss with Bentley. Her heart was in turmoil, caught between the connection she felt with him and the reality of her complicated relationship with Chase.

As Raelynn went about her daily life in Music City, her mind kept wandering back to that moonlit night on the beach. The waves crashing, the warm breeze, and Bentley's presence, it was all etched in her memory. She had been surprised by the depth of the connection they had formed, even if just for a few hours. The intense conversation about music and life had left a lasting impact on her, and she couldn't deny that Bentley had touched a part of her soul.

At the same time, her relationship with Chase remained rocky. His return to Camp LeJeune only added another layer of strain. Raelynn had been trying to rebuild trust after he had cheated on her, and his absence only seemed to intensify her insecurities. The thought of him being far away, surrounded by people who didn't know their history, weighed heavily on her. She wondered if he would repeat his mistakes, and the anxiety was taking a toll on her.

Raelynn needed to sort through her feelings, and she decided to confide in her cousin, Kendall, who was home visiting from the Air Force Academy.

One evening, Raelynn invited Kendall over to her cozy apartment. As they sat on the worn-out couch, sipping on cups of steaming tea, Raelynn took a deep breath, trying to find the right words to convey the turmoil inside her.

"Kendall, there's something I need to talk to you about," Raelynn began, her voice steady but tinged with vulnerability.

Kendall looked at her, concern etched in her features. "Of course, Rae. You know you can talk to me about anything. What's going on?"

Raelynn hesitated for a moment; her eyes focused on the swirling patterns in her tea. "You remember that trip to Cancun, right? The one with Chase?"

Kendall nodded, her expression gentle. "Yes, of course. It was supposed to be a romantic getaway, right?"

Raelynn nodded, her heart pounding in her chest. "It was... but something happened. I... got into an argument with Chase. Chase stormed off and left me at the bar alone. Well, there was this handsome guy. He was probably about six foot even, with these deep blue eyes, dirty blonde hair, and a muscled physique. We talked, and... things got heated, thankfully we only kissed. I told Chase about it, and he suggested that we go to counseling."

Kendall listened attentively; her eyes filled with empathy. "Rae, that sounds incredibly complicated. I can't imagine how you must be feeling right now."

Raelynn let out a shaky breath, her hands trembling slightly. "It's like I'm being pulled in two different directions, Kendall. On one hand, there's this connection with Bentley that I never expected. And on the other, there's Chase, who I love, but the trust has been so fragile since he cheated on me."

Kendall reached out and gently squeezed Raelynn's hand. "I can't pretend to have all the answers, but I do know that your feelings are valid. It's okay to be confused and torn in a situation like this."

Raelynn nodded, grateful for Kendall's support. "The thing is, Chase is stationed at Camp LeJeune now, and the distance... it's killing me. It's hard enough trying to navigate this rocky road, and now with him so far away, it feels almost impossible."

Kendall's expression softened even further. "I can only imagine how tough that must be, Rae. Long-distance relationships are incredibly challenging, especially when trust is already an issue."

Raelynn's eyes welled up with tears, and she blinked them back, determined to be strong. "And the counseling... I want to try, I really do. But without being married, it's even more complicated. The logistics, the distance, it all feels like a mountain we have to climb."

Kendall nodded in understanding. "It's a difficult situation, no doubt. But remember, Rae, you have to prioritize your own well-being and happiness. If something doesn't feel right, you have to trust your instincts."

As Raelynn looked into Kendall's kind eyes, she felt a surge of gratitude for having such a supportive person in her life. She knew that she couldn't rush her decisions.

"You're right, Kendall," Raelynn whispered, her voice filled with determination. "I need to take things one step at a time and figure out what's best for me, even if it's not easy."

Kendall smiled warmly. "That's the spirit, Rae. I'll be here for you, no matter what path you choose."

Taking a deep breath, Raelynn hesitated for a moment, as if she had one more piece of the puzzle to share. "There's something else, Kendall. Bentley... he said something to me that night in Cancun. Something that's been on my mind ever since."

Kendall leaned in, her curiosity piqued. "What did he say, Rae?"

Raelynn's eyes sparkled with a mix of intrigue and uncertainty. "He heard me sing karaoke at the bar. He said that I had a real gift and that I should pursue music. He made me believe in myself and my abilities in a way I haven't felt in a long time."

Kendall's eyes widened with surprise. "That's incredible, Rae! You've always had a beautiful voice, but it sounds like this Bentley guy helped you see your talent in a whole new light."

Raelynn nodded, a hint of excitement in her voice. "He did, and it's been lingering in my mind ever since. I've been thinking about it, Kendall. About giving music a real shot, not just as a hobby, but as a career. Maybe even recording some of my songs and sharing them with the world."

Kendall beamed with enthusiasm. "Rae, that's amazing! You've got the talent and the passion, and if Bentley's words have encouraged you to take that leap, I say go for it. Follow your heart and your dreams."

Raelynn smiled, feeling a glimmer of hope. "Thank you, Kendall. You've always been so supportive, and I'm lucky to have you as my cousin. You and Cassidy are my true lifesavers."

With Kendall's support and the newfound encouragement to pursue her passion for music, Raelynn felt a spark of excitement in her heart. She began to imagine a future where she could share her talent with the world, where her voice and her songs could touch the hearts of many.

Later that evening, Raelynn sat on her balcony, the city lights of Nashville twinkling in the distance. The night air was cool against her skin, a soothing contrast to the whirlwind of emotions she'd been experiencing. The conversation with Kendall had been a lifeline, and the encouragement to pursue music had ignited a fire within her.

As she gazed at the stars overhead, Raelynn's mind raced with possibilities. She could imagine herself on stage, pouring her heart out through her music. It was a dream she'd always carried, but now, it felt more tangible than ever before.

Feeling a surge of determination, Raelynn decided to call Chase. She wanted to hear his voice, to share her newfound excitement with him. She dialed his number and waited, her heart pounding in anticipation.

Chase's voice came through the phone, a mix of familiarity and distance. "Hey, Rae. How's it going?"

Raelynn could sense the hesitation in his words, a subtle shift in his tone. It made her pause for a moment, a small knot of worry forming in her stomach. "Hey, Chase. I'm... I'm doing okay," she replied, her voice carrying a hint of uncertainty. "How about you? How's it going being back in North Carolina?"

There was a brief pause, as if Chase was carefully considering his response. "It's... it's going great," he finally said, but there was something guarded in his voice, something that didn't quite match the enthusiasm he was trying to convey.

Raelynn's brow furrowed in concern. She could feel a disconnect between them, a barrier that hadn't been there before. She took a deep breath, gathering her thoughts, and decided to share her newfound dream with him.

"Chase, I've been thinking a lot lately," she began, her voice steady. "About music, about my voice, about what it means to me. And I've come to a decision. I want to start a band."

There was a brief silence on the other end of the line, and Raelynn could almost hear the gears turning in Chase's mind. When he finally spoke, his words were blunt and cold, like a bucket of ice water on her enthusiasm.

"That's a stupid idea, Rae," he said flatly.

Raelynn felt her heart sink. It was like a punch to the gut, an unexpected blow that left her breathless. She had expected support, or at least some understanding, but Chase's reaction was the opposite.

"What? Why would you say that, Chase?" she asked, her voice tinged with hurt.

"I'm just being realistic, Rae," Chase replied, his tone unyielding. "You're talking about starting a band? That's not something you just do, especially when you're trying to figure out everything else in your life. Like our relationship. It's a distraction."

Raelynn felt a mix of anger and disappointment surge within her. She had hoped for encouragement, for Chase to be excited about her newfound passion. Instead, she was met with resistance, with doubt.

"It's not a distraction, Chase," she insisted, her voice firm. "It's something I've always wanted to do, and now feels like the right time. Music is a part of me, and I can't ignore that anymore."

There was a tense silence on the line, a palpable shift in the air. Raelynn could sense the distance growing, the gap widening between them. It was as if they were standing on opposite sides of a chasm, unable to bridge the divide.

Finally, Chase spoke, his voice softer but no less resolute. "Look, Rae, I'm just trying to be honest. I don't think this is the right move for you right now. You have other things to focus on."

Raelynn felt a mixture of frustration and determination wash over her. She knew that she couldn't let Chase's opinion dictate her decisions, especially when it came to something as important to her as music.

"I appreciate your honesty, Chase," she said, her voice steady. "But this is something I need to do for myself. With or without your support. I hope you understand that."

As they said their goodbyes and hung up, Raelynn sat in the quiet of her apartment, the weight of Chase's words still lingering in the air. But alongside them was the flicker of determination, the ember of a dream she was unwilling to let go of.

In the coming days, Raelynn threw herself into her music. She started attending open mics, meeting fellow musicians, and even began writing her own songs. Each note, each lyric, was a step towards the future she envisioned.

7

Let's Start a Band

After weeks of diligently pursuing her musical aspirations, Raelynn believed she had reached a point where she could establish a band. Having collaborated with several musicians during this period, she felt confident enough to approach them and propose forming a band together. While Raelynn was overjoyed about embarking on this next stage of her career, Chase remained somewhat apprehensive about this new chapter in her life.

Raelynn understood Chase's concerns, but her determination to follow her passion for country music was unwavering. She knew that forming a country band was the right path for her, and she had already visualized the band's name, "Southern Harmony," and the kind of music they would create together.

Raelynn eagerly reached out to the musicians she had worked with over the past few weeks, sharing her vision for "Southern Harmony." Some were excited and intrigued by the opportunity, while others, for various reasons, declined the invitation. Raelynn respected their decisions, knowing that the right group of musicians would eventually come together.

After a couple weeks of networking and persistence, the puzzle pieces of her band began to fall into place.

Raelynn found Owen, a talented guitarist at an open mic night. He had a flair for both acoustic and electric styles. Although Owen possessed the look of a heavy metal guitarist, his passion for country music was evident, and he had a knack for weaving captivating melodies into every note he played. Owen was as excited about "Southern Harmony" as Raelynn was, and he eagerly joined the band, eager to contribute his skills to Raelynn's growing vision. He was even on board to help her find members to complete the band.

After a couple tiring weeks meticulously seeking out musicians that Raelynn and Owen thought would fit the sound they were trying to produce, "Southern Harmony" was finally a complete band.

With everything in place, the excitement among the band members was palpable. The rhythm section locked in tight, the harmonies blended seamlessly, and Raelynn's voice soared over the music like it had finally found its home. Owen, with his signature blend of acoustic warmth and electric fire, played off Raelynn's vocals beautifully, adding depth and emotion to the songs they had begun to craft.

One evening, after a long night in the studio recording, the band gathered around in Raelynn's cozy Downtown Nashville apartment. The walls were adorned with posters of iconic country artists, and the air buzzed with the energy of their recent practice. It was clear that "Southern Harmony" was ready to move to the next level, but the question now was how to get their music out into the world.

"We've got the songs, we've got the sound," Raelynn said, her voice filled with the same determination that had driven her to form the band in the first place. "Now, we need to figure out how we're going to promote ourselves."

"Social media is key," one of the band members suggested. "We should start putting out teasers, maybe do a few live-streamed performances to build a following."

"I agree," Owen chimed in, "but we need something more. We need to think bigger, something that will really get us noticed."

The group fell into thoughtful silence, tossing around ideas and strategies. It was Owen who eventually spoke up with a suggestion that made Raelynn's heart skip a beat.

"Raelynn, there's something I think you should really consider." Owen said cautiously.

She looked at him curiously. "What's that?"

Owen glanced at the other band members before meeting her eyes. "Your father. I know it's not the route you want to take, but he's got all the connections, the resources. Maybe he could help us out, get us some gigs, or even just some advice on how to break through."

Raelynn hesitated, her mind racing. Jim Hart, her father, was a force to be reckoned with in the music industry. As the CEO and owner of Harts Entertainment and Management, he had the power to turn unknown artists into superstars. But Raelynn's relationship with her father had always been complicated, especially when it came to her music career. He'd never been shy about his opinions, and Raelynn wasn't sure she was ready to hear what he might have to say.

Finally, Raelynn let out a chuckle, "Yeah right, We would have better luck with a brick wall helping us."

The band members exchanged glances, sensing the tension behind Raelynn's words. Owen leaned forward, his voice gentle but firm. "I get it, Rae. But it's worth a shot. Even if he says no. Like the great Michael Jordan once said, you miss a hundred percent of the shots you don't take."

Raelynn sighed, weighing the suggestion in her mind. She had always prided herself on making it on her own terms, but Owen had a point. This was bigger than just her now—it was about the whole band, and their dreams were all tied together. Talking to her father was definitely worth a shot.

"Alright," Raelynn finally agreed, "I'll talk to him. No promises, but I'll give it a shot."

Later that night, Raelynn decided to pay her father a visit. As she made the dreadful drive, she could feel the anxiety making its presence known. She knew that her father, Jim Hart, was not only a successful businessman but also a no-nonsense individual. She had seen him make tough decisions in the corporate world, and asking for his help in pursuing her dream made her feel vulnerable.

During the drive, Raelynn muttered to herself, rehearsing various ways to approach the conversation. She knew she had to be strategic and careful in her approach. Her father's reputation was one of a shrewd and tough negotiator, and she needed to find the right words to convince him.

In front of her parents mansion, Raelynn took a deep breath and reminded herself of her bandmates' encouragement. She had to believe in herself and her passion for music. With a determined spirit, she made her way to the front door.

As Raelynn entered the house, she could feel the weight of her decision pressing on her. She knew her parents had no idea about her pursuit of music, let alone her band "Southern Harmony." The secret she was carrying felt like a burden, and she hoped that her father's reputation wouldn't stand in the way of her dream.

She finally found her father in his home office, surrounded by a stack of documents. With a deep breath, she cleared her throat and summoned the courage to speak.

Jim Hart, Raelynn's father, was a tall and imposing figure, with salt-and-pepper hair and a perpetually serious expression. He exuded an aura of authority, a man who had spent most of his life navigating the complex world of business and finance. He dressed in well-tailored suits, and his stern demeanor was known to strike fear into many.

"Dad, can I talk to you about something important?"

Jim Hart looked up from his paperwork, his gaze sharp and focused. "Of course, Rae. What is it?"

Taking a deep breath, Raelynn began, "Dad, you know how passionate I am about music. I've formed a band called "Southern Harmony", with some incredibly talented musicians, and we believe we have the potential to make a significant impact in the music industry."

Jim Hart listened, his expression inscrutable, waiting for her to get to the point.

"I've been thinking, Dad," Raelynn continued, "whether Harts Management, your company, could provide us with support. We need help in taking our first steps in the industry, and I believe your expertise and resources could make a big difference for us."

Jim Hart's expression remained unchanged, and Raelynn couldn't read his thoughts. Finally, he spoke, and his words were far from what she expected.

"Raelynn, this is a foolish idea. The music industry is unpredictable and full of disappointments. You should be focusing on your studies and building a stable future. This band of yours won't lead to anything substantial. I won't waste my time and resources on it."

Raelynn felt deflated. She had hoped for support, but her father's blunt rejection stung. She knew he was a pragmatist, but she had thought he might understand her passion.

As Raelynn left her father's office, a heavy silence seemed to hang in the air. Her father's words had dashed her hopes of support, leaving her feeling disheartened and vulnerable. She knew her bandmates were counting on her, and she was determined to make their musical dreams a reality, even if it meant doing it without her father's help.

But as she walked away from the office, she was met by her mother, Olivia Hart.

Olivia Hart, Raelynn's mother, was a woman of elegant poise. She had a refined appearance, her auburn hair neatly styled, and her outfits always impeccably coordinated. Her social circles often consisted of affluent individuals who shared her views on the importance of wealth and social status. She had strong opinions about the path Raelynn should take in life.

Olivia, who had overheard the conversation between Raelynn and Jim, couldn't resist adding her opinion.

"You see, Raelynn," Olivia said with a condescending smile, "your father is right. This music dream of yours is nothing but a foolish idea. You should be focusing on your studies and securing a stable future."

Raelynn's frustration grew as her mother echoed her father's sentiments. She had expected a more empathetic response from her mother, but Olivia's words only added to the weight of her disappointment.

"And," Olivia continued, her tone growing more critical, "you need to leave that no-good-for-nothing Chase behind. Find yourself a wealthy husband who can take care of you and provide you with the future you deserve."

Raelynn bit her lip, struggling to hold back her irritation. She had never been one to conform to traditional expectations, and her dreams of making music with "Southern Harmony" were deeply ingrained in her heart and soul. She knew she had to prove her parents wrong.

After the devastating encounter with her parents, Raelynn needed the support of her bandmates more than ever. She knew it was time to call them and share the heartbreaking news that her father, and even her mother, had rejected the idea of pursuing music.

Raelynn drove home in silence, her thoughts racing. As she pulled into the parking lot of her apartment complex, she sat in the car for a moment, staring at the dashboard. The conversation with her parents had left her feeling crushed but she knew she couldn't let it break her spirit.

With a deep breath, Raelynn grabbed her phone and dialed Owen's number. The phone rang a few times before Owen picked up, his voice cheerful as ever. "Hey, Rae! What's up?"

Raelynn tried to muster some enthusiasm, but the heaviness in her heart made it difficult. "Hey, Owen. Are you free right now? I need to talk to you about something."

"Sure," Owen replied, his tone becoming more serious. "What's going on?"

Raelynn hesitated for a moment, trying to find the right words. "I just got back from my parents' house. I talked to my dad about helping us out, you know, with the band."

Owen could sense the tension in her voice. "And how did it go?"

Raelynn sighed, leaning her head back against the car seat. "Not good. He shot the idea down completely. He doesn't think 'Southern Harmony' is worth his time, and he made it clear he doesn't want to be involved."

There was a brief silence on the other end of the line before Owen spoke. "I'm sorry, Rae. I know you were hoping he'd come around."

Raelynn nodded, even though Owen couldn't see her. "Yeah, I was. And my mom… well, she wasn't any better. She basically told me to give up on music and find a rich husband instead."

Owen let out a soft chuckle, though it was tinged with sympathy. "Wow. That's… something."

"Yeah," Raelynn replied, her voice weary. "It's frustrating, but I knew there was a chance they'd react this way. I just… I guess I was hoping for a miracle."

"Rae, don't let this get you down," Owen said, his voice firm. "We don't need your dad's help to make it. We've got something special here, and we're going to keep pushing forward, no matter what."

Raelynn smiled faintly at his words. "Thanks, Owen. I needed to hear that."

"Anytime," Owen replied. "So, what now?"

Raelynn took a deep breath, gathering her resolve. "Now, we keep going. I'll call the others and let them know what happened, but I want them to know that this doesn't change anything. We're still in this together, and we're going to make it work."

"That's the spirit," Owen said, his voice filled with encouragement. "We've got your back, Rae. We'll figure this out."

After Raelynn called and informed the rest of the band of the news, she knew there was one more call she needed to make. Raelynn hesitated for a moment, staring at Chase's name on her phone screen. She knew that, despite the distance and the turbulence between them, he was the one who could still cheer her up.

After a few rings, Chase picked up, his voice casual and uninterested. "Hey, what's up?"

"Chase," Raelynn began, her voice still carrying the weight of her emotions, "I need to talk to you about something important."

Chase let out a sigh on the other end. "Can it wait? I'm in the middle of something."

Raelynn hesitated before she let her frustration get the best of her, "You know what, Chase? Just forget it. Whatever you're doing must be more important than talking to your girlfriend."

Raelynn ended the call abruptly, her heart racing with a mix of anger and disappointment. She stared at her phone, feeling a wave of frustration crash over her. The conversation with Chase had been the final straw in a series of setbacks, and it left her feeling even more enraged. As Raelynn made her way inside her apartment, her phone began to ring — it was Chase calling back.

Raelynn hesitated for a moment before answering, her emotions still raw. "Hello?"

"Rae, what's wrong," Chase's voice came through the phone, sounding more serious.

Raelynn took a deep breath, trying to steady her voice. "I just had a really tough day. I talked to my parents about this band I just started, and it didn't go well. They're not supportive at all, and my mom even told me to give up on music, break up with you, and find someone wealthy instead. And I just need to really hear your voice."

Chase was quiet for a moment, processing her words. "Rae, I dont know what you want me to say. I actually agree with your parents. I told you to stop letting that guy Brantley, Brentley, whatever his name is get inside your head. Chasing after music is just crazy talk."

Raelynn's heart sank at Chase's words, a crushing disappointment settling over her like a heavy fog. She had hoped for empathy and encouragement, especially after the devastating encounter with her parents. Instead, Chase's response was just as bitter cold.

"Chase," Raelynn said, her voice trembling with hurt, "I really thought you'd be understanding. I thought you'd be the one I could count on to support me.

Chase's voice was firm but detached. "I'm sorry, Rae. You've been so caught up in this dream since Cancun, and I can't keep pretending it's going to work out. You don't have the charisma to make it in the music industry."

"And you don't have the dick size to be such an asshole but here we are." Raelynn's voice was filled with raw anger as she abruptly hung up the phone.

Raelynn's heart sank at Chase's words, a heavy disappointment settling over her like a dense fog. She had been looking for empathy and encouragement, especially after the painful encounter with her parents. Instead, Chase's response was just as cold.

"Chase," Raelynn said, her voice trembling with hurt, "I really thought you'd understand. I thought you'd be the one person I could count on for support."

Chase's voice was firm but detached. "I'm sorry, Rae. You've been so obsessed with this dream since Cancun, and I can't keep pretending it's going to work out. You don't have the charisma to make it in the music industry."

"And you don't have the dick size to be this much of an asshole, but here we are." Raelynn's voice crackled with raw anger as she abruptly hung up the phone.

As Raelynn angrily sat in the silence of her apartment, her mind drifted back to Cancun and her brief encounter with Bentley. Remembering his words offered her solace as she faced the backlash for pursuing her dream. A part of her wished she had gotten Bentley's contact information just to hear his words of encouragement once more.

It wasn't long before Raelynn found herself lost in thought, wishing Chase could show the same level of support for her dreams that a complete stranger like Bentley had. Instead, she was left yearning for Chase's support, hoping that one day he might come around.

8

Eight Years Later: Bentley's Path to Superstardom

Camera lights flashing, another sold out show with fans screaming "Bentley", and a stage waiting for him to rip it to shreds; what was just a dream 8 years ago, is now Bentley's life. When Bentley and Cameron discussed him taking his music more serious, he wasn't being serious at all. He was just blowing smoke, joking with Cameron.

In the weeks after that conversation, Bentley started turning his emotions into powerful song lyrics. It was his outlet to keep his mind occupied from all the pain he endured with Michelle leaving him at the altar, to him coming back from their "honeymoon" to find out that she had died in a car crash. It was also a way for him to express his feelings about the encounter he had in Cancun with Raelynn. However, that brief but powerful connection with Raelynn was now a faded memory that he had long forgotten about.

As Bentley started recording the songs he wrote, he found the courage to post "Cinderella," a song inspired by his encounter with Raelynn in Cancun. To Bentley's surprise the song went viral.

Over a 7-month period Bentley released song after song, and just like "Cinderella" went viral, all his other songs followed suit. With his songs going viral all over the internet it was only a matter of time before he landed himself a record deal.

And just that happened.

One of the executive producers for Warner Bros. Records was strolling the internet trying to find a new breakout artist and that's when he stumbled across Bentley's music. At first the producer wasn't impressed with Bentley's sound, but astonished by the fan base he had, the producer kept listening. That's when he clicked on Bentley's song "Cinderella." Amazed by the sound of that song, he knew he couldn't let Bentley slip away and he just had to reach out.

Bentley still remembers the day he got the call from Warner Bros. Records, it was December 20th, 2012, at 8:30 in the morning when his phone started ringing. He was reluctant to answer the phone, as he didn't recognize the number. Looking back on it, Bentley is thankful that he did because that phone call changed his life.

Warner Bros. Records scheduled the meeting for after the holidays so that Bentley could spend Christmas and New Years with his family. It also allotted him the time and opportunity to break the big news to his family. Everyone was overly excited for the opportunity that Bentley had been given.

On January 4th, 2013, Warner Bros. Records flew Bentley out to Los Angeles, California for their big meeting. When the plane touched down at LAX Bentley felt the excitement consume him. He got off the plane and walked out the terminal gate wearing the biggest smile you had ever seen as he begin looking for his chauffeur that Warner Bros. Records had arranged to pick him up. Bentley saw a tall black guy decked out in the sharpest black suit and topper hat that you'd ever seen standing in front of a stretched-out Cadillac Escalade limousine holding a personalized sign with his name. Bentley was in state of awe. He could not believe all of this was happening to him.

When the limo pulled up to the front of the record label Bentley just took a deep breath as he knew he was moments away from changing his life. He stepped out of the limo, shook the driver's hand and thanked him for the hassle of being his chauffeur. As the driver pulled off Bentley just stood there looking up at this gigantic building, and he could feel his heart began to pound out of his chest. He slowly started taking steps toward the entrance of the building and with every step he took he could feel his hands become more and more sweatier.

Once inside the building Bentley was amazed at what he saw, plaque on top of plaques lined up and down each and every hallway wall. He was in so much awe that he began thinking to himself, "One day that's going to be my name on one of these plaques." While standing there the receptionist at the fronts desk noticed him standing there as if he were lost.

Once Bentley assured the receptionist that he wasn't lost she escorted him to a large conference room with a giant oval see-through glass table, where he patiently awaited the arrival of the producers, managers, and their legal team to come into the room.

Upon the team's arrival, Bentley rose from his seat, greeted everyone with a firm handshake, and settled back down. The label representatives initiated the meeting by expressing their interest in learning more about Bentley. They inquired about the inspiration behind his musical journey, prompting him to share his backstory.

Bentley explained to them his love for music, how he felt that when words couldn't speak music could. He also explained how his music was never meant to be taken seriously that it was more so a hobby to keep his mind occupied, as he explained to them the events that had transpired in his life over the past year. The label representatives were blown away by Bentley's backstory.

Not wanting to waste time, the team began explaining the ins and outs of what they were expecting. Their expectations of him were to have fan interaction to build his fan base. They expected him to become more social on social media. They also expected him to do interviews with the media periodically to also help build a relationship with fans and the media outlets by putting a face with a name. They also explained that if he were to sign, they would want him to begin recording music as soon as possible. Since his song "Cinderella" had become so popular over his current fan base, they wanted him to begin working on that with a producer for a re-release.

The team's lawyer pulled out the contract from his briefcase and laid it on the table with a smile. Bentley, without legal representation, anxiously awaited to hear the full extent of his contractual obligations. He was relieved to find the terms straightforward: meeting deadlines, engaging with fans and media, and Warner Bros Records owning the copyrights. Bentley would retain copyrights for select songs, maintain 50% creative control, and earn 35% in royalties for certain tracks. The label expected three albums in six years, with an upcoming recording budget. Warner Bros. Records showed remarkable faith in Bentley, offering him a contract usually reserved for seasoned artists due to his viral success. To support his career, they provided a manager from Harts Management, responsible for scheduling, bookings, interviews, and any other assistance Bentley might require.

That day marked a life-altering moment for Bentley as he pressed his pen onto the paper, letting the ink flow as he signed a contract worth $10 million with a $1,00,000 signing bonus. After signing, Bentley pushed the contract to the center of the table, leaned back in his chair, and released a deep sigh of relief. After a year and a half, Bentley finally felt on top of the world.

In present time, Bentley, now a sensational superstar ripping stages in half, and stealing girl's hearts, has been living his life like a rolling stone since the day he signed that contract. Although Bentley was now a three-time Grammy Award winner, and millionaire, he never forgot his roots. He kept his promise to his best friend Cameron. He gave Cameron $1.5 million to pay off all his debt and to build the nightclub of his dreams. With that money Cameron built club Electric. A club which became well known thanks to Bentley performing there.

Tonight, Bentley was up on stage at a sold-out show in Orlando, Florida performing the song that helped him get the Grammy Award for "Best New Artist." You could hear the words echoing throughout the venue, but it was something about tonight.

Everyone on Bentley's team could tell he was off. Even the fans in the crowd could tell something was up, just by the way he sounded and the way he was carrying himself. No one knew that on this date May 13th, 2011, 8 years ago Michelle, Bentley's bride-to-be passed away. Every year on this date for Bentley it's been hard to handle. Tonight was the first time he's had to perform on that date. Trying to fight back all the emotions he was feeling was taking its toll on his performance. Somehow Bentley was still able to make it through and close his set with his first hit, "Cinderella."

"You're calling my phone all hours of the night
That just means y'all had a fight
Looking for me to make it right
Though you don't plan on staying the night
You just want somebody to relax ya mind
While you come undone
But like Cinderella
You'll be gone before the morning sun
Leaving another piece of clothing behind
Just for me to find
Until the next time
I swear
This is another Cinderella story
With a romantic twist"

The lights dimmed as the closing chorus ended, and the fans erupted in cheers. Bentley, aware of his subpar performance, decided to stay on stage and requested a spotlight. He spoke from the heart, "Hey everyone, that was the last song of the set. I should be backstage right now, but I want to apologize for not being at my best tonight. My mind was elsewhere, and you all deserve better. To explain, not many people know this, but eight years ago on May 7th, 2011, I was supposed to marry my high school sweetheart, the love of my life. However, that didn't happen. I was left standing at the altar. On May 13th, 2011, she tragically passed away in a car crash. Today, May 13th, 2019, is the hardest day of the year for me. It's the first time I've had to perform on this date. I wanted to personally apologize to all of you. Thank you for being here tonight. Have a great night; I love you all." Bentley left the stage and was embraced by his team, who had tears in their eyes. Not many of them knew his story until that moment, and they encircled him like a family, providing support. Bentley felt like a weight had been lifted, as his past was no longer a secret, but something people could now understand.

Later that night, Bentley was at the after-party, doing what he's done best for the past 8 years. He'd spot an attractive girl, whisper sweet nothings, and sweep them off their feet. Tonight, his attention was on a tall, hazel-eyed blonde with a stunning outfit. He wasted no time and bought her a drink, asking playfully, "How many drinks to leave with a superstar?" With a mischievous grin, she replied, "One. Your place or mine?" Bentley, accustomed to such quick responses, smiled, took her hand, and led her to the nearest exit.

When they returned to Bentley's hotel room, the drinks were starting to take their toll as they stumbled through the door. As the door swung open, the blonde pushed Bentley against the wall and began kissing his neck. Suddenly, a high-pitched female voice interrupted them. Bentley recognized the voice, and it sent shivers down his spine. He knew he was in for a lecture when he heard, "Well hey there, son, I hope me, and your father aren't interrupting anything?" his mom said.

Shocked to see his parents in Orlando, he pushed the blonde away, "Mom, Dad, what a surprise! Why didn't you tell me you were coming?" The blonde looked disgusted and left in a hurry, slamming the door behind her.

"Seems like you've become quite the ladies' man," his dad said with a grin. Bentley's mom, less enthused, gave his dad a scolding look.

After Faye gave Steve the look, she turned to Bentley with a smile and said, "Son, do you not remember sending your father and me tickets to the show?"

Bentley's face revealed his forgetfulness, which was understandable given everything on his plate. He had to perform on the 8-year anniversary of his fiancée's death. Besides, he'd been too preoccupied living a bachelor's life, indulging in one-night stands.

"Mom, I completely forgot. You guys never told me you were coming, so I assumed you wouldn't. You've never attended any of the shows I sent tickets for, and you didn't even accept the money I sent you to ease your financial burdens. So, why are you here now, and how did you get into my hotel room?"

His mother smiled and, after taking a deep breath, said, "I suppose you have a point. Your father has always wanted to visit Florida, and with the plane tickets and show tickets you sent, we decided why not. Plus, we needed a break from reality and what better way than to see our superstar son perform in front of thousands of fans? Oh, and the concierge let us in. He called your manager Mike and verified it."

Bentley sensed something more significant was bothering his parents, but he initially chose to let it go. However, his love for his family led him to ask, "Mom, I'm glad you're here, but I wish you had called ahead so I could be better prepared and not have a random girl here. But, what's wrong? I can tell something's up by your tone and choice of words. You're hiding something. What's going on?"

His mother remained silent, and he could tell she thought she had hidden their problems well. She turned to Steve, and they exchanged glances before Steve spoke up, "Son, there is something wrong. Several things. First, you rarely come home since you found stardom. It's as if you've forgotten where you came from. I get it, you're young, living the high life, but you're 28, and it's time to settle down and start a family. Having a child out of wedlock while living the fast life would be a disgrace. We're ready to be grandparents, but the right way – meet a girl, marry her, have kids. We saw you with that girl tonight; you didn't even know her name. We raised you better than this. Lastly, your mother and I didn't want to burden you with our problems, but we're broke and struggling. We don't want your handouts, so keep your money. We're here because your mother thought it would be a good break from the stress we've been under lately."

Bentley was stunned by his father's lecture, as he had never seen him so stern. His parents being broke and not accepting his help left him baffled. His mother, typically a peacekeeper, sat in silence with tears in her eyes.

"Faye, I think it's best we go and give him some time to process everything," his father said as they got up to leave. Bentley walked them to the door, gave them both a hug, and told them he loved them before shutting the door behind them.

Shortly after his parents left, Bentley sat on the couch with a Bud Light, still trying to process his dad's stern words. He'd never seen his father so agitated, and he knew things must be tough for his parents. His mother, usually the strong one, had been unable to hide her anxiety. Bentley contemplated ways to help his parents without their knowledge.

His idea was to return home and stay there until they were back on their feet. The challenge was that he was in the middle of his first headliner tour, and canceling it would disappoint his fans, the record label, and promoters. However, he realized his final eight shows were all within a three-state radius—Tennessee, North Carolina, and South Carolina. What if he could combine these shows into one massive concert; A Cinderella Fan Fest and end the tour?

The next day, Bentley pitched the idea to his team, revealing his family issues behind the decision and how he wanted to ensure he didn't disappoint his fans or the record label. Surprisingly, the team loved it, and Bentley was taken aback by their enthusiasm. Bentley had a history of trying to satisfy everyone's needs, and this was another attempt to do just that.

With little time to execute the plan, his team was under immense stress. They had to notify the venues expecting Bentley, inform fans of the cancellation, and secure a large venue with adequate security for the fan fest. They considered Raleigh, North Carolina, Bentley's home state, but no existing venue could accommodate the expected crowd. They settled on the Bank of America Stadium, near the North Carolina-South Carolina border.

With the date set for May 23, 2019, Bentley was relieved. He decided to surprise his parents with the news and headed home. At the Orlando International Airport, he avoided paparazzi, opting for anonymity. As the flight to Raleigh Durham International boarded, he thought, "I'm coming home."

On the plane, he texted Cameron to arrange a pickup, keeping the surprise to himself. Then he settled in, closed his eyes, and took a nap, imagining the familiar scent of Carolina air as he prepared to return to his roots.

9

Eight Years Later: Raelynn's Struggles

Eight years had passed since Raelynn's life took an unexpected turn, and it had been a tumultuous journey. As she sat in her new home in Raleigh, North Carolina, she couldn't help but reflect on the trials and tribulations that had brought her here. Her journey was marked by heartache, lost dreams, and surprising new beginnings.

Raelynn and her band, "Southern Harmony", had faced numerous challenges and setbacks. Despite their undeniable talent and passion for music, record labels had repeatedly shut their doors to them. Raelynn couldn't escape the looming shadow of her father, Jim Hart, who had used his influence to blackball her and her band from the industry.

It was a bitter pill to swallow, knowing that her own father was the source of their struggles. She had grown up around the music industry, believing it was a world of opportunity and creativity. But her father's actions had shattered that illusion, leaving her to question her place in the industry she loved.

However, being blackballed by the industry wasn't the only thing that plagued the bands rise to stardom, but also Raelynn's pivotal decision to move to Raleigh.

One fateful night, Raelynn's best friend Cassidy Brooks called her in tears, revealing a life-altering moment. Confessing that she had conceived a child during a frat party with a complete stranger. Uncertain about her next steps, Cassidy made the courageous choice to keep the baby and forgo her education at NC State, where she had been attending college. In due time she gave birth to a baby boy, Skylar Jax Brooks. The challenges of single motherhood were a struggle to Cassidy.

Raelynn, faced with her own set of struggles, knew that she had to take action. She made the bold choice to leave Nashville behind and move to Raleigh to support Cassidy in raising Skylar. Her bandmates also believed that it was best to part ways. The band was stuck in a rut and not getting anywhere. They also weren't willing to uproot their lives and relocate to Raleigh, and Raelynn respected their decisions. Which marked the end of "Southern Harmony", a chapter of her life that was filled with dreams and memories.

Raelynn's personal life was no less tumultuous. Her relationship with Chase had been a rollercoaster of emotions. The trust issues that had plagued them since he cheated on her still lingered, casting a dark cloud over their love.

Then there was the unforgettable encounter with Bentley, the stranger who had walked into a dive bar where Raelynn was singing karaoke. They had shared an inexplicable connection that left a lasting impression on her. However, as time passed, she had pushed those memories to the deepest corners of her mind as she tried to focus on her future with Chase. Life had taught her that dwelling on such connections only led to heartache.

Additionally, an unresolved tension existed between Raelynn and Chase, casting a perpetual shadow over their relationship. Chase never wholeheartedly embraced Raelynn's musical aspirations and her involvement in the band. This ongoing source of discord had tarnished their bond for years. Though his affection for her ran deep, his reservations regarding her career path persisted, serving as an enduring barrier between them.

In spite of the tumultuous path they had navigated, Raelynn and Chase found themselves engaged after her relocation to Raleigh, finally able to spend more time together. It appeared to be a step toward a brighter future, yet their engagement would ultimately crumble beneath the weight of their unresolved issues.

The final nail in the coffin for their relationship came when Raelynn discovered that Chase had once again betrayed her. Raelynn walked in on Chase having sex with the same girl from his unit that he had previously cheated on her with. He had the girl face down in the pillows on their shared bed as he stood behind her plowing his weight into her. The heartbreak and betrayal cut deep, leaving Raelynn with no choice but to end their engagement and part ways. Not first without laying hands of Jesus on Chase.

The pain was excruciating, but it also allowed her to see the relationship for what it truly was—a cycle of betrayal, mistrust, and pure disrespect. It was time for her to move on and find her own path, unburdened by the weight of a broken heart.

Life in Raleigh proved to be difficult for Raelynn as she encountered the familiar ache of depression. She contemplated her decision on leaving Nashville, was it really worth it? Her relationship with Chase had met its demise since her move. Raelynn's musical career was also at standstill because of her decision to leave. During this period Raelynn began to question her purpose. She loved helping Cassidy raise Skylar, but she felt that her decision was putting her life and dreams on the backburner.

To get out of the slump she was in, Raelynn decided to try and start over by creating a band in Raleigh, hoping that collaboration and shared passion could reignite her musical journey. She placed ads in local music shops and online forums, looking for like-minded musicians who were willing to commit to the dream of making music their livelihood.

But as she began to audition potential bandmates, the challenges became apparent. None of the musicians she encountered shared the same vision as her. Some were only interested in playing gigs on weekends for fun, while others had commitments that made a full-time music career impossible. It seemed that everyone she met had a different idea of what music meant to them.

Frustration began to creep in, and Raelynn felt a sense of isolation. It was disheartening to witness her dream slipping through her fingers, and the weight of depression clung to her even more firmly.

Although Raelynn quickly realized forming a new band was no easy feat, she still refused to give up on chasing her dreams. In the midst of navigating through the struggles of helping Cassidy with Skylar and trying to form a band, it was Owen who offered her a glimmer of hope.

Owen eventually agreed to move to Raleigh to help Raelynn in her musical pursuit but only if she agreed to focus on a solo career. Owen believed that Raelynn's talent deserved to shine. With Owen's unwavering support and experience, the weight on Raelynn's shoulders felt a little lighter.

Owen's presence made all the difference, and together, they began building a band that aligned with Raelynn's vision. They meticulously handpicked musicians who shared her passion for music and understood the commitment it took to turn their dreams into reality.

They spent countless hours rehearsing, writing songs, and honing their sound. The chemistry among the band members was palpable, and Raelynn knew she had finally found the right team.

As they started performing together, the energy and connection they shared on stage were electric. The audience could feel it too, and their fan base began to grow steadily. Word spread about Raelynn and her band throughout North Carolina, and soon they were playing even more gigs.

With each successful show, Raelynn's confidence grew. She sensed a deeper connection to her music and her band while on stage, surpassing any feeling she'd ever experienced with "Southern Harmony."

The journey wasn't without its challenges. They faced long nights, financial struggles, and the inevitable creative differences that come with any artistic endeavor. But Raelynn and Owen had seen all this before during their stint with "Southern Harmony." Their experience helped navigate the band through those struggles as they continued to perform and build their reputation.

Through the band's passion and determination, they eventually saw Raelynn's solo career thriving as they began being booked up and down the East Coast.

In present time, Raelynn and her band sensed they were on the verge of a major breakthrough, even though they continued to play in intimate venues. While their reach had extended beyond Raleigh, Raelynn and her band cherished every chance to perform in the city, particularly at Club Electric. The strong rapport they had established with the owner, Cameron, made these performances especially meaningful. The connection they had forged with the venue and its audience was something they deeply valued.

Raelynn and her band were slated to play at Club Electric this weekend and Raelynn was beyond excited.

As Raelynn finished reflecting on the path that led her to now, she couldn't help but feel a sense of pride and accomplishment. The struggles of the past had molded her into a stronger and more determined artist.

Raelynn was still taking in the quiet when she heard the front door open, and Cassidy walked in. She looked tired, worn out and worried, and Raelynn knew that something was bothering her friend.

Cassidy slumped onto the couch across from Raelynn, and with a heavy sigh, she began to speak. "Raelynn, you won't believe the day I've had. Skylar had a doctor's appointment today, and they told me that he might have leukemia and may need a bone marrow transplant. But there's a catch... I'm not a match."

Raelynn's heart sank as she listened to Cassidy's words. The weight of the situation was palpable, and she could see the pain in her friend's eyes. She reached out and placed a reassuring hand on Cassidy's shoulder.

"Oh, Cass," Raelynn said softly, "I'm so sorry to hear that. That's just... it's unimaginable. How is Skylar?"

Cassidy's eyes welled up with tears as she spoke, "He's just a little boy, Raelynn. He doesn't fully understand what's going on, but he knows he's sick, and it breaks my heart to see him so confused and scared."

Raelynn squeezed Cassidy's shoulder gently, trying to offer as much comfort as she could. "I can't even imagine how tough this must be for you both. But, Cassidy, you're a great mother, and you're doing everything you can to take care of Skylar. Sometimes life throws us curveballs, and we have to face them head-on."

Cassidy wiped away her tears and nodded, her voice shaky but determined. "I know, Raelynn, but it's just... I feel so helpless. As his mom, it's my job to protect him, to keep him safe, and now I can't even provide him with what he needs the most – a match for the bone marrow transplant. I feel like I'm failing him."

Raelynn leaned in closer, her voice gentle and understanding. "Cassidy, you're not failing him. Sometimes, we can't control everything, no matter how much we want to. What you can do is be there for Skylar and let him know that you love him and that you'll support him through this. And who knows, there might be other potential donors out there who could be a match. We can spread the word, get the community involved, and do everything we can to find a donor for Skylar."

Cassidy nodded, her eyes still filled with worry but with a glimmer of hope as well. "You're right, Raelynn. I'll do whatever it takes to help my son. And I'm so lucky to have you as a friend, always being there for me."

Raelynn smiled, offering Cassidy her unwavering support. "We're in this together, Cass. We'll find a way to get through this, I promise."

As the two friends held onto each other in that moment of shared sorrow and determination, Raelynn had an idea spring into her mind. Instead of taking the proceeds from performing at Club Electric this weekend she was going to donate them to Cassidy for future medical bills. She also was going to speak to Cameron about possibly turning the show into a fund-raising event.

Raelynn's heart swelled with determination and a sense of purpose. She knew that she had the opportunity to make a significant impact, not just as a friend but as an artist with a platform. She looked into Cassidy's eyes, her own filled with newfound resolve.

"Cassidy, I want to do something for Skylar. I want to donate the proceeds from our performance at Club Electric this weekend to help with Skylar's future medical bills. It's the least I can do to support you both through this difficult time."

Cassidy's eyes widened, a mixture of surprise and gratitude. "Raelynn, that's... that's incredibly generous. Are you sure about this?"

Raelynn nodded firmly. "I'm sure, Cassidy. Music has the power to bring people together, and I want to use it to help you and Skylar. We'll dedicate this performance to your family, and I hope it can make a difference in some small way."

Tears welled up in Cassidy's eyes once more, but this time they were tears of gratitude and hope. She reached out and embraced Raelynn tightly, whispering, "Thank you, Raelynn. You have no idea how much this means to me and Skylar."

But Raelynn's determination didn't stop there. After their heartfelt conversation, she picked up her phone and reached out to Cameron, the club owner.

"Cameron, I have an idea," Raelynn began. "I want to turn our show at Club Electric into a fundraising event for Skylar's medical expenses. We can use our music and our fan base to make a real difference."

Cameron, on the other end of the line, was silent for a moment before responding, "That's a brilliant idea, Raelynn. I'll get to work on organizing it right away. We can collaborate with local charities and raise awareness within the community."

With the support of club Electric's owner Cameron and the rest of the band, Raelynn felt empowered. They would turn their upcoming performance into an event that would not only uplift the spirits of their fans but also help provide the financial assistance that Cassidy and Skylar so desperately needed. It was a way for them to give back and be there for their friend during her time of need, and Raelynn was determined to make it a night to remember.

10

Welcome Home Bentley!

As Bentley's plane touched down at Raleigh-Durham International, he quickly rushed outside to the terminal pick up where he spotted Cameron. Cameron was leaned up against his nice fancy all white sports car in a blue collared Polo, khakis, Sperry's, and aviator sunglasses, trying to look cool. When Cameron saw Bentley, he rushed over, greeted him with a hug, and helped him with his bags. "BENTLEY!!! HOW HAVE YOU BEEN MAN? LIKE HOW'S LIFE?" Cameron said with excitement.

Bentley smiled from ear to ear, "Man, I've been great. Actually, I'm doing excellent now that I'm here. I'm going to be home for a few months. How's the..." and before he could finish asking Cameron how he had been, Cameron cut in cutting him off.

"Wait, wait, what do you mean you'll be here a few months? Since you became Bentley, the superstar, you rarely come back home anymore other than the periodic visits."

Bentley laughed, "Man, it means exactly what it means. I'm here to stay for a few months. My team and I devised a plan to end the tour earlier by combining the last 8 shows into my first annual Another Cinderella Fan Fest so I could spend time at home with my friends and family. I really miss you guys. How have you been anyways, and how's my club."

Cameron laughed, "Sound like a case of the prodigal son returning home, and by the way, you mean MY club; it is doing great. Now that you're home for a while, maybe you can do a couple performances there for me, and I might be able to franchise it." Cameron said.

"We'll see," Bentley said with a chuckle.

Bentley found solace during the car ride home from the airport with Cameron, a rare high that didn't require alcohol. It felt like the chaos of his high-speed life was finally slowing down, or so he hoped. However, his thoughts kept drifting to his parents and their financial struggles. While he hadn't devised a concrete plan yet, he was determined to assist them discreetly by paying off all their bills. Bentley anticipated their anger when they discovered his actions, but he believed it was better to seek forgiveness than permission. After all, he was an adult, and it was his money to use as he saw fit.

As Cameron pulled into Bentley's driveway, Bentley was surprised to see both his parents' vehicles at home. He was more disappointed because he wanted to be in the house with dinner cooked to surprise them when they got home. This threw a wrench in his plans, but it was still possible to surprise them this way.

As Bentley walked through the door, he thought he had walked into the wrong house as he walked in on his parents in a shouting match with one another. Something Bentley had never seen his parents do ever.

"Mom, Dad, what the hell is happening here?" Bentley asked as he walked through the kitchen.

His mom was looking over a stack of bills at the kitchen table with tears while his dad stood at the kitchen bar. "Hey, son, what are you doing here?" His mom asked with a shaky voice as she tried wiping the tears from her eyes.

With a confused look, Bentley answered, "I'm going to be home for a couple of months and thought I was going to surprise you guys. Instead, y'all are surprising me with a warzone. What the hell is going on?"

His parents looked shocked when he said he was staying home for a couple of months. His dad was the slightest bit thrilled, "Oh great, another mouth to feed." Still no answers on what was going on.

Bentley decided the only way to get to the bottom of the hostility was to partake in the warzone as he too raised his voice. "WHAT THE HELL IS GOING ON? WHAT DOES HE EVEN MEAN ANOTHER MOUTH TO FEED?"

Tears started falling uncontrollably from his mother's eyes as she looked up at him, "Everything's gone wrong. I lost my job at the firm 2 months ago, and everything has fallen on your father. We've been struggling to make it work. Today he lost his job at the plant. So now we have no money coming in, and your father refuses to ask you for help. Son, we could use your help, but your father is too proud to ask for it."

At that moment, his father shouted across the kitchen, "OH, I'M TOO PROUD BECAUSE I BELIEVE IN WORKING AND BUSTING MY ASS FOR THE THINGS I OWN. I DON'T NEED NO HANDOUT," as he stormed out the backdoor, slamming it shut behind him. His mother just placed her face in the palm of her hands and continued crying.

Bentley's heart felt like it had been shattered. He finally understood how bad his parents were struggling and couldn't believe his dad didn't want his help. He wanted nothing more in the world than to help his parents; after all, they supported him financially for 20 years.

Bentley walked over to his mother, took the stack of bills from her, and began looking them over. He saw the foreclosure notice on their house, the electric bill, the cellphone bills, his sister's tuition and rent bills, and all the other miscellaneous bills. He shook his head in acknowledgment as he looked up at his mother, grabbed her hands, and held them in his.

"Mom, don't worry about this. I'm going to have my accountant take care of all of this. Don't worry about Dad; he'll come around. Right now, he's depressed, stressed, and ashamed because he can't take care of his family, but what is family if they don't help each other? So don't worry about this, Mom; I got this." Bentley said with assurance.

Bentley got up from the table and went out the backdoor to find his dad. He walked into his dad's work shed, where he found Steve sitting on his workbench crying with a .45 in his right hand. Immediately adrenaline started pumping throughout Bentley's body as he feared what might happen next. Bentley took a deep breath as he carefully approached his father.

"Dad put the gun down and look at me; talk to me," Bentley said as calmly as possible in a situation like that.

Steve slowly put the gun down as he looked up at Bentley, "You shouldn't be in here. Please, son, get out."

Still not believing the situation, Bentley took another deep breath just to keep calm. "I'm glad I'm in here. Had I not got in here when I did, there's no telling what I might have walked in on. So, I'm not leaving, not until you give me that gun." Bentley said, continuing to remain as calmly as he could.

Steve took a deep breath, handed Bentley the gun, and just broke down crying as Bentley grabbed his father, embracing him in a hug, holding him tightly. "I'm sorry, son, I'm sorry." Steve cried out repeatedly.

Bentley was shaking as he was slowly coming down from the adrenaline high. "Dad, we're keeping this between us. No one needs to know, especially not Mom." Bentley said, continuing to hold on to his dad.

"Son, I feel like a failure; I feel like I'm not a man because I can't provide for my family. That's my job, not yours." His father said with a shaky voice.

"Dad, we're family. And family helps family when they're in need. I love you, and I love your work ethic, but I owe you both so much for supporting me all these years. I'm taking care of everything, so you don't need to worry about it. I'm also providing extra money so you and Mom can stop working if you want. It's not a handout; it's a way to give back and let you be your own boss." Bentley assured his dad.

Steve looked at Bentley, his eyes filled with gratitude and pride. He couldn't believe how much his son had grown, not just in stature, but in heart and soul.

"You've always had a good heart, son," Steve whispered, his voice choked with emotion. "But I never imagined you'd be the man you are today. I'm so proud of you."

Bentley smiled, his own eyes glistening with tears. "We're a team, Dad. We've always been. And I'll do whatever it takes to make sure you and Mom are taken care of."

As Steve and Bentley let go of each other's embrace, Bentley playfully chuckled, "Damn, this was a helluva welcome home." His dad sighed and apologized for the millionth time.

Later that night, Bentley recounted the day's events to Cameron over the phone. Cameron was shocked to hear that Mr. and Mrs. Riggs were facing financial difficulties, as they always seemed so composed. Bentley mentioned that his father had even attempted to end his life to secure an insurance policy for the family, instead of reaching out for Bentley's help, despite Bentley's willingness to support them.

"Cam, it's crazy," Bentley told his friend, "They were in Orlando at my show just two nights ago, and I could sense something was wrong. I had no idea how bad it was until I got home. I am so grateful that I decided to cut the tour short and organize this fan fest to be here with them."

Cameron agreed that Bentley's decision was wise and suggested that Bentley come to Club Electric over the weekend to relax and clear his mind before the upcoming fan fest. Bentley agreed, acknowledging that the 3-day event would be both stressful and fun, making some downtime essential.

After talking to Cameron, Bentley checked social media to gauge the fans' reactions to the announcement of the inaugural Another Cinderella fan fest. Many fans expressed their excitement about being part of this event. However, there were some who expressed disappointment due to the last-minute changes, as they couldn't make it due to work or travel constraints.

Despite feeling sorry for those who couldn't attend, Bentley remained confident in his decision and was enthusiastic about the fan fest. He was also eager to see which other artists his team would bring on board to perform.

As Bentley lay in his childhood bedroom that night, he couldn't help but think about Cameron's offer to visit Club Electric. The room felt smaller than he remembered, the walls adorned with posters of his favorite bands from his teenage years. It was a stark contrast to the glamorous life he led on tour, and for a moment, it was a comforting feeling.

The events of the day had taken a toll on Bentley's emotions. His parents' financial struggles and the revelation of his father's desperate act had left him reeling. Bentley couldn't shake the image of his dad, sitting in that work shed with a gun in hand, and the relief he felt when he managed to intervene.

He stared at his phone, contemplating whether to text Cameron to confirm his plans for the weekend. Cameron's invitation seemed like a lifeline in the midst of chaos. The idea of letting loose and taking a break from the chaos of his life as a superstar was tempting. Bentley considered the fun he could have at Club Electric, surrounded by friends and familiar faces. The idea of leaving his family temporarily to relax and clear his mind was becoming increasingly appealing.

As he weighed the options, Bentley couldn't help but feel torn. He wanted to spend as much time with his parents as possible and be there to support them in every way he could. But he also needed a moment to breathe, to gather his thoughts and find the strength to face the road ahead.

As he typed out a message to Cameron, Bentley couldn't help but feel a sense of guilt for leaving his parents during such a challenging time. However, he also recognized that he needed to take care of himself and find some balance in his life.

With the message sent, Bentley took a deep breath, hoping that a night at Club Electric would provide the mental break he desperately needed. It was a chance to unwind, celebrate his homecoming, and prepare himself for the upcoming fan fest.

11

It's Electric

It was the Saturday before Fan Fest and Bentley showed up at Club Electric taking Cameron up on his offer. Tonight, would be the first time Bentley had been inside Electric and not performed. He was looking forward to enjoying himself.

"Hey Bentley, I'm glad you could make it, man. Hope you're enjoying yourself; God knows you need it. Just cut loose and do what Bentley does." Cameron said as he spotted Bentley come through the door.

Bentley laughed and nodded as he walked through the crowd to the bar. He really couldn't speak too much to Cameron because the club was insanely busy, and so was Cameron.

As Bentley made his way to the bar he accidently bumped into a gorgeous, yet feisty woman. "Watch where you're going, asshole." Bentley heard her say as she disappeared into a sea of people.

Bentley couldn't quite place a finger on it, but something about the woman's five-foot-four curvy frame, platinum shoulder-length blonde hair, and her soul-piercing blue eyes seemed very familiar. With his stardom, Bentley had encountered numerous women, making it almost impossible to remember them all. However, there was an aura of recognition about her that piqued his curiosity.

As he sat at the bar with his drink in hand, Bentley's mind raced to connect the dots. He couldn't help but wonder if this woman had crossed paths with him in the past, perhaps during one of his performances or meet-and-greets. Her striking presence hinted at a deeper connection that he was struggling to recall. Either way, Bentley knew he had to get with her by the nights end.

About an hour later, Bentley turned around to signal the bartender for two more beers when he spotted the familiar girl he had bumped into earlier. "Hey," Bentley greeted her. The blonde continued to sway to the music, seemingly ignoring him, waiting for the bartender to prepare her drink. Slightly perplexed, Bentley made another attempt. "Hey, how are you?" Finally, the blonde acknowledged him, but with an eye roll.

Determined not to be discouraged, Bentley persisted. "Why are you ignoring me? What have I done to you?" he inquired.

The blonde turned to him, her expression now clearly aggressive as she sharply retorted, "Fuck off, asshole."

Bentley, now looking puzzled, remarked, "Dang, feisty, are we?"

The blonde responded with a disgusted look, clearly irritated by his persistence. She retorted, "No, I don't have time for fuck-boys like you, Bentley."

Bentley's jaw dropped in disbelief when she mentioned his name. For a moment, he had forgotten his superstar status. "Wait, how do you know my name?" he inquired, genuinely curious.

The blonde looked at him, her expression incredulous. "Um, are you stupid Mr. Superstar? How about your hit song 'Cinderella,' or the fact that my dad is the CEO of the company your manager works for?" she replied, her tone laced with attitude as she stormed off.

Bentley was completely unaware that the blonde he accidentally collided with was Raelynn, the girl he had shared such a profound connection with during their one-night encounter in Cancun. He found himself too preoccupied savoring the sting of rejection to connect the dots about the blonde's identity. Especially since it had been quite some time since a woman had turned down his advances. He shook his head and took the last sip of his beer, pondering the unexpected twist of fate that had just transpired.

Backstage getting ready to go on, Raelynn found herself venting to Owen about what had happened with Bentley. She couldn't believe the audacity of Bentley to try and spit game. Especially, since he was plastered on almost every magazine and media outlet as a playboy.

"I really can't believe him Owen, like who does he think he is? I'm not one of his little groupies! I'm not going to fall for his antics and throw myself at him for sex. I don't know him. I don't want to know him." Raelynn pleaded to Owen while he was pre-tuning his guitar.

Owen looked up at Raelynn as he continued to tune his guitar, "Well, Rae, the guy is a famous rapper with a lot of popularity right now. I mean he is also on the cover of Forbes magazine as the hottest man alive right now and women probably are throwing their selves at him and he's more than likely not saying no to very many. At this point, Bentley probably thinks every woman in America does want to sleep with him."

The expression on Raelynn's face was pure disgust as she felt like Owen was trying to justify Bentley's actions. "So basically, what I heard is you would be doing the same thing if you were in his shoes Owen."

"No. That is not at all what I am saying. Bentley is a prick that just so happens to be in a position of a lot of attention from women and he's only thinking with his dick. Honestly, it's embarrassing to watch for us good guys." Owen pleaded.

At that moment, a lightbulb went off inside Raelynn's head, "Owen, you just gave me an idea! What do you think about me pointing him out tonight. Maybe call him on stage and publicly embarrass him in front of everyone?"

"Well Rae, this is your show. You call the shots here. If this is something, you want to do then I will support you like I have from day one." Owen said as he got up to head towards the stage entrance.

As Raelynn stood at the bottom of the steps to the stage entrance, she knew what she had to do. She knew she couldn't be the one to let Bentley continue to get by with his playboy antics. She wasn't going to let him keep embarrassing the good guys.

Just as Raelynn was set to come on stage the DJ stopped spinning the music and came on the mic, "Alright, Alright, Electric, it's that time.

No, not last call but time to welcome the hottest artist in the Triangle area with us here tonight up on stage."

Bentley's eyes grew wide as he just knew that the DJ was going to call his name. If the DJ called his name, he was going to be pissed because he told Cameron that he was only coming to drink, not perform, and Cameron agreed.

"Welcome to the stage Miss Raelynn Hart." The DJ shouted.

Bentley sighed a huge sigh of relief as his eyes grew bigger when Raelynn stepped onto the stage. He couldn't believe his eyes. It was the girl he had tried talking to earlier in the night that so ruthlessly shut him down. He was now even more intrigued by this mysterious woman as he now had a name to go with the face.

"Hey everybody, y'all ready to party," Raelynn asked the crowd.

Bentley was finally able to hear Raelynn voice loud and clear, now that it wasn't being covered up over the loud club music. Something about the innocence in her country twang voice sounded very familiar. Bentley just couldn't place it, but he was infatuated.

"I'm ready to party too, but first, let me share a quick story about tonight. I had an unpleasant encounter with a guy earlier – no 'excuse me' or anything. Later, I'm at the bar, grabbing shots to muster the courage to stand in front of all of you, and guess who's there? That same guy, trying to flirt with me. Seriously, can you not." Raelynn conveyed to the crowd, glancing in Bentley's direction. Bentley had the biggest smile on his face.

"Y'all want me to embarrass him by inviting him up here?" Raelynn asked the crowd. Bentley's smile quickly faded.

Bentley started looking around as the crowd erupted into a chant, "DO IT DO IT."

"Alright, alright, y'all got it. Bentley, c'mon, get your ass up here on this stage." Raelynn demanded.

Bentley took a huge breath as he knew there was no escaping this. He started making his way through the crowd of people, making sure this time he said "Excuse me" every time he maneuvered around someone or bumped someone. As he climbed on the stage, the equipment manager shoved a microphone into his chest.

Once Bentley was on stage standing in the bright spotlights and Raelynn could see him up close and personal, bells started going off inside her head. Bentley looked strikingly familiar to her and not because of his fame but like someone she knew. It was something in his demeanor and the way he looked, his five-foot-ten stature, five o'clock shadow, high skin fade, blueish green eyes, tattoos going up and down his right arm, and the way his muscles filled out the tight black t-shirt he was wearing was piquing Raelynn's curiosity. However, in the moment, Raelynn knew she didn't have time to figure out how or if she did know Bentley.

"Now, Bentley, do you want to redeem yourself in front of all these people and tell your side of the story," Raelynn asked Bentley as she was still looking at him with curiosity on her face. Bentley just smiled at Raelynn and shook his head "no" jokingly. He was trying not to stare, but her beauty was hard not to stare at, as he too was still trying to figure out if they had a previous connection.

"Well, no, not really. But since you've so kindly put me in the spotlight, I guess I will give my side of the story. Yes, I did bump into you earlier tonight, and before I could apologize, you disappeared into a crowd of people, I guess cause you're so short. It's easy for little people to get lost in a crowd. Oh, and as far as the bar, I was trying to apologize until you called me a fuck-boy, and yeah, maybe I was trying to flirt who knows." Bentley responded as he was looking deeply into Raelynn's eyes trying to figure out her game.

Raelynn just laughed. "Aw, that's so cute; Bentley has a soft side. He doesn't like to be called a fuck-boy. We've all read the articles; we know who you are. A single superstar living the bachelor life breaking girl's hearts, too bad I'm out of your league."

The crowd went berserk when Raelynn told Bentley that she was out of his league, screaming, "BURNED!"

Bentley couldn't believe he had just got roasted like that. Raelynn on the other hand looked at Bentley with a huge smile knowing she had defeated him as Bentley didn't have a comeback. Raelynn felt like she accomplished her goal in getting a win for the good guys. However, she knew she couldn't let this opportunity pass her by, for her career's sake.

"So Electric, what are the odds you guys have two artists in the same building at the same time, and one of those artists being a 3-time Grammy award winner? You know, I think that calls for a song together. How about 'Cinderella' goes country, I do the chorus, and Bentley here does his famous rap verse's?" Raelynn looked out at the crowd and asked.

Bentley didn't want to perform tonight, but Raelynn and her fans insisted, "Raelynn, I think you're right; let's do it. I don't want to steal your spotlight, but since you're insisting, let's do it." Bentley said as he nodded in agreement.

The crowd cheered as the song faded out, and Bentley jumped off the stage. When he jumped off the stage, he decided to stay near the stage to watch Raelynn's performance. Not only did Raelynn look familiar but her voice was also strikingly familiar. Bentley just couldn't remember how or why. The only thing he knew for sure was Raelynn was so beautiful with the voice of an angel.

After Raelynn's performance, she bowed and thanked the audience, including Bentley, who had joined her on stage. "Thanks for performing with me, Bentley, you asshole," she playfully quipped as she left the stage. Bentley raised his beer in response and decided to find Raelynn backstage.

Raelynn stood out to Bentley; she didn't fall for his usual charm, and she seemed to harbor a strong dislike for him. Her rejection only intrigued him further, and he wanted to understand why. He also wanted to know why she felt so familiar.

"That was quite a stunt you pulled back there," Bentley said as he approached Raelynn on her way to the dressing room.

She glanced back and smiled, teasing, "Should have known Bentley would come looking for me."

Raelynn, though small in stature at five-foot-four, her attitude made her seem ten feet tall and unshakable. "You should know that I've read all the tabloid stories about your one-night adventures and the hearts you've broken," she remarked. "So, let's cut to the chase. I'm Raelynn. It was nice to meet you, but I don't fall for one-liners or guys like you, so this conversation is now over."

Bentley, undeterred by her shade, smiled politely and shook his head. "Don't believe everything you read in those tabloids; they love to twist stories for a headline. Here, give me your phone and I'll give you my number. When you want to get to know the real Bentley Riggs, just give me a call."

Raelynn hesitated but eventually handed over her phone, thinking there was no harm in taking his number, even if she had no intention of calling.

12

The Connection

The next morning Raelynn woke up to find that her performance with Bentley was going viral. She almost couldn't believe it. She felt as if she were dreaming. Although Raelynn wasn't very fond of Bentley, she knew this is what her career needed to get her in the national spotlight.

As Raelynn lay in bed, she kept replaying the night over as Bentley's face kept flashing in her head. She knew about Bentley's reputation through the media and wanted nothing to do with him. She didn't care if he was famous or the hottest man alive according to Forbes, that didn't impress her. However, after encountering Bentley in person, Raelynn found herself oddly attracted to him. She couldn't quite grasp what it was about Bentley that was drawing her in. Was it Bentley's strangely familiar presence or the fact that he had singled her out in the crowded club that piqued her curiosity. All that Raelynn was sure of was her growing curiosity about Bentley, as she stared at the phone number he had entered, contemplating whether she should give him a call.

After a few moments of contemplation, Raelynn's curiosity got the best of her. With her heart pounding, she dialed the number and brought the phone to her ear.

As the phone rang, Raelynn's nerves got the best of her. She couldn't believe she was actually doing this against her better judgement. After a few more rings, just when she thought he might not answer, she heard a groggy voice on the other end.

"Hello?" Bentley mumbled, clearly still half-asleep.

Raelynn hesitated as she didn't know what to say. She honestly didn't think Bentley would pick up her phone call.

"Bentley?" Raelynn replied with a slight tremble in her voice.

There was a pause, and Raelynn could almost picture Bentley rubbing his eyes as he tried to wake up. "Yeah, this is Bentley. Who's this?"

"It's Raelynn," she said, her confidence growing as she spoke.

Bentley quickly recognized her voice. He honestly couldn't believe Raelynn actually decided to call him. Especially after how she kept shutting him down last night.

"Hey, Raelynn! I'm glad you called. I honestly didn't think you would, though, especially the way you quickly blew me off every time I tried to talk to you." Bentley said with a tad bit of excitement in his voice.

Raelynn laughed as she tried to explain herself. "About last night, I'm sorry. However, today's a new day, so maybe we can get a fresh start. What do you say we go get some coffee? My treat, and maybe you can help me get to know the real Bentley Riggs."

Uh, sure, just give me time to get up and take a shower. Just text me the location and the time." Bentley said with disbelief that Raelynn was given him some sort of chance.

That afternoon, Bentley and Raelynn met a local coffee shop in Downtown Raleigh. Both were visibly nervous to the other as they greeted each other. As they sat at a high-top table on the outside patio looking at the pedestrians walking the streets and cars go by, Bentley couldn't help but notice that familiar aura still surrounding Raelynn. For Raelynn, it was likewise. There was something strange about Bentley that was pulling her to Bentley, almost like she had known him all her life.

"So, I guess I will start since I invited you here." Raelynn said as she folded her hands on the table-top in front of her. "I guess I'm here to get to know the real Bentley Riggs, so tell me." Raelynn finished as she took a sip of her coffee.

Bentley took a deep breath as he prepared to tell Raelynn the real story of Bentley Riggs. "A few nights ago, at my show in Orlando, I revealed something that hasn't hit the tabloids yet. So, here's the unfiltered truth. Eight years ago, I was a different person. Engaged and ready to settle down, until my fiancé left me a note on the dresser, saying we were too young. I went on our honeymoon to Cancun alone, trying to heal. When I returned, I learned she'd been killed in a car accident. Music became my solace, and Warner Bros. Records discovered me. Fame brought excesses - women, booze, and money. I became a partying sensation, trying to numb the pain. Until my parents confronted me in Orlando, reminding me of the person they raised. It stung. That's why I'm back home, planning to stay for a while. That's my story. What's yours?"

In that instance Raelynn understood her curiosity that had been drawing her into Bentley. It finally clicked for her why Bentley felt so familiar – because he was. "Wait a second," Raelynn said as she paused to look Bentley up and down with confusion on her face before continuing. "You're Bentley, Bentley?" She said with a questioning tone.

Bentley could see the lightbulbs going off in her head as he watched her eyes studying him with deep focus. Bentley was lost at was going on inside her head as he had still not made the connection.

"What do you mean? I'm confused right now because yes, I'm Bentley, as in famous rapper Bentley." he said with a confused look on his face.

"No, you idiot. I know you're Bentley the famous rapper, but you're also Bentley from Cancun. Remember, I was singing karaoke, you walked up to me and my boyfriend Chase, and we hung out on the beach that night?" Raelynn replied as she was still in disbelief.

Bentley's eyes widened in realization. The memories came flooding back, crashing against the walls he had built around that time in his life. "Raelynn...?" he stammered; his voice tinged with disbelief.

Raelynn nodded, a mixture of surprise and amusement dancing in her eyes. "Yes, Bentley. It's me."

A smile spread across Bentley's face, a blend of astonishment and sheer joy. "I can't believe it's you! I knew you seemed familiar! I honestly never thought I'd see you again after all these years and kicked myself for not getting your number. "

Raelynn chuckled, the sound of it filling the space between them. "Well, it seems fate had other plans for us. I can't believe we found each other like this, in the most unexpected way. Shit, I can't believe you've been right in front of my face all this time and I didn't recognize you! You look so different with all of them tattoos and muscles," Raelynn said as she caught herself admiring Bentley's new attracting physical attributes.

Bentley blushed, a rare occurrence for a man who was used to the spotlight. "Yeah, a lot has changed over the years. I guess life has a way of shaping us in unexpected ways."

Raelynn couldn't help but smile, charmed by Bentley's humility. "Well, you wear it well," she said with a grin sliding across her face.

Bentley found himself drawn to Raelynn's smile, a radiant and captivating expression that seemed to light up the entire coffee shop patio. It was as if the years had melted away, and they were back in Cancun, sharing the same connection that had initially brought them together.

"So, now that we've put the pieces to the puzzle together. Tell me about you. How's things with you and Chase?" Bentley asked as he was still blushing.

"After our conversation in Cancun, where you encouraged me to pursue music, I did just that. However, my journey hasn't been as successful as yours. It's been an uphill battle. When I formed the band 'Southern Harmony,' Chase wasn't supportive at all; he thought it was a foolish idea. My parents also disapproved of my musical ambitions. I approached my father for help with a record deal, but it backfired, and we got blackballed from the industry. My best friend Cassidy had a baby from a one-night stand, and I moved to Raleigh to help her raise her son while finishing my degree online. I thought it would work out with Chase, as he was stationed nearby at Camp LeJeune. We even got engaged, but I caught him cheating, and we broke up about six and a half years ago. It sent me into a depression spiral. Owen, my guitarist from the 'Southern Harmony,' eventually moved to Raleigh to help me with my musical career, on the condition that I pursue a solo path. We've been doing well, but we still haven't had any calls from record labels. Last night, though, performing with you might have opened some doors in the industry. Our performance is going viral, and it feels like a breakthrough." Raelynn confessed.

Bentley listened intently to Raelynn's story, a mixture of empathy and admiration in his eyes. He couldn't help but feel a deep sense of connection to her, given their shared history in Cancun. Her journey in the music industry resonated with his own struggles to find his path, and he admired her determination and resilience.

"That's quite a journey you've been on," Bentley said with a supportive tone. "I'm sorry to hear about the challenges you've faced, especially with your father and Chase. But it's inspiring to see that you've continued pursuing your passion. And it's great to hear that our performance together might be a turning point for your career. You definitely have the talent. I thought that back in Cancun."

Raelynn smiled, appreciating Bentley's kind words. "Thank you, Bentley. It means a lot coming from someone like you, who's made it big in the industry. But enough about me. What about you? What made you decide to come back home and take a break from the fame and the fast life?"

Bentley took a sip of his coffee, contemplating how much he wanted to share. After a moment, he began to speak, his voice tinged with sincerity. "Like I mentioned earlier, I lost sight of who I was after my fiancée left me and then passed away. The fame and success were a way to numb the pain, but they also turned me into someone I didn't recognize. When my parents confronted me, it was a wake-up call. I realized I needed to reconnect with my roots, rediscover the person I used to be before all this."

Raelynn nodded in understanding. "It takes a lot of courage to step back and reevaluate your life like that. I'm glad you're finding your way back to your true self. I must admit; I was initially skeptical of meeting you, given your reputation. But now, that I remember who you are I'm far from skeptical. I remember how hurt you were in Cancun when your fiancé left you at the altar. I met the vulnerable Bentley, not superstar Bentley. Only if the media could see the side of you that I've seen. Only if they could see that you've been dealt a great deal of hurt resulting in walls being built and the things you do are to numb that pain."

Bentley let a slight smile creep across his face, "I can't blame you for being skeptical. I know I've done my fair share of wild and crazy things. I fully understand I still have a lot of healing I still need to do as well as a lot of growing up to do. Also, I really appreciate your kind words, but I don't think the media is ready for a vulnerable Bentley."

Raelynn nodded, her eyes softening with understanding. "You're right, the media doesn't often show the real person behind the celebrity façade. But sometimes, it's those vulnerabilities and struggles that make you relatable to people. It's what connects us all, in the end."

Their conversation flowed effortlessly, and time seemed to slip away as they shared stories, dreams, and aspirations. It was a beautiful feeling that after all the years that had passed there was still a connection between the two.

As the evening sun painted the sky with shades of orange and pink, Bentley found himself captivated by Raelynn's presence. Her warm smile, her genuine interest in his story, and the way she saw through his fame to the person he once was had him hooked. He couldn't deny that he was increasingly drawn to her, not just out of curiosity but a genuine connection that transcended their past.

Their coffee cups were long empty, and the patio lights began to twinkle as night settled in. Bentley couldn't help but muster the courage to ask, "Raelynn, would you be interested in continuing this conversation over dinner? I know a great Italian restaurant nearby with some amazing lasagna."

Raelynn grinned, her eyes sparkling with anticipation. "I'd love that, Bentley. It sounds perfect."

With the decision made, Bentley and Raelynn left the coffee shop, their footsteps filled with a sense of excitement and possibility. The night held the promise of more revelations, laughter, and the rekindling of a connection that had been buried in the sands of Cancun.

As Bentley and Raelynn sat at the Italian restaurant, their conversation flowed seamlessly. They talked about their dreams, their fears, and everything in between. It felt like they had known each other for a lifetime, despite the years that had passed since their chance encounter under the Mexico stars.

As the evening wore on, Bentley couldn't shake the feeling that there was something special about this moment. It was as if fate had intervened, bringing them back together for a reason. And then, it hit him.

"Raelynn," Bentley said, his voice filled with a newfound determination, "I have an idea. You know about me canceling my tour and combing the remaining shows into the Cinderella Fan Fest, right?"

Raelynn nodded, her curiosity peaked. "Yeah, of course. It's supposed to be a huge event."

"Well," Bentley continued, "what if you were to perform at the fest? I think it could be a game-changer for you. It's a chance to showcase your talent on a national stage, and with the buzz from our performance last night, I think the organizers would be open to it."

Raelynn's eyes widened in surprise. The idea was both exciting and daunting. The Cinderella Fan Fest was a major event, and performing there would undoubtedly be a turning point in her career.

"You really think they'd consider us?" Raelynn asked, a mixture of hope and disbelief in her voice.

Bentley nodded, his gaze unwavering. "I do. I mean it is MY festival after all. All I got to do is put the word in."

Raelynn couldn't believe what she was hearing. This was an opportunity of a lifetime, one that could change the trajectory of her music career. She looked into Bentley's eyes, gratitude and excitement welling up inside her.

"I... I don't know what to say," Raelynn stammered, overcome with emotion.

Bentley smiled, his eyes filled with sincerity. "Just say yes, Raelynn. And I'll make it happen."

Raelynn's heart raced as she processed the magnitude of Bentley's offer. It was an incredible opportunity, one that she had never even dared to dream of. She took a deep breath and looked into Bentley's eyes with determination.

"Yes, Bentley," she said, her voice unwavering. "I would love to perform at the festival."

Bentley's face lit up with joy, his eyes sparkling with excitement. "That's fantastic, Raelynn! We're going to blow the roof off that place. I'll make sure everything is arranged with the organizers. You're going to be amazing."

As they left the restaurant that evening, the air was filled with a sense of anticipation and possibility. Bentley couldn't help but feel a growing connection to Raelynn, one that went beyond their shared past. He wanted to spend more time with her, getting to know the woman who had captured his attention in such a profound way.

"Raelynn, I was thinking, maybe we could spend some more time together before the festival. You know, to rehearse, hang out, and just get to know each other better. What do you say?" Bentley asked before parting ways.

Raelynn's heart skipped a beat at the thought of spending more time with Bentley. She had come to admire and appreciate him in ways she never expected. "I'd love that, Bentley," she replied, her voice filled with genuine enthusiasm. "Let's make some magic happen."

As they parted ways, little did they know that magic was certainly going to be made in more ways than just music.

13

Once in a Lifetime

Bentley woke up feeling determined to get Raelynn added to the Cinderella Fan Fest setlist as he began making calls. He knew it wasn't going to be an easy task, but he was not going to budge until Raelynn was added.

After numerous negotiations with team managers and organizers, Bentley finally got the confirmation that Raelynn was going to be added. He couldn't help but share a sense of excitement for her. After Raelynn's story about her struggles in the music industry the previous night Bentley knew she truly deserved it. He couldn't wait to tell her later that evening when they met for dinner.

On cloud nine from all the feelings that he was feeling, Bentley decided to call Cameron and fill Cameron in on who Raelynn was. Bentley knew that Cameron was going to struggle to believe that Raelynn was the girl Bentley encountered in Cancun. Bentley himself was still struggling to believe it.

After a few rings Cameron answered the phone. "What's up Bentley? I see you performed at the club the other night after you told me you weren't going to perform." Cameron said with a laugh.

"Yeah, your artist was very ruthless. I kind of was left no choice. I actually called to talk to you about her." Bentley said with a chuckle before switching to a more serious tone.

"No, Bentley. I can't help you hook up or whatever it is you are trying to accomplish." Cameron said over the phone with a deliberate tone.

Bentley felt a shot of discouragement. Is that really what Cameron and the rest of the world thought of him? That all he wanted to do was sleep with every woman he possibly could? Was he really that bad…a full out playboy.

"Cam, man, that's not what I want to tell you. Do you remember my honeymoon to Cancun?" Bentley asked still trying to brush off Cameron's words.

"Yeah. That was eight years ago, what about it?" Cameron asked with confusion.

"Do you remember the girl I told you I met while there?" Bentley asked, as he was mischievously trying to build the suspense.

"Yeah. Again, what about it?" Cameron asked with confusion steadily growing in his tone.

Bentley could sense Cameron's confusion through the phone and let out a chuckle, "Well, you're not going to believe this but your artist, Raelynn, she's also the girl from Cancun."

Cameron fell silent for a moment, processing Bentley's revelation. Bentley could almost hear the gears turning in Cameron's mind as he tried to make sense of what he had just heard.

"Wait, what?" Cameron finally responded, his voice a mixture of disbelief and amusement. "Raelynn? Are you serious, Bentley?"

Bentley couldn't help but smile on the other end of the line. He knew how absurd it sounded, and he had gone through the same disbelief when he first made the connection. "I kid you not, Cam. As you know I ran into her at the club, and after some... let's call it heated banter, and meeting for coffee yesterday we figured out we met in Cancun all those years ago.

There was a pause before Cameron spoke again, his voice now tinged with intrigue. "You're telling me that the girl you met on your honeymoon is now the same artist, I've been hiring to perform at the club the past few years? Wow, what a plot twist."

Bentley took a deep breath, the weight of the revelation settling in. The connection between Raelynn and his past was undeniable, and the unexpected twist of fate left him both intrigued and bewildered. As he listened to Cameron's astonished response, Bentley couldn't help but wonder how this reunion would impact both his life and Raelynn's. The air hung with anticipation, as Bentley knew that this unexpected reunion could be a monumental turning point in his life.

As the phone call with Cameron came to an end, Bentley began to get ready for his evening out with Raelynn. He was eager to spend more time getting to know her. He was also excited to relay the news that she had been added to the Cinderella Fest line up.

That evening Bentley sat across from Raelynn at a local steakhouse where he found himself lost in her deep blue eyes. They were pulling him in like the oceans current. The connection between them was also growing more electric as their conversation flowed effortlessly.

As they finished eating Bentley wiped his mouth and looked at Raelynn with such excitement on his face as he couldn't contain it. "So, Raelynn. I've got some exciting news for you."

Raelynn looked up from her plate of food at him as she was still picking at what was left on her plate, "Oh." She said with a do-tell tone in her voice.

Bentley let out a slight chuckle as he could see the anticipation building on her face. "After working very hard this morning, I've managed to get you your shot," Raelynn's eyes widened as she patiently waited for Bentley to finish, "You have successfully been added to the Cinderella Fest line up."

As the words left Bentley's mouth, Raelynn let out a loud squeal of excitement as eyes began to water with tears.

"Bentley, I can't thank you enough for this opportunity! This means so much to me. Like, you have no idea. This is a once in a lifetime opportunity for me and my band." Raelynn pleaded as she wiped the tears from her eyes.

"You're welcome, but there is one more thing. So, you and your band are set to perform the last day of the festival, I however personally want you there the whole weekend." Bentley said.

Before he could finish Raelynn interrupted, "May I ask why?" she asked with confusion.

"Well, as you know I headline all three nights and I want to add a segment where we perform two to three songs together. Obviously, we must perform Cinderella after the buzz we created Saturday night. For the other song I was thinking, taking one of your songs and I create rap verses, but you still do the choruses and the bridge. The next song we can either write a song together or completely cover a song. What do you say?" Bentley asked with sincerity.

Raelynn's eyes widened in surprise, a mix of joy and disbelief written across her face. Bentley's proposition hung in the air, and the weight of the opportunity settled on her shoulders. She blinked, processing the magnitude of what he was offering.

"Bentley, are you serious?" she asked, her voice a mixture of excitement and amazement.

He grinned, nodding. "Absolutely. Plus, it's a chance for you to showcase your talent the whole weekend, not just one night."

Raelynn's mind raced with possibilities. The thought of sharing the stage with Bentley for not just one but multiple performances at Cinderella Fest was beyond anything she had imagined. She leaned back in her chair, a smile spreading across her face.

"I...I don't even know what to say other than yes." Raelynn said as she was swimming in a mix of emotions.

"It's settled. We're doing this. Which means we probably should get to work since we only have three days until the festival." Bentley said with a smile as he signaled for the waiter to bring the check.

"Do you want to start working tonight?" Raelynn asked anxiously.

"Actually, that would be great. However, I am staying with my parents while I'm in town and they're probably asleep which would make it a little hard to practice music." Bentley said with a hint of disappointment in his voice.

"No worries! You can come to my house and practice. I mean this is a big deal for me, so… yeah you can come over." Raelynn said with excitement.

Bentley's eyes lit up at Raelynn's invitation. "That sounds perfect, Raelynn. Let's make this weekend unforgettable," he said, paying the bill as they got ready to leave the restaurant.

As they walked out into the cool night, Bentley held the door open for Raelynn. The air was filled with a mix of excitement and anticipation, and the connection between them seemed to spark and sizzle like the energy in the air before a storm.

Once they arrived, Raelynn led Bentley into her home studio, a cozy space filled with musical instruments, recording equipment, and a warm ambiance. As Bentley settled in, Raelynn went to the kitchen and returned with two wine glasses and a bottle of wine.

"Let's give a toast to the power of music for reconnecting us." Raelynn said as she finished pouring wine into her glass, raising it in the air.

"To the power of music." Bentley said with a grin as he raised his glass, clinking it together with Raelynn's.

As the hours passed seemingly so did the music and wine. Bentley was finding it easy to write lyrics as the idea just kept coming to him. Writing for his fourth studio album had become a bit of a struggle as he had hit a mental block, but being in Raelynn's presence working on music with her everything was just coming to him.

Raelynn was having a great time working on music with Bentley. She could also tell that he was enjoying it himself. Raelynn also picked up on the sense that a weight had been lifted off Bentley's shoulders as he became more lively with his lyrics. The story that he was able to tell with his words and music really inspired her.

After a few hours of working non-stop on music Bentley and Raelynn decided to take a much needed break to relax. As Bentley reached for the wine bottle to refill his glass, Raelynn was also reaching for the bottle, and

Bentley's hand just slightly grazed Raelynn's. They locked eyes as the touch sent a shock of electricity through them both.

In that moment, Bentley leaned in, and Raelynn met him halfway as they interlocked into a passionate kiss. After a few seconds that felt like an eternity, Raelynn put her hand on Bentley's rock-hard chest pushing him away.

"Woah, what was that." Raelynn said in shock as she was shaking her head in disbelief, trying to grasp what just happened.

"I am so sorry." Bentley said in pure panic mode, as he was not sure if the kiss was welcomed or not.

"Don't be sorry, but like what the fuck was that?" Raelynn asked with uncertainty in her voice.

"Honestly, I don't know. It felt like the universe was pulling us together." Bentley said as he ran his fingers through his hair.

"Yeah, I know. I felt it." Raelynn said still in shock.

For a moment the room was filled with silence as they both sat there contemplating their next move.

Raelynn knew she would be lying if she said that the kiss was just a kiss because it just wasn't any kiss. This kiss created a warm fuzzy feeling inside her chest that she hadn't felt in a very long time. That kissed also sparked an explosion inside her brain as flashbacks started flooding in taking her back eight years ago to that night on the beach in Cancun when Bentley first kissed her. Raelynn also knew she couldn't deny how bad she wanted to rip Bentley's shirt off for a closer look after feeling the hardness of his chest against her hand.

Bentley sat in the silence reflecting on the kiss hoping it hadn't crossed the line. Bentley really felt a connection with Raelynn that was larger than life and didn't want to jeopardize that. He really wanted to help Raelynn with her career and didn't want anything to prevent that from continuing.

As they sat in reflecting silence, Raelynn leaped up grabbing both sides of Bentley's face pulling him into her kiss. The kiss was long, deep, and passionate, lasting longer than the first. As their breathing heightened,

Bentley grabbed Raelynn's face with both hands pulling her kiss deeper into his.

Just as the tension of Bentley's erection started to press against his jeans, he pulled away. Her lips tasted just like the wine they had been sharing.

"I think we should slow down before we get to ahead of ourselves." Bentley in a low-husky voice said as he was trying to adjust himself discreetly.

Raelynn leaned back, still locking eyes with Bentley, "I think you're right." Raelynn said as she cleared her throat trying to catch her breath.

It wasn't an easy decision as they could see the burning desire for more reflecting in each other's eyes. Raelynn and Bentley finally knew how undeniable the connection between them truly was, reminding them of that night in Cancun. The sparks were brighter than ever.

As Bentley sat fighting the wanting, he was losing the battle as he couldn't help but imagine the unknown territories of Raelynn's body that her clothes hid from him. Bentley knew that it was best for him to leave before he ended up contradicting himself, giving into the desire.

"Raelynn, I think I'm going to call it a night and get out of here." Bentley said as he got up trying to again discreetly adjust himself.

As Bentley stood up Raelynn couldn't help but notice the prominent imprint through his jeans. She couldn't help but imagining him deep inside of her. She wanted it. She wanted it so bad that her vagina ached for it.

"Umm…yeah ok. Let me walk you to the door." Raelynn said trying to shake off the vivid daydream.

Raelynn and Bentley shared a kiss as he walked out into the cool early morning air.

Out on the curb, Bentley patiently waited for his Uber to get him back to his car. As Bentley waited, he couldn't help but smile thinking about what had just occurred. That smile quickly faded away as he began to kick himself for just not going for it, for not giving into the temptation. Especially, since Raelynn was eagerly wanting it just as bad as he did too.

The next afternoon Bentley found himself back at Raelynn's to once again work on music for the upcoming festival. The tension between them was undeniable as it had become awkward with how hard they tried to ignore the gravitational pull, pretending last night hadn't happened, and trying to keep their distance. The tension quickly started to affect the music making process as lyrics were now harder to formulate compared to the previous night.

"Ok. Fuck this!" Bentley blurted out in frustration, leaning over his guitar as he began rubbing his eyes with his hand. "We need to talk about last night, because this…us…it's making it awkward." Bentley continued with a more serious tone.

Raelynn let out a sigh, "Oh thank God it wasn't just me feeling this tension." She said under her breath, barely loud enough for Bentley to still hear it.

"Look, maybe the wine did the talking and guided our actions but truthfully," Bentley paused as he found Raelynn's eyes locking focus onto them. "I don't think that's the case." Bentley continued.

"Oh." Raelynn interjected.

"Look Rae, we have a very brief history. That connection we found in Cancun, we never got to fully explore. It left us wondering about could've been's. Now, the universe has somehow led us to cross paths again, years later. The connection is still there. That spark from Cancun is more alive than ever. I haven't believed in love since Michelle, and I don't know that if I ever will but there's definitely something here. There's no denying that." Bentley said staring deeply into Raelynn's eyes.

Bentley's stare was making Raelynn squirm and the tone in his voice with the words he spoke was making her warm in places that she wanted him so badly to touch. "I want you to fuck me." Raelynn blurted out as she quickly turned red as a beet soon as the words rolled off her lips. She couldn't believe she had actually said that as she thought she was only thinking it inside her head.

"OH MY GOD! I DID NOT MEAN TO SAY THAT!" Raelynn shouted in sheer panic.

Bentley was taken back as he let out a chuckle, "Rae. C'mon, please be serious right now."

"I am so sorry, Bentley. I did not mean to actually say that, but yes. All of what you said is true. The connection, the spark, and the wanting… It's all there." Raelynn said still in panic mode.

"Then what do we do about it? And no, I will not just fuck you." Bentley said with a wondering look as he let out a slight chuckle.

"This is painful for me to say just as it's going to be painful to do, but I guess let's take it slow. It's probably for the best anyways because I don't know if I'm ready for the media attention that comes with being your girlfriend or whatever it is that we're trying to accomplish here." Raelynn said as she let a slight smile come across her face.

"Okay then. Then we're taking it slow." Bentley said with a reassuring tone in his voice as he let a huge smile out, knowing how challenging this was going to be for the both of them.

As they resumed their work on the music, a newfound ease settled between them. The tension that had threatened to overshadow their collaboration began to dissipate, making way for the genuine camaraderie they had shared before the unexpected turn of events.

As they continued to spend time together, Bentley and Raelynn navigated the complexities of their evolving relationship, finding solace in the music they created together. They also discovered the joy in exploring each other's worlds beyond the music. They shared stories, laughter, and the occasional stolen glance that spoke volumes. The connection between them deepened, and they found solace in the unspoken understanding of what they were building.

14

The Space Between Us

The night before the festival's opening day, Bentley loaded his dad's truck up gave his parents a hug and headed to Charlotte to check into his hotel room. He knew the following morning was going to be hectic running through stage setup and soundchecks before the gates opened. Bentley who was used to the spotlight was feeling pretty nervous. That only meant Raelynn's nerves had to be through the roof. Deep down Bentley hoped that Raelynn was ready to take on a stage and crowd of this magnitude.

While on his drive to Charlotte, Bentley called Raelynn to see if she had left home yet. Since she was expected to be checking into her hotel tonight as well. The sound of Raelynn's voice on the other end of the phone immediately put a smile on Bentley's face. It was warm and welcoming.

Bentley and Raelynn's conversation flowed effortlessly as they talked about their respective drives to Charlotte. Bentley could sense the nervousness in Raelynn's voice increase. The closer to Charlotte she got, the more surreal all of it started to become. Raelynn couldn't believe that without a record deal she was getting treated to the same luxuries as Bentley.

As Bentley pulled into the hotel parking lot, he hung up the phone but not before making sure Raelynn had Mike, his managers contact information.

Inside the hotel lobby Bentley was greeted by Mike who escorted Bentley to the check in counter. Once checked in, the hotel concierge gave Bentley his room key card and Bentley made his way towards his room but not before turning back to Mike.

"Hey, Mike!" Bentley shouted from across the lobby as he made his way back.

"Yes sir." Mike said as Bentley now stood directly in front of him.

"I gave Raelynn your phone number. She is supposed to call you when she gets here," Bentley paused looking at the time on his phone. "Which she should be here in the next forty-five minutes. Please take good care of her Mike. If she asks, give her my room number." Bentley continued as he turned to walk off.

Forty-five minutes later, Raelynn was pulling into the parking lot of the hotel as she gave Mike a ring to meet him in the lobby. Just as he did for Bentley, Mike got Raelynn all checked in and squared away. He even managed to get her room directly across the hall from Bentley's.

"Miss. Hart, I would like you to know that your room is right across the hall from Mr. Riggs. Mr. Riggs has instructed me to take care of you this weekend. So, if you have any issues or questions, you have my number, feel free to give me a ring." Mike said.

Raelynn just smiled and thanked him as she made her way to her room. She was in awe of Mike's deep British accent.

Once inside her room Raelynn was left speechless. The room was huge. The bathroom was huge. The shower huge. However, what really took her breath was the view. Her room overlooked the city lights of uptown Charlotte. She was in awe as she looked out at bustling city traffic and the pedestrians walking up and down the sidewalk in and out of the bars and clubs below. She was struggling to wrap her head around this being her reality instead of a crazy dream. Raelynn had experienced luxurious things throughout her life thanks to her father, Jim Hart, but not on her own without his presence. Especially, not since she started pursuing music and he cut her off from almost all financial support.

Later that night after Raelynn had settled in, she decided to walk across the hall to Bentley's room rather than call or text him. She really wanted to see him.

Outside Bentley's door Raelynn knocked twice as she waited anxiously with butterflies in her stomach excited to see Bentley. However, Raelynn was not prepared for the sight that blessed her eyes when his hotel door swung open as her mouth dropped in honest surprise.

Bentley stood before her wearing nothing but a pair of black basketball shorts. She could tell Bentley was free balling as his imprint was largely noticeable. As Raelynn continued to admire the view before her, she couldn't distinguish between reality and make believe. She didn't know if she was imaging the steam rolling out behind Bentley or if he had just gotten out the shower. But his damp hair made it evident it was real.

Raelynn continued to look Bentley up and down as she admired his chiseled chest which had a tattoo going from one side to the other that read the phrase, "The pain you feel today is the strength you feel tomorrow." Raelynn admired Bentley's rock-hard abs, and his perfect V-shaped lines peaking over the waistband of his shorts. It was a lot for Raelynn to take in, but it was hot.

Raelynn's admiration over Bentley's half naked body was only a few seconds but it felt like a lifetime as she had so many thoughts and emotions flood her brain at once. She wanted so bad to push him inside the room and let Bentley have his way with her body. It was an internal struggle for Raelynn when it came to balancing her wanting and her agreement to take things slow. As she was crumbling under the pressure of burning desire, she was becoming very irritated with how slow things were actually moving.

"Not leaving much to the imagination, I see." Raelynn said with a mischievous smile as she glanced down at Bentley's waist before flinging her arms around him giving him a kiss.

Bentley chuckled, "Well, hey there!" he said as he pulled back from Raelynn's kiss, shutting the door behind them.

Raelynn let out a chuckle as she stretched out across Bentley's bed, one arm propping her head up as she continued to admire his gorgeous body. Seeing, Bentley this way made it all make sense as to why he was on the cover of Forbes magazine as the hottest man alive.

Bentley walked over to the bed stretching out beside her, one arm propped holding up his head while his other hand gripped firmly at

Raelynn's waist looking into her eyes. "I'm really glad you decided to come see me tonight." Bentley said with a slight touch of vulnerability in his voice.

Raelynn let out a smile as she bit her bottom lip, "Where else would I be?" she asked playfully.

"I really don't know. Maybe in your room fangirling over the size of it." Bentley joked back before Raelynn interjected.

"Oh, Bentley you're behind schedule. I already did that. I need you to keep up superstar." Raelynn said playfully.

The minutes passed seemingly as they continued to tease back and forth. Their laughs filled Bentley's hotel suite like a comedy show.

Meanwhile, Bentley couldn't help but revel in the fact that Raelynn was there with him. Her playful banter and the way she effortlessly occupied the space on his bed made him feel alive in a way that went beyond the pulsating energy of the city outside. As he lay there beside her, he traced patterns on her waist with his fingers, enjoying the warmth of her skin.

Bentley's mind, however, was not entirely free from the internal tug-of-war that mirrored Raelynn's conflicting desires. On one hand, he felt the undeniable chemistry between them, a magnetic force that seemed to pull them closer with each passing moment. On the other hand, Bentley respected their decision to take things slow, a desire he found both endearing and challenging.

He shifted his gaze from Raelynn's eyes to the ceiling, contemplating the delicate dance between passion and restraint. The vulnerability in his voice resurfaced as he spoke, "God, I want you so fucking bad right now."

Bentley's words gave Raelynn visible goosebumps all over her skin. She wanted him too and hearing him say those words melted away the barriers built to protect her heart. Raelynn knew she should keep her guard up with Bentley, but the desire and the connection between them made that a losing battle. Especially, in this moment, hearing Bentley release the words she had been dying; craving to hear Bentley say since their kiss Monday night.

With the temptation burning, Raelynn found restraint as she sat up on the bed looking down at Bentley. "Why don't you take me then." Raelynn said seductively.

Bentley huffed in frustration, "I can't."

As a confused look came across Raelynn's face she blurted out, "And why not?"

Bentley let out a sigh of frustration as he looked Raelynn in the eyes, "Because we agreed to take it slow. Plus, I know I have a reputation with the media that goes far and beyond the vulnerable Bentley you met in Cancun. I want to prove to you and to myself that it's a made-up narrative."

Raelynn listened intently, the conflict in Bentley's eyes reflecting the internal struggle he was facing. She admired his honesty, the vulnerability he was willing to share with her. The room was charged with a palpable tension, desire intertwining with the understanding that some things were worth waiting for.

Bentley continued, his voice carrying a sincerity that resonated with Raelynn, "I want us to be more than just a headline, Raelynn. I want you to see the real me, not the persona the media has created. Taking it slow is my way of showing you that I'm serious about us."

Raelynn's heart fluttered with a mix of emotions, desire, frustration, and a growing sense of admiration for Bentley's commitment to authenticity. She nodded, acknowledging the depth of his words. "So, let's get to know each other Bentley. For once this week, let's not talk about music or the festival. Let's talk about our past, our future, our dreams, our goals, hell even our favorite color and foods. "

"Our likes and dislikes?" Bentley asked jokingly as he was still starring into Raelynn's eyes.

Raelynn grinned, appreciating Bentley's playful response. "Exactly. Let's knock down those walls we've both built around her hearts."

Bentley's eyes sparkled with anticipation as Raelynn's proposition opened a new chapter in their conversation. He welcomed the opportunity to share more about himself, to peel back the layers of fame and reveal the person behind the headlines.

Bentley's eyes wandered for a moment, lost in memories, before he started to unveil the tapestry of his life. "Well, you know I'm a Carolina boy through and through. Grew up in a small town, spent most my childhood with my grandma. She was the one who got me into music."

A soft smile played on Bentley's lips as he recounted his early years. "Grandma pushed me to play piano, perform in the church choir, and act in school plays. It wasn't just about the music; it was about storytelling for me. Music became my outlet for emotions, a way for my words to speak when I couldn't."

Raelynn's eyes widened with interest, captivated by the intimate details Bentley was sharing. "And the tattoo," he continued, tracing the ink on his chest, "it's her mantra. 'The pain you feel today is the strength you feel tomorrow.' She used to tell me that every time life got tough."

As Bentley bared his past, Raelynn felt a newfound connection, understanding the roots that anchored him. "Blue is my favorite color," Bentley confessed, "like the endless Carolina skies. And steak, well, that's the way to my heart."

Raelynn chuckled, "Noted. Steak dinners from now on."

Bentley's eyes twinkled with mischief. "As for sports, I bleed Carolina blue. Tar Heels and Panthers all the way. And when I'm not touring, I love spending quality time at the beach. There's something about listening to the waves that grounds me."

Raelynn nodded, appreciating the glimpse into Bentley's world. The conversation took a more serious turn as Bentley shared his dislikes. "You know," he said with a wry smile, "I'm not a fan of women throwing themselves at me, even though I rarely say no. It's just not my thing."

Raelynn couldn't help but smirk at his honesty. Bentley's sincerity resonated with her, making her feel more connected to the man behind the celebrity facade.

As Bentley hesitated before divulging his romantic history, Raelynn listened, recognizing the vulnerability in his gaze. "I've only been romantically involved with two people," he admitted, locking eyes with her. "You and Michelle."

The room held a moment of silent acknowledgment before Bentley spoke again, "But when it comes to... well, you know, let's just say there have been too many encounters to count. It's a part of this crazy life, but it's not what defines me."

Raelynn raised an eyebrow, playfully teasing, "Should I be worried?"

Bentley chuckled, "Not at all. Just trying to be honest. It's been a journey, Raelynn, and I want you to know all of it."

Bentley looked deep into Raelynn's eyes before continuing, "My biggest fear is getting close to someone again. Letting them see the vulnerable side of me just for them to walk away and leave again."

Raelynn felt a pang of empathy as Bentley exposed his fear, the vulnerability in his eyes piercing through the playful banter. She reached out, her hand finding his, intertwining their fingers in a reassuring grip.

"Bentley, you're not alone in that fear," she said, her voice soft yet unwavering. "We've both got our walls, and it's scary to think about letting someone in."

Bentley's gaze softened, gratitude and relief flickering in his eyes. The shared vulnerability deepened their connection, creating a space where both Bentley and Raelynn could be real with each other.

Raelynn then leaned in, pressing a gentle kiss to Bentley's forehead. Bentley's eyes sparkled with a newfound curiosity as Raelynn invited him into the realms of her preferences and history.

"Alright, Raelynn," Bentley said, a mischievous grin playing on his lips, "tell me your favorite color. Don't keep me in suspense."

Raelynn chuckled, her eyes gleaming with amusement. "Hot pink. It's bold, just like me."

Bentley nodded appreciatively, his fingers gently tracing imaginary patterns on Raelynn's arm. "I like that. It suits you."

Raelynn continued, "I absolutely love pizza. It's my go-to comfort food. And I have this thing for spur-of-the-moment trips. No planning, just spontaneous adventures."

Bentley's eyebrows raised in interest. "Spontaneous trips, huh? That sounds like a blast."

"Yeah, it's the thrill of not knowing what's next," Raelynn explained. "And rude people—can't stand them. Life's too short for negativity."

Bentley nodded in agreement, "Amen to that."

As the conversation flowed, Raelynn delved into her academic background, sharing her degree in criminal justice from Tennessee University. "I bleed orange for the Volunteers and blue for the Titans," she laughed. "It's a dream of mine to make it big and show my father that I didn't need his help."

Bentley admired Raelynn's determination, a shared fire burning between them. "I get that, Raelynn. Proving the doubters wrong is a powerful motivator."

Their conversation seamlessly shifted to Raelynn's goals. "I want to make music that fans can connect with," she confessed. Bentley admired her sincerity, realizing the depth of her passion for her craft.

The exchange of dreams continued, the connection between Bentley and Raelynn deepening with each revelation. Raelynn's love for country music and punk rock resonated with Bentley's eclectic taste. They found common ground in their appreciation for different genres.

Bentley, in turn, shared more about himself. "I love all kinds of music, but my go-to is heavy metal. It's raw, intense—the stories told through the music resonate with me."

Raelynn's eyes widened with interest. "Heavy metal, huh? That's unexpected for a rapper."

Bentley nodded, a smile playing on his lips. "I've got this dream, you see. I want to either make a heavy metal album or collaborate with some of my favorite heavy metal vocalists, especially Oli Sykes from Bring Me The Horizon."

Raelynn's eyes lit up with excitement. "Wow. That sounds incredible, Bentley. Breaking barriers in the music industry."

Bentley grinned, appreciating Raelynn's enthusiasm. "Exactly. It's about pushing boundaries, doing something unexpected."

As the night wore on, their conversation flowed seamlessly between laughter, shared dreams, and moments of vulnerability. The dim light in Bentley's hotel suite created a warm ambiance, casting a soft glow on the two figures sprawled across the bed. Raelynn's head eventually found a comfortable resting place on Bentley's chest, her fingers absentmindedly tracing patterns on his skin, as fatigue began to creep in.

In the midst of discussing favorite childhood memories, Bentley's voice gradually softened, his gaze fixed on Raelynn's profile. Raelynn, too, felt the soothing rhythm of Bentley's heartbeat beneath her ear, and the fatigue she had tried to shake off finally caught up with her. The words between them slowed, the pauses between sentences lengthened, until their conversation became a lullaby, gently coaxing them into the embrace of sleep.

With each passing moment, Bentley and Raelynn drifted into a peaceful slumber, tangled in a web of shared stories and unspoken emotions. The room, once filled with laughter, now echoed only with the soft cadence of their breathing. The warmth of the connection they had forged lingered, creating a cocoon of comfort that wrapped around them as they surrendered to the tranquility of the night. In the quietude, Bentley's arm instinctively tightened around Raelynn, pulling her closer, as if to ensure that the fragile intimacy they had discovered wouldn't fade in their dreams.

15

Festival Fever

The following morning was the start of a hectic day, opening day. As Bentley and Raelynn laid snuggled peacefully asleep in each other embrace, Bentley's alarm began blaring. As his eyes slowly began to part open, he couldn't help but mischievously smile.

Bentley's morning wood had him hard as a rock, but that's not what made the smile creep across his half sleep face. It was the deadweight of Raelynn's hand firmly gripping around his penis while she peacefully slept.

"Raelynn" Bentley just above a whisper said as he gently nudged her.

As Raelynn opened her eyes and saw the placement of her hand, she quickly jerked it back in sheer panic, "OH MY GOD! I AM SO FUCKING SORRY!"

Bentley couldn't help but chuckle at Raelynn's reaction. Her reaction was far more animated than his.

"Don't be sorry. I actually liked your hand being there." Bentley said as he chuckled through his words.

Although Raelynn felt embarrassed, she couldn't deny that she liked her hand being there too. Feeling the hardness of Bentley's penis in her palm, only further deepened her imagination. Further proving taking things slow was going to be hard.

As Raelynn was gathering her composure from the pure embarrassment she felt, she looked up at Bentley locking eyes, "What happened to the 'let's take this slow' energy from last night mister." Raelynn said as she tried to mirror Bentley's playful banter through her embarrassment.

Bentley rolled over as he elevated his upper body overtop of Raelynn. "What if I said after last night, I feel like we're ready?" Bentley said with a serious tone as he looked down into Raelynn's eyes with sincerity.

Without a moment's hesitation, Raelynn seized Bentley by the back of his head, drawing him down onto her in a passionate and eager kiss. As the kissing became more intense, and more passionate Bentley's hands began to roam Raelynn's body.

Bentley's touch sent shockwaves throughout Raelynn's body as she had longed for this moment, and it was finally happening. Bentley's touch was soft, gentle, and caring as she felt the warmth of his hands all over her. She couldn't get enough. She wanted more. She could tell Bentley wanted more too as she could feel the tension growing in his pants. She could feel the hardness of his cock in between her legs as he continuously pressed his body weight back and forth making her crave it even more.

As the moment continued to intensify, Bentley's hands continued to freely roam Raelynn's body alternating between her ass and breast. As the grinding of their bodies intensified, Bentley couldn't help but notice the warmth between Raelynn's legs increasing with each passing second.

As Bentley slid his hands under Raelynn's t-shirt, lifting it over her head, revealing her sexy black bra, he was left breathless. Bentley's kisses soon started to take a new route as they left Raelynn's lips creating a trail from her neck down to the tops of her breast that he continuously followed.

As Bentley continued kissing up and down Raelynn's upper body, Raelynn reached her hand up grabbing Bentley hard throbbing cock in the palm of her hand and began stroking it through his basketball shorts. Just as she did that Bentley let out a moan of pleasure.

As Bentley and Raelynn were finally letting their desires freely burn like a wildfire, Bentley's phone began to ring but he ignored it as they continued to explore each other's bodies. Then it rang again.

A clearly sexually frustrated Bentley pulled away from Raelynn's burning embrace, "Fuck." Bentley grunted as he reached for his phone.

It was Mike calling to inform Bentley that he and Raelynn had five minutes to be downstairs to leave for Bank of America Stadium. In the heat of the moment, Bentley had almost forgotten about needing to be at the venue for set walk throughs and soundchecks.

Bentley, frustration evident in his expression, answered the call with a hurried "Yeah, Mike. We'll be there in five," before hanging up.

Raelynn, still caught in the heat of the moment, looked at Bentley with a mix of desire and amusement. "Well, that's quite the wake-up call," she teased.

Bentley chuckled, the tension from the interrupted passion lingering in the air. "Yeah, not exactly how I pictured my morning going," he admitted, a mischievous glint in his eyes.

With urgency Raelynn gathered herself and her shirt off the floor and quickly hurried across the hall to her room. Bentley and Raelynn quickly got dressed and remerged in the hallway smiling at each other's presence.

As they made their way downstairs to the hotel lobby Bentley couldn't stop himself from stealing glances at Raelynn before it dawned on him how hectic the day was going to be.

"Raelynn, before we get to this lobby, I want you to know just how crazy this day is going to be." Bentley said with seriousness in his voice as he put the playful banter away.

Raelynn felt Bentley's words strike a chord within her as all the nerves started to rush into her body. "What do you mean?" Raelynn asked worriedly.

Bentley could sense Raelynn's nervousness as he grabbed her hands stopping in the middle of the hallway. As he looked into her eyes, he could see the fear slowly creeping in.

"Listen Rae, I know you're nervous and that's okay. I get nervous every time I step out onto the stage, its normal. I didn't mean to startle you; I just wanted you to be aware of what's to be expected." Bentley said calmly as he tried calming Raelynn's nerves.

"And what's that?" Raelynn asked as her nervousness was quickly starting to grow.

"Alright, let me paint the picture. You're accompanying us for the moment because our return isn't on the agenda until after the show. The thing is, you're a crucial part of the show, but your grand entrance is scheduled for later, meaning you go with us now or you don't. I also want you to be aware that our weekend won't leave us with much, if any, breathing space for personal conversations or quiet moments. While you'll find yourself with ample downtime, my world will be a whirlwind, with meet and greets, media interviews, and photoshoots pulling me in about a million different directions." Bentley said as he tried to lay out the agenda for Raelynn the best he could without knowing a hundred percent himself what the itinerary included.

Raelynn listened intently to Bentley's words, the reality of the chaotic day sinking in. As Bentley spoke, she could see the genuine concern in his eyes, and it comforted her in a strange way. Despite the whirlwind that awaited them, Bentley took a moment to reassure her, to let her know what to expect.

"Okay," Raelynn replied, a mixture of nerves and determination in her voice. "I signed up for this, right? I'm ready for whatever."

Bentley smiled appreciatively, squeezing her hands gently. "That's the spirit. Just remember, you're free to go to all the different stages and see whatever artist you want. Or, if you choose, you can hideout in the dressing room and take a nap. Whatever you do just make sure you're back in the dressing room by eight."

Bentley's words hung in the air as they entered the hotel lobby, the anticipation of the day's events settling between them. The hotel staff had prepared a quick breakfast spread for the entourage, but Bentley's mind was already racing ahead to the festival grounds.

As they stepped outside, the morning air was crisp, the city still waking up around them. The convoy of vehicles waited, ready to transport everyone to Bank of America Stadium. Bentley's eyes scanned the surroundings, absorbing the transformation of the streets into festival spaces.

"Mint Street barricaded off," Bentley noted, a mix of surprise and excitement in his voice. "Looks like they've turned the whole area into part of the festival grounds."

Raelynn followed his gaze, taking in the sight of a stage set up in the middle of what used to be a busy street. The energy of the festival was already palpable, even at this early hour.

The convoy rolled through the streets, and as they approached the stadium, Bentley pointed out the Panther practice facility with a stage set up in front of it. "Two main stages side by side inside the stadium too," he explained. "It's going to be wild."

The vehicles pulled up to the backstage entrance, and the entourage began to disembark. Bentley took Raelynn's hand, leading her through the bustling backstage area. There was a sense of controlled chaos as crew members hurriedly prepared for the day's events.

They entered the stadium, greeted by the enormity of the venue. The morning sun cast a warm glow over the empty seats, a stark contrast to the vibrant chaos that would soon fill the space.

Bentley guided Raelynn through the backstage labyrinth, passing dressing rooms, production areas, and the hum of activity that surrounded them. The gravity of the moment hit Raelynn as she realized the scale of the event she was about to be a part of.

As they approached the main stage, Bentley's eyes lit up. "This is where the magic happens," he said, his voice filled with a mix of excitement and reverence. "The main stage, with the energy of thousands of people out there. It's a feeling like no other."

Raelynn took it all in, the enormity of the stages, the anticipation in the air, and the distant echoes of soundchecks filling the stadium.

Bentley's passion for his craft was contagious, and she couldn't help but feel a surge of excitement.

The entourage continued their journey through the stadium, pausing for a brief walk-through on the main stage. Bentley discussed cues with the production team, ensuring that every detail would be perfect when the time came.

As they left the stage, Bentley turned to Raelynn. "I have to dive into some last-minute preparations, but I want you to explore a bit. Get a feel for the place. And remember, no matter where you are, be back in the dressing room by eight tonight."

Raelynn nodded, a mix of nerves and eagerness bubbling within her. She watched Bentley disappear into the backstage chaos, the weight of the day settling on her shoulders.

With Bentley occupied by the demands of the festival, Raelynn took a deep breath and decided to embrace the chaos in her own way. She roamed through the backstage area, catching glimpses of various artists in preparation for their performances. The distant sounds of music checks and the hum of excitement filled the air.

As the festival gates finally swung open, fans started pouring in, transforming the once-quiet stadium into a vibrant sea of anticipation. Raelynn decided to venture into the heart of the festival, eager to experience the diverse range of performances.

She found herself at Lil Tracy's set, the beats reverberating through her as the crowd around her danced and swayed. From there, she explored Lil Aaron's energetic performance, the crowd feeding off his infectious energy. The festival offered a kaleidoscope of genres, and Raelynn soaked it all in, moving from 24kGoldn's hip-hop vibes to the hauntingly beautiful melodies of Billie Eilish.

Ava Max electrified the stage with her pop anthems, and Dua Lipa brought an undeniable energy, making the stadium feel like a massive dance floor. Raelynn even ventured into the punk rock scene, enjoying the high-energy performances of State Champs, All Time Low, and Neck Deep.

The festival grounds buzzed with energy, and Raelynn felt a sense of liberation as she moved between stages, immersing herself in the music and the collective spirit of the crowd. The day unfolded in a whirlwind of beats, melodies, and the diverse expressions of artistry.

As the clock neared eight in the evening, Raelynn made her way back to the dressing room. The backstage area retained a sense of controlled frenzy, a mixture of anticipation and nervous energy. She opened the door, expecting to find the room empty.

To her surprise, Bentley was there, having managed to slip away from his media commitments for a brief moment. His eyes lit up as he saw her, a silent understanding passing between them. The festival had been a whirlwind, and the desire that had been building since the morning rekindled in that shared glance.

Without a word, Bentley closed the door behind Raelynn. The air in the dressing room crackled with tension as they moved toward each other. Bentley's hands found their place on Raelynn's waist, pulling her into an embrace that erased the distance of the chaotic day.

Their lips met in a passionate kiss, a fusion of longing and urgency. The room, filled with the muffled sounds of the festival outside, became a sanctuary for their shared desires. Bentley's fingers traced the contours of Raelynn's body, each touch sending shivers down her spine.

As the intensity grew, Bentley guided Raelynn toward the plush couch in the corner of the room. He gently laid her down, their lips refusing to part. The world outside, with its chaos and noise, disappeared as they surrendered to the moment.

Bentley's hands roamed over Raelynn's body, exploring every inch with a familiarity that only heightened the intensity. Raelynn's fingers found their way through Bentley's tousled hair, pulling him closer.

In the midst of their passionate embrace, Bentley's lips trailed down Raelynn's neck, leaving a trail of kisses that sent shivers through her entire body. The atmosphere in the room was charged with desire, and every touch, every caress, felt like an electric current connecting them.

As Bentley's hands continued their exploration, Raelynn's breath hitched. The festival's distant beats seemed to synchronize with the pounding of her heart. In that stolen moment, the world narrowed down to the two of them, tangled in the intoxicating dance of longing.

Just as their passion reached its peak, the dressing room door flung open without warning, revealing a crew member with a surprised look. "Sorry to interrupt, Bentley, but we need you for the next round of interviews."

The interruption was jarring, and Bentley and Raelynn froze, their eyes locking in shared frustration.

Bentley sighed, a mix of irritation and amusement in his eyes. "Alright, give me a minute."

The crew member quickly retreated, leaving Bentley and Raelynn in a state of suspended desire. Bentley turned back to Raelynn, a wistful smile playing on his lips. "Looks like we'll have to continue this later, if the universe will allow."

Raelynn chuckled, a mix of frustration and amusement mirroring Bentley's expression. "Seems like the universe has a sense of humor."

Bentley leaned down, placing a lingering kiss on Raelynn's lips before pulling away regretfully. "I'll make it up to you, promise."

As the evening progressed, the moment approached for Bentley to take the stage. Raelynn accompanied him to the stage entrance, where they eagerly awaited MGK's set to conclude. As MGK's performance reached its conclusion, the stadium reverberated with thunderous cheers, and the lights dimmed, casting an intense darkness over the venue.

As Bentley's entrance video began to play, it illuminated the atmosphere, and he turned to Raelynn, sharing a kiss before vanishing onto the stage. The video heightened the crowd's excitement to a deafening level, and when Bentley finally stepped into the spotlight, the eruption of cheers reached an even more exhilarating crescendo.

Raelynn stood at the side of the stage, a mix of anticipation and pride in her eyes as she watched Bentley effortlessly command the attention of the roaring crowd. The energy in the stadium was palpable, and Bentley's magnetic presence electrified the atmosphere.

As the set progressed, Bentley's voice and music resonated throughout the venue, creating an unforgettable experience for the audience. Then, with a mischievous smile, Bentley took a moment to acknowledge Raelynn. He called her onto the stage, describing her as a talent he discovered in a bar just last weekend. However, he added a twist, mentioning a chance meeting eight years ago in Cancun at a karaoke bar. Bentley even mentioned the video that was going viral from their performance of Cinderella.

The crowd's curiosity heightened as Bentley and Raelynn took center stage, the connection between them evident. They launched into the final three songs of the setlist, the result of a week's hard work and dedication. The chemistry between Bentley and Raelynn was undeniable, and the audience was swept away by the synergy of their performance.

Closing out the set with Bentley's major hit song "Cinderella," Bentley and Raelynn poured their hearts into the music. The crowd swayed to the rhythm, captivated by the emotional intensity of the performance. As the last note resonated through the stadium, Bentley seized the moment. He pulled Raelynn into a passionate kiss, their silhouettes casting a captivating image against the backdrop of cheering fans.

In that moment, Raelynn felt a whirlwind of emotions—joy, exhilaration, and a profound sense of connection. As they shared the stage, the echoes of their performance lingered in the hearts of the audience, as well as Raelynn's. The spotlight dimmed, but the memory of that magical night would forever be etched in the hearts of Bentley, Raelynn, and the countless fans who witnessed their electrifying performance.

16

Uninterrupted

Day one of Cinderella Fest was officially in the books as Raelynn and Bentley ventured back to the hotel with their entourage. The energy amongst the group was very high in excitement.

Bentley couldn't have been happier. It was very evident with the radiant smile that he was wearing.

Raelynn was still relishing in the moment trying to take it all in. She couldn't believe she had just fulfilled her dream of performing in front of thousands of screaming fans. She was more than ready for the next two nights, to be out on that stage again. Especially, with Bentley by her side. Raelynn also hoped her performances with Bentley would bring a large gathering of fans to her own set Sunday afternoon.

Back at the hotel, Bentley and Raelynn found their selves alone in the elevator. As the elevator doors shut, Bentley looked over to Raelynn with a mischievous smirk on his face. He couldn't contain the pent-up sexual frustration any longer.

Raelynn looked at Bentley with knowing eyes as she braced herself for the electrifying intensity that was about to come. She wanted this. She had been wanting this since the first time they kissed in Cancun, from their kiss Sunday night, from the week spent working on music, since seeing Bentley's half naked body standing in front of her, to the heated passionate moment they shared this morning and in the dressing room. She longed for this.

Bentley reached out clinching Raelynn by the back of the head pulling her into his kiss, as her hair fell all around his hand. Raelynn more than willingly fell into his kiss and their surroundings began to fade.

As the kisses became more passionate, Bentley's hands began to roam freely up and down Raelynn's body. Bentley's hands continuously alternating between one hand gripping her ass and the other squeezing her breast. Eventually, he started kissing up and down Raelynn's neck to the tops of her breast and Raelynn could feel Bentley's teeth scraping against her neck as he followed his continuous trail of kisses.

The temperature in the elevator began to rise when Bentley cupped Raelynn's ass cheeks, lifting her onto the elevator wall railing, holding her up with his body weight pushed firmly against hers. As Raelynn's legs straddled him, he could feel the warmth between her legs. It made him crave her that much more. He couldn't handle the ache in his penis from all the built-up tension anymore.

Raelynn could feel Bentley's built-up tension as it was throbbing against the most sensitive part of her body. She couldn't wait to actually feel him inside her. Her mind raced almost as fast as her heartbeat as it played out the vivid scenes before they even transpired.

After a minute or two that felt like an eternity the elevator finally reached their floor. As the elevator doors slowly opened, Bentley helped Raelynn down from the railing, their lips never parting as they fell out into the hallway. The kisses were still passionate as they fell against the walls, all the way down the halls to their rooms.

Standing outside their respective rooms, an out of breath Bentley managed to get the words "Your room or mine?" out.

"I don't care." Raelynn managed to get out in between the kissing, her voice hitched, as they fell against Bentley's hotel room door.

"My room it is." Bentley said with a husky voice, as he opened the door without parting from Raelynn's kiss.

As they fell into Bentley's room the door closed behind them. Bentley pushed Raelynn against the wall, pressing his body firmly against hers. Gyrating his hips against her body.

As the kissing grew even more intense, with a sense of urgency lifted Raelynn's up and sat her on the entertainment center a few steps away from the door. She now replaced the hotels decor that Bentley managed to sling into the floor.

Bentley's hands, firm yet gentle, explored every inch of Raelynn's body as if trying to memorize the contours of her soul. The objects shattered and scattered on the floor from the entertainment center were forgotten, replaced by the palpable heat of their connection. Bentley's kisses trailed down from Raelynn's lips to the hollow of her neck, leaving a trail of fire in their wake.

Raelynn's fingers tangled in Bentley's hair, pulling him closer. Every touch, every kiss, sent electric shocks through her body, igniting a fire that threatened to consume them both. Bentley, lost in the depth of their connection, began to explore the curves of her body with a hunger that mirrored Raelynn's own.

As Bentley's hands moved down her sides, Raelynn could feel the anticipation building, her breaths coming in ragged gasps. She couldn't wait much longer as she grabbed the bottom of Bentley's shirt, pulling it over his head with urgency.

Raelynn began scaping her nails up and down Bentley's bare chest and abdomen, feeling his chiseled sculpture against her fingertips.

Bentley groaned at the sensation of Raelynn's nails on his skin, the pleasure coursing through his veins. He reciprocated by unhooking the straps of Raelynn's dress, pulling it over her head, tossing it beside his shirt into a pool of fabric. Her body, bathed in the soft glow of the hotel room's ambient light, was a masterpiece that Bentley couldn't get enough of.

The room was charged with an intoxicating blend of desire and anticipation. Bentley, overcome by the sight of Raelynn standing before him in nothing but her bright red lingerie, felt a surge of admiration for the woman who was slowly but surely capturing his heart and soul.

With the passion burning bright as ever, Raelynn unbuttoned Bentley's jeans as he slid his hand under his waistband slowly pulling them down. Without breaking away from Raelynn's kiss, Bentley brought his legs up one by one as he finished removing his jeans.

Now standing in just his plaid boxers, Bentley reached his arm around to the small of Raelynn's back unhooking her bra with one hand. As Raelynn's bra hit the floor, Bentley gently squeezed both of her breast as Raelynn let out a slight moan. Eventually, kissing his way down to her nipples, placing one in his mouth as he gently sucked on it.

Raelynn could feel Bentley's teeth on her breast as he sucked on her nipple, sending even more waves of shock throughout her body.

As Bentley kissed his way back up to Raelynn's neck, his hands flirted with her panties waistband. Raelynn couldn't handle the teasing as she grabbed both his wrists, holding them in place, urging him to pull them down.

Bentley kissed his way down Raelynn's body until he was kneeling, kissing on her inner thighs. Bentley slowly pulled her panties down. With anticipation building, Bentley kissed his way back up to the hollow of Raelynn's neck as he slid of his boxers revealing his rock-hard cock.

Raelynn's eyes widened. It was much bigger than she had visualized. Although, she felt it in her hand that morning.

In one swift motion Raelynn reached her hand out cupping Bentley's penis into the palm of her hand and pulled him closer. She could feel his dick throbbing as she began to slowly stroke it.

Their desire surged to new heights as Raelynn's bold move sent a jolt through Bentley's body. The room became a playground of sensations, a canvas for the unrestrained passion between them. Raelynn, still seated on the entertainment center, took charge, exploring Bentley's arousal with a sense of confidence that fueled their connection.

Bentley's breath hitched as Raelynn's hand wrapped around him, the warmth of her touch sending shivers down his spine. He groaned in response to her touch, surrendering to the pleasure that coursed through him. As her strokes became more deliberate, Bentley's knees weakened, and he leaned into her, his hands finding refuge in her tousled hair.

The room echoed with the rhythm of their shared desire. Bentley's eyes, locked onto Raelynn's, conveyed a mixture of appreciation and surrender. Raelynn, emboldened by the control she held, reveled in the power she had over him.

As Bentley's arousal intensified, Raelynn felt a surge of satisfaction. Her movements became a dance, a symphony of pleasure that resonated through the room. Bentley, lost in the intensity of the moment, let out a primal growl as the sensations overwhelmed him.

In the midst of their heated exchange, Bentley, fueled by an insatiable desire, decided to take control. With a sudden surge of strength, he lifted Raelynn off the entertainment center, her legs instinctively wrapping around his waist. The air crackled with electricity as he carried her effortlessly toward the bed.

Raelynn's hands, now gripping Bentley's shoulders, met his intense gaze with a mixture of surprise and anticipation. The room seemed to spin as Bentley tossed her onto the bed, the softness of the sheets offering a contrast to the intensity of their connection. Raelynn landed with a gasp, her eyes never leaving Bentley's.

Bentley, driven by a hunger that mirrored Raelynn's, followed her onto the bed. Their eyes locked in a heated exchange, the anticipation between them palpable. Bentley crawled over Raelynn, his body hovering just inches above hers. The room echoed with the sound of their heavy breaths, a symphony of desire.

Without breaking eye contact, Bentley's hands traced a path from Raelynn's thighs up to the curves of her hips, teasingly brushing his lips against hers. Their connection deepened as Bentley's kisses traveled down, leaving a trail of fire in their wake. His exploration continued, moving lower, down her neck, her collarbone, until his breath danced over the valley between her breasts.

Raelynn's fingers wound through Bentley's hair, pulling him closer, a silent plea for more. Bentley responded with a hunger that mirrored her own. His kisses descended further, exploring the contours of her stomach, each touch sending waves of pleasure through her body.

With a swift, decisive motion, Bentley positioned himself between Raelynn's thighs. He looked up, locking eyes with her, seeking permission.

The air buzzed with anticipation as Raelynn nodded, her eyes filled with desire.

Bentley's lips met the soft, delicate skin of her inner thighs, leaving a trail of feather-light kisses. His hands, now gripping her hips, held her in place as he teased her with the warmth of his breath. The room echoed with the sounds of Raelynn's sighs, a symphony of pleasure that fueled Bentley's determination.

As Bentley's tongue traced delicate patterns, Raelynn's breath hitched. The sensations became a whirlwind of pleasure, building with each flicker of his tongue. Her fingers tightened in Bentley's hair, an instinctual response to the escalating ecstasy.

Emboldened by the intoxicating sounds escaping Raelynn's lips, Bentley delved deeper, fully immersing himself in the act of giving her pleasure. Bentley's movements were deliberate, his tongue dancing across Raelynn's most intimate places, heightening the sensations that surged through her body.

Raelynn, lost in the intensity of the pleasure, arched her back, her fingers still entwined in Bentley's hair. She could feel the rising crescendo within her, the anticipation of release building with every tantalizing touch. Bentley's expert ministrations had her on the edge, teetering between ecstasy and surrender.

In an unexpected yet bold move, Raelynn, fueled by the desire to reciprocate, tightened her grip on Bentley's hair and gently pulled him back up toward her. Bentley, sensing her intentions, met her gaze with a smoldering intensity, a silent acknowledgment of the unspoken exchange of control between them.

With a seamless motion, Raelynn flipped Bentley onto his back, her movements guided by a newfound confidence. She straddled him, a vision of empowered sensuality, and looked down at him with a fiery determination in her eyes. The room pulsed with an electric charge as Bentley gazed up at her, his desire mirroring the intensity reflected in her eyes.

Raelynn wasted no time in exploring Bentley's body with a hunger that matched his. Her lips traced a path down his chest, leaving a trail of heated kisses. The room echoed with Bentley's appreciative groans as Raelynn moved lower, teasingly brushing her lips against his abdomen.

Bentley's anticipation heightened as Raelynn's kisses trailed lower, inching toward his throbbing arousal. The room seemed to vibrate with desire as Raelynn reached her destination. With a teasing look in her eyes, she locked onto Bentley's gaze, savoring the intensity of the moment.

As Raelynn took his throbbing cock and placed it into her mouth, Bentley's breath caught in his throat. The warmth and wetness enveloped him, sending waves of pleasure through his body. Raelynn's movements were both deliberate and sensual, a dance of passion that left Bentley yearning for more.

Raelynn enjoyed the taste of Bentley as her tongue worked its magical circles around the head of his penis, making him beg for more. As Raelynn looked up at Bentley with the length of his hardness in her mouth, she could see his pleasure as his eyes were rolled into the back of his head, his hands finding solace in her tousled hair.

Bentley couldn't handle the sensation anymore as he reached down pulling Raelynn back up to his kiss. In a quick burst of energy, Bentley flipped Raelynn onto her back, locking eyes, positioned himself in between her thighs.

As Bentley hovered over Raelynn with locked eyes, he leaned down engaging in a slow, deep, and passionate kiss before he entered inside her.

"Oh fuck." They both moaned in unison, as it was finally happening with no interruptions.

Their bodies moved in perfect harmony, a dance of passion and desire that transcended the physical realm. Bentley and Raelynn were lost in the intoxicating rhythm of their connection, each movement driving them closer to the edge of ecstasy.

The room became a symphony of moans and sighs, punctuated by the creaking of the bed and the rhythmic slapping of their bodies coming together. Time seemed to stretch, and the outside world faded away as they surrendered to the pleasure that consumed them.

Bentley's hands roamed Raelynn's body, tracing the curves and contours as if he were sculpting a masterpiece. Raelynn's nails dug into

Bentley's back, her breaths coming in short gasps as waves of pleasure radiated from their joined bodies.

As their passion reached its peak, Bentley's movements became more urgent, each thrust a declaration of their shared desire. Raelynn met him with equal fervor, her hips rising to meet his in a synchronized dance of intimacy.

The air crackled with the electricity of their connection, and the room echoed with the symphony of their pleasure. Bentley's name tumbled from Raelynn's lips in a breathless mantra, each utterance fueling the fire that burned between them.

In the throes of passion, Bentley and Raelynn found a profound connection that went beyond the physical act. Their eyes locked, conveying a depth of emotion that words could never capture. It was a union of souls, a moment of vulnerability and raw authenticity.

As the intensity built, Bentley felt the familiar tension coiling within him, signaling the impending climax. Raelynn, sensing his nearing release, clung to him with an intensity that mirrored his own. In the final crescendo, they reached the pinnacle of pleasure together, their bodies trembling in unison.

Spent and breathless, Bentley collapsed beside Raelynn, their bodies still entwined. The room was hushed, the only sound their synchronized breaths as they basked in the afterglow of their shared ecstasy.

"That was quite an experience," Raelynn remarked, resting her head on Bentley's chest and gazing up at him.

"Tell me about it. That was fucking intense." Bentley replied, still trying to catch his breath.

"Was it worth the wait?" Raelynn teased.

Bentley let out a contented chuckle, running a hand through Raelynn's tousled hair. "Absolutely," he said, his eyes still reflecting the lingering intensity of their shared experience. "More than worth it."

Feeling a renewed surge of energy, Bentley reluctantly untangled himself from Raelynn's embrace, sitting up on the edge of the bed. "I need a shower," he announced, a mischievous glint in his eyes.

Raelynn shot him a playful grin, feeling a magnetic pull toward him. As Bentley got up and headed toward the bathroom, Raelynn couldn't resist the temptation. With a stealthy and swift movement, she rose from the bed and followed him.

The shower's sound masked her approach, and as Bentley stepped into the cascading water, he turned, only to find Raelynn joining him with a sly smile. The water droplets glistened on their skin as they stood together under the warm spray, the intimacy of the shower amplifying the connection they had just shared.

Bentley's surprised expression shifted to one of delight as Raelynn closed the distance between them, the steamy air adding to the allure. Without a word, she reached for the bar of soap, her movements deliberate and sensuous, continuing the dance of intimacy that had begun in the hotel's elevator.

Accidently on purpose, Raelynn dropped the bar of soap, "Oops!" She said teasingly as she knelt down to pick it up. Only she didn't pick it up.

As Raelynn remained on her knees, she met Bentley's gaze with a playful glint in her eyes.

Bentley's anticipation heightened, his eyes locked on her with a mix of surprise and desire. The steamy air enveloped them in an intimate embrace as Raelynn, still maintaining eye contact, playfully swiped her fingers across Bentley's thighs.

With a sudden surge of boldness, Raelynn pushed Bentley gently against the shower wall, her gaze unwavering. With a slow, deliberate movement, Raelynn's hands trailed up Bentley's thighs, fingers dancing lightly over his skin. Bentley's breath caught as he watched her every move, the anticipation of what might come next adding to the charged atmosphere.

In an unexpected yet tantalizing maneuver, Raelynn's hands reached for Bentley's arousal, her fingers wrapping around him with a firm yet gentle touch. Bentley's eyes widened in surprise and delight, his breath hitching as Raelynn's touch sent shivers down his spine.

The steamy air seemed to thicken with desire as Raelynn continued her intimate exploration as she placed his penis in her mouth. Bentley, pressed against the shower wall, succumbed to the sensations, his hands finding real estate on the tiled surface for support.

Raelynn's gaze remained locked onto Bentley's, a mischievous smile playing on her lips as she began a slow, rhythmic movement. The warmth of the water combined with the tender touch created a sensory experience that left Bentley both breathless and enraptured.

Bentley, overwhelmed by the sensations, braced himself against the shower wall as Raelynn's actions brought him to the brink of ecstasy. The intensity of their gaze deepened the connection, each glance and touch speaking of the unspoken understanding that bound them together.

As Bentley reached the peak of pleasure, Raelynn continued her bold exploration, swallowing with a sense of confidence and desire that left no room for hesitation. She looked up at him, her lips glistening, and with a swipe of her hand, she mischievously cleaned any remaining remnants from her lips with a smile.

"The pleasure was mine." Raelynn teased, as she got up, exiting the shower.

"You are a mean woman Miss Raelynn Hart." Bentley teased back, while trying to catch his breath.

As Raelynn wrapped herself in a towel, she looked back at Bentley still leaned up against the shower wall defeated, "You can tell Mike to cancel my room. I don't think I'll be needing it the rest of the weekend." She said with sly grin, before exiting the bathroom.

Bentley emerged from the bathroom wearing nothing but a towel and found Raelynn reclining on the bed, wrapped in a towel, her eyes filled with a mix of satisfaction and playfulness.

Bentley approached her with a teasing glint in his eyes. "You know, Miss Hart, you've made quite an impression. Canceling your room, are we?" he said, a smirk playing on his lips.

Raelynn chuckled, her gaze meeting Bentley's. "Well, it seems I've found a much more interesting accommodation for the weekend."

Bentley sat down on the edge of the bed, his eyes tracing the contours of Raelynn's figure. "I must say, canceling your room is a bold move. What if I turn out to be a terrible roommate?"

Raelynn leaned in with a sultry smile, her fingers tracing patterns on Bentley's chest. "I have a feeling you'll be anything but terrible."

With a playful twinkle in her eyes, Raelynn removed the towel from her body, tossing it to the floor, revealing the curves that had captured Bentley's attention earlier. Bentley, in response, discarded his own towel, and the room became a canvas of bare vulnerability. They met in the middle of the bed, the warmth of their bodies creating an irresistible magnetism. As they embraced, the echoes of their laughter and whispered promises blended seamlessly into the soft hum of the night.

The sheets cradled them as they settled into each other's arms, their skin still flushed from the lingering heat of the shower. Bentley's fingers traced gentle patterns on Raelynn's back, a silent reassurance that spoke of more than just physical connection. Raelynn, in turn, nestled closer, her head finding a comfortable nook on Bentley's shoulder.

In the soft glow of the room, Bentley and Raelynn, now completely entwined, surrendered to the gentle pull of sleep. Their nude forms became a testament to the intimacy they had shared, a silent celebration of a connection that burned deep between them. As they drifted off to sleep, Bentley cuddled Raelynn with his warm embrace.

17

Afterglow

The following morning Bentley woke up with the sun beaming through his hotel room as the rays of light danced off his and Raelynn's skin. The sun reflected off Bentley's pearly whites, as a huge smile came across his face seeing Raelynn still wrapped in his arms.

As Bentley laid there cuddling Raelynn, he couldn't help but replay last night over in his mind. After all the obstacles that prevented last night from happening sooner made it worth the wait. It was hands down the best sexual encounter that he had ever experienced. It was an experience that left Bentley wanting more.

As the flashback continued, Bentley became aroused and his hard erection pressed against Raelynn's bare cheeks, sending chills of sensation throughout his body reminding him of last night's burning passion. Remembering, Raelynn's gracious acts of pleasure in the shower, a mischievous smirk danced across his face. Bentley began kissing on Raelynn's neck and ear while his hand roamed up and down her thigh.

"Good morning." Raelynn mumbled as she was starting to wake up, wearing a big smile on her face.

Without a word, Bentley continued kissing on Raelynn's neck, as his hand now massaged her butt cheek. Raelynn turned her head meeting Bentley's intoxicating kiss, igniting an early morning flame.

Bentley gently withdrew from Raelynn's kiss, their gazes locking in a fiery exchange. With a smoldering intensity, he brought his hand to his lips, licking his fingers with a seductive allure, and then sensually traced them along the curve of Raelynn's backside, inserting his fingers inside of her.

Raelynn let out a slight moan as she caved into his touch, as she could feel his fingers deep enough to hit that right location. Bentley's 'come here' motion against her G-spot pushed her to the brink, as she clinched the back of Bentley's head pulling him into her kiss.

Just as Raelynn was on the brink of releasing, Bentley withdrew his fingers teasing her as she craved for that release. Bentley let out a mischievous chuckle as he could see the frustration in her eyes and on her face as she was so close.

With sense of urgency, Bentley dominantly rolled Raelynn flat onto her stomach as he positioned himself above her. He kissed his way down her back until his face was face-to-face with her ass. With both hands firmly planted on Raelynn's ass, he pulled her cheeks apart, burying his face into the most sensitive part of her body.

"OH...FUCK," Raelynn moaned as Bentley's tongue worked its magic on her clit.

Again, Bentley pushed Raelynn to the brink of release as her body trembled with anticipation of her climax. Again, Bentley teased, coming back up for air as Raelynn was on the edge. The frustration building inside her.

As Bentley was still positioned above Raelynn, he still held her cheeks apart as he dropped a ball of spit to act as a lubricant on the most sensitive part of her body. Using his penis, Bentley began to spread the spit ball around, teasing Raelynn beyond measure.

With a powerful thrust Bentley, inserted his hard throbbing cock inside Raelynn, he let out a moan of pleasure as he began to stroke in and out.

"OH, FUCK YES" Raelynn screamed out, as she bit down on her pillow, hands clinching the sheets, and her eyes rolling into the back of her head with the pleasure.

Bentley's thrusts were different from last night. They weren't slow and passionate instead they were powerful and demanding, increasingly getting harder and faster. The smacks of their bodies colliding getting louder and louder as they echoed in the hotel room. Raelynn alternated between moans and screams of pleasure as Bentley pounded her hard and good.

As Raelynn neared her release her body began to uncontrollably tremble. Right, as she was about to climax, she tried to lift her head up to scream out the pleasurable release that was inbound, but Bentley quickly shoved her head back down, burying her face into her pillow, muffling the sound of her release. Bentley in return let out a growl, as they reached their ceiling together.

"Now it's a good morning," Bentley said with a sly grin as he finally responded to Raelynn with words, getting up to get dressed for the busy day ahead.

"That's one way to start a morning," Raelynn said, still trying to catch her breath.

Later that morning, Bentley and Raelynn were both dressed to head down to the lobby to meet Mike for the short trip over to Bank of America Stadium for day two of fan fest. They both felt rejuvenated as they had a newfound energy.

Descending in the elevator, the very same one where their passionate night had unfolded, Bentley and Raelynn exchanged playful glances, sharing smiles and laughter as they reminisced about the unforgettable moments.

"Oh, Raelynn before I forget. Mike canceled your room this morning like you wanted. Don't worry about your things, he has instructed housekeeping to move them into my room." Bentley looked at Raelynn and said as the elevator reached the hotel lobby.

Silently, Raelynn beamed at Bentley, her eyes sparkling with affection. She wrapped her arm around him, resting her head on his chest as they gracefully exited the elevator.

"Thought I was going to have to send a search party for you two," Mike said as Bentley and Raelynn approached him in the hotel lobby.

Bentley and Raelynn glanced at each other as they begin to chuckle.

At Bank of America Stadium, day two of Cinderella fest was filled with the same routine as the previous day. Raelynn, Bentley, and his team were escorted to their dressing room. Just as they settled in Bentley, just like the previous day was pulled away to go handle record label obligations. Raelynn, again patiently waited in the dressing room with full range to explore the festival grounds just as yesterday as long as she was back in place by eight that evening.

As it neared time for the gates to open for the start of day two, Raelynn decided to venture out into the festival on her own. That morning she had caught a glimpse of the set times and wanted to see some of the artist performing.

After watching the sets of Lawson, Fever 333, 24hrs, Schoolboy Q, and Kirko Bangz, Raelynn decided to take a break from music. She decided to catch a glimpse of Bentley's life in the fame aside from being up on stage.

Raelynn quickly made her way to a pop-up tent that was heavily guarded with security, and as she stood to the side, she caught glimpses of Bentley as fans one by one entered inside the pop-up tent to meet him and get their photo-op. As she watched on from the side, she couldn't fight the pang of jealousy that entered her chest. Watching all of Bentley's fans enter the tent vying for his attention, throwing their arms around him, flashing him their tits, or even trying to throw their lustful lips on him made her feel some type of way.

Raelynn really didn't know why she was feeling jealous considering her and Bentley hadn't defined their relationship, it was still fresh and they hadn't had that discussion yet. Although there was a part of Raelynn that hoped they eventually would define things. However, the jealousy was still there. Raelynn knew she was beautiful, and she knew the connection her and Bentley had was something deeper than she could explain but she still felt uneasy at seeing this side of his stardom firsthand.

As Raelynn's jealousy was at its peak her phone buzzed with a text. It was Owen letting her know that he had the rest of her bandmates had arrived.

Raelynn quickly retreated from the meet and greet tent and went to meet her bandmates. With a quick stride, Raelynn navigated through the bustling festival grounds to find her band. Her heart, still fluttering with a touch of jealousy, welcomed the distraction of seeing familiar faces. She spotted Owen first, his tall frame with his long shaggy hair and easy smile making him easily recognizable. Beside him stood the rest of Raelynn's bandmates, Levi, Elijah, and Jake.

Owen caught sight of Raelynn approaching and flashed her a bright smile, signaling the others to turn their attention toward her. The festival buzzed around them, but in that moment, their excitement centered on the reunion with their lead singer.

"Raelynn!" Owen called out, and the bandmates greeted her with warm smiles and friendly gestures.

Raelynn felt a mix of relief and joy as she joined the group. The warmth radiating from her bandmates eased the remnants of jealousy that lingered from witnessing Bentley's meet and greet.

"Hey, guys! It's so good to see you," Raelynn exclaimed, embracing each of them in turn. The camaraderie among the bandmates was palpable, and Raelynn felt an instant connection with the group.

Levi grinned, his laid-back demeanor shining through. "We've been waiting for this moment all week. How's it been, hanging out with Bentley all week? Better yet how was performing with him in front of thousands of fans last night?"

Raelynn chuckled, her cheeks tinged with a faint blush. "Performing with Bentley was unreal. The energy, the crowd—it was an experience like no other. And hanging out with him... well, let's just say it's been interesting."

Owen raised an eyebrow, a mischievous glint in his eye. "Interesting, huh? Do tell."

"Well, turns out I actually know Bentley! We met briefly eight years ago in Cancun at a karaoke bar." Raelynn said, as she put air quotes around the word "know."

The revelation about Raelynn and Bentley's previous encounter in Cancun sparked intrigue among her bandmates. Owen's mischievous grin widened, and Levi raised his eyebrows, clearly eager to hear the details.

"Wait, seriously?" Owen asked, his tone a mix of amusement and curiosity. "You've known Bentley for eight years?"

"No. I just met him, and we shared a moment. A moment that I had long forgotten until Sunday when we met for coffee. After talking, it clicked that we remembered each other." Raelynn said.

The bandmates exchanged surprised glances, absorbing Raelynn's revelation. Owen leaned in, a teasing smile on his face. "So, what kind of moment are we talking about?"

Raelynn playfully smacked Owen as she gave him a stern look, "That's none of your business."

Owen chuckled, raising his hands in mock surrender. "Alright, alright, your secret's safe with us. But this is one hell of a plot twist, Raelynn."

"Raelynn, I know it's only been a week since we've seen you last but you look very different. You look…happier." Elijah chimed in as he was looking Raelynn up and down.

Raelynn smiled at Elijah's observation. "Well, I guess you could say it's been an eventful week," she replied with a playful twinkle in her eyes.

Levi nudged Owen with a smirk. "Looks like our girl here has some stories to spill. spill 'em, Raelynn!"

Raelynn laughed, a soft, knowing sound that seemed to dance in the air. "Maybe, maybe not," she teased, keeping her secret tucked away, savoring the warmth of her bandmates' company.

Elijah raised an eyebrow, a curious grin playing on his lips. "Come on, Raelynn. Spill the details. What's making you glow like that?"

Levi joined in with a playful smirk. "Yeah, spill the tea, or should we say, the coffee?"

Owen chuckled, enjoying the banter. "Seriously, though, Raelynn, you've piqued our interest. What's the story?"

Raelynn feigned innocence, batting her eyelashes. "Oh, it's just been a crazy week, you know? Connecting over music…lots of music. But some stories are meant to be kept under wraps."

Jake, who had been silent until now, finally spoke up. "Well, whatever it is, we're happy to see you in good spirits. And speaking of music, are you ready for our set tomorrow afternoon?"

Raelynn grinned, the playful banter of her bandmates bringing a welcome lightness to the moment. "Absolutely, Jake. I'm more than ready. This whole experience with Bentley has fueled my energy, and I can't wait for us to rock the stage together."

As the bandmates continued to catch up and exchange stories about their week apart, Raelynn couldn't help but glance over her shoulder toward the pop-up tent where Bentley was still engaging with fans. The remnants of jealousy had dissipated, replaced by a sense of appreciation for the unique world Bentley inhabited. She knew they both had separate lives in the spotlight, and navigating this newfound connection would require some understanding on both ends.

The festival day unfolded with the bandmates enjoying the various performances, exploring the vibrant atmosphere, and sharing laughter. Raelynn felt a renewed sense of camaraderie with her band, and she cherished the moments they spent together.

As the sun dipped below the horizon, signaling the approach of her performance, Raelynn led her bandmates backstage. The excitement bubbled within her, a mix of nerves and anticipation. She couldn't wait to share the stage with Bentley once again, this time with her bandmates backstage to watch on.

In the backstage chaos, Bentley spotted Raelynn approaching with her band. His eyes lit up, and he excused himself from the ongoing conversation to meet them halfway.

"Hey there, rockstar," Bentley greeted Raelynn with a smirk, pulling her into a brief but warm hug. His eyes flickered over to her bandmates, offering nods and casual greetings.

Raelynn couldn't help but smile, the shared energy between them palpable. "Ready for another unforgettable performance?" she asked, a playful glint in her eyes.

Bentley leaned in, his lips brushing against her ear. "With you by my side? Always."

"Well, I'd like you to meet my band, Owen, Jake, Levi, and Elijah. We are all gracious of the opportunity you have given us to perform her tomorrow." Raelynn, she said as she gestured over to her bandmates.

Bentley turned his attention to Raelynn's bandmates, offering a genuine smile. "It's a pleasure to meet all of you. I've heard great things about your music, and I'm looking forward to seeing you guys rock the stage tomorrow."

Owen, ever the charismatic one, stepped forward with a firm handshake. "Likewise, Bentley. We appreciate the chance to be part of this festival."

Levi, with his easygoing demeanor, clapped Bentley on the shoulder. "Thanks for having us, mate. It's an honor." His Australian accent stronger than usual.

Jake, the quiet one, nodded appreciatively.

Elijah, always full of energy, just grinned.

As they continued to chat, Mike approached the group, a clipboard in hand. "Alright, folks, we've got a tight schedule. Bentley, we need you and Raelynn to head up to the stage and get ready to go on after Post Malone. Raelynn you know the deal. You'll stand in the wings of the stage until he calls you on for the last three songs, just like last night. Let's go guys."

Raelynn looked back at her band as Mike started herding her and Bentley away, "I'll catch you guys later."

As Bentley and Raelynn made their way toward the stage, the festival buzzed with anticipation. The energy in the air was electrifying, and the distant thump of music echoed through the stadium.

Bentley kept a reassuring hand on Raelynn's lower back as they navigated the backstage chaos. The occasional glance, the unspoken connection between them, spoke volumes. As they reached the side of the stage, Bentley turned to Raelynn, his eyes locking onto hers.

"Just like last night Rae, just like last night. You got this." Bentley said with a reassuring smile.

Raelynn just looked up at Bentley and smiled as they stood there watching Post Malone finishing up his set.

Just like the previous night, soon as Post Malone's set concluded, Bentley introductory video began blaring throughout the stadium and fans erupted.

Just like the previous night, Bentley navigated the stage with such demand, also just like the previous night Bentley introduced Raelynn. Again, they closed out the show with the last three songs, ending with Cinderella.

That night back at the hotel, Bentley, Raelynn, and her bandmates hung out in the hotel's luxurious lounge, laughing, joking, and drinking as they all shared stories.

The laughter and chatter echoed in the upscale lounge, creating a lively atmosphere as Bentley, Raelynn, and her bandmates relished the post-performance glow. The night unfolded with a blend of shared stories, clinking glasses, and the occasional burst of laughter that drew curious glances from other patrons checking in.

As the night progressed, Bentley found himself captivated not just by Raelynn but by the dynamic of her band. He appreciated the genuine friendships they shared and the easy way they included him in their circle. Owen's charisma, Jake's quiet strength, Levi's laid-back charm, and Elijah's infectious energy—it was a mix that seemed to complement each other perfectly.

At one point in the evening, Jake, who had been observing the subtle exchanges between Bentley and Raelynn throughout the day, the glances, the shared smiles, and the way Bentley's hand found its way to the small of Raelynn's back—it was evident that there was something more between them.

"Oh, they are definitely fucking fucking," Jake blurted out, his words breaking through the laughter and causing a momentary hush in the conversation. Bentley and Raelynn both turned toward Jake, their eyes locking with a mix of surprise and amusement.

Bentley couldn't help but burst into laughter at Jake's straightforward comment. Raelynn, though momentarily taken aback, joined in the laughter, shaking her head in mock disbelief.

"Jake, mate, subtlety is a lost art on you," Levi quipped, raising an eyebrow with a smirk.

Elijah added with a chuckle, "Well, it's not like they're hiding it very well."

Bentley, still grinning, raised his hands in mock surrender. "Alright, you got me. Guilty as charged."

Raelynn playfully nudged Bentley with her elbow. "Looks like our secret's out, huh?"

The banter continued, the atmosphere light and filled with camaraderie. As the night wore on, Bentley and Raelynn found themselves stealing glances and subtle touches, the unspoken connection deepening with each passing moment.

The luxurious lounge echoed with the shared stories of the night, blending the worlds of fame and ordinary moments. Eventually, the laughter softened, and Bentley suggested, "How about we call it a night? Tomorrow's another big day."

Agreeing, the group bid farewell to the upscale lounge and retreated to their respective rooms. Bentley and Raelynn, still sharing playful glances, made their way to Bentley's room, where a comfortable silence enveloped them as they prepared for a night of peaceful sleep. But more like another night fueling the burning passion between them.

18

Here's Your Moment

The following afternoon Raelynn and her band stood on the wing of the stage ready to embrace their once in a lifetime opportunity to perform in front of thousands of fans. Raelynn stood there, nervous as hell as she looked out at the sea of people waiting for them to come on stage. It was a different feeling than the one she had the past two nights performing with Bentley in front of a crowd like this. It was her first-time performing solo in front of a crowd this large.

Raelynn wished that Bentley could be there to watch her performance, but she knew he had another day filled with label obligations.

While Raelynn, stood there consumed by her nerves, out of nowhere she felt someone wrap their hands around her waist and pull her close to them. She then heard the familiar voice that made the butterflies fly away.

"Did you miss me?" Bentley whispered into her ear.

Raelynn turned to face Bentley and planted a kiss on his lips. "I didn't think you could make it to watch us?" Raelynn asked as she pulled from Bentley's kiss, locking eyes.

"You thought I was missing this? No way I was missing this! I had Mike push some things back so I could be here." Bentley said as he pulled Raelynn into his warm embrace.

138

As Raelynn melted into Bentley's embrace, the nervous energy that had gripped her began to dissipate. Bentley's presence was a soothing balm to her anxieties, and she couldn't help but smile up at him.

"Really? You rearranged your schedule for me?" Raelynn's eyes sparkled with a mix of surprise and delight.

Bentley nodded, his gaze never leaving hers. "I wouldn't miss this for the world. You and your band are about to rock this stage, and I wouldn't want to be anywhere else."

She felt a swell of gratitude, not just for Bentley being there, but for the unwavering support he consistently showed. "Thank you," she whispered, leaning in for another quick kiss.

The stage manager motioned to Raelynn and her band letting them know it was time. Owen, Levi, Jake, and Owen's eyes widened as if they were suddenly battling nerves their selves.

"Here's your moment Rae. You got this!" Bentley said reassuringly as Raelynn pulled from his embrace to head out on the stage.

Stepping into the spotlight, Raelynn was accompanied by Owen's rhythmic chords for the opening song. The audience burst into cheers. Before long, Elijah added the vibrant tones of his keyboard, Levi set the drums in motion, and Jake joined in with the bass, collectively giving birth to a fusion of rock and country melodies.

Meanwhile, Bentley stood at the side of the stage, watching Raelynn with a mix of pride and adoration. Seeing her under the spotlight, commanding the stage with a confidence that captivated the audience, filled him with a sense of accomplishment. Yet, beneath the surface, a pang of jealousy gnawed at him as he observed the undeniable chemistry between Raelynn and Owen.

As Raelynn sang her heart out, Bentley couldn't shake the feeling that Owen's hands on her waist were a little too possessive, his whispers a little too close. The smile on Raelynn's face, the way her eyes lit up when she looked at Owen—it stung. Bentley tried to push away the jealousy, reminding himself that this was part of the performance, just a show for the audience.

However, as the set continued, Bentley found it increasingly difficult to suppress his emotions. A tight knot formed in his stomach, and he grew more distant. The cheers of the crowd became distant echoes as jealousy clouded his thoughts. Unable to bear the sight any longer, he turned on his heels and walked away from the stage, disappearing into the backstage shadows.

Raelynn, in the midst of her performance, couldn't help but notice Bentley's abrupt departure. A flicker of concern crossed her face, but she pushed it aside, focusing on the music. The show must go on.

As the final notes of the song echoed through the venue, Raelynn took a moment to catch her breath. She scanned the wings of the stage, hoping to find Bentley, but he was nowhere in sight. Confusion and worry crept into her eyes as she exchanged glances with Owen and the rest of the band.

Bentley, seething with frustration and hurt, found solace in the quiet dressing room backstage. He paced back and forth, grappling with the conflicting emotions that threatened to overwhelm him. His mind replayed the moments on stage, the way Raelynn and Owen seemed to share an unspoken connection.

Back on stage, Raelynn powered through the next few songs, her mind occasionally wandering to Bentley's sudden exit. She couldn't shake the feeling that something was amiss. As the set reached its climax, Raelynn poured her heart into the performance, hoping to convey her emotions through the music.

Breathless from the final song, Raelynn rushed off the stage, leaving her bandmates in a state of confusion. She couldn't ignore the nagging worry about Bentley's sudden departure any longer. The backstage corridors seemed to stretch endlessly as she frantically searched for him.

Meanwhile, Bentley, still grappling with his conflicting emotions, had retreated to the quiet dressing room. The echoes of the performance still lingered in his mind, but the hurt and frustration were more palpable. He hadn't expected the surge of jealousy to hit him so hard, and now he found himself wrestling with the aftermath of witnessing Raelynn's on-stage connection with Owen.

As Raelynn pushed open the door to the dressing room, the atmosphere changed instantly. The tension between them was thick, and Bentley's eyes, once filled with adoration, now held a storm of conflicting emotions. Raelynn, determined to address the issue, took a deep breath.

Raelynn approached Bentley with determination, gently yet assertively taking his hand. Leading him to a small room within the dressing area, partially closing the door behind them.

Bentley, still reeling from the rush of emotions, avoided Raelynn's gaze. The room felt suffocating with unspoken tension. Raelynn took a deep breath, searching for the right words to bridge the gap between them.

"I saw you leave during the performance, what's going on," Raelynn ask, her eyes searching Bentley's for answers.

Bentley sighed running a hand through his hair, "I... I couldn't take it."

"Take what?" Raelynn asked with her voice heightening with frustration.

"I couldn't take the connection you and Owen had on stage alright." Bentley said as he starred at the floor.

"Bentley, it was just a fucking performance, why are you so jealous right now?" Raelynn asked with the frustration building in her voice.

"YEAH, IT WAS JUST A FUCKING PERFORMANCE, RIGHT? IT LOOKED LIKE Y'ALL WANTED TO FUCK ON STAGE, THE WAY Y'ALL TOUCHED EACH OTHER, AND UNDRESSED EACH OTHER WITH YOUR EYES." Bentley shouted, unable to contain his emotions any longer.

Raelynn was in pure shock, and she couldn't decide what shocked her more. Was it the fact Bentley was jealous of Owen or was it the fact Bentley just shouted at her.

"YOU'RE JEALOUS OF OWEN, AND ACCUSING ME OF WANTING TO FUCK HIM? THAT'S FUCKING HILARIOUS BENTLEY. ONE BECAUSE OWEN IS GAY. WHY ARE YOU SO FUCKING MAD RIGHT NOW ? I DIDN'T GET MAD

YESTERDAY WHEN I WATCHED FROM THE SIDELINES AT YOUR MEET AND GREET, GIRLS LITERALLY THROWING THEIR SELVES ON YOU AND FLASHING YOU THEIR FUCKING TITS.' Raelynn shouted back.

At this point, Owen, Levi, Jake, and Elijah, entered the dressing room giving each other 'what the fuck' glances as they could hear the shouting match coming from the small room inside the dressing area.

"Sounds like trouble in paradise." Jake said just loud enough for the group to hear.

"Yeah, but why the fuck is my name being mentioned, or my sexual orientation." Owen responded with anger in his voice.

"I don't know mate, but maybe we should get out of here and let them have their moment." Levi chimed in.

"To hell with that, I want to know why my name is being mentioned." Owen said with anger apparent in his voice and on his face.

The band hesitated for a moment, unsure whether to intervene or give Raelynn and Bentley some space. However, the escalating tension in the room made it clear that something needed to be addressed.

Owen pushed open the door to the small room, confronting the tense scene inside. Raelynn and Bentley turned their attention to him, both wearing expressions of shock and frustration. Bentley was clearly caught off guard by the sudden intrusion.

"What the hell is going on in here?" Owen demanded, his eyes narrowing as he focused on Bentley.

Raelynn turned to Owen, frustration evident in her eyes. "Apparently, Bentley thinks our on-stage chemistry was more than just a performance. And now he's accusing me of wanting to 'fuck' you."

Owen's face contorted in a mixture of confusion and anger. "Seriously, Bentley? Do you even know me? I'm gay, for God's sake. There's nothing like that between Rae and me."

Levi, Jake, and Elijah sat in the dressing area witnessing the unfolding drama. Jake muttered, "Well, this escalated quickly."

Inside the room, Bentley's initial outburst had given way to a realization of his mistake. He ran a hand through his hair, looking genuinely regretful. "I... I didn't know. I just saw you two up there, and I let jealousy get the best of me."

However, Raelynn wanted answers, "But why Bentley? We have only been doing whatever it is we're doing for a week. We haven't even defined a relationship between us yet."

Bentley sighed, realizing the weight of his actions. "I know, Rae. I messed up, and I let my insecurities get the best of me. I've never been good at this communication stuff and seeing you up there with Owen just triggered something in me. It's not an excuse, but it's the truth."

Raelynn's anger softened as she saw the sincerity in Bentley's eyes. She took a deep breath, trying to find a way to navigate through the mess. "Bentley, we need to figure out if we can trust each other. Communication is key, and accusations like this won't help us build anything meaningful. Especially, if this is even something you really want."

Owen, still standing in the doorway, added, "And for the record, Bentley, if you have an issue, talk to her. Don't make baseless accusations. It's not fair to anyone involved."

Bentley nodded, remorse written all over his face. "You're right. I should have talked to you, Raelynn, instead of letting my emotions control me."

The room fell into an awkward silence, and the rest of the band exchanged glances. Jake broke the silence, "So, are we all good here, or do we need to form a therapy circle?"

Raelynn managed a small smile, "I think we need some time to talk, figure things out. But we're adults, we can handle this."

Just as things were calming down Mike entered the dressing room, "Hey, Bentley are you still good with opening the show with your new song tonight?" Mike began hesitating on his question as he started sensing the tension in the room.

Bentley glanced at Raelynn, silently seeking her approval before responding to Mike. Raelynn nodded, signaling that the show must go on despite the emotional turmoil they were navigating.

"Yeah, Mike, we're good," Bentley replied, his tone more composed than before. "Let's stick to the plan."

Mike, sensing the need for a moment of privacy, nodded and left the room, closing the door behind him. The band members exchanged glances once more, understanding that Raelynn and Bentley needed time to address their issues as they too left the room.

Raelynn turned her attention back to Bentley, her expression softening. "We need to talk, Bentley. About us, about trust, and about figuring out what we want from this."

Bentley nodded, his eyes reflecting a mix of regret and determination. "I know, Raelynn. I overreacted, and I want to make things right. Can we talk after the show?"

"Of course," Raelynn replied, appreciating Bentley's willingness to confront the situation.

Bentley left to go finish his media obligations for the day as Raelynn stayed in the dressing room replaying everything that had just happened over in her head.

As the day went on and Bentley navigated through his media obligations, he couldn't shake the weight of the situation. The echo of his own accusations lingered in his mind, and he couldn't help but feel a sense of shame for letting his insecurities control him.

Backstage, Raelynn took the time to think things through. She understood that emotions could run high, especially in the chaotic world of the music industry. However, she needed assurance that Bentley could communicate openly and honestly. As she pondered the complexities of their budding connection, she couldn't deny the spark of something real between them.

Later that evening, Bentley returned to the dressing area. You could tell he was behind schedule the way he moved through the room with an urgency to change clothes for the performance.

"Bentley, we need you and Raelynn stage side ready to go now." The voice of a stage manager shout inside the dressing area while Bentley was changing.

As Bentley and Raelynn swiftly left the room, Raelynn could hear the music of the band on stage, it was a lot different from the artist that they had gone on after the previous two nights. The music was a lot heavier to be a rapper, or a pop artist.

"Who are you going on after Bentley?" Raelynn asked with curiosity in her voice.

"Honestly, I don't even know. They told me it was a surprise a surprise headliner," Bentley responded as he tried listening to the music coming from the stage. "HOLY SHIT! That's Bring Me The Fucking Horizon." Bentley shouted with excitement in his voice as you could see him on the verge of geeking out!

Raelynn could see the sparkle in Bentley's eyes the moment he realized that it was 'Bring Me The Horizon' performing. They quickly hurried to stage side so they could catch the remnants of the performance.

As Bentley and Raelynn made their way to the stage side, the pulsating beats and electrifying energy of Bring Me The Horizon's performance filled the air. The crowd roared, caught up in the intense atmosphere created by the renowned rock band.

Bentley, still buzzing with excitement, couldn't help but share his enthusiasm with Raelynn. "I can't believe we're getting to see Bring Me The Horizon live! They're freaking legendary!"

Raelynn smiled, appreciating Bentley's genuine passion for music. The two stood side by side, absorbing the powerful sounds and captivating stage presence. The chaotic emotions from their earlier confrontation seemed momentarily forgotten during the thrilling performance.

As Bring Me The Horizon wrapped up their set, Bentley stood there in awe and amazement. It was a surreal experience witnessing his favorite band perform live for the first time. However, as the time for Bentley's own performance approached, he couldn't shake the fanboy excitement within him. Hoping for a chance to speak to Oli Sykes, the lead singer, Bentley lingered like a dedicated groupie.

While waiting to see if he could catch a moment with Oli, Bentley found himself overwhelmed with shock, especially when Oli Sykes approached him and initiated a conversation.

"Hey mate, you and your crew put on an incredible festival. Thanks for having us," Oli expressed with his distinct British accent.

Struggling to find his words amidst the surprise, Bentley managed to respond, "Thanks, man! You guys are incredible. Maybe we can collaborate on a song sometime."

"I think that'll be a great idea, mate. Get your guys to reach out, and maybe we can figure something out," Oli suggested before disappearing into the backstage frenzy with the rest of his band.

Bentley turned to Raelynn, who was smiling at his excitement. She understood the significance of the moment for him.

"I can't believe he knew who I was, Rae," Bentley mumbled.

"Well, I can! You're Bentley, for crying out loud. Now, pull yourself together. You've got a show to put on," Raelynn said, leaning up to give Bentley a kiss before he pulled away to take the stage.

As Bentley prepared to enter the stage, the production team sounded his suspenseful intro like they had the previous two nights. Quickly, the intro faded into Bentley's new song "Ghost". The song had a dark but vibey intro as Bentley began with the opening the lyrics.

"She said I only come around
When I'm feeling lonely
When I'm looking for some company
She said I lead her on
Just to cut her off"

The crowd erupted in excitement as they realized they were being treated to a brand-new song. The anticipation heightened as the beat dropped, and Bentley delved into the opening verse.

"So if I ghost you
Don't take it personal baby
I promise
It's me not you
You said it best yourself
I only come around
When I'm feeling lonely

146

I just want sex
With no strings attached
No emotional connection
Just physical attraction
But you're so complicated
Always wanting relations"

The fans found themselves pleasantly surprised when the chorus hit—a dark, rock-infused hook that marked a departure from Bentley's previous sound. Despite its unexpected nature, the audience embraced the fresh vibe. The instrumental arrangement, Bentley's vocals—all of it was a departure from Bentley's old sound, yet a captivating one that held their attention.

"She said I only come around
When I'm feeling lonely
When I'm looking for some company
She said I lead her on
Just to cut her off
She said I'm a ghost in the night
And she might just be right
She might just be right
Cause sometimes I feel like a ghost
Creeping through the night"

As Raelynn observed Bentley performing his latest song, she found herself genuinely enjoying his new sound. However, a nagging curiosity about the lyrics lingered in her mind. Would Bentley eventually ghost her? Was his time with her solely driven by loneliness? Were their interactions merely about physical intimacy? A cascade of thoughts flooded her mind, causing her to become absorbed in contemplation for the majority of Bentley's set. She nearly missed her cue to join him on stage for the final three songs, a routine they had followed for the past two nights.

As Bentley and Raelynn concluded the final song of his setlist, Raelynn hurried off the stage, but Bentley remained, lingering in the moment. She assumed he stayed behind to soak in the atmosphere and savor the occasion, especially since it marked the last night of the festival hastily organized by Bentley on a whim. Until she heard his voice come through the speakers.

"Cinderella Fest! I extend my heartfelt gratitude to all the fans who embraced this impromptu idea and made the effort to join us this weekend. To those who couldn't make it due to the last-minute changes, I assure you, I'll find a way to make it up to them in the future," Bentley expressed, addressing the enthusiastic sea of fans.

Raelynn observed from the stage wing, admiring Bentley's commitment to his fans, both present and absent due to the sudden alterations. Little did she know what was in store.

"Furthermore, I want to express my gratitude to everyone for warmly welcoming Miss Raelynn Hart throughout this weekend, from her time on stage with me to her solo performance today. Thank you!" Bentley continued.

Raelynn couldn't help but smile, genuinely appreciating Bentley's hospitality for allowing her to share the stage and showcase her talent.

"With that said, I'd like to invite Raelynn and her band to the stage for a moment to give them the recognition they deserve," Bentley declared, casting a glance at Raelynn, who stood in the wings with a smile on her face.

As Owen, Jake, Elijah, and Levi joined Raelynn, confusion marked their expressions, as if they expected Raelynn to have answers to the unfolding events. Raelynn, however, remained in the dark.

The group, now standing alongside Bentley in the spotlight, received thunderous cheers and applause from the crowd.

"A few moments ago, I learned that Miss Raelynn Hart and her band are being offered a 2-year contract with Warner Bros. So, if you've enjoyed her angelic voice this past weekend as much as I have, rest assured, this isn't the last time you'll hear it," Bentley announced, beaming at Raelynn and her band.

The thoughts Raelynn had during Bentley's new song quickly faded as shock and disbelief took over, tears welling up in her eyes. A sense of relief washed over her as the weight of hard work and dedication to music finally paid off. The trials she faced to reach this point now seemed insignificant, making every challenge worthwhile.

Backstage in the dressing room, the air buzzed with a vibrant energy that matched the rhythm of Raelynn's racing heart. The walls echoed with laughter, and the euphoria of success danced in the air like musical notes. Raelynn, Owen, Levi, Jake, and Elijah couldn't contain their elation, each member of the band reveling in the contract offer from Warner Bros. that promised to propel them into the limelight.

As the celebration continued, Bentley entered the room, a smile playing on his lips as he observed the joyous scene unfolding before him. Raelynn, surrounded by her bandmates, radiated a happiness that mirrored the glimmer in her eyes. The camaraderie was palpable, a harmonious symphony of dreams coming true.

Bentley, overcome with pride and affection, made his way through the jubilant group, his steps light but purposeful. He reached Raelynn, who was still caught up in the surreal moment of success. With a warmth that transcended words, Bentley enveloped her in a gentle hug, feeling the heartbeat that echoed the rhythm of their shared dreams.

Whispering softly into her ear, Bentley conveyed his heartfelt sentiments, "You deserve this! Enjoy this moment with them, and we'll talk back at the hotel." His warm breath against her ear sent chills down Raelynn's spine.

Before pulling away, Bentley pressed a tender kiss to her forehead, a gesture that spoke volumes of his love and support. As he retreated, leaving Raelynn to bask in the glow of her achievement, the room continued to reverberate with laughter, music, and the sweet anticipation of what lay ahead.

19

Pillow Talk

Later that night back at the hotel Bentley and Raelynn sat on the edge of the bed in the hotel room, the weight of the day's events lingering in the air. The celebratory atmosphere had given way to a more subdued mood as they both processed the highs and lows of the day.

Bentley, with a mix of pride and humility, broke the silence. "I'm genuinely happy for you, Rae. This contract is a big deal, and you and your band deserve every bit of success that comes your way."

Raelynn nodded, grateful for Bentley's support. "Thank you, Bentley. I couldn't have imagined this happening so quickly. It's surreal, and I want to thank you for the chance at making this all happen."

Bentley sighed, a hint of seriousness in his eyes. "I need to apologize again for the way I acted earlier. It was unacceptable, and I let my insecurities get the best of me. I promise it won't happen again."

Raelynn appreciated Bentley's sincerity, but she also needed to address the underlying issues. "Bentley, we need to have an honest conversation about us. About trust, communication, and where we see this going. Today showed me that we both have our own worlds, and we need to figure out how to navigate them together."

Bentley nodded, understanding the gravity of the situation. "I agree, Rae. I don't want my issues to get in the way of what we could have."

"Bentley, you're not the only one with issues here… just the only one to put yours on display. I have my share of insecurities that surfaced this weekend to. I just hid mine because I don't know what this is." Raelynn said with sincerity reflecting in her eyes.

Bentley's face contorted with a puzzled look, "What do you mean?"

Raelynn sighed a deep breath as she knew there was no way around this conversation and needed to face it head on. Even if it was difficult to talk about her feelings with Bentley. "Well, for starters seeing your interaction with the fans yesterday at the meet and greet tent. Seeing all the girls that tried kissing you for their photo-op, the ones that flashed you their tits, and the ones professing their love for you, really gave me an uneasy feeling."

Bentley could see the uneasy feeling Raelynn was talking about mirrored in her eyes. It was difficult for her to talk about it.

"I understand your concerns there. I have experienced a lot of crazy shit during my meet and greets, I just hope you know I don't encourage that behavior." Bentley said with sincerity.

"I understand that. It's just… you're fucking Bentley. You can have any girl in the world why would you choose some country girl from Nashville. Ya know?"

Bentley sighed, recognizing the weight of Raelynn's insecurity. He took her hand in his, his gaze sincere. "Raelynn, you're not just 'some country girl.' You're talented, genuine, and there's something about you that drew me in. It's not about having anyone in the world; it's about connecting with someone on a deeper level. But I get it."

Raelynn nodded, appreciating Bentley's reassurance but realizing that the conversation needed to go deeper. "And what about the song you performed today? 'Ghost'... Is that how you see us?"

Bentley hesitated for a moment, searching for the right words. "Rae, that song isn't about us and it damn sure isn't how I want things to go between us. I recorded that song two weeks ago before you were in the picture. It's about the struggles I've faced in the past, the mistakes I've made, and the walls I've built. It's a reflection of my own journey and the challenges of balancing personal connections with the demands of my career."

Raelynn listened attentively, her heart softening as Bentley explained the meaning behind the song. "Bentley, I get it. We both have our baggage, our own stories. Just after hearing those lyrics, I got a bit worried. I don't want you as a ghost in my life. However, I do want us to be on the same page, you know?

Bentley nodded, understanding the gravity of her concerns. "I get it, Rae. And I don't want that either. I know we've only known each other for a week, but this weekend has been... different. It made me realize that I want to give this an honest try."

Raelynn looked at him, curiosity in her eyes. "An honest try at what, Bentley?"

Bentley took a deep breath, his gaze unwavering. "At us. I know it's only been a week of getting to know each other, but this weekend, seeing you on stage, the way we connected musically and personally, it felt like more than just a fleeting moment. I want to see where this could go. I want to see if we can make it work, even with our crazy lives and different worlds."

Raelynn's heart skipped a beat as she processed Bentley's words. A warmth spread through her, and a smile tugged at the corners of her lips. "So, are you saying you want to define the relationship? Or should we keep feeling things out?"

Bentley chuckled, a genuine smile lighting up his face. "Honestly, Rae, I haven't romantically been with anyone since Michelle. I've been scared. So, for the past eight years I've been doing my own thing. But there is something so unique about you. So yeah, I want to give 'us' a shot. I want you to be my girlfriend, Raelynn Hart."

Raelynn's eyes widened in surprise, and then a radiant smile broke across her face. "Well, in that case, Bentley, I'd be honored to be your girlfriend."

Bentley's grin widened, and he pulled her into a warm embrace. "Good, because I can't imagine not having you in my life after this weekend."

Raelynn tilted her head upward, gently placing a kiss on Bentley's lips. "Well, the first kiss as a couple definitely has a fantastic flavor," she remarked playfully, pulling back to meet Bentley's gaze.

In response, Bentley wordlessly grasped Raelynn by the back of her head, drawing her back into the kiss. It lingered, profound and passionate, with an undeniable warmth emanating from the shared connection.

Bentley's fingers tangled in Raelynn's hair as the kiss deepened, a slow burn igniting between them. Their lips moved in sync, dancing to an unspoken rhythm that only they could hear. Bentley's hands traced delicate patterns down Raelynn's spine, sending shivers through her body.

In a daring move, Bentley shifted their positions, bringing Raelynn's leg over the top of him. She straddled him, her legs on either side, intensifying the intimacy between them.

As their kisses grew hotter, more urgent, Raelynn could feel the tension building in Bentley's jeans. And Bentley could feel the warmth radiating off Raelynn's most sensitive part of her body.

Breaking the kiss, Raelynn gazed into Bentley's eyes, her own filled with a wildfire that seemed to consume her. "Bentley," she whispered, her voice a seductive murmur, "I want you to do something for me."

Bentley, still caught in the haze of their shared desire, nodded. "Anything, Raelynn."

A mischievous grin played on her lips as she spoke, "I want you to yell at me again, like you did in the dressing room earlier today. I want to feel that raw passion, that possessiveness. It turned me on, Bentley."

Bentley's eyes widened in surprise, a mix of confusion and curiosity flickering across his face. He wasn't expecting her request, and for a moment, he hesitated. "You want me to yell at you?" he asked, his voice tinged with disbelief.

Raelynn nodded, a playful glint in her eyes. "Yes, Bentley. I want to feel the intensity, the fire. I want to lose myself in the heat of the moment with you." As her fingers trailed Bentley's chest, tracing the contours of his muscles.

He hesitated, uncertainty playing in his eyes. "I can't just do it on command, Raelynn. It was a moment, a reaction."

But Raelynn wasn't one to back down. She leaned in, her lips brushing against his ear. "Try, Bentley. Give it an honest try. I want to feel that fire again."

Bentley took a deep breath, his fingers tightening in her hair. Then, with a low, controlled growl, he spoke, "Raelynn, you're mine. No one else gets to touch you like this."

A thrill ran down Raelynn's spine. It wasn't as explosive as in the dressing room, but the possessiveness in his tone sent a shiver through her. She grinned, challenging him further. "Louder, Bentley. Let it out."

He shot her a questioning look, but then, as if succumbing to her desire, he raised his voice, "You. Are. Mine."

A surge of satisfaction filled Raelynn. She leaned back, looking into Bentley's eyes. "See? That wasn't so hard."

Bentley, caught between amusement and arousal, chuckled. "You're something else, Raelynn."

She leaned in, capturing his lips in another searing kiss. "And you like it."

As their passion escalated, Bentley's hands explored the curves of Raelynn's body. The atmosphere became charged with electricity, desire reaching its peak. Raelynn broke the kiss again, breathless but determined.

"Bentley," she whispered against his lips, "I don't want you to make love to me right now. I want you to fuck me like you did yesterday morning, but harder."

Bentley's eyes darkened with a mix of surprise and desire at Raelynn's bold request. The intensity between them skyrocketed, and he could feel the anticipation coursing through his veins. He held her gaze for a moment, searching for any sign of hesitation, but Raelynn's eyes sparkled with confidence.

"Are you sure about this, Rae?" Bentley asked, his voice laced with a hint of concern.

She nodded, her lips curling into a sultry smile. "I've never been more sure."

Bentley didn't need any more encouragement. Without a word, tightened his grip on Raelynn, he stood up, lifting her effortlessly with him, her legs still wrapped around him.

Their lips remained connected as Bentley carried her across the room, their bodies pressed together in a fervent embrace. He could feel Raelynn's heartbeat against his chest, matching the rhythm of his own. The urgency of their desire heightened, the air thick with anticipation.

Bentley found a suitable surface, and with a swift, deliberate motion, he pinned Raelynn against the wall. The impact sent a jolt through both of them, igniting the fire that had been smoldering since their first kiss. Raelynn's hands roamed over Bentley's shoulders, down his chest, as she reveled in the raw masculinity that consumed him.

Bentley's kisses became more aggressive and his touch more possessive. As he ripped Raelynn's t-shirt right down the middle, revealing her black bra.

"Yes Bentley." Raelynn chuckled through the sultry in her voice.

Bentley's eyes flared with desire as he absorbed the sight of Raelynn in the torn shirt, her black bra exposed. With a devilish grin, he yanked his own shirt off, the muscles in his torso flexing as he revealed the inked artwork decorating his skin. The room seemed to pulse with an electrifying energy as Bentley's primal instincts took over.

Bentley's hands, strong and confident, moved to unhook her bra. Bentley skillfully unhooked Raelynn's bra with a one hand flick. As the bra clung loosely to Raelynn, Bentley slid his hands under the bra squeezing on her bare breast.

In response, Raelynn let out a slight moan as she flung her head into Bentley's chest biting down. As her teeth grazed his skin, she felt his muscles tense in response. Raelynn reveled in the taste of his skin, her nails digging into his back as she sought to deepen the connection.

As Raelynn marked Bentley's chest and shoulder with bites, Bentley raised his right hand to her mouth with his left hand still in place. In a mutual understanding, she sensually sucked on his fingers, occasionally playfully nibbling and giggling. Bentley then traced his right hand back down Raelynn's body, slipping it beneath the waistband of her jeans and panties, where he gently inserted his fingers.

Raelynn squirmed under Bentley's touch, a mixture of pleasure and anticipation coursing through her veins. Bentley enjoyed the sight of her reveling in the sensations he was creating. With a swift, assertive motion, Bentley ripped open Raelynn's jeans, exposing the lacy edge of her black panties.

The room crackled with an electrifying energy as Bentley, consumed by desire, yanked her jeans down, leaving them pooled at her ankles. Raelynn, now only in her torn shirt, bra, and panties, arched into Bentley's touch, a silent plea for more.

Bentley, not one to hold back from a challenge, turned Raelynn to slam against the wall. The impact sent a thrill through both of them, the raw passion of the moment unfolding. With a deft movement, Bentley pulled down her panties, exposing Raelynn's most intimate desires.

As Bentley's fingers explored her, Raelynn's breath hitched, and she moaned in response. The room seemed to shrink around them, encapsulating their shared moment of vulnerability and desire. Bentley, attuned to Raelynn's every reaction, relished in the power he held over her pleasure.

Raelynn, pressed against the wall, couldn't help but surrender to the intensity of the moment. She bit her lip, her nails digging into the wall as Bentley's touch ignited a fire within her. Her body, a canvas of desire, responded to Bentley's every move with a rhythmic dance of passion.

In a husky whisper, Raelynn, still tingling from Bentley's touch, voiced her yearning. "More, Bentley. I want more."

With Bentley firmly in command, he knelt behind Raelynn, his hands caressing her bare ass. He tenderly parted her cheeks and indulged in the intimate exploration of the most responsive and delicate regions of her body.

Raelynn moaned loudly as Bentley skillfully propelled her toward the brink of ecstasy. Her hands instinctively reached out, desperately seeking anything to grasp onto.

While Bentley continued to push Raelynn to the brink of release, he began undoing his jeans. In a swift move, he stood up dropping his jeans and boxer to the floor, pooled around his ankles.

Hard as a rock Bentley stood behind Raelynn fully exposed as he spit in his hand, rubbing the wetness on his throbbing cock. With a powerful thrust Bentley inserted his length inside Raelynn, driving her into the wall.

"YES, FUCK YES," Raelynn screamed out in pleasure as Bentley slapped her ass as hard as he could.

Each thrust was more powerful than the last and with each one Bentley let out grunts of pleasure. With each stroke Bentley continued to periodically slap Raelynn's ass, leaving his red handprint perfectly visible.

"MORE. BENTLEY. MORE." Raelynn screamed out as the pleasure was completely consuming her.

Bentley tangled his fingers in Raelynn's hair, wrapping it into a tight bundle within his grasp. His hand clenched, exerting a firm but gentle pressure, eliciting a gasp from Raelynn. "Pull harder," she pleaded, her voice filled with a mix of desire and anticipation. Bentley pulled harder.

Beginning to fatigue in energy from his powerful thrust, Bentley, with Raelynn's hair still knotted in his hand pushed her down to her knees. Bentley assertively guided her mouth onto his cock. Bentley wanted Raelynn to taste her own passion.

As Raelynn aggressively worked magic on Bentley's length, he couldn't contain his moans. With his eyes rolling to the back of his head with the pleasure, he pushed Raelynn's head further down on his dick. Raelynn gagged with all of Bentley in the back of her throat.

With a second wave of energy Bentley assertively guided Raelynn to his kiss, tasting the mix of his own pleasures as well as Raelynn's. The kisses were passionate and forceful, each taking turns biting each other's lips.

"I want you to choke me," Raelynn whispered into Bentley's ear just before he lifted her, pressing her against the wall, thrusting into her with determination.

Raelynn was now suspended between the solid wall and Bentley's chiseled frame, her legs wrapped around him. Bentley, with a firm grip around her neck and supporting her with one hand and his body weight, intensified the connection.

As Raelynn reached her ceiling, Bentley continued with unyielding intensity, causing her to scream in ecstasy. Even after her climax, Bentley persisted, feeling his own climax drawing near.

"I want to taste you," Raelynn whispered in Bentley's ear, sensing the pulsating anticipation of his impending climax.

As Bentley's release became inevitable, with a sense of urgency lowered Raelynn from the wall. Gracefully sinking to her knees, she sensually followed the descent, taking Bentley into her mouth as he approached the pinnacle of pleasure.

With a gratifying groan, Bentley released, and Raelynn sensually continued to pleasure him through his climax. Her eyes locked onto his, she swallowed every manifestation of passion between them. Even after Bentley had climaxed, Raelynn continued to bring him pleasure, sending tingling sensations coursing through his entire body, heightened by his newfound sensitivity.

Bentley, aware of the shared vulnerability and desire that had unfolded between them, gently withdrew from the intense connection. He let his fingers trail over Raelynn's skin, a tender gesture to bring her back from the heightened pleasure she had experienced.

Raelynn, breathless and still tingling from their intimate encounter, looked up at Bentley with a mixture of satisfaction and desire. He extended a helping hand, and she accepted, allowing him to guide her to her feet. The room, once filled with the energy of passion, now settled into a quiet intimacy.

"Is this what sex with Bentley is going to be like? Because I can definitely get used to this," Raelynn quipped playfully, still catching her breath.

Bentley chuckled, a playful glint in his eyes, "You got it all wrong. Is this what sex with Raelynn Hart is going to be like? Because I can get used to this, because this was all you."

Raelynn chuckled with a mischievous grin on her face, "I must warn you Bentley, I am a very naughty girl. I need my spankings from time to time."

Bentley's eyes sparkled with amusement at Raelynn's playful admission. "I might just enjoy giving you those spankings more than you think."

The playful banter continued between Bentley and Raelynn, the air thick with a mixture of satisfaction and anticipation. Bentley, with a devilish grin, continued, "But you'll have to earn those spankings."

Raelynn responded with a sly smile, "Challenge accepted. Mr. Superstar."

With a twinkle in his eye, Bentley gestured toward the disheveled room around them. "I think we've created quite a mess here. Care to join me in a shower?"

Raelynn nodded, "Lead the way, Bentley."

Bentley took Raelynn's hand, and together they walked into the bathroom, the warm glow of satisfaction lingering between them. The shower, once again, became a sanctuary where the outside world ceased to exist. The water cascaded over them, a gentle reminder of the sensual connection they shared.

As Bentley and Raelynn stood under the soothing spray, the playful banter continued, creating a melody of laughter and whispered promises. They washed away not just the physical remnants of their passion but also any lingering doubts or fears. In the intimate space of the shower, they discovered a profound comfort in each other's arms.

With the water turned off, Bentley grabbed a couple of towels and handed one to Raelynn, his eyes never leaving hers. The air in the bathroom was filled with a quiet tenderness as they dried each other off, their movements slow and deliberate.

As they ventured back into the bedroom, Bentley pulled back the covers of the bed, inviting Raelynn to join him. The soft sheets cradled them as they lay side by side, limbs entwined. Bentley pressed a lingering kiss to Raelynn's forehead, savoring the warmth of the moment.

In the hushed stillness of the room, Bentley whispered, "Sleep tight, Raelynn."

Raelynn nestled closer, finding comfort in Bentley's embrace. "Goodnight, Bentley," she murmured, her voice a gentle caress.

They drifted into a peaceful slumber, their dreams entangled with the promise of a future filled with laughter, passion, and the shared intimacies that bound them together. The moonlight spilled into the room, casting a soft glow over the two lovers snuggled up, content in the quietude of the night.

20

Festival Hangover

The following day the euphoric feeling Cinderella Fest weekend created still lingered in the air as the stagehands had already began breaking down the makeshift festival grounds. Mint Street, which had been bustling with fans the past three days, now looked like a mere ghost town.

As Raelynn made her commute back home to Raleigh, she found herself lost in thought. She had a lot to reflect on after her weekend at Cinderella Fest. When Raelynn arrived in Charlotte, she was an unsigned artist just trying to make it but was leaving with a two-year contract with Warner Bros. She also arrived in Charlotte single but was leaving with a boyfriend. A boyfriend that was superstar. A boyfriend that was pretty good looking with his sculptured muscles, tattoos, and his charming smile. A boyfriend that was pretty good in bed too. Bentley was more than Raelynn could have dreamed.

Raelynn sat in her car, the hum of the engine providing a rhythmic backdrop to her thoughts. The memories of the weekend continued to play like a film in her mind, and Bentley's face was the star of every scene. She couldn't shake the euphoria that clung to her, an intoxicating blend of success and newfound love.

Bentley made Raelynn's heart flutter every time he was near. Every time they kissed, she felt as if the world stopped spinning. Every time Bentley touched her, she felt the sparks shooting throughout her body, igniting a fire that burned deep. A fire that made her crave his touch in every way possible. It was a feeling that she couldn't put into words no matter how hard she tried. It was a feeling Raelynn had never experienced with any other love interest.

As Raelynn continued her drive home, she pictured Bentley's perfect diamond bright smile, the warmth of his hand in hers, and the way he looked at her with an intensity that sent shivers down her spine. Bentley's laugh also echoed in her mind. In this moment she realized the undeniable.

Raelynn was in love with Bentley Riggs.

The weight of that realization settled in Raelynn's chest like an anchor, dragging her euphoria into the depths of uncertainty. Bentley, with all his charm and superstar status, had become the unexpected occupant of her heart, and she couldn't ignore the fear that crept into her thoughts.

The drive back to Raleigh felt longer than usual for Raelynn. The landscape blurred as she grappled with the whirlwind of emotions that had taken over her life. Bentley had swept her off her feet in more ways than one, and the speed at which it all happened left her breathless. She couldn't deny the intensity of her feelings, but she couldn't help wondering if her heart was playing a dangerous game.

With the Raleigh skyscrapers in sight, Raelynn couldn't help thinking about the media scrutiny awaiting them. It clawed at the edges of her consciousness. Raelynn knew that being in a relationship with someone as high-profile as Bentley Riggs meant sacrificing a degree of privacy. The paparazzi, the headlines, they were all looming threats, ready to pry into the affairs of her romance with Bentley. The very thought made her stomach churn with anxiety.

Her parents, conservative and protective, also loomed in her mind. Her parents were already against her dreams to pursue music. Now she had a record deal thanks to Bentley; the one man her father truly could not stand in the world of superstardom. Her father couldn't stand Bentley because Mr. Hart's company was responsible for managing Bentley's career and mitigating all his wild playboy antics. Raelynn knew her parents wouldn't be pleased with the news of either life changing occurrence.

Then, there were the career hurdles. Raelynn had just inked a deal with Warner Bros., and Bentley's fame brought with it a set of challenges she hadn't fathomed. Would their careers align or collide? The uncertain future of their professional lives weighed on her mind like an impending storm.

But perhaps the most daunting fear of all was the fear of heartbreak. Raelynn had been through it before, with Chase, and the scars from that experience still lingered. The vulnerability of opening her heart to someone, especially someone in the unpredictable world of fame, sent shivers down her spine. The fear of history repeating itself added a layer of caution to her blossoming love with Bentley.

As Raelynn pulled into her driveway, she sat in the car for a moment, grappling with the mix of emotions that threatened to overwhelm her. The engine's hum now seemed to underscore the uncertainty that lay ahead. Taking a deep breath, she gathered her belongings and headed into her cozy home.

The apartment felt different now, quieter and less comforting than when she had left for Cinderella Fest. She walked through the door, and the familiar scent of her vanilla-scented candles did little to ease the weight on her shoulders. As she began to wonder how she was going to tell her best friend Cassidy everything. Raelynn knew that was going to be troublesome all on its own.

Raelynn knew Cassidy hated Bentley with a burning passion although she never quite understood why. Bentley used to be Cassidy's favorite artist but now she couldn't stand him. Anytime he would come on the radio or TV, Cassidy was quick to change the channel. And Raelynn never pried on why the sudden change. She just knew breaking the news to Cassidy that she was dating Bentley was going to cast a huge thunder cloud on their friendship.

The weight of her thoughts clung to Raelynn as she settled into her living room, the dim glow of the evening sun casting long shadows across the walls. She sank into the couch, contemplating the challenges ahead. Bentley, though an unexpected blessing in her life, came with complications she couldn't ignore.

The decision to keep their relationship quiet nagged at the edges of her mind like an unanswered question. The fear of media scrutiny and the potential backlash from her parents and Cassidy loomed large. She knew that unveiling her romance with Bentley could spark a storm of attention, and that was something she wasn't sure she was ready to face.

Taking a deep breath, Raelynn began to weigh the pros and cons. On one hand, the world knowing about her relationship with Bentley might bring attention to her music career. It could be a publicity boost that could elevate her status in the industry. On the other hand, it could also attract unwanted drama and invasive questions into her personal life, overshadowing her musical achievements.

The conflict with her parents added another layer of complexity. Raelynn loved her parents, but their conservative values clashed with the whirlwind romance she found herself in. Bentley's image in the media, coupled with her newfound success, would undoubtedly be a bitter pill for them to swallow. She couldn't shake the worry that their disapproval might cast a shadow on her happiness.

As she sat in her quiet apartment, the decision became clear. Raelynn couldn't risk it all for the sake of a public spectacle. She valued her privacy, her relationship with her parents, and her friendship with Cassidy too much to throw it all to the mercy of media scrutiny.

With a determined sigh, Raelynn decided to keep her relationship with Bentley under wraps, at least for now. She would continue to enjoy the blissful moments with him in private, away from the prying eyes of the world. Her heart, though filled with love for Bentley, also harbored a practical understanding of the challenges they faced.

✳✳✳✳

Across town Bentley also had returned home to his parents from the weekend Cinderella Fest. Much like Raelynn, he also engaged in deep reflection on the week and the time spent with her over the weekend. He cherished how her presence had the power to make him momentarily escape the bustling world of fame that surrounded him.

Bentley's mind lingered on the memories of Cinderella Fest, where the roar of the crowd and the dazzling lights of the stage had faded into the background every time he locked eyes with Raelynn. Her presence was a sanctuary, a place where he could momentarily shed the weight of his superstar persona and just be Bentley, the guy who found solace in the simplicity of love.

As he reclined on his childhood bed, Bentley's gaze drifted to the ceiling. The posters of his own face, frozen in various stages of rockstar intensity, adorned the walls around him. It was a stark contrast to the serenity he found in Raelynn's company. Her music had become the soundtrack to his quiet moments, the lyrics resonating in his mind even in the absence of the festival's noise.

He couldn't help but smile as he recalled the way Raelynn's eyes lit up during their performances together. It was as if she saw beyond the superstar facade and into the heart of the man behind the fame. Bentley had been in the music industry long enough to recognize when someone was genuine, and Raelynn was the real deal. Her authenticity had captivated him from the very first moment they met in Cancun, and he felt a connection that went beyond the glitz and glamour of the stage.

The memories from the week brought a mixture of joy and contemplation to Bentley. Raelynn's authenticity had pierced through the chaotic swirl of fame, and he found himself drawn to her in a way he hadn't experienced in years. The realization hit him like a gentle wave, a soft whisper in the cold depths of his heart.

Bentley was falling hard and fast for Raelynn.

However, Bentley was no stranger to the complexities of love. While lying there, he couldn't escape the realization that Raelynn was the first person he'd allowed into his heart since Michelle, the woman who had left him standing at the altar eight years ago. The pain of that memory still lingered, a ghost that haunted the corners of his mind. Michelle's sudden departure and the subsequent tragedy had left Bentley with a fear of opening up to love again.

The idea of falling for Raelynn both excited and terrified him. The warmth he felt when she was near was undeniable, a stark contrast to the numbness he'd grown accustomed to. Bentley couldn't deny the magnetic pull of her presence, but the fear of getting hurt again gnawed at the edges of his newfound happiness.

The paparazzi, those relentless hounds of the media, were a familiar annoyance to Bentley. He had learned to navigate their intrusive questions and flashing cameras with practiced ease. But now, with Raelynn in the picture, he worried about her. He knew she wasn't accustomed to the constant invasion of privacy that would come with dating a celebrity. Bentley understood the importance of shielding Raelynn from the harsh spotlight.

The road, both literal and metaphorical, was a challenging one. Bentley's life on tour was a whirlwind of screaming fans, late-night performances, and the constant lure of temptations. He couldn't ignore the reality that he was a magnet for the kind of attention that could strain even the strongest relationships. The worry gnawed at him — could he withstand the relentless onslaught of adoration and stay faithful to Raelynn?

Their careers posed another significant hurdle. The clash between the demands of their respective musical journeys raised questions about how much time they would truly get to spend together. Bentley cherished the moments they shared, but he couldn't shake the fear that the relentless pace of their professional lives might threaten the fragile balance they were trying to build.

As Bentley lay on his childhood bed, surrounded by the echoes of his thoughts, he knew it was time to confront these concerns. The weight of the uncertainties loomed over him, but Bentley realized that these were conversations he needed to have with Raelynn. Boundaries and expectations needed to be established; the foundation of their relationship required careful construction. Especially after his outburst of jealousy Sunday during Raelynn's performance.

In the midst of Bentley's contemplations, he felt a surge of excitement about sharing the news with his parents and his best friend, Cameron. Bentley was aware that they might find it hard to believe, but he knew they would still share in his happiness. They had consistently been his greatest support system, standing by him through the ups and downs of his musical journey. Bentley eagerly anticipated witnessing the joy in their eyes as he disclosed the newfound happiness that Raelynn had brought into his life.

As he stood up from his childhood bed, a burst of energy propelled Bentley into action. He reached for his phone, fingers dancing over the screen to compose messages to his parents and Cameron. The words flowed effortlessly, a testament to the genuine excitement and happiness that Raelynn had ignited within him.

"Hey Mom and Dad, can we go out to dinner tonight? I've got some big news to share!"

Bentley grinned at the thought of their reaction. His parents, who had witnessed the highs and lows of his career, would surely be curious about the nature of this 'big news.' As for Cameron, Bentley couldn't wait to see the disbelief and joy on his best friend's face when he revealed the details.

A similar message was sent to Cameron, punctuated with an exclamation mark to convey the urgency and excitement of the impending announcement. Bentley envisioned the camaraderie, the shared laughter, and the inevitable teasing that would follow once Cameron learned the details.

With the messages sent, Bentley felt a mix of anticipation and nerves. He knew that introducing Raelynn into his inner circle would be a significant step, and he hoped that his loved ones would embrace the happiness radiating from this new chapter of his life.

21

Notes of Change

The evening arrived, and Bentley found himself seated at a cozy corner table in a local mom and pop restaurant with his parents, Steve and Faye, and his best friend, Cameron. The ambiance was warm, with soft lighting and the comforting aroma of home-cooked meals.

As they looked over the menu, Bentley couldn't help but steal glances at his parents and Cameron. The excitement bubbling within him threatened to burst forth at any moment. He could sense their curiosity, and a mischievous smile played on Bentley's lips.

"So, what's this big news you've got for us, son?" Steve, Bentley's father, asked with a twinkle in his eye. Faye, his mother, leaned forward, her expression a mix of curiosity and parental concern.

Bentley glanced at Cameron, who raised an eyebrow, clearly intrigued. Taking a deep breath, Bentley decided to dive right in. "Well, Dad... Mom... do you remember Raelynn, the country artist who performs at Cameron's club, Club Electric?"

His parents exchanged a quick look before nodding. "Of course," Faye replied. "The talented young woman with the soulful voice. What about her?"

A grin spread across Bentley's face as he locked eyes with his best friend. "Well, Cam already knows this, but I met Raelynn while I was in Cancun…"

"Oh, this is about to be good." Cameron snickered under his breath, briefly interrupting Bentley.

Disregarding Cameron's comment, Bentley pressed on with his revelation. "Coincidentally, I quite literally bumped into her at the club last weekend. I didn't recognize her, and she didn't recognize me… well, she did recognize me as Bentley, but not from our encounter in Cancun. Anyway, we spent the week working on music together, and this past weekend, we performed at Cinderella Fest. I must say, she's truly special."

Steve and Faye exchanged surprised glances, and Cameron's eyes widened in realization. Bentley continued, his voice carrying a mixture of excitement and vulnerability, "But here's the thing, guys. It's not just about the music anymore. Raelynn and I... we've connected on a much deeper level. I think I'm falling for her."

Cameron's playful expression shifted to one of genuine surprise. He leaned back in his chair, eyeing Bentley with a mix of amusement and curiosity. "Wait, wait, wait. Are you telling me that the infamous Bentley, the guy who's practically been allergic to commitment the last eight years, has caught feelings?"

Bentley rolled his eyes, playfully nudging Cameron. "Yes, Cam, believe it or not. Love has a strange way of sneaking up on you."

Cameron chuckled, shaking his head. "Well, I'll be damned. The man's in love. Raelynn must be something special to have tamed the untameable Bentley."

Bentley rolled his eyes, though a smile lingered. "You're insufferable, you know that?"

"That's what you keep me around for," Cameron quipped, earning laughter from Bentley's parents.

Steve, Bentley's father, spoke up, a mixture of happiness and caution in his voice. "Bentley, it's wonderful that you've found someone special, but things seem to be moving quite fast. Have you thought about the implications, especially with the media always poking around your life?"

Faye, Bentley's mother, added her perspective. "Your father's right, sweetheart. Fame can be a tricky thing, and relationships in the public eye are under constant scrutiny. Are you sure about this? I mean, you just met her… again, and now you're already... falling?"

Bentley nodded, understanding their concerns. "I know it might seem fast, but there's something different about Raelynn. It's like we've known each other for a long time, and I can't explain it. And as for the media, well, that's something we'll have to discuss and figure out together. Until we do I want everything kept quiet. I just couldn't hide this from y'all."

Cameron, catching the serious undertone, chimed in with a grin. "Looks like our rapstar here is turning into a romantic. Who would've thought?"

As Bentley's parents finish dinner, they bid their goodbyes and left the restaurant. Bentley and Cameron stayed behind, settling into a more relaxed atmosphere. Bentley leaned back in his chair, a thoughtful expression on his face.

"You're not messing with us, right?" Cameron asked, his playful demeanor giving way to a more sincere curiosity.

Bentley chuckled, shaking his head. "No, Cam, I'm dead serious. This is different. Raelynn's different."

Cameron leaned forward, his eyes narrowing as if trying to decipher Bentley's thoughts. "Okay, spill. Give me all the details. How did you go from not recognizing her in the club to falling for her in a week?"

Bentley released a sigh before delving into the specifics. "Well, Cam, you're aware of the connection I had with that girl in Cancun... and you know that girl was Raelynn. You're also aware that we met for coffee the night after the club and connected the dots about knowing each other from Cancun. So, I suppose this is where my story begins. After coffee, I got the idea to include her in the Cinderella Fest lineup and feature a segment in my set where she performed with me each night."

Cameron nodded, a knowing look in his eyes. "So, you invited her to perform with you. Smooth move, Bentley. But how did things progress from there?"

"Well, we spent the whole week working on our collaboration and every time we were together, I felt this gravitational pull towards her. I mean it pulled me into kissing her the night of our coffee date before she was even a part of the lineup as a solo performance." Bentley said as he recalled the moments shared with Raelynn.

"Oh shit. How did that go over? I'm assuming good since she performed with you all three nights." Cameron asked with a curious tone.

"Uh, it was a shock to both of us. I mean we both felt the pull, and we agreed to slow it down and try to keep it strictly professional." Bentley said.

"What happened to strictly professional?" Cameron joked.

Bentley laughed, shaking his head. "Well, that went out the window pretty quickly. We couldn't resist the chemistry, and, honestly, it added something magical to our performances. The crowd loved it, and so did we."

Cameron raised an eyebrow. "And the falling in love part? When did that happen? I mean, besides the obvious connection on stage."

Bentley's gaze turned introspective. "It was during the late-night jam sessions, the quiet moments when it was just us and the music. We talked about everything, our dreams, our fears, our pasts. Raelynn's authenticity, man, it's like a breath of fresh air. I found myself opening up to her in ways I haven't in years."

Cameron leaned back, a thoughtful expression on his face. "So, you're telling me you're head over heels for this girl after a week of intense collaboration and soul-baring conversations?"

Bentley nodded, a mix of vulnerability and excitement in his eyes. "Yeah, Cam, I am. It's scary how fast it happened, but it feels right. I can't ignore the way she makes me feel; alive, grounded, and like there's something more to life than just the spotlight."

Cameron smirked. "You've got it bad, my friend. This isn't the Bentley I've known for the past eight years."

Bentley chuckled. "Tell me about it. I never thought I'd be the one talking about falling in love ever again… especially after Michelle."

Cameron's expression turned more serious. "What about the media, though? You know they'll eat this up. How are you planning to handle that?"

Bentley sighed, rubbing his temples. "That's the part I'm still figuring out. I want Raelynn to have her privacy, especially with the media's obsession with every move I make. We haven't discussed that yet and we really need to before the media catches wind of it."

Cameron nodded, understanding the gravity of the situation. "You're right. You need to have a game plan before the media catches wind of it. It's not just your story anymore; it's both yours and Raelynn's."

Bentley ran a hand through his hair, contemplating the challenges ahead. "I know. I'll talk to her about it tomorrow. We need to be on the same page and figure out how to navigate this without it overshadowing what we have."

As Bentley and Cameron continued their conversation, Bentley's phone buzzed with a text notification. He glanced at the screen to see Raelynn's name, and a smile crept across his face.

"What's that grin for?" Cameron asked, noticing Bentley's reaction.

Bentley held up his phone. "It's Raelynn. She just texted me."

Cameron raised an eyebrow. "Well, spill. What's the country sensation saying?"

Bentley opened the message, his eyes scanning the words. "She says she misses me and wants to see me. She suggested I come over tomorrow afternoon."

Cameron wiggled his eyebrows. "Looks like someone can't get enough of our rapstar."

Bentley chuckled at Cameron's teasing, a warmth spreading through him. "Yeah, well, the feeling is mutual. I miss her too, Cam."

Cameron leaned back, crossing his arms with a sly grin. "Love looks good on you, Bentley. Who would've thought you'd be the one caught up in the whirlwind of emotions?"

Bentley rolled his eyes but couldn't hide the affectionate smile tugging at his lips. "You're enjoying this way too much, aren't you?"

"Oh absolutely," Cameron replied, his eyes twinkling. "But in all seriousness, I'm genuinely happy for you. Raelynn is a great person, and if she's got you smiling like that, then she must be something special."

Bentley nodded, gratitude filling his voice. "She is. I've never felt this way before, and it's both thrilling and a bit terrifying."

Cameron raised an eyebrow. "Terrifying? You? The man who faces crowds of thousands without breaking a sweat?"

Bentley chuckled. "Performing on stage is one thing, but this... this is different. It's like stepping into the unknown, and I want to make sure I don't mess it up."

Cameron's expression softened. "You won't, Bentley. Just be yourself, and if Raelynn has captured your heart, then she must see something incredible in you too."

Taking a final sip of his drink, Bentley appreciated the unwavering support from his best friend. As they stood to leave the restaurant, he felt a mix of anticipation and nervousness about what lay ahead.

The city lights shimmered in the distance as Bentley and Cameron walked out into the cool night air. Bentley couldn't help but reflect on the evening, on the unexpected turn his life had taken. Love had entered his world in a way he never anticipated, and the journey ahead was both thrilling and unknown.

Cameron clapped a hand on Bentley's shoulder, breaking him from his thoughts. "Well, my friend, it looks like you're in for an interesting ride. Who knows, maybe we'll be planning a double date soon."

Bentley chuckled, appreciating Cameron's ability to lighten the mood. "Let's not get ahead of ourselves, Cam. You've got to find a woman who can put up with you for more than five seconds first."

Cameron feigned offense, placing a hand over his heart. "Ouch, Bentley, that hurts. But fair point, fair point."

As they reached the parking lot, Bentley and Cameron went their separate ways. Cameron unlocked his car, while Bentley headed towards the familiar figure of his dad's truck.

"Take care, Bentley," Cameron called out, leaning against his car with a grin. "And remember, if you need any relationship advice, I'm your guy."

Bentley chuckled. "I'll keep that in mind, love guru. Goodnight, Cam."

With a wave, they parted ways for the night. Bentley climbed into the driver's seat of his dad's truck, a comforting familiarity surrounding him. The engine roared to life, and as he drove through the quiet streets, he couldn't shake the feeling that his life was on the verge of a new and exciting chapter.

22

Sky is the Key

The next afternoon, Bentley stood outside Raelynn's door, eagerly awaiting her to answer. As the door opened, Raelynn greeted him with a radiant smile that illuminated the room. As Raelynn stood in the doorway Bentley quickly took notice that she was wearing one of his shirts from the concert souvenir stands, paired with white board shorts, Bentley leaned in and kissed her.

"Hey handsome!" Raelynn said as their lips parted.

Bentley couldn't help but grin, captivated by the way Raelynn's eyes sparkled. "Hey yourself," he replied, a playful glint in his eyes. "Nice choice of attire, by the way."

Raelynn chuckled, a light blush gracing her cheeks. "Thought I'd borrow a bit of your style. It's surprisingly comfortable."

As they walked into Raelynn's living room, Bentley couldn't ignore the gentle strumming of a guitar and a faint melody playing in the background. Skylar, a little boy sitting on the floor surrounded by toys, looked up with curiosity.

The little boy possessed strikingly large blueish-green eyes that held a twinkle of innocence. He had tousled dirty blonde hair, and his cheeks were starting to flush with shyness in the presence of Bentley. Bentley knew the boy couldn't be much older than five or six, given his small stature.

Raelynn followed Bentley's gaze, laughing softly. "Oh, don't mind Skylar. His mom, Cassidy, is running a bit late. She should be here soon to pick him up." Raelynn said to Bentley before speaking to the little boy, "Hey Skylar, this is Aunt Rae's friend Bentley. Can you say hi?"

Bentley smiled, appreciating Raelynn's easygoing nature. "No worries. Hi there, Skylar," he greeted, crouching down to the little boy's level.

Skylar looked at Bentley with wide eyes, then back at his toys. "Hi," he mumbled shyly.

Bentley chuckled. "Looks like he's got quite the setup here."

Raelynn nodded. "Yeah, we were having a little jam session before you arrived. Skylar loves music."

Bentley glanced at Raelynn with a playful grin. "Starting them young, I see."

She winked, playfully nudging him. "Got to share the love for music, right?"

Raelynn glanced at Skylar, who was engrossed in playing with his toys. "Hey, Bentley, do you mind keeping an eye on Skylar for a bit? I'll just go get ready, and we can continue our chat. His mom will be here soon."

Bentley nodded, smiling. "Sure, take your time. We'll be right here."

As Raelynn swiftly left the room to go get ready, Bentley sat on the floor next to Skylar, "Hey, kiddo, you mind if I play with you?" Bentley asked.

Skylar was clearly timid, and Bentley could see it in his body language as Skylar looked up at him and shyly said "Sure."

"Hey Skylar, how old are you, buddy?" Bentley asked the little boy as they continued to play with his matchbox cars and action figurines.

"I just turned 5," Skylar said looking down at the John Cena action figure he held in his hand.

Bentley had always been good with kids. Even though he had none of his own, Bentley had always wanted to have at least six kids. However, with everything that happened with Michelle, Bentley had become content with not having any kids at all.

"So, Sky, what do you think about your Aunt Raelynn?" Bentley asked as he crashed two matchbox cars together.

Skylar smiled as he looked up at Bentley with his little sparkling eyes, "I love my Aunt Rae-Rae, she's pretty, and she's fun. You like her, don't you?" Skylar asked as Bentley just smiled and let out a chuckle.

Bentley's chuckle was a little loud as Raelynn heard it while she was in the bathroom. Raelynn playfully acknowledged Bentley's chuckle, as Bentley heard her shout from the bathroom, "You boys better not be in there talking about me; I will beat y'all up."

Skylar and Bentley both laughed at Raelynn's playful remark as they continued to play with Skylar's toys. "You know what Skylar? I think I really like your Aunt Rae… a lot." Bentley confessed as he replied to Skylar's question with a huge smile on his face.

Time passed rather quickly as Bentley and Skylar sat in the floor playing. Skylar had Bentley channeling his inner childhood imagination as they laughed and joked amongst each other.

Skylar and Bentley both jumped when they heard the front door swing open. They both turned to face the sound of the door as a flustered woman's voice echoed down the hall.

"I'm sorry, I'm late. I hope he wasn't any trouble…" As the woman approached the living room doorsill and saw Bentley and Skylar sitting on the floor playing, she stopped mid-sentence, she looked like she had just seen a ghost. "Raelynn, I need to speak with you right now." The woman shouted as her tired voice shifted to a more angrier tone.

As Bentley starred at the angry woman, he took in the sight of her brunette hair in a messy bun, her dark hazel brown eyes that were currently filled with rage, her sun-kissed tan, and her white diner uniform, which was covered in food remnants. Bentley couldn't help but wonder who she was.

"Hey, Skylar, who is that woman buddy," Bentley asked just loud enough for Skylar to hear him as the angry woman stormed through the living room towards the bathroom where Raelynn was getting ready.

"That's my mommy. She works a lot, so I stay with Aunt Rae-Rae a lot." Skylar said as he looked up at Bentley.

Bentley finally knew who the woman was. Although he didn't know much about her, he knew it was Cassidy, Raelynn's best friend.

In the bathroom, Raelynn was greeted by an angry Cassidy. "Raelynn, what the fuck? What the fuck is he doing here? Why the fuck is he playing with my son?"

Raelynn, still doing her make-up, turned to face Cassidy. Raelynn could see the blood boiling inside Cassidy as her face was bloodshot red. Cassidy's reaction to seeing Bentley entertaining Skylar truly had her baffled. She knew Cassidy didn't like Bentley, and she knew having him over while Skylar was there was risky, but she also had expected Skylar to have been gone before Bentley arrived. She also didn't think Cassidy's reaction would be like this. She figured Cassidy would have been more cordial despite her disdain for Bentley. However, Raelynn was wrong.

"Whoa. Calm down, Cassidy. He's here to take me out. What's the deal here." Raelynn said in shock as she was struggling to find the words to diffuse the situation.

"Don't tell me to calm down. You got a stranger in the house playing with my son that you were supposed to be watching, yet you're in here doing your make-up, not paying any attention to them. Anything could have happened to my son!" Cassidy barked at Raelynn, who was still wearing a confused look on her face.

"Calm down, Cassidy; what the fuck has gotten into you. Your son is fine. Just like he always is and always will be when he's with me." A confused Raelynn said.

"No, I'm not calming down. I'm leaving. I can't deal with you right now." Cassidy shouted as she stormed out of the bathroom, leaving Raelynn there standing in confusion.

Bentley was still sitting on the living room floor playing with Skylar trying to make enough noise so the boy couldn't hear the shouting match in the bathroom. Bentley could only hear bits and pieces of what was happening, and he could tell Cassidy was not a happy camper.

Cassidy flew out of the bathroom into the living room, grabbing Skylar aggressively by the arm. "Let's go! We'll get your toys later."

As she yanked the boy up and led him down the hall, Bentley could hear the boy begin to pout. "But mommy…" the boy pleaded but was cut off by an angry Cassidy.

"No, son. We're leaving now. I'm sorry, but you'll have to get your toys later." Cassidy barked at the boy.

As the door slammed shut, Bentley sat there in the now quiet living room, the echo of Skylar's fading sobs lingering in the air. The sudden tension left Bentley perplexed, and he couldn't shake the feeling that there was more to the situation than met the eye.

Raelynn emerged from the hallway, her expression a mix of confusion and concern. "What just happened?" she asked, glancing towards the closed door through which Cassidy and Skylar had just departed.

Bentley rose from the floor, his gaze shifting between the closed door and Raelynn's bewildered eyes. The atmosphere in the room seemed heavy with unspoken tension as Skylar's fading sobs continued to echo in the background.

"I have no idea," Bentley admitted, his brow furrowed in concern.

Raelynn sighed, running her fingers through her hair as if trying to make sense of the chaos that had just unfolded. "This is… whatever. I'm going to finish my make-up and I'll be ready in five minutes."

Bentley nodded, understanding that sometimes a bit of distraction and a change of scenery could be the best remedy for a tense situation. As Raelynn headed back to the bathroom, he couldn't help but feel a sense of responsibility to turn the day around.

With a gentle knock on the bathroom door, Bentley called out, "Hey, Rae, don't spend too much time on your hair and make-up. We've got an adventure planned for the afternoon. Bring your swimwear!"

Raelynn's voice, though muffled by the door, carried a hint of curiosity, "An adventure? What's the plan?"

Bentley chuckled, deciding to keep it a surprise. "You'll see. Just be ready in five minutes, okay?"

He could hear Raelynn's laughter through the door. "Alright, mystery man, you've got it. Five minutes it is!"

Bentley stepped back into the living room, a determination to salvage the day etched on his face. He glanced around, noticing the scattered toys and remnants of the interrupted playtime with Skylar. Taking a moment to tidy up, he couldn't shake the feeling that this unexpected twist might turn into an opportunity to build stronger connections.

As Raelynn emerged, looking refreshed and ready for the unknown adventure, Bentley flashed a mischievous grin. "You ready for this?"

Raelynn laughed, the earlier tension temporarily forgotten. "I have no idea what 'this' is, but let's do it!"

With that, they left Raelynn's apartment, leaving behind the echoes of the chaotic afternoon.

23

Hidden Currents

After ninety minutes, Bentley and Raelynn arrived at Steele Creek Marina, located in the quaint country town of Townsville, North Carolina, the home of Kerr Lake. This town straddled the Virginia-North Carolina border, just beyond the lively city limits of Raleigh.

The marina was a picturesque scene with boats of various sizes bobbing gently in the water, and the sunlight casting a golden hue on the lake's surface. Bentley led Raelynn toward a familiar pontoon boat docked at the marina, a vessel that held cherished memories of family outings and lazy afternoons on the water.

As they stepped onto the boat, Bentley's eyes reflected the serene beauty of the lake. "Welcome to the family pontoon boat," he announced with a proud grin.

Raelynn looked around, absorbing the calming atmosphere. "This is incredible."

Bentley nodded, steering the boat away from the dock. "Yeah, it's been a part of the family for years. Thought we could use a little lake time to shake off the tension from earlier."

Raelynn appreciated Bentley's thoughtful gesture, realizing that he was trying to create a positive atmosphere despite the unexpected disruption. The boat glided across the lake's smooth surface, the gentle breeze whispering through the air.

They found a quiet spot in the middle of the lake, surrounded by the serenity of nature. Bentley cut the engine, allowing the boat to float gently. The only sounds were the lapping of the water against the boat and the distant calls of birds.

Bentley anchored the boat, and they decided to bask in the warmth of the sun. They stretched out on the boat's cushioned seats, letting the gentle rocking of the water create a soothing rhythm. The lake, with its vast expanse, seemed to absorb the troubles of the world, leaving only tranquility in its wake.

Raelynn lay there, gazing at the sky with a contemplative expression. Bentley couldn't help but notice the furrowed lines on her forehead, a sign that her mind was still occupied by the earlier events. He turned his head, taking in the view of the lake, but his attention remained tethered to Raelynn.

After a few moments of comfortable silence, Bentley spoke softly, "Hey, Rae. You seem a bit distant. Is everything okay?"

Raelynn sighed, her eyes never leaving the sky. "It's just... Cassidy. I've never seen her so angry and upset."

Bentley propped himself up on his elbow, looking at Raelynn with concern. "Do you want to talk about it?"

Raelynn turned to look at Bentley and let out a deep sigh, "It's complicated, Bentley. I really think you being there is what had her so angry."

Bentley furrowed his brow, trying to comprehend Raelynn's words. "Me being there? Why would me being there upset her?"

Raelynn hesitated for a moment before sighing. "Honestly Bentley, Cassidy doesn't like you and I've never understood why. When you first made it big, Cassidy was obsessed, like I mean she was a huge fan. I mean she chose to attend NC State, with hopes of a chance encounter with you. After she got pregnant, there was a change in her attitude towards you. Every time your music would come on the radio, she would change it. If you appeared on TV, she would change it. I have no idea what changed."

Bentley listened in surprise as Raelynn revealed the strange history between Cassidy and himself. The peaceful surroundings of the lake seemed to contrast sharply with the unexpected revelation. He furrowed his brow, processing the information.

"So, she was a fan, and then something changed after she got pregnant?" Bentley asked, seeking clarification.

Raelynn nodded, her expression a mix of confusion and concern. "Exactly. It's like she has this grudge against you, and I can't figure out why. I've tried talking to her about it, but she shuts me down every time."

Bentley ran a hand through his hair, a puzzled expression on his face. "That's bizarre. How can you hate someone you have never even met? Especially, after you were a big fan?"

Raelynn sighed, acknowledging the absurdity of the situation. "I know, right? It doesn't make sense. I've tried to understand her perspective, but every time I bring it up, she just gets defensive and avoids the conversation. It's like there's some secret she's keeping, and I'm stuck in the dark."

Bentley glanced at Raelynn, his concern deepening. "It sounds like there's more to this story."

Raelynn hesitated; her gaze fixed on the rippling water beneath the boat. "Bentley, do you remember when I told you I moved here was to help my best friend because she got pregnant after a one-night stand? Well, as you know that best friend is Cassidy. The trust is, she doesn't know who Skylar's dad is. It's been bothering her because Skylar is at that age where he's asking questions. It also doesn't help that doctor's think he may have leukemia and may need a bone marrow transplant and she wasn't a match."

Bentley's eyes widened with a mix of surprise and concern. The weight of Cassidy's situation, the uncertainty surrounding Skylar's health, and the revelation about his potential connection to the child left him speechless for a moment.

"Wow. That is a lot." He finally said, his voice a mixture of empathy and shock. "That's an incredible amount of stress and uncertainty for her to bear."

"Yeah, so she's super protective over Skylar." Raelynn said as she wiped a tear from her eye. "But anyways let's not let this ruin our day."

Bentley nodded, understanding the need to shift their focus away from the heavy revelations for a while. He gently reached out, wiping away a tear from Raelynn's cheek, a silent gesture of support.

"You're right," Bentley agreed, his voice filled with a mix of concern and determination. As he leaned in and planted a soft but assuring kiss on Raelynn's lips.

Raelynn smiled through the lingering emotions, grateful for Bentley's comforting presence. As they pulled away from the kiss, Bentley looked into her eyes, his gaze sincere.

As they lay back on the boat, Raelynn's mind turned to a different curiosity. With a playful smile, she looked at Bentley and asked, "So, Mr. Bentley, I know you're staying with your parents while you're in town, but where do you usually live? I mean, you're a big shot in the music industry. Do you have a mansion somewhere?"

Bentley chuckled; the tension of the earlier conversation momentarily lifted. "Well, yeah. I have a place down in Miami, an oceanfront mansion. I love the warm weather year-round. It's my little sanctuary."

Raelynn's eyes widened in amazement. "An oceanfront mansion? That's incredible!"

Bentley grinned, appreciating her enthusiasm. "It's not too shabby. I find inspiration in the sound of the waves. But I have to admit, there's something special about being back home, away from all the chaos and paparazzi."

Raelynn tilted her head, her curiosity growing. "How long do you plan on staying in town? I mean, it's nice that you're here, but it seems like you've got a whole other world waiting for you in Miami."

Bentley pondered the question for a moment, his eyes scanning the horizon. "I haven't decided, honestly. I love being home, having a sense of normalcy. Miami can be overwhelming sometimes, you know? Here, I can just be Bentley, not the celebrity. Plus, I get to spend time with you" Bentley leaned smiling, giving Raelynn a kiss on the forehead.

Raelynn blushed at Bentley's affectionate gesture, a warmth spreading through her. "Well, I'm honored to be part of your escape from the chaos aside from Cinderella Fest."

Bentley chuckled, his gaze lingering on her. "You make it sound like being here is an escape. Maybe it is. I love the simplicity of it all. And Cinderella Fest, that was different. That was fun kind of chaos."

Curiosity sparkled in Raelynn's eyes. "Tell me more about your life in Miami. What's it like living in an oceanfront mansion? And what's a typical day like for Bentley, the international music sensation?"

Bentley grinned, enjoying Raelynn's interest. "Well, Miami is vibrant, full of life. My mansion sits right on the beach, so every morning, I wake up to the sound of the waves crashing against the shore. It's like having a piece of paradise at my doorstep."

Raelynn's eyes lit up with fascination. "That sounds dreamy. What do you do on a regular day?"

Bentley leaned back, propping himself up on his elbows. "Honestly, it varies. Some days, I'll spend hours in the studio, working on new music. Other times, I just want to relax by the pool, maybe catch some rays. And of course, there are those spontaneous moments where I might decide to take my new yacht out for a spin."

Raelynn playfully nudged him. "Must be nice."

Bentley laughed. "It has its perks, for sure. But it also comes with the constant scrutiny of the media, the never-ending demands. That's why coming back home feels like a breath of fresh air. No paparazzi, no expectations, just the simplicity of being."

Raelynn nodded, understanding the need for such simplicity in the midst of a whirlwind career. "I get it. Must be nice to trade the spotlight for a bit of normalcy."

Bentley's expression softened. "Exactly. And who knows how long I'll stay this time. I'm still figuring it out. I love being home, but the industry always pulls you back in."

Raelynn's gaze turned thoughtful. "Do you ever get tired of it all? The fame, the constant attention?"

Bentley sighed, a hint of weariness in his eyes. "Sometimes. It's a double-edged sword. I love making music, connecting with people through it. But the invasion of privacy, the constant scrutiny—it can be draining. That's why I savor moments like these, away from it all."

They lay back on the boat, the sun casting a warm glow on the lake. Raelynn nestled closer to Bentley, and he wrapped his arm around her, finding comfort in the simplicity of the moment. As the boat gently rocked on the tranquil waters, they shared stories, laughter, and the promise of genuine connection, leaving behind the complexities of their lives for a while.

24

A Heartfelt Test

The following morning Bentley laid in bed still bothered by Cassidy and Skylar's struggles. He was also bothered by her not liking him as a person when she didn't even know him. Thoughts raced continuously through his mind as Bentley knew he had to do something to help Cassidy and Skylar but didn't know exactly what.

Later that morning while in the shower, it finally dawned on him on what to do. He remembered Raelynn explaining to him that Skylar was sick and would potentially need a bone marrow transplant and Cassidy wasn't a match. An insult to injury to a single mother already struggling to stay afloat. That's when Bentley came up with the idea to get tested to see if he was a match.

Bentley knew his act of kindness and attempt to help may not change Cassidy's opinion of him, but he didn't care. Bentley always had a soft spot in his heart for sick kids and struggling single parents, that's why he wanted to help despite her views towards him. It wasn't an attempt to buy her fanship back but an attempt to save Skylar's life.

Determined to make a difference, Bentley dressed quickly after his revelation. He could feel the weight of the decision he was about to make, understanding the potential impact on Cassidy and Skylar's lives. As he drove to the doctor's office, thoughts swirled in his mind, alternating between hope and apprehension.

Upon arriving at the medical facility, Bentley approached the front desk, his heart pounding with a mix of nerves and determination. "I'd like to schedule a test to see if I'm a potential match for a bone marrow transplant," he explained to the receptionist.

The receptionist looked up, surprise flickering across her face at the unexpected request. "That's usually a scheduled process, sir. Do you have an appointment?"

Bentley shook his head. "No, it's not scheduled. I didn't know that I needed to. I'm sorry."

The receptionist regarded Bentley with a mixture of understanding and curiosity. "No need to apologize, sir. Let me see what I can do. Can I get the name of the patient you're wanting to be tested for?"

"The patient's name is Skylar…" Bentley hesitated for a moment, realizing he hadn't anticipated this question. "… ma'am I'm sorry. I don't know his last name. I know that he just turned five and his mother's name is Cassidy. That is all the information that I know."

The receptionist nodded, her expression softening as she sensed Bentley's genuine concern. "That's okay. We'll do our best to work with the information you provided. Please have a seat, and I'll see what we can arrange for you."

Bentley took a seat in the waiting area, his mind racing with a mix of anxiety and hope. He fidgeted with his hands, glancing around the sterile, white-walled room. The minutes felt like hours as he waited, contemplating the potential impact of his decision.

After a brief period, the receptionist returned, holding a clipboard and wearing a reassuring smile. "We're going to proceed with some preliminary tests today. It might take a bit longer for us to gather more information about Skylar, but we'll start the process. If you could fill out these forms, we'll get started as soon as possible."

Bentley took the clipboard, expression grateful. As he filled out the forms, his thoughts lingered on Skylar and Cassidy. The idea of being a potential match filled him with a sense of purpose, but the uncertainty of the situation weighed heavily on his mind.

Once the paperwork was complete, Bentley handed it back to the receptionist, who thanked him before guiding him to the examination room where Bentley waited for the doctor's arrival.

As Bentley sat in the examination room, the sterile surroundings emphasized the gravity of the decision he had made. He glanced at the door anxiously, waiting for the doctor to arrive. The hum of fluorescent lights overhead seemed to echo the rapid beating of his heart.

The door opened, and a middle-aged doctor walked in, his face marked by a warm, reassuring smile. "Good morning, Mr. Riggs. I'm Dr. Reynolds. I understand you're interested in being tested for a potential bone marrow transplant?"

Bentley nodded, his expression earnest. "Yes, that's correct. I want to see if I could be a match for a little boy named Skylar. He's five years old and may potentially need a transplant. His mother's name is Cassidy. I'm sorry doc, but that's all the information that I have. I just want to help in case it does come down to him needing the bone marrow transplant."

Dr. Reynolds listened attentively, studying Bentley's determined expression. "I appreciate your willingness to help, Mr. Riggs. The fact that you've come forward for a procedure like this without knowing much about the patient is quite unusual. Can you tell me more about your connection to Skylar and Cassidy?"

Bentley took a deep breath, considering how to explain the situation. "Skylar is my girlfriend's godson. I only met him and Cassidy yesterday, but learning about Skylar's condition and the struggles Cassidy is facing struck a chord with me. I want to help. I might not know them well, but I believe this is the right thing to do."

Dr. Reynolds nodded, understanding evident in his eyes. "It's not every day we encounter someone with such a selfless drive to help others. Just to clarify, Skylar Brooks and Cassidy Brooks, right?"

Bentley's expression went grim as he wasn't sure if that was their last names. "Possibly. I'm sorry doc, I don't know their last names."

The doctor chuckled as he was still admiring Bentley's modesty to get tested without knowing Skylar or Cassidy. "What's your girlfriend's name Mr. Riggs?" Dr. Reynolds asked.

Bentley hesitated on answering the question because he and Raelynn still hadn't discussed if they were ready to go public with them dating. However, if there was chance that this information could speed up the process Bentley wasn't going to be the one to hold it up any longer.

"My girlfriends name is Raelynn Hart." Bentley said with a big smile as that statement felt so good rolling off his lips.

"Ah. Ok, so this is for Skylar Brooks." Dr. Reynolds said as he paused to scroll through his tablet. "Mr. Riggs, we usually only start with preliminary test first but due to the nature of Skylar's case and not knowing what the issue is, I'm going to go ahead and authorize the full examination panel for you today. If that's ok."

Bentley nodded, appreciating the doctor's proactive approach. "Yes, of course. Whatever it takes to expedite the process and help Skylar as soon as possible."

Dr. Reynolds proceeded to conduct a thorough examination, involving various tests to assess Bentley's overall health and compatibility for a potential bone marrow transplant. As the examination progressed, the doctor engaged in casual conversation to ease the tension in the room.

"Mr. Riggs, I must say, your decision to step forward in this manner is quite extraordinary. We often see family members coming forward for such procedures, but your willingness to help someone you've only recently met is commendable."

Bentley, now more at ease with the doctor's friendly demeanor, opened up about his motivations. "I may not know Skylar and Cassidy, and that's ok because sometimes you just feel a calling to help people that are in more need than yourself."

As the tests progressed, Bentley couldn't help but reflect on the fragility of life and the unexpected turns it could take. He marveled at the idea that a decision made in a shower, born out of compassion for someone he barely knew, could potentially alter the course of Skylar's life.

Once the extensive examination concluded, Dr. Reynolds offered a reassuring smile. "Thank you for your cooperation, Mr. Riggs. We'll process the results as quickly as possible. In the meantime, please understand that Skylar's condition is still being investigated, and we'll keep you informed every step of the way."

Bentley expressed his gratitude, eager for any updates. As he left the examination room, he couldn't shake the mix of emotions that accompanied this unexpected journey. The weight of the decision lingered, but so did a spark of hope that he might be able to make a difference in Skylar's life.

Feeling accomplished Bentley decided to drive to head to Raelynn's to see her and tell her about his generous act. He was nervous on how she would take the news.

As Bentley drove to Raelynn's house, his mind was filled with a mix of nervousness and anticipation. He couldn't wait to share the news with her, yet a part of him wondered how she would react to the impromptu decision he had made.

Pulling up to Raelynn's driveway, Bentley took a deep breath to steady his nerves. He grabbed the bouquet of roses he had bought for her, a small gesture to lighten the mood before he shared the potentially life-altering news. As he approached the front door, he couldn't help but smile at the thought of seeing Raelynn's reaction.

Bentley knocked on the door, and after a moment, Raelynn opened it with a warm smile. The sight of her made Bentley's heart skip a beat, and he couldn't help but feel grateful for her presence in his life.

"Hey, surprise!" Bentley greeted her, holding out the bouquet of roses.

Raelynn's eyes lit up with delight. "Bentley, you didn't have to bring flowers, but they're beautiful. Thank you!"

Bentley grinned, glad to see her happy. "Well, I thought they might brighten your day. Mind if I come in?"

Raelynn stepped aside, welcoming Bentley into her home. As they settled in the living room, Bentley couldn't contain the excitement any longer.

"So, I have something to tell you," Bentley began, his eyes gleaming with a mix of nerves and joy.

Raelynn raised an eyebrow, curious. "Okay, spill it. What's the big news?"

Bentley took a deep breath, searching for the right words. "I went to get tested today, to see if I could be a match for Skylar's bone marrow transplant."

Raelynn's eyes widened in surprise, and then a mix of emotions crossed her face. "Bentley, that's... that's incredible. Why did you decide to do that?"

Bentley explained the entire sequence of events, from hearing about Cassidy and Skylar's situation, the shower revelation and finally the decision to get tested. Raelynn listened attentively, her admiration for Bentley growing with each word.

"I just felt this calling to help, Raelynn. I may not know them well, but if there's a chance I can make a difference, I want to take it," Bentley said earnestly.

Raelynn reached out, taking Bentley's hand in hers. "That's an amazing thing you're doing, Bentley. Skylar and Cassidy will be so relieved if you are a match and he does need this transplant."

Bentley smiled, relieved by Raelynn's supportive reaction. "I was nervous about how you'd take the news. I didn't want you to think it was too impulsive or anything."

Raelynn squeezed his hand. "No, Bentley, it's not impulsive. It's incredibly generous, and it shows the kind of person you are. I'm proud of you."

Bentley's heart swelled with gratitude for Raelynn's understanding. "I'm just hoping it all works out, and I can be a match for Skylar. The tests are done, and now we just have to wait for the results."

Raelynn nodded, her eyes reflecting a mix of emotions. "Whatever happens, Bentley, the fact that you tried means a lot. You've already made a difference in Skylar's life just by taking this step."

Bentley leaned in, giving Raelynn a gentle kiss. A kiss that seemed to stop their busy minds from wandering.

As they pulled away from the kiss, Bentley looked into Raelynn's eyes with a grateful smile. "Thank you for the vote of confidence, Raelynn."

Raelynn returned the smile. "Of course, Bentley. Now let's just hope everything works out for the best."

Bentley's gaze shifted to the bouquet of roses he had brought. "And speaking of making things better, I have another idea."

Raelynn raised an eyebrow, intrigued. "Oh? Do tell."

Bentley nodded, feeling a deep connection with Raelynn in that moment. "I was thinking... What do you say we take a little break from everything? A getaway trip, just you and me."

Raelynn's eyes sparkled with excitement. "A getaway trip? That sounds amazing. Where are we going?"

Bentley grinned, his eyes glinting mischievously. "How about we head to my place in Miami? We can relax and take our minds off things."

Raelynn's eyes widened in surprise. "Your Miami mansion? Are you serious?"

Bentley chuckled. "Absolutely. A change of scenery might do us good. Plus, it'll be a nice distraction from everything."

Raelynn's eyes sparkled with excitement. "A getaway sounds amazing! But how do you propose we get there?"

Bentley leaned back, a mischievous glint in his eyes. "Well, my dear, I have a few options for you. Do you want to drive down, enjoy a scenic road trip? Or perhaps, we can fly first class commercial, make it a comfortable journey. And then, there's the third option – I could arrange a private jet for us."

Raelynn's eyebrows shot up in surprise. "A private jet? That sounds... extravagant."

Bentley shrugged, a playful smile on his lips. "Why not? We could use a bit of extravagance in our lives. Plus, it's faster, and we'll have the entire jet to ourselves. Imagine the luxury."

Raelynn's eyes widened playfully. Well, Mr. Bentley, let's do it then since we're talking about escaping reality. Let's make it truly luxurious. Plus, there's something I've always wanted to do."

Bentley's curiosity piqued, and he raised an eyebrow. "Oh, really? What's this mysterious thing you've always wanted to do?"

Raelynn grinned, her eyes sparkling with a mischievous glint. "Ever heard of the 'mile-high club'?"

Bentley's expression shifted from curiosity to amusement. "Oh, I'm very familiar with it. Is that on your bucket list?" Bentley chuckled through his response.

Raelynn nodded with a playful smile. "Guilty as charged. What better time than now, on our way to Miami in a private jet? It's the perfect setting for a little dirty adventure, don't you think?"

Bentley chuckled, appreciating Raelynn's spontaneity. "Well, I can't argue with that. It's settled then. A private jet it is."

Raelynn laughed, the sound filling the room with a carefree energy. "I can't believe we're doing this, Bentley. A spontaneous trip on a private jet? This is like a scene out of a movie."

Bentley joined in her laughter, feeling the weight of the world momentarily lift off his shoulders. "Sometimes, you just have to embrace the unexpected, right?"

With an enthusiastic nod, Raelynn replied, "Absolutely! Life is too short to not enjoy these moments. Now, when do we leave?"

Bentley checked his watch, a glint of excitement in his eyes. "How about we leave for the airport right now? The jet is actually already waiting for us."

Raelynn agreed, "Sounds perfect. Let me grab a few things, and we'll head to the airport."

"You don't need to pack clothes because honey, you won't be needing them." Bentley chuckled with a devilish grin.

Raelynn turned back with a mischievous glint in her eyes, "Well, looks like I'm traveling light."

As Raelynn gathered a few essentials, Bentley couldn't help but feel a sense of exhilaration. The prospect of a spontaneous trip with Raelynn and the anticipation of the unexpected made his heart race.

Within moments, Raelynn returned with a small bag, her smile reflecting a mix of anticipation and playfulness. "Alright, Mr. Bentley, I'm ready for whatever this adventure holds."

Hand in hand, they made their way to the car, and Bentley couldn't shake the feelings that he was experiencing. He knew they both could greatly benefit from the beautiful scenery Miami had to offer.

25

Mile High Club

After a quick car ride across the city, Bentley and Raelynn were parked outside the tarmac in front of a flashy blacked-out private jet. The jet, with its sleek design and tinted windows, exuded an air of luxury. As they approached, the pilot and crew greeted them, and Bentley exchanged a few words with them before leading Raelynn up the steps to board the jet.

The interior of the private jet was as luxurious as one would expect, with plush leather seats, ambient lighting, and an overall opulent atmosphere. Bentley guided Raelynn to a spacious seating area, and they settled in as the door closed behind them. Raelynn and Bentley sat directly across from each other face to face.

Raelynn glanced at Bentley, her eyes sparkling with anticipation. "So, Mr. Bentley, what's the plan for our Miami getaway?"

Bentley grinned, savoring the thrill of the moment. "No concrete plans, just a desire to enjoy the sun, the beach, and you. Wherever the day takes us."

Raelynn nodded, her playful spirit shining through. "Sounds like a great plan!"

The pilot's voice came over the intercom, announcing the flight details and welcoming Bentley and Raelynn aboard. Bentley couldn't help but feel a sense of exhilaration as the jet taxied down the runway, ready to take them to the warm embrace of Miami.4

As the jet ascended into the night sky, Bentley couldn't help but look at Raelynn with a devilish grin as they shared a toast with glasses of champagne. The city lights below sparkled like a sea of stars in Raelynn's eyes as Bentley began biting on his bottom lip imagining her on top, riding him on that big spacious couch at back of the plane.

They spent the initial part of the flight stealing sly glances at each other, exchanging occasional chuckles. Their teasing escalated with each passing moment, resembling a silent dance of undressing through lingering gazes.

Feeling the urge for a more tangible connection, Raelynn, unable to resist the temptation, decided to take things further. A mischievous smile played on her lips as she initiated playful teasing with Bentley.

Nonchalantly kicking off her heels, Raelynn began a subtle exploration, tracing her foot along Bentley's leg. Her movements became more provocative, eventually reaching the center where she could sense his arousal. Gently rubbing her foot up and down, she continued the teasing before retracing her path down his other leg.

As the jet reached cruising altitude, Bentley found himself unable to resist Raelynn's playful teasing any longer. Rising from his seat, he gently helped her to her feet, drawing her into a passionate kiss. Their lips locked, and with a sense of urgency, Bentley led Raelynn toward the rear of the plane where the spacious white couch awaited.

In their eager haste, they stumbled toward the back of the aircraft. Upon reaching their destination, Bentley reached behind him, swiftly pulling the privacy curtain shut, creating an intimate space for the two of them.

Behind the closed curtain, the ambient lighting cast a warm glow, creating an intimate atmosphere. Bentley and Raelynn, their eyes locked with desire, shared a moment of silent understanding. Bentley, overcome by the magnetic pull of Raelynn's sensuality, took a step closer, his hands finding the curve of her waist.

Feeling the need to assert control, Raelynn pushed Bentley gently down onto the plush couch. Their lips remained connected, a symphony of passion echoing in the confined space. Raelynn's hands, skilled and teasing, began to unbutton Bentley's shirt, revealing the sculpted contours of his chest.

Bentley, feeling the electricity in the air, reciprocated by sliding his hands along the curves of Raelynn's body. The soft touch of his fingers made her shiver with anticipation. As the last button on Bentley's shirt was undone, Raelynn broke the kiss, her eyes locking onto his with a fiery intensity.

Raelynn rose from her seat, her gaze fixed on Bentley, and she initiated a seductive dance in rhythm with the music resonating through the aircraft speakers. Bentley watched with impatience as the enticing performance unfolded.

As Raelynn sensually removed pieces of clothing, Bentley, unable to contain his desire, attempted to draw her nearer by reaching out. However, Raelynn playfully swatted his hands away, further fueling his longing.

Eventually, standing in nothing but her lingerie, Raelynn descended to her hands and knees, embarking on a tantalizing crawl toward Bentley. Once in close proximity, she skillfully undid his belt, and began unbuttoning his pants with a provocative intent.

The hum of the jet's engines served as a backdrop to the escalating tension between Bentley and Raelynn. Raelynn's eyes locked onto Bentley's as she continued her deliberate movements, teasingly undoing his pants one button at a time. Bentley, entranced by her every move, felt a surge of anticipation coursing through him.

With each undone button, Raelynn's mischievous smile widened. She maintained eye contact with Bentley, her gaze daring him to lose himself in the rising desire. The confined space behind the privacy curtain became a playground for their shared fantasies, and Bentley willingly surrendered to the allure of Raelynn's seduction.

As Raelynn finally released the last button, she met Bentley's gaze with a tantalizing grin. Sensing the intensity of the moment, Bentley raised his hips slightly, allowing Raelynn to slide his pants down, revealing the growing desire beneath.

With his pants now discarded, Bentley was left in a state of anticipation. Raelynn, still maintaining eye contact, leaned in closer, her warm breath sending shivers down Bentley's spine. She continued her exploration, her hands tracing the contours of his thighs, inching closer to the source of his mounting arousal.

Raelynn playfully kissed the tip of Bentley's arousal, teasing it gently, before taking his rigid length into her mouth. Bentley couldn't help but release a pleasure-filled moan in response.

As Raelynn sensually moved up and down Bentley's shaft with her mouth, his hands found their way into her hair, guiding and enhancing every pleasurable motion she made.

Sensing Bentley nearing climax, Raelynn pulled away, locking eyes with him mischievously. In a slow, seductive motion, she stood up, removing her panties before climbing on top of Bentley and straddling him.

As Raelynn positioned herself over Bentley, feeling his length penetrating deeply, she slid her hands under the halves of Bentley's unbuttoned shirt, finishing the job by peeling it off his shoulders.

Raelynn experienced a sense of fulfillment as she checked joining the mile-high club off her bucket list. Bentley attempted to assert control and switch positions, but Raelynn firmly rejected his request, asserting her dominance.

This was her moment, and she intended to make it unforgettable. Riding Bentley just like a pornstar with an increasing intensity, she took charge of the encounter, showcasing her prowess. The passionate exchange reached its peak as they both climaxed together.

As Raelynn nestled on top of Bentley while they reclined on the couch, both still unclothed, the plane began its descent. Sensing the movement, Bentley lifted his head, planting a gentle kiss on Raelynn's head. "Rae, we should get dressed. We'll be landing shortly."

Raelynn, still catching her breath, nodded in agreement with Bentley, as she reluctantly disentangled herself from Bentley's embrace, reaching for her scattered clothing.

"How does it feel to be a part of the mile-high club now?" Bentley asked jokingly.

"It feels surreal. I can't believe it actually happened," Raelynn replied as she was putting her shirt back on.

Once fully clothed, Bentley and Raelynn emerged from behind the curtain, their expressions a blend of satisfaction and anticipation. The pilot's voice came over the intercom, preparing them for the landing. Bentley and Raelynn took their seats, the private jet gliding smoothly toward its destination, bringing an end to their clandestine escapade in the skies.

26

Miami Heat

The private jet touched down in Miami, bringing Bentley and Raelynn to the vibrant city illuminated by the warm glow of night lights. As they exited the aircraft, a chauffeur-driven car awaited them on the tarmac to take them to Bentley's mansion.

As they approached Bentley's mansion, Raelynn couldn't help but be awestruck by the opulence that surrounded her. The mansion stood as a testament to Bentley's success, with its modern architecture, pristine landscaping, and an air of extravagance that permeated the entire property.

"Welcome to mi casa," Bentley said with a playful grin as they entered the mansion.

Raelynn's eyes widened at the sight before her eyes. The interior was a blend of modern design and luxury, with high ceilings, marble floors, and contemporary artwork adorning the walls. The air was filled with the scent of expensive candles, creating an inviting ambiance.

Bentley led Raelynn through the mansion, showcasing its various rooms. The kitchen boasted state-of-the-art appliances, and the living room featured oversized windows offering a breathtaking view of the beach. Bentley made sure to highlight the mansion's amenities, from the private theater to the impressive wine cellar.

Eventually, Bentley guided Raelynn to the master bedroom, which featured a California king-sized bed with luxurious linens and a balcony that overlooked the beach. The room exuded an air of sensuality, with dimmed lights and soft music playing in the background.

Raelynn's breath caught as she took in the master bedroom. The walls were adorned with rich, deep-colored tapestries that added warmth to the room. A massive chandelier hung from the ceiling, casting a soft, golden glow that accentuated the plush furnishings. The king-sized bed, with its silk sheets and an abundance of pillows, beckoned them in.

Bentley moved closer, his fingers gently tracing the contours of Raelynn's cheek. "What do you think?" he asked, his eyes filled with a mixture of anticipation and desire.

"It's... incredible," Raelynn replied, her voice barely above a whisper. She felt a surge of emotions, a blend of excitement and nervousness, as she took in the intimate setting.

As the days unfolded, Bentley and Raelynn explored the mansion's every nook and cranny. The enormous waterfall shower in the master bathroom became a favorite spot for them. The high-pressure water cascaded down, enveloping them in a cocoon of warmth and luxury. It was an experience that left them both rejuvenated and eager for more.

Their passion spilled over into every corner of the mansion. The kitchen, with its sleek countertops and top-of-the-line appliances, witnessed culinary experiments that went far beyond the realm of cooking. Laughter and pleasure echoed through the hallways as they found joy in each other's company.

By the pool, they basked in the sun and the opulence of their surroundings. Bentley's mansion had a private outdoor area that rivalled a five-star resort, complete with a poolside bar and plush loungers. The two of them reveled in the pleasure of each other's company, the sound of laughter mingling with the gentle lapping of the water.

The balcony of the master bedroom provided a breathtaking view of Miami's beaches. Bentley and Raelynn spent moments of quiet intimacy there, surrounded by the soft hum of the city below and the warm night breeze.

Their escapades weren't confined to the mansion either. Bentley's yacht became a playground for their desires as it sailed through the serene waters of the sound. The rhythmic motion of the yacht only heightened the intensity of their connection as they embraced the freedom of the open sea.

Before they knew it three days had flown by like a blur. The dawn of the third day echoed the previous two, as sunlight gently infiltrated the master bedroom windows of Bentley's mansion. The sun's rays danced across their intertwined, naked bodies ensnared in the embrace of tangled sheets.

The warmth of the morning sun was interrupted by the persistent buzz of Bentley's phone on the bedside table. Bentley groaned, attempting to ignore the disturbance as he tightened his grip around Raelynn. The call persisted, interrupting the peaceful cocoon they had woven together.

With a reluctant sigh, Bentley finally released Raelynn and reached for his phone. The screen illuminated with missed calls and notifications. He swiped them away without checking, focusing instead on the here and now.

Ignoring the call, Bentley tossed the phone aside, more interested in the woman lying beside him. Raelynn, now fully awake, propped herself up on one elbow and looked at him with a teasing smile.

"Someone's eager to interrupt our little paradise," she said, her voice filled with playful sarcasm.

Bentley chuckled, his attention solely on her. "Whoever it is can wait. I have more important things to focus on right now."

Raelynn's eyes sparkled with mischief as she leaned in, her lips brushing against Bentley's ear. "Well, aren't you the charmer? I like your priorities," she whispered, sending a shiver down his spine.

Bentley couldn't help but smile at Raelynn's playful demeanor. He leaned in, capturing her lips in a lingering kiss. Their connection was undeniable, a magnetic force that drew them closer with each passing moment.

As Bentley pulled Raelynn closer, he traced a finger along the curve of her spine, savoring the warmth of her skin. "I believe we were in the middle of something," Bentley murmured, his voice low and filled with desire.

Raelynn's teasing smile deepened, and she responded with a languid kiss. The room, bathed in the soft morning light, became a sanctuary of shared intimacy. The world outside, with its demands and distractions, faded away as they surrendered to the magnetic pull drawing them together.

The balcony door stood ajar, allowing the gentle breeze to caress their entwined bodies. Bentley and Raelynn, lost in the ebb and flow of passion, were oblivious to the city awakening beyond their sanctuary.

As their connection reached its crescendo, Bentley and Raelynn found solace in each other's arms. The morning sunlight, now fully embracing the room, painted their entangled forms with a golden glow.

After their shared moment of bliss, Raelynn gently disentangled herself from Bentley's embrace, a satisfied smile playing on her lips. "I really need a shower to wash off the sins of this morning."

Bentley watched her with admiration as she gracefully moved toward the bathroom. Bentley appreciated the way the morning light accentuated the curves of her silhouette. As the door closed behind her, the sound of running water soon filled the air, a soothing backdrop to the distant waves crashing against the shore.

Deciding to take advantage of the serene atmosphere, Bentley grabbed his pack of cigarettes from the nightstand and headed toward the balcony. The view was breathtaking—the sun casting a golden hue on the ocean waves below, and the beach was gradually coming to life with beachgoers. The cool breeze tousled his hair as he stepped outside, and he took a deep breath, savoring the salty scent of the sea. The rhythmic sound of the waves below seemed to carry away any lingering tension.

As Bentley lit his cigarette, inhaling deeply as he leaned against the balcony railing, allowing his thoughts to wander.

As Bentley listened to the waves crashing on the shore below and the laughter of the people on the beach reverberate through the gentle breeze, he decided to check the missed call from earlier.

As he pulled up his call log, Bentley saw that the missed call was from Dr. Reynolds doctor office. The missed call was accompanied by a voicemail which Bentley quickly listened to.

"Hello, Mr. Riggs, it's Dr. Reynolds. I'm calling regarding the recent panel of tests we conducted to determine your compatibility for Skylar's bone marrow transplant. While I haven't received the results yet, there are some findings from the tests that have caught my attention. Please call me back at your earliest convenience. Have a great day." Dr. Reynolds said in the message.

As Bentley's thoughts began to whirl, Raelynn emerged on the balcony after her morning shower, wearing only a towel that she draped around herself, enveloping Bentley in her embrace.

"It's your turn to shower honey," Raelynn whispered, intensifying her hold on Bentley and drawing him nearer, her head resting firmly against his back.

Bentley took one last drag from his cigarette, savoring the taste before flicking the remaining stub over the balcony railing. The worry in his mind intensified as he pocketed his phone and turned to face Raelynn. Her radiant smile faltered as she sensed a shift in his demeanor.

"Everything okay, babe?" Raelynn asked, her concern evident in her eyes.

Bentley hesitated as he didn't want to bother Raelynn but ultimately knew being quiet would only worry her more. He then took a deep breath as he told her about the voicemail from Dr Reynolds.

A hush fell over the balcony as the waves continued their rhythmic dance below, the backdrop to a conversation neither of them had anticipated. Raelynn's fingers traced comforting circles on Bentley's back, a silent reassurance that they were in this together.

"Dr. Reynolds mentioned some findings in the tests," Bentley continued, choosing his words carefully. "I haven't heard the results yet, but it sounds like there might be something they need to discuss. I need to call him back."

Raelynn nodded, a mix of worry and support in her gaze. "I think you should call him back, but perhaps after you have taken a hot and relaxing shower first."

"Alright, alright, I'll call him back soon as I get out of the shower." Bentley confirmed as he kissed Raelynn's forehead before heading towards the shower.

Bentley stepped into the marble-tiled bathroom, the worries of the moment clinging to him like a shadow. As the warm water cascaded down, he couldn't shake off the nagging thoughts about the voicemail from Dr. Reynolds. The steaming shower, usually a source of comfort, felt more like a temporary distraction.

As Bentley let the water wash away the sins of the morning, his mind was preoccupied with the unknowns that lay ahead. The soothing rhythm of the falling water failed to drown out the concern that echoed in his thoughts.

27

This Changes Everything

After Bentley's much needed shower, he reemerged back onto the balcony with Raelynn, who had now settled into one of the lounge chairs, her gaze fixed on the vast expanse of the ocean. Bentley, still damp from the shower, took a seat beside her, wrapping a towel around his waist.

The atmosphere was charged with a mix of anticipation and anxiety. Bentley's mind raced with the possibilities of what Dr. Reynolds might reveal. He fumbled with his phone, hesitating before making the call. Raelynn, sensing his inner turmoil, reached for his hand, offering a reassuring squeeze.

"You've got this, Bentley," Raelynn whispered as she got up, planting a kiss on his forehead, before retreating back inside to give Bentley his privacy.

Bentley took a deep breath, his heart pounding in his chest as he dialed Dr. Reynolds' number. The seconds felt like hours until finally, the doctor's voice crackled through the phone.

"Hello, Bentley. I've been expecting your call," Dr. Reynolds said, his tone serious.

Bentley's mind raced, trying to find the right words. "Doc, you've got to level with me. What's going on?"

Dr. Reynolds sighed on the other end. "Bentley, I need you to understand the gravity of what I'm about to share. I've been going through the test results, and I've discovered something that changes everything."

Bentley's grip tightened on the phone. "Just tell me, Doc. No beating around the bush. Am I match or am I not a match?"

"Bentley, it's crucial for you to grasp the situation. When I became a doctor, I pledged to uphold patient privacy through an oath. What I'm about to share with you could potentially breach HIPAA regulations, leading to serious consequences for me. However, considering the unique circumstances, there exists a significant grey area, and I believe I'm not violating HIPAA. Also, as a man I would want someone to tell me." Dr. Reynolds managed to get out before Bentley cut him off.

"Come on Doc, I think you've built the suspense enough. Get to the point." Bentley said as he was beginning to become flustered with the situation.

"Ok. I still don't know if you are a perfect match for the transplant but given what I know I believe you will be. Considering there is a fifty-fifty chance between parents, and Cassidy already isn't a match." Dr. Reynolds explained.

There was slight pause as Bentley was still trying to figure out what Dr Reynolds meant. "Ok, so what does that mean doc." Bentley said with the frustration steadily growing in his voice.

Dr. Reynolds sighed deeply before asking Bentley, "You aren't grasping what I'm laying down are you?"

"Obviously not doctor. I'm not good at guessing games. I need you to paint the picture clear as day for me." Bentley said back to Dr Reynolds with the frustration still apparent in his voice.

"Ok, Bentley I will dumb it down for you. After going through some of the test. It has been discovered that Skylar is your son. Which means you are Skylar's biological father." Dr. Reynolds stated with frustration growing in his voice.

Bentley's world seemed to come crashing down around him. The words hung in the air, echoing in his mind, and for a moment, he couldn't comprehend what Dr. Reynolds had just revealed.

"What? That's not even possible," Bentley stammered, his mind reeling with disbelief. "Skylar is not my son! I've never even met Cassidy until the other day. There must be a big misunderstanding."

Dr. Reynolds sighed, understanding the shock Bentley was experiencing. "I assure you, Bentley, the results are conclusive. The DNA tests don't lie. Skylar is your biological son."

Bentley's towel-clad figure tensed, his jaw clenched as he struggled to absorb the revelation. His mind raced through the recent events, connecting the dots in a way he hadn't considered before. The implications of being Skylar's father hit him like a tidal wave, and panic began to set in.

"Doc, this can't be happening. If Skylar is my son, why didn't Cassidy tell me? Why has she let me miss five years of my son's life." Bentley fired questions in rapid succession, his voice betraying a mix of confusion and anxiety.

Dr. Reynolds maintained a composed demeanor, empathizing with Bentley's emotional turmoil. "I understand this is a lot to process, Bentley. Cassidy may have her reasons, and it's crucial to approach this situation with sensitivity. I recommend having a calm conversation with her to gain clarity on the circumstances surrounding Skylar."

Bentley's mind was a whirlwind of emotions — disbelief, anger, and a profound sense of loss. The balcony, once a serene retreat, now felt like a battleground for his conflicting emotions. He took a moment to collect himself, then nodded slowly.

"Yeah, you're right, Doc. I need to talk to Cassidy," Bentley muttered, his gaze fixed on the horizon as if searching for answers in the vastness of the ocean.

As Bentley hung the phone up, he lit up a cigarette to try and calm his nerves as his mind was racing all over the place. As he sat there, it finally clicked to why Cassidy acted the way she did when she saw him and Skylar together the other day at Raelynn's. It finally clicked to him why she was no longer a fan of his. Everything was starting to click except his encounter with Cassidy. He was still struggling to recall meeting her, much less having sexual relations with her.

As Bentley sat there smoking on his cigarette dealing with all the thought inside his brain, he knew that he couldn't let Raelynn know about this. At least not until he had the chance to address this with Cassidy first.

Bentley took a long drag from his cigarette, the smoke swirling around him like a shroud of uncertainty. His mind raced with questions and emotions, yet he knew he couldn't burden Raelynn with this revelation just yet. He needed to sort things out with Cassidy first, find the truth, and figure out how to navigate the newfound complexities of his life.

Raelynn stepped back onto the balcony, concern etched across her face as she saw Bentley lost in thought. She walked over and sat down beside him, her hand gently resting on his shoulder. "Bentley, what did the doctor say? Is everything okay?"

Bentley hesitated, his gaze fixed on the glowing tip of his cigarette. "Doc needs to run more tests. It's not confirmed yet, but he thinks I might be a match for Skylar. They need more time to figure it out."

As they sat there in a heavy silence, Bentley's mind was a battlefield of conflicting emotions. The weight of the revelation about Skylar being his son bore down on him, but he couldn't let Raelynn in on the truth just yet. The timing was all wrong, and he needed to confront Cassidy before anything else.

Breaking the silence Bentley leaned in kissing Raelynn on the forehead, a token of his appreciation for her being so supportive. "Rae, I think we should head back to North Carolina tonight. I'll start arranging the jet."

Raelynn, sensing the gravity of the situation, nodded understandingly. "Of course, Bentley. Whatever you need to do, I'm here for you." She gave his hand a reassuring squeeze, silently offering her support.

Bentley took one last drag from his cigarette, extinguishing it on the balcony's edge. His mind was a storm of emotions, and the impending conversation with Cassidy weighed heavily on him. As they made their way inside to pack for their trip back to North Carolina, Bentley couldn't escape the whirlwind of thoughts.

How did this happen? Why did Cassidy not reach out to him? Was it because Cassidy didn't know who Skylar's father was? Would she even let him get to know Skylar? There were so many questions swirling in his mind that he knew the only way he'd get the answers to them was to have a sit down with Cassidy.

The thought of a sit down with Cassidy not only made Bentley anxious and nervous but it truly terrified him. He didn't know how to bring this up. He didn't know how she would react to his discovery of this. So many things terrified him about the situation at hand, but he knew he couldn't wait any longer. Bentley knew he needed to rush back to North Carolina to initiate the talk with Cassidy that he was very much dreading.

28
The Truth Hurts

After Bentley and Raelynn landed back in North Carolina, Bentley hurriedly got Raelynn home so he could face the consequences of his prima donna behavior. Bentley was beyond nervous as he felt his heart racing a thousand miles a minute. It also didn't help matters with the fact that he had to hide this from Raelynn.

Although Raelynn was a very important part of Bentley's life, she was not his priority. It was getting to the bottom of things with Cassidy and getting to formally meet Skylar as his dad. However, keeping this from Raelynn hurt Bentley. He wanted nothing more than to vent to her about this. Bentley even feared how she would react learning that Skylar was his son. Especially, with Cassidy being her best friend.

As the chauffeur arrived at Raelynn's house, Bentley stepped out of the car and assisted her with her belongings, escorting her to the front door. As Bentley leaned in for a goodbye kiss, he couldn't hold back the three little words that slipped out, "I love you."

Raelynn took a step back with the biggest grin on her face as she playfully smacked Bentley across the chest.

"Not Bentley Riggs, America's hottest bachelor telling me that he loves me right now. Oh my!" Raelynn said playfully although she could feel some sort of distant tension between them.

Raelynn's grin persisted, but beneath the playful banter, she sensed a distant tension with Bentley. His admission of love took her by surprise, and she couldn't help but feel a mixture of joy and concern.

Bentley's half-smile concealed the internal turmoil he grappled with, uncertainty lingering in his eyes. "Well, it seems I can surprise even myself sometimes," he responded, his tone betraying a hint of vulnerability.

As they stood on the threshold of Raelynn's home, Bentley knew the impending truth would bring pain. Despite Raelynn's significance in his life, she remained temporarily overshadowed by the urgent need to address matters with Cassidy and embrace his role as Skylar's father. The weight of keeping these secrets from Raelynn gnawed at him, but he couldn't delay the confrontation any longer.

With sincerity in his voice, Bentley took a deep breath and confessed, "Raelynn, I can't deny this any longer. I am madly and deeply in love with you! I don't know what you did or what kind of spell you put on me, but I love it. I really hope we can make this last forever and navigate any obstacles we might face together or individually."

The words hung in the air, a bittersweet moment marked by the conflicting emotions swirling within Bentley. Raelynn, though surprised, sensed the sincerity in his voice. The joy of Bentley's love was tinged with the anticipation of the challenges that lay ahead, challenges Bentley was determined to face head-on.

"I love you too." Raelynn said through tears as she leaned into kiss Bentley before he turned to head back to the car.

Seated in the car, Bentley pondered the best approach to address Cassidy. As he sat there, a strategy took shape in his mind. He decided to reach out to the diner, intending to speak with the manager. Bentley aimed to inquire about Cassidy's schedule and inform the manager that he needed to arrange a meeting with her.

The diner manager gave Bentley the green light for a meeting with Cassidy. He instructed Bentley to come by and request to be seated in Cassidy's section later in the evening when the restaurant was expected to be less busy.

Later that evening Bentley pulled into the diner. As he sat in the car contemplating on going in or just driving off and leaving it be, he could see Cassidy through the diner windows, as she gracefully moved table to table taking care of her customers.

Bentley knew despite the difficulty of this situation he had to go inside the diner, he just didn't know what he was going to say. It was awkward to him that she was the mother of his child, yet he didn't even remember her. It was awkward how she was his girlfriend's best friend. Bentley eventually pulled himself together and made his way inside the diner where he was greeted by the hostess whose eyes grew wide in shock. As Bentley made his way closer to the hostess, he could feel her eye fucking him making the situation even more tense.

"Hey, it's just one. Can you put me in Cassidy Brooks section?" Bentley said nervously.

As the hostess led him to a back corner booth, he caught a glimpse of Cassidy attending to a table. As Bentley sat down, he continued to stare Cassidy down, trying to connect the dots on how they had met, but nothing was registering.

As Cassidy was attending to her table Bentley saw her look back towards where he was sitting, and she rolled her eyes. Bentley watched her whole bodily expression change in mere seconds. He saw her go from happy and cheerful to dreadful.

After a few moments of Bentley waiting, Cassidy finally made her way to his table. "Why are you here?" Cassidy asked with strong tone of disdain in her voice.

Bentley looked up at Cassidy and starred nervously into her green eyes. He couldn't help but to realize that Skylar got his eyes from his mother.

"I know." Bentley said nervously.

Bentley could instantly tell that Cassidy had no idea of what he was talking about as he watched the confusion creep across her angry face.

"You know what?" Cassidy said with a confused but angry tone as she folded her arms.

Bentley took a deep breath as he prepared to lay the hidden truth out. "I know that Skylar is my son." Bentley said nervously as he could feel his heart beating in his throat.

Cassidy looked like she had seen a ghost when those words rolled off Bentley's lips. She took a step back and stared at him as her eyes began to water.

"You need to leave right now." Cassidy said as her voice began cracking through the tears.

"Cassidy, I'm not leaving until we talk. I called your boss before I got here, to make sure this was ok. Hell, I'll give you the money for the tips you miss but we need to talk." Bentley said as stared at her with a serious but scared expression on his face.

"I don't need your money. We're not some charity case." Cassidy shouted as she turned to walk away.

As she started to walk away, Bentley noticed her boss looking their way as he gave Cassidy a nod to return to Bentley's table. As Cassidy made her return to the table, she aggressively slid into the booth seat across from Bentley. Bentley could tell that this moment felt forced for her by her body language and actions. Also, by the way she was avoiding making eye contact.

"You said you wanted to talk, so talk." Cassidy said with an attitude as she crossed her arms looking away from Bentley.

Bentley took a deep breath, trying to find the right words amidst the tension that hung in the air. The clinking of dishes and murmurs of other patrons created a background hum to their conversation.

"Cassidy, I honestly don't even know where to begin other than, have you always known that I was Skylar's father?" Bentley asked as he wasn't sure how to navigate getting to the bottom of this.

Bentley could tell that this was a lot for Cassidy to take in as he could visibly see the inner struggle she was having as her eyes watered up with tears of realization that there was no more hiding the truth.

"Yes, Bentley. I have known since day one of finding out I was pregnant that you were the father. The question I want to ask right now is how the hell did you find out?" Cassidy said with anger still apparent in her voice.

"It doesn't matter how I found out. All that matters is that I now know. Why didn't you have me subpoenaed for a paternity test? Do you know how many women have done that too me since my rise to fame?" Bentley said as frustration began to settle in.

"And that comment right there is exactly why I didn't. I knew my son would be better off without an egotistical fuckboy father in his life. Listen to these words carefully and understand them, we don't need you Bentley." Cassidy said as her angry tone was becoming more potent.

Bentley winced at Cassidy's words, the harsh truth cutting through the air. He hadn't expected a warm welcome, but the intensity of her resentment caught him off guard. He leaned back in the booth, grappling with the reality of the situation.

"I don't mean to come off as an insensitive asshole, but the reality is, you may actually need me. There's a significant likelihood that I'm a perfect match for Skylar's bone marrow transplant." Bentley paused briefly before continuing, "Ironically, that's how I discovered Skylar is my son. I attempted to do a good deed for a stranger I believed I didn't know, only to have my world flipped upside down when I found out I have a five-year-old son with that very stranger." Bentley pleaded with frustration apparent in his voice.

Bentley could tell that he struck a chord as tears began to free fall from Cassidy's eyes. It almost made him feel bad for his word choices. The reason he didn't feel bad is because he knew that these were words that needed to be said no matter how insensitive they may seem.

"There you go again. The same inconsiderate self-centered asshole I met the night we hooked up. You don't even fucking remember me yet just because you've found out that you're my son's sperm donor and can potentially save his life, that it gives you some almighty right to enter our lives. That's comical" Cassidy pleaded as she began to chuckle through her angry tone.

"Cassidy he's my son too and I deserve the right to know my son. Hell, he deserves the right to know his father too. Like it or not he is our son Cassidy." Bentley pleaded.

Cassidy scoffed, the bitterness in her tone cutting through the air. "Our son? He's my son, Bentley. You don't get to claim that title just because you found out you share some DNA with him."

"Cassidy don't be that bitter. You never gave me the chance, nor the opportunity to be a father in the past five years." Bentley pleaded.

Cassidy's eyes bore into Bentley's, her anger still smoldering as she listened to his pleas. The air in the diner seemed thick with tension, and Bentley could feel the weight of the past five years pressing on his shoulders.

"Don't play the victim here, Bentley. You can't honestly tell me you would have been interested in being a father. You were living your most glamorous life, different girl every night. The ability to go and come as you pleased. So not subpoenaing you was for the best for all of us." Cassidy retorted; her voice laced with bitterness.

"Cassidy, what did I ever do to you for you to hate me this much. Please enlighten me since I don't even recall meeting you. So please explain." Bentley asked as he wanted to finally connect the dot on how he knew Cassidy.

Cassidy's voice quivered as she began, memories of the past surfacing in the vulnerable lines of her face.

"It was the first time you ever performed at Electric. You called me up on stage, when I got up there, I could tell you were on another planet, but I didn't care. You were hot, every female that night would have died to be in my shoes."

Her words echoed with a mixture of bitterness and lingering desire. Bentley listened, his expression unreadable.

"You gave me a lap dance, and when you were done, you told your team to keep me backstage until you got done."

Cassidy's eyes narrowed, reliving the surreal experience. Bentley shifted uncomfortably, his eyes avoiding hers.

"That's when you came and told me about this frat party your friend was throwing and you wanted me to go, so I went."

Cassidy's pacing slowed, her gaze piercing through the recounting of that fateful night.

"We got to the frat party, and you led me to a room where we had sex."

Bentley winced, the weight of the consequences hanging in the air. Cassidy's hand gestured, recreating the path that led to their entanglement.

"After we had sex, it was like you forgot all about me and left me at this frat party all alone, not knowing a single soul while you went and did your own thing."

Cassidy's bitterness reverberated in the words, and Bentley couldn't meet her accusing gaze.

"I left and didn't want to have anything to do with you since. When I found I was pregnant, I knew it was yours, but I knew I would be better off without you in the picture, so I painted you out of the picture."

Cassidy's hands moved with deliberate strokes, as if erasing an unwanted memory. Bentley's jaw clenched, a mix of regret and acknowledgment in his eyes.

"When everyone asked who the father was, I didn't lie. I told everyone the truth, I went to a party and had a one-night stand with someone that I didn't know because honestly, I didn't know you."

Bentley's gaze fell, the admission of his own ignorance hanging heavily between them.

"I knew who I wanted you to be, but you were the furthest thing from that, and I don't regret it. Given the choice, I'd do it all over."

Cassidy's defiance clashed with the vulnerability in her eyes. Bentley's silence spoke volumes.

"I still don't want not a damn thing from you. This conversation I don't even want to be having. Life was so much better without you knowing."

Cassidy's arms crossed protectively, a defensive barrier against the resurgence of emotions. Bentley sat still, absorbing the impact of her words.

"I will say this though, you gave me the greatest gift ever when you made me a mother, and I wouldn't want to change that for nothing."

Cassidy's voice softened, a genuine note of gratitude breaking through the layers of resentment. Bentley's eyes met hers, a complex mix of regret and acknowledgment flickering in their depths.

Bentley felt a whirlwind of emotions crashing over him as Cassidy's words echoed in the dimly lit diner. He had unknowingly left a mark on her life, a mark that had shaped the course of hers and, as he was discovering, his own life as well.

For a moment, silence hung heavy between them, broken only by the distant sounds of clinking dishes and subdued chatter from other patrons. Bentley's mind raced, grappling with the reality of his past actions and the consequences that had unfolded without his knowledge.

"Cassidy, I had no idea. I genuinely don't remember any of it, and I'm truly sorry for the pain I've caused you," Bentley finally spoke, his voice carrying a mix of regret and sincerity.

Cassidy's gaze remained fixed on him, her eyes revealing a complex interplay of emotions. "Sorry doesn't change the past, Bentley. It doesn't erase the nights I spent wondering if I made the right choice, if Skylar deserved to know his father," she responded, her tone softened but resolute.

Bentley nodded, absorbing the weight of her words. "I understand that, Cassidy. But now that I know about Skylar, I want to be there for him. I want to be a part of his life, to make up for lost time," he pleaded, a newfound determination in his eyes.

Cassidy sighed, her shoulders slumping as if she carried the burden of their shared history. "You can't just waltz into his life and expect everything to be okay, Bentley. Skylar has grown up without you, without even knowing you exist. And I've worked hard to make sure he's had a stable and loving environment."

As their conversation concluded somewhat amicably, Bentley made his way out the diner. Before exiting he looked back at Cassidy, and he couldn't help but feel guilt wash over him.

"Cassidy, I'd like to officially meet Skylar as his father and get to know him." Bentley said nervously as he looked back at Cassidy and said before exiting the diner.

"No, it's not happening. Now leave." Cassidy said with a stern tone as Bentley exited the diner.

Despite the overwhelming emotions of the night, Bentley was determined not to back down from getting to know his son. However, he recognized that both he and Cassidy needed time to process everything, making it clear that this discussion would need to be postponed for another day.

29

Don't Let This Get Ugly

The following day after sleeping on the confrontation with Cassidy, Bentley was back at the diner. He was back with a mission to carve a role for himself into Skylar's life.

The atmosphere inside the diner was markedly different from the previous night. Bentley could sense the weight of the unresolved conversation hanging in the air as he approached the hostess. His demeanor, however, reflected a newfound determination.

"Hey, I'm here to see Cassidy again," Bentley stated, a firmness in his voice that matched his resolve.

The hostess, remembering him from the previous night, eyed him with a mix of curiosity and skepticism, as she was biting at her bottom lip. Nevertheless, she led Bentley to the same back corner booth from the night before.

As Bentley settled into the booth, he couldn't shake the lingering tension that surrounded him. He glanced around the diner, searching for any sign of Cassidy. The clinking of dishes and the subdued chatter of patrons served as a backdrop to his mounting anticipation.

After what felt like an eternity, Cassidy appeared, making her way toward Bentley with a guarded expression. The air crackled with unspoken emotions as she took her seat across from him. The defensive barrier from the night before was still evident in the crossed arms and wary eyes.

"Bentley, we had this conversation already. What more is there to say?" Cassidy's voice carried a mix of exhaustion and defiance.

"Cassidy, I want to get to know my son." Bentley pleaded firmly.

"And I said no. It not happening." Cassidy said aggressively as she slammed her hand on the table.

"Cassidy, come on now be reasonable right now. Don't do this. Don't let this get ugly." Bentley said.

Bentley held Cassidy's gaze, his eyes pleading for understanding as he leaned back, assessing Cassidy's demeanor.

"Is that a threat? Talking about being reasonable. Bentley, you show up out of nowhere, claiming to be Skylar's father, and you expect me to just accept that? It doesn't work like that." Cassidy said as she aggressively slid into the booth across from Bentley.

"No, that's not a threat. That's a promise. I will not hesitate to get my lawyers involved. We can either do this the easy way or the hard way, the balls in your court you decide. I want to get to know my son." Bentley said with a serious tone and look on his face.

Cassidy's eyes widened at Bentley's stern words. The threat of legal action hung heavy in the air, intensifying the already charged atmosphere. The diner seemed to quiet down, as if the universe itself was holding its breath, waiting for Cassidy's response.

She leaned back, her defensive posture giving way to a mixture of anger and frustration. "Bentley, please don't do this. I'm begging you. Just let it be. We're just fine without you. Plus, you think bringing lawyers into this will make everything right? Bentley, this isn't just about paperwork. This is about Skylar's life, his emotions, and the trust he places in me."

Bentley's resolve softened as he witnessed the genuine distress in Cassidy's plea. He took a deep breath, trying to find a middle ground amidst the emotional storm that surrounded them.

"Cassidy, I don't want to make this harder for you or Skylar. I just want a chance to be a part of his life. I understand it's complicated, and I'm willing to work through it with you. But I can't let the opportunity slip away. Skylar deserves to know his father and I deserve to know my son," Bentley said, his tone more empathetic.

"Bentley, please just let this go. Please, I'm begging you." Cassidy pleaded with her voice cracking as the tears began to fall down her face.

"Cassidy, I can't walk away from this. Missing five years of my son's life is tearing me apart. I've missed so many milestones, and I refuse to miss any more. I can't be the absent father, it's just not who I am. I could choose to leave right now, but I won't. I can't live with that. So, it's your call—either we find a way to make this work, or I involve lawyers. The choice is yours," Bentley pleaded, his eyes reflecting the pain, guilt, and shame he felt.

Cassidy's tears mirrored the conflict within her. Bentley, sensing the fragility of the moment, softened his approach.

"Cassidy, I understand your fears, and I don't want to hurt you or Skylar. But we can't ignore the reality here. I want to be a part of Skylar's life, to make up for lost time. Please, give me a chance to prove that I can be the father he deserves," Bentley implored, his voice gentle but resolute.

Cassidy's tear-streaked face softened as Bentley's words sank in. The weight of the unresolved past hung heavily in the air, but there was a flicker of hope amidst the tension.

"Fine." Cassidy whispered, wiping away tears with the back of her hand. "But if we're doing this, we're doing this my and without lawyers."

Bentley's eyes softened, gratitude and determination glinting within them. "Thank you, Cassidy. I'll respect your terms, and I promise, I'll do everything in my power to make this as smooth as possible for Skylar."

"Okay, well, my terms are as follows." Cassidy's voice held a mix of determination and caution. Bentley leaned forward, attentive.

"You will not, under any circumstance, tell Raelynn that Skylar is your son," she declared, her gaze unwavering. Bentley nodded, acknowledging the gravity of her first stipulation.

"I will do that when I am comfortable," Cassidy continued, her hand gesturing subtly as if laying down invisible boundaries. Bentley respected her need for control in this delicate situation.

"This is a forever stipulation," she emphasized, the weight of the words hanging in the air. Skylar's privacy was non-negotiable.

"Skylar will never be put into the media spotlight." Cassidy's gaze bore into Bentley's, ensuring he grasped the significance of keeping their lives private.

"I will allow for you to tell your parents," She conceded, a slight softening in her expression. Bentley recognized this as a gesture of trust.

"And I will allow for them to meet him." Cassidy's eyes held a mix of caution and consideration, gauging Bentley's reaction to her concessions.

"I will determine when you meet him," she asserted, regaining control of the narrative. Bentley, though eager, nodded in agreement, accepting her terms.

"I will be the one to tell him in your presence that you are his father," Cassidy declared, her protective instincts evident. Bentley listened, realizing the weight of the responsibility Cassidy was entrusting him with.

"And, for the love of God, don't expect him to call you dad right away," she pleaded, her tone softening. Cassidy's concern for Skylar's emotional well-being was palpable.

"I need you to understand Skylar is always and will always be a top priority." Cassidy's final words hung in the air, a reminder of the central focus of their agreement. Bentley met her gaze with a solemn nod.

"Are we clear, Bentley?" Cassidy's question echoed in the silence, the terms of their agreement settling between them like unspoken promises. Bentley took a deep breath, fully comprehending the gravity of the path ahead.

"Yes, Cassidy. Crystal clear," he affirmed, understanding the significance of each condition she had set forth.

In the aftermath of Cassidy's terms, Bentley took a moment to absorb the weight of the agreement. He could see the mix of vulnerability and strength in Cassidy's eyes, the silent plea for understanding. The diner's atmosphere seemed to echo the intensity of their conversation, each word carving a path into the uncharted territory of Skylar's future.

"Thank you, Cassidy. I'll respect your terms, and I promise, I'll do everything in my power to do right by Skylar," Bentley assured, a genuine sense of gratitude emanating from him. He was determined to honor Cassidy's conditions and prove himself worthy of Skylar's life.

"You better or you want have to worry about lawyers or seeing him again after I'm finished with you." Cassidy assured.

Bentley nodded solemnly, acknowledging the gravity of Cassidy's warning. He knew that the journey ahead wouldn't be easy, and gaining Cassidy's trust was just the first step. As they navigated this delicate dance of co-parenting, he was acutely aware that any misstep could shatter the fragile foundation they were building.

As Cassidy wiped the remaining traces of tears from her cheeks, she pulled out her waitress pad handing it to Bentley. "Here write your number down so I can call you when I am ready for this next step."

Bentley took the pad and pen, carefully jotting down his phone number. He handed it back to Cassidy, who accepted it with a nod. The exchange felt like a tentative bridge between two worlds, a connection forged through the written digits on a small piece of paper.

"Thank you," Cassidy whispered, her gaze sincere. Bentley could see a hint of exhaustion in her eyes, but also a glimmer of relief. They were embarking on an uncharted journey, but the first step had been taken, and an understanding had been reached.

As Cassidy jetted off to assist other customer, Bentley got up to leave the diner. Before leaving the table Bentley placed two-thousand dollars under a napkin for Cassidy to find when she cleaned the table. He knew Cassidy didn't want his money, hell she didn't even want him in the picture, but he felt it was the least he could do.

As Bentley left the diner that day, he couldn't shake the mixture of emotions swirling within him. Excitement, anxiety, and a profound sense of responsibility weighed on his shoulders. The road ahead was uncertain, and the challenges of co-parenting with Cassidy were bound to test the strength of their fragile agreement.

30

A Moment to Remember

That following Friday morning, Bentley got woken up by Cassidy calling his phone. Bentley was honestly shocked to see her calling him, it must have meant that she was ready to put a plan in motion for Bentley to meet Skylar as his dad officially.

When Bentley answered the call, he could sense Cassidy's nervousness from the tone of her voice.

"Hey, Bentley. Skylar finishes school at three-fifteen. Would you be interested in meeting me at the diner around two forty-five, and we can go together to pick him up from school? After that, we can take him for ice cream and break the news that you're his dad," Cassidy suggested, her voice trembling.

Bentley's heart raced with a mix of anticipation and anxiety as he listened to Cassidy's proposal. The gravity of the moment struck him— meeting Skylar officially as his father. He knew this time meeting Skylar was going to be very important. Very emotional. This meeting with Skylar was more than a simple introduction; it was a profound, life-altering event.

"Cassidy, that sounds perfect. I'll be at the diner at two forty-five. Thank you for allowing this." Bentley replied, his voice reflecting a mix of gratitude and anticipation.

Cassidy sighed deeply before responding, "Bentley, after thinking on this the past couple days, I must admit you were right. It isn't fair that I keep Skylar from his dad, or his dad from him. I just hope you don't let me or my little boy down."

"I'm very glad you had that realization, and I promise I'm not going to disappoint you guys." Bentley said as he tried reassuring Cassidy this was in fact the right decision.

"We'll see. Have you told anyone? Your parents? Raelynn?" Cassidy asked as her tone shifted towards a more serious note.

Bentley hesitated for a moment, grappling with the weight of the truth he was about to unveil. "No, not yet. My parents are out of town on vacation, and I haven't had the chance to talk to them. As for Raelynn, I've been avoiding her," Bentley admitted, his voice going lower.

Cassidy's voice peaked with surprise. "Avoiding her? Why?"

Bentley sighed, the burden of his secret pressing upon him. "I'm afraid I might unintentionally spill the beans, you know? Tell her about Skylar before you get the chance to do it. I don't want to jeopardize the agreement we have, Cassidy. It's crucial that you're the one to tell Raelynn. And hopefully it's soon. I know you'll do it when you're ready and I'm on your clock, but I can't keep avoiding Rae in fear I might jeopardize our agreement."

Cassidy took a moment to absorb Bentley's explanation. She understood the delicate nature of the situation and the need for careful timing. "I get it, Bentley. This is a big deal for everyone involved. But I promise, once Skylar knows about you, I'll talk to Raelynn. Just try to keep it together a little longer."

"Thanks, Cassidy. I appreciate your understanding. This is just as nerve-wracking for me as it is for you," Bentley admitted, feeling a mixture of emotions.

As the day unfolded, Bentley found himself glancing at the clock more frequently than usual. The minutes seemed to drag on, each passing moment carrying the weight of anticipation. Finally, it was time to head to the diner.

Bentley arrived a little early and as he was sitting in his dad's truck scrolling on his phone, Cassidy pulled up beside him in what appeared to be a beat up 2004 Honda Civic that looked like it had more days in its rearview than it did out its windshield.

Bentley looked up, a smile playing on his lips as Cassidy parked the worn-out Civic next to his dad's truck. She stepped out, glancing at the truck with a raised eyebrow.

"Nice ride," Cassidy said with a hint of snarkiness in her voice.

Bentley chuckled as Cassidy slid in the passenger seat, "Well, it's my dad's, He's letting my drive it while I'm in town."

As they drove to Skylar's school, the atmosphere inside the truck was thick with tension. Bentley couldn't help but feel the weight of the upcoming revelation pressing down on them.

The radio played softly in the background, an attempt to fill the silence that seemed to stretch on forever. Bentley stole a glance at Cassidy, noticing the way she gripped the edge of her seat. Her knuckles were turning white, a clear sign of the nerves bubbling beneath the surface.

"Everything okay?" Bentley asked, breaking the silence.

Cassidy sighed, her shoulders slumping. "Yeah, just anxious, you know? This whole thing is surreal. I never thought this would be happening."

Bentley nodded, understanding the sentiment. "I get it. It's a lot to take in for both of us."

The rest of the ride continued in a somewhat awkward silence. Bentley couldn't shake the feeling that the air in the truck was charged with anticipation, both of them bracing for the unknown. Occasionally, their eyes would meet, and a half-smile or a nod would pass between them, silent reassurances that they were in this together.

As they pulled into the parking lot of the school, kids were already starting to file out of the building with their classes as parents were meeting their kids and walking them to the cars.

"So do you want me to park, or do you want me to stay in the car?" Bentley asked.

"Stay in the car it'll take just a second." Cassidy said with her nerves showing by the tone in her voice as she got out the car.

Cassidy walked to the sidewalk and as she reached the sidewalk, Skylar, who seemed full of energy came running up to his mother. He wrapped his arms around her legs, embracing her in a tiny hug. Together, hand in hand, Cassidy and Skylar walked back to the car, the bond between them evident in the tender connection they shared.

"Skylar, you remember Bentley from Aunt Rae-Rae's, right?" Cassidy asked.

"Yeah, he played with me while you two were in the bathroom talking." Skylar replied.

"Well Bentley was nice enough to give me a ride to pick you up today because my car messed up." Cassidy said.

As Cassidy and Skylar walked back to the car Bentley couldn't help but watch with amazement. He couldn't believe that was a living and breathing part of him.

Skylar's eyes widened as he looked up at Bentley. His eyes big and blue were filled with innocence but held a mixture of curiosity and recognition in his gaze. Bentley couldn't help but feel a surge of emotion as Skylar studied him, feeling a lump forming in his throat, realizing the gravity of the moment. He was about to reveal a truth that could reshape Skylar's understanding of family and identity.

"Hey, Skylar. How's it going?" Bentley greeted, trying to keep his tone casual despite the whirlwind of emotions inside him.

Skylar studied Bentley for a moment before returning the smile, "Hi, Bentley! Thanks for driving Mommy today."

Bentley chuckled, "Anytime, buddy. Ready for an adventure?"

Skylar's eyes sparkled with excitement, "Yeah! What are we gonna do?"

Bentley exchanged a glance with Cassidy, both sharing a moment of silent acknowledgment that this was the juncture where their lives would take a new turn. Bentley took a deep breath, his voice steady as he began, "Well, Skylar, the adventure starts with some ice cream. How does that sound?"

Skylar's face lit up with delight, "Ice cream? Yay!"

The tension in the car eased slightly as they drove to the nearby ice cream shop. Bentley couldn't help but admire the way Skylar's eyes widened with excitement at the sight of the colorful array of ice cream flavors. As they sat in a cozy corner booth, Bentley contemplated how to navigate the upcoming conversation.

After a few bites of ice cream, Cassidy approached the task at hand, breaking the news to Skylar.

"Skylar, there's something special I need to tell you," Cassidy began, her voice shaky but gentle. Skylar looked at her with curious eyes, still unaware of the profound revelation awaiting him.

Cassidy took a deep breath, glancing at Bentley as if she were looking for reassurance before continuing, "You know how I haven't wanted to talk about your dad much? Well, what if I told you that you have met him a couple of times now?" There was a pause before Cassidy continued, "What if I told you that you were sitting beside him eating ice cream right now?"

Skylar's eyes widened with surprise, and he turned to look at Bentley. Bentley, feeling a mix of nerves and excitement, offered a warm smile to Skylar. Bentley could feel the weight of the revelation in the air as Cassidy took another deep breath.

"Hey son," Bentley greeted, a nervous undertone in his voice as he gazed at Skylar. It was as if he had stepped into a time machine, seeing his own five-year-old reflection in the mirror. The familiarity was uncanny, observing Skylar display mannerisms so similar to his own, all while realizing they had never been a part of each other's lives until this moment.

"That's your dad, Sky!" Cassidy interjected, as tears began to form in her eyes.

Skylar's eyes widened even more, his innocent gaze switching between Cassidy and Bentley. The realization slowly settled in, and Skylar's face transformed into a mixture of awe and excitement.

"Dad?" Skylar said, the word looked foreign yet strangely comforting on his lips.

Bentley nodded, a mixture of emotions playing on his face. "Yeah, buddy. I'm your dad."

"But how? Your aunt Rae's boyfriend." Skylar said with a hint of confusion mixed in with the excitement in his voice.

Bentley took a deep breath, trying to find the right words to explain the complex situation to Skylar. "It's a bit complicated, buddy. You see, sometimes families are made in unexpected ways. Your mom and I, we had a connection a long time ago, and you're the beautiful result of that connection."

Skylar's confusion lingered, but he seemed eager to understand. "So, you and Mom knew each other before?"

Bentley nodded, a soft smile on his face. "Yeah, sorta, a long time ago. Life took us on different paths, and thankfully they have crossed again because now here I am with you."

As Bentley and Skylar embraced their newfound connection, the day unfolded into a series of shared adventures. After the ice cream shop, they strolled through a nearby park, Skylar chattering animatedly about his friends, favorite toys, and the games he loved playing. Bentley, absorbing every detail of Skylar's world, couldn't help but marvel at the innocence and wonder contained in his son's simple joys.

The atmosphere inside the apartment was cozy but held the scent of struggles and resilience inside its tight space. As Bentley glanced around, he couldn't help but notice the worn-out furniture, faded curtains, and the dim lighting that painted the rooms. Cassidy, however, navigated the space with a sense of pride, making it a home for her and Skylar.

Skylar eagerly showed Bentley his collection of toys and drawings, each one a testament to the vibrant imagination of a five-year-old.

While Skylar dove into his backpack to retrieve his kindergarten homework, Bentley, felt an overwhelming sense of responsibility and love take over his body as he knelt to help Skylar with his homework.

The tiny kitchen table became a makeshift study space. Bentley marveled at Skylar's eagerness to learn and the way his eyes lit up with every correct answer. Bentley found himself transported back to his own childhood, a mixture of nostalgia and pride filling his heart as he assisted Skylar with the alphabet and simple arithmetic. It was a small but precious father-son moment, one Bentley hadn't anticipated but cherished, nonetheless.

As Bentley helped Skylar with his homework, he couldn't help but marvel at the pictures that adorned the apartment's walls. They captured Skylar's journey from infancy to the present, showcasing his growth, milestones, and the unwavering love Cassidy had showered upon him as a single mother.

The photos told a story of determination, love, and countless cherished moments. Skylar, in various stages of childhood, smiled back at Bentley from the frames. Each picture held a piece of their shared history, and Bentley couldn't help but feel a swell of emotion as he witnessed the tangible evidence of the life he had unknowingly been a huge part of.

Once Skylar completed his homework and had a light dinner, Cassidy ushered him to the bathroom for his bath. While Cassidy tended to Skylar in the bath, Bentley stayed in the living room continuing to look at the pictures of Skylar surrounding the walls of the tiny apartment. This time, he moved closer to the pictures, studying them with more attention.

Amid the pictures, Bentley's attention was drawn to one particular photograph. Skylar's first-ever baby picture. The image captured a moment of pure innocence, a tiny bundle cradled in Cassidy's arms. Bentley couldn't tear his eyes away from the snapshot that encapsulated the beginning of Skylar's journey. His son, in that tiny frame, represented a new chapter in Bentley's life—a chapter that had remained unwritten until now.

As Bentley stared at the photo, he felt a tidal wave of emotions crashing over him. Regret, for the moments he had missed; joy, for the chance to be a part of Skylar's future; and a profound sense of responsibility, knowing that his actions would shape Skylar's perception of family and fatherhood. The weight of that responsibility settled on Bentley's shoulders like a mantle, urging him to be the father Skylar deserved.

In that quiet moment, Cassidy reemerged into the living room. She stood there silently, observing Bentley as he lost himself in the memories captured by the photograph. Tears began to form in her eyes as she witnessed Bentley's emotions unfold. The vulnerability on Bentley's face was apparent, and Cassidy, too, felt the weight of the moment.

She cleared her throat, a subtle interruption that broke Bentley's reverie. The air in the room seemed to shift as Cassidy gently reminded Bentley that it was time to tuck Skylar into bed. The words hung in the air, carrying the unspoken acknowledgment of the depth of what had transpired that day.

Bentley reluctantly tore his gaze away from the baby picture, a mixture of emotions etched on his face. He followed Cassidy to Skylar's room, the walls adorned with more pictures capturing the essence of Skylar's childhood.

As they stood by Skylar's bedside, Bentley's gaze lingered on his son's peaceful expression. Skylar, wrapped in the security of sleep, seemed blissfully unaware of the seismic shift that had occurred in his life that day. Bentley, however, was acutely aware of the impact of his presence, his newfound role as Skylar's father.

Cassidy, still watching Bentley closely, sensed the internal struggle he was experiencing. She placed a hand on Bentley's shoulder, a gesture of understanding and support. Together, they whispered goodnight to Skylar, the room filled with a sense of shared responsibility and the promise of a new beginning.

After Skylar was tucked in and the room fell into a gentle hush, and Bentley went to leave because he didn't want to outwear his welcome. However, to Bentley's surprise Cassidy invited him to the living room.

"Don't go just yet. Take a seat on the couch, I have something I want to show you." Cassidy said as she walked to her room.

Bentley stood still by the door, in case he needed to make an exit, however when Cassidy returned from her room carrying a box, plopping down on the couch, Bentley joined.

"These are more of Skylar's baby pictures." Cassidy said as she opened up the box pulling out a photo album handing it to Bentley.

As Bentley opened the photo album the first picture he saw was a picture of Skylar naked as a jay bird with weight and full birth name that Bentley read out loud to himself "Skylar Jax Brooks. 8 pounds and 4 ounces."

"So, this photo must be his first baby picture and not that one." Bentley said as he looked up, pointing at the picture he was lost in moments ago.

Cassidy chuckled, "Yes, this is true first photo. I couldn't put this one on display for everyone to see though."

Bentley chuckled as he could slowly start to see the regret and the guilt dance in Cassidy's eyes.

"I love his name! Where did it come from?" Bentley asked trying to hide his emotions.

Cassidy smiled, "Honestly, I was just playing with names, and it stuck. Eventually we can talk about you signing his birth certificate and maybe changing his last name to yours."

"Cassidy I would love to sign the birth certificate and for him to have my last name, but I'm scared the media might catch wind of that." Bentley said with a hint of uncertainty in his voice. He wasn't expecting Cassidy's change in persona.

Cassidy smiled as she looked at Bentley, "If the media gets a hold of it then so be it. That's your son and your name deserves to be on that birth certificate too. If not for you I wouldn't...we wouldn't have that beautiful baby boy in there."

Bentley was taken aback as he was a bit startled by Cassidy's shift in demeanor towards him. "Thank you, Cassidy, but why the sudden change?"

Cassidy's grin faded as she poured her feelings out. "I was mad at you for so long, without even knowing why. I wanted to hate you, to keep you away from our lives. But when you came into the diner and I saw the hurt in your eyes, I felt guilty. You deserved to know about Skylar, no matter how angry I was. If I had sought you out when I first found out I was pregnant, who knows where we'd be now. Maybe we could have been a family living somewhere tropical, raising Skylar together. All I know is you're here now, and that's what matters."

She paused, her emotions welling up. "I can't change the past, neither can you. I'd love to give you back the first five years of Skylar's life, but I can't. I can only show you pictures and hope you stick around as he continues to grow. I want our son to be happy. Today, when he found out you were his father, that's the happiest I've seen him in a long time. It stung, knowing I held back on his happiness by keeping you both in the dark. It hurt when you said you were a perfect match for his bone marrow transplant, and I wasn't. I've been there every step of the way, keeping him safe. Yet, the one thing I couldn't do was save his life if he needed the bone marrow, and you could. It didn't feel fair, but that's my fault for not telling you, and I can't apologize enough," Cassidy confessed, tears filling her eyes.

Cassidy's words even made Bentley began to tear up. He could hear just how hurt she was. He could also hear the guilt that she felt. He was just glad that she was opening up and telling him.

"Cassidy it's okay. You want somewhere tropical to raise our son I can make that happen. I know you said you don't want my money but if it'll make you and my son happy, I will do it. Ever since I found out I was Skylar's dad this protective instinct has come out of nowhere. Like there's not a damn thing in this world that I will not do for my son to see him happy or you for that matter because you are the mother of my child." Bentley pleaded.

"Bentley that's a nice gesture but no thank you. I don't need the money. Just be there for your son that's all I'll ever need." Cassidy said as she was wiping tears from her eyes still.

Bentley looked around the apartment before responding, "No offense, me getting you out of this dump would be me being there for my son."

After Bentley and Cassidy's heart to heart the night pressed on and Cassidy shared more stories, more pictures, and Bentley found himself engrossed in the narrative of Skylar's life. Each photograph, each anecdote, was a puzzle piece contributing to the story of a family reuniting.

As Bentley prepared to leave, Cassidy gave Bentley the approval to pick Skylar up from school Monday as she handed him a couple of photographs, tangible memories to carry with him. Bentley held them with care, knowing that they represented not just Skylar's past but also the beginning of his journey as Skylar's father.

31
The Heart of the Matter

Monday morning arrived in a whirlwind for Bentley, who found himself navigating a world of emotions as he embraced his new role in fatherhood. Excitement and trepidation intertwined, and the inability to share these feelings with Raelynn weighed heavily on him. He had to keep his emotions hidden, a challenging task during such profound changes.

It didn't help matters that Raelynn was nagging at him. Raelynn sensed a shift in their relationship, feeling a wedge growing between them. Despite spending a lot of time together, Bentley's recent emotional distance raised concerns. She wanted him to open up about what was on his mind, sensing an internal struggle beneath his surface.

Despite the urge to confide in Raelynn, Bentley remained steadfast in honoring the agreement he made with Cassidy. The delicate balance between newfound fatherhood and the complexities of his relationship with Raelynn tested Bentley's resilience.

The day unfolded as Bentley navigated his work responsibilities, the anticipation building as the clock ticked closer to the moment he would pick Skylar up from school. The photographs Cassidy had given him were safely tucked into his wallet, a constant reminder of the new chapter in his life.

As the school bell rang, Bentley parked his dad's truck near the school, eager yet nervous about meeting Skylar in the pickup line. As the children poured out of the building, Bentley spotted Skylar among them, his eyes searching for the familiar face.

Skylar's face lit up with recognition as he spotted Bentley. With a backpack bouncing on his small shoulders, Skylar rushed towards the truck, the excitement evident in his every step. Bentley opened the door, and Skylar hopped in, his eyes sparkling with joy.

"Hey, Bentley!" Skylar greeted, his enthusiasm contagious.

"Hey, buddy! How was school today?" Bentley asked, a genuine smile on his face.

Skylar began recounting his day, animatedly sharing stories about his friends, a new drawing he made, and the adventures of the playground. Bentley listened with rapt attention, savoring every detail of Skylar's life.

"Sky, I got some people I want you to meet." Bentley said with nervousness apparent in his voice. Bentley could sense the curiosity growing within Skylar before he continued, "I call them mom and dad."

Skylar's eyes widened with surprise and curiosity, and a smile spread across his face. "Really, Bentley? You mean, like, my grandparents?"

Bentley nodded, his heart pounding with a mix of nervousness and excitement. "Yeah, exactly. I haven't told them about you yet but what do you say we do it together? Maybe grab a quick snack while were there too?"

Skylar's eyes widened even more, and he nodded enthusiastically. "Sure, Bentley! I'd love to meet them! What do they like to eat? Do they like ice cream?"

Bentley chuckled at Skylar's excitement. "Well, I'm not sure about their favorite foods, but I'm pretty sure they'd love to spend time with you. And hey, if they have ice cream, that's a bonus, right?"

Skylar's grin widened, and Bentley drove towards his parents' house, Skylar chattering away about what kind of ice cream he hoped they would have. The anticipation filled the truck as they approached Bentley's childhood home.

As Bentley and Skylar pulled up at his parents' house, he noticed Cameron was already there, chatting with Faye and Steve in the driveway. Skylar, unaware of the dynamics, hopped out of the truck, eager to meet Bentley's mom and dad.

"Fuck," Bentley muttered quietly as he stepped out of the truck. Cassidy had greenlit introducing Skylar to his parents only, but now, with Bentley's best friend unexpectedly present, there was no concealing Skylar, who had already eagerly hopped out the truck.

Approaching Skylar at the truck's front, Bentley knelt down to offer some reassurance, noticing Skylar's growing nervousness. "It's going to be alright, buddy. They're going to love you. And guess what? You also get to meet your Uncle Cam, but let's keep that between us, okay?" Bentley suggested, receiving a nod of agreement from Skylar. "Your mom told me I could only introduce you to my parents, and I wasn't expecting him to be here," Bentley explained.

Bentley took a deep breath, realizing the complexity of the situation. He didn't want to create tension, but he also couldn't hide Skylar's presence. As they approached the group, Cameron turned, a curious expression on his face.

"Bentley, who's this little guy?" Cameron asked, extending a hand towards Skylar.

Bentley smiled nervously, "Mom, Dad, Cam, this is Skylar. He is, uh my son. He is your grandson and your nephew Cam."

Faye's eyes widened with surprise, a mix of shock and joy reflected on her face. She exchanged a quick glance with Steve, who raised his eyebrows in disbelief. Bentley could sense a swirl of emotions in the air – anticipation, curiosity, and a touch of apprehension.

"Skylar, this is your Grandma Faye and Grandpa Steve," Bentley introduced with a warm smile, his hand gently resting on Skylar's shoulder. "And this here is your Uncle Cam," he added, gesturing towards Cameron.

Faye recovered quickly from the initial shock, a wide smile breaking across her face. "Oh my goodness! Bentley, he's adorable!" She approached Skylar and crouched down to his eye level. "Hello, sweetheart! It's so wonderful to meet you."

Steve, though taken aback, managed a smile as well. "Hey there, sport. Bentley, when were you planning on telling us about this little guy?" There was a mix of curiosity and mild reproach in Steve's voice.

Bentley hesitated for a moment, meeting Steve's disappointed gaze. "I... I wanted to, Dad. It's just been a lot to process, and things have been complicated the last week since learning of his existence. Plus, you guys were out of town on vacation, and this isn't news you drop over the phone."

Cameron, sensing the tension, decided to break the ice. "Well, little man, welcome to the family! I'm your Uncle Cam. We're gonna have some good times together, alright?" He offered a fist bump to Skylar, who reciprocated with a shy grin.

As the awkwardness began to dissipate, Faye took charge, her maternal instincts kicking in. "Come on, let's head inside. I'm sure you're hungry, Skylar. We've got some snacks waiting for you."

Bentley felt a mix of relief and nervousness as they all moved towards the house. The dynamics had shifted, and he hoped that the love and warmth of his family would envelop Skylar in acceptance.

Steve, though still wearing a thoughtful expression, put a hand on Bentley's shoulder. Squeezing tightly sending a pain throughout Bentley's body, "We'll talk about this later, son, but for now, let's focus on making Skylar feel at home."

Inside the house, Bentley, Skylar, and Cameron followed Faye, who was leading the way to the cozy living room. The air was filled with a mix of emotions, and Bentley couldn't shake the feeling that he was standing on the precipice of a significant shift in his family dynamics.

As they settled on the comfortable sofas, Skylar was still absorbing the new surroundings. Faye disappeared into the kitchen, promising to bring some snacks for Skylar. Bentley took a deep breath, feeling the weight of the unspoken tension in the room.

Cameron, ever the peacemaker, tried to lighten the mood. "So, Skylar, tell us a bit about yourself. What's your favorite subject in school?"

Skylar, though a bit shy, warmed up to Cameron's friendly tone. "Um, I really like art! And recess is super fun. I have this friend, Jake, and we play superheroes every day."

Cameron chuckled, exchanging a glance with Bentley. "That sounds awesome, buddy! Maybe you can teach me some superhero moves later."

Faye returned with a tray of snacks, a mix of cookies and fruit. She placed it on the coffee table, smiling warmly at Skylar. "Help yourself, sweetheart. We're so happy to have you here."

Skylar's eyes widened at the array of treats before him. "Wow, thank you!" he exclaimed, reaching for a cookie.

Bentley, still processing the evening's events, took a moment to observe the scene. His parents, though surprised, were making an effort to welcome Skylar, and Cameron was doing his best to keep the atmosphere light.

As they indulged in snacks and casual conversation, Bentley's mind raced with thoughts of how to navigate the delicate situation with Raelynn. He knew he needed to talk to her, to explain the complexity of the circumstances and reassure her of his commitment to their relationship. The weight of the unspoken words lingered, and Bentley felt torn between the various aspects of his life that were colliding.

After some time, Faye turned her attention to Bentley. "Bentley, sweetheart, let's have a talk. Skylar, you can stay here with Uncle Cam and enjoy the snacks, alright?"

Bentley nodded, exchanging a glance with Cameron, who gave him an encouraging smile. As Faye led Bentley into another room, Steve followed behind.

Once inside the room, the atmosphere became charged with tension. Faye gestured for Bentley to take a seat, and Steve leaned against the closed door, his arms crossed. Bentley could feel the weight of their expectations and the unspoken questions hanging in the air.

Faye wasted no time, her expression stern. "Bentley, care to explain what's going on? You bring a child home, and we find out he's your son and our grandson all in one go?"

Bentley swallowed hard, feeling a lump forming in his throat. He tried to find the right words, the words that would convey the complexity of the situation without causing further disappointment.

"I... Mom, I never expected things to unfold like this," Bentley admitted, his eyes fixed on the floor. "I just found out about Skylar a week ago. Cassidy, his mother, confirmed it and it's been a whirlwind since then. I haven't even shared it with Raelynn because Cassidy, who happens to be her best friend, wants to break the news. It's straining things between Raelynn and me because I want to open up to her about all of this, but I can't. She senses the distance and knows something's not right, and I'm drowning trying to navigate through all of it, Mom."

Faye's stern expression softened, sympathy replacing some of her initial disappointment. She exchanged a concerned glance with Steve, who unfolded his arms, leaning against the doorframe with a more thoughtful expression.

"Bentley, you're a grown man now, but you're still our son. We want to understand what's going on," Faye said, her voice gentle but firm. "Start from the beginning. How did this happen? And why are you keeping it a secret from Raelynn?"

Bentley steadied himself, his breath deliberate, as he began to share the unexpected turn of events.

"Cassidy, Skylar's mother, and I crossed paths at a frat party during the early stages of my rise to fame. What I didn't know then was that our brief encounter resulted in her getting pregnant. However, she chose not to inform me about it, disapproving of the person I was at that time."

A pause hung in the air as Bentley let the weight of that revelation settle.

"Recently, I stumbled upon Cassidy and Skylar at Raelynn's place. To my surprise, I had no recollection of Cassidy, but she vividly remembered me, harboring resentment from that frat party encounter. Raelynn then shared that Skylar was unwell and might require a bone marrow transplant."

Another pause followed as Bentley grappled with the complexities of the situation.

"Determined to help, I agreed to undergo testing to check if I could be a match. It was during this process that the doctor dropped the bombshell—Skylar is my son."

The room hung in a heavy silence as Bentley's words lingered, the weight of the revelation sinking in.

Faye and Steve exchanged glances, absorbing the gravity of Bentley's story. Bentley continued, his voice tinged with vulnerability.

"I had no idea, Mom, Dad. I didn't know I had a son until a week ago. Cassidy kept it a secret all these years, and I can't imagine what Skylar and she have been through. It's overwhelming, and I'm trying to do the right thing by Skylar, by Cassidy, and by Raelynn. But the more I try to navigate this, the more complicated it becomes."

Steve sighed, his initial sternness softening. "Bentley, we understand it must be a shock for you too. But keeping this from Raelynn... that's a tough spot you're in. She deserves to know the truth."

"I know, Dad," Bentley replied, his gaze still fixed on the floor. "But Cassidy wants to be the one to tell her. She feels like it's her responsibility, and I promised her I'd respect that. It's tearing me apart, Dad. I want to be honest with Raelynn, but I also want to honor Cassidy's wishes."

Faye spoke up, her voice filled with understanding. "Bentley, honesty is crucial in any relationship. Raelynn is your partner, and she deserves to know what you're going through. Keeping secrets only leads to more complications."

Bentley nodded; his internal struggle evident. "I know, Mom. I just need to find the right time and way to tell her. It's just... everything is happening so fast, and I'm trying to be there for Skylar too. I want to be the father he needs."

Steve uncrossed his arms and approached Bentley, placing a reassuring hand on his shoulder. "Son, we'll figure this out together. Skylar is family now, and we're here to support you. But you need to communicate with Raelynn. The longer you keep her in the dark, the harder it'll be for both of you."

Feeling a mixture of gratitude and apprehension, Bentley looked up at his parents. "I appreciate that, Dad. I know I need to talk to Raelynn, and I will. I just hope she understands the complexity of the situation."

Faye squeezed Bentley's hand, offering a supportive smile. "We'll be here for you, Bentley. And for Skylar. Now, let's go back to the living room and try to make Skylar feel at home. We'll take one step at a time, alright?"

Bentley nodded, appreciating the support from his parents. As they walked back to the living room, he couldn't shake the weight of the unresolved issues hanging in the air. Skylar and Cameron looked up as they entered, the atmosphere cautiously optimistic.

The evening unfolded with mixed emotions, snacks, and attempts at normalcy. Bentley watched as Skylar gradually warmed up to his newfound family, sensing the acceptance growing. However, the unspoken tension with Raelynn still lingered in Bentley's mind, a challenge he knew he couldn't avoid for much longer.

As night fell, Bentley found himself contemplating the next steps. Skylar was settled in, laughing with Cameron in the living room, while Faye and Steve worked on making dinner. Bentley knew he had to confront the difficult conversation with Raelynn, facing the consequences of his actions and the complexities of his newfound role as Skylar's father.

32

The Price of Love

Six weeks had passed since Bentley's life had taken an unexpected turn, revealing Skylar as his 5-year-old son. In that time, he immersed himself in building a strong father-son bond, cherishing every moment spent getting to know the little boy who had entered his life so abruptly.

As Bentley navigated the complexities of parenthood, he grappled with a secret weighing heavy on his conscience. Despite the deep connection he shared with Raelynn, his girlfriend, he hadn't yet mustered the courage to reveal the truth about Skylar's parentage. He believed Cassidy, Raelynn's best friend and Skylar's mother, would eventually break the news herself, but she seemed to be treading cautiously, awaiting the opportune moment. Cassidy harbored nervousness, not just for herself but also for how Raelynn would react to this life-altering revelation. Bentley, too, understood the gravity of the situation and was patient, giving Cassidy the space, she needed.

Meanwhile, Raelynn's life continued to unfold on a different front. She found herself flying to California, embarking on a journey that held significant professional importance. At the Warner Bros Records headquarters, she, along with her manager Mike and her bandmates Owen, Levi, Jake, and Elijah, stood poised to sign a two-year record deal. The excitement in the air was palpable as they ventured into this new chapter of their musical journey, unaware of the intricate web of personal revelations waiting to be unveiled.

In the midst of their separate worlds, Bentley and Raelynn were bound by a shared secret, one that would inevitably reshape the foundations of their relationship. As they stood at the crossroads of their individual lives, both were yet to comprehend the complexities that lay ahead—complications that would test the strength of their love and the resilience of their connection.

"Good morning, babe!" Bentley said as he rolled over kissing Raelynn.

The morning sun streamed through the curtains, casting a warm glow across Raelynn's bedroom. Bentley's greeting, filled with genuine affection, marked the beginning of another day in their intertwined lives. As he rolled over to kiss Raelynn, a mixture of emotions played on his face, masking the internal turmoil that accompanied the secret he carried.

Raelynn reciprocated Bentley's kiss with a soft smile, but a sudden wave of nausea disrupted the tranquility of the moment. Without warning, she pushed Bentley gently back and hurriedly hopped out of bed. Rushing to the toilet, she barely made it in time before the queasiness overwhelmed her. Bentley, concerned, followed her to the bathroom, his worry deepening as he watched Raelynn's unexpected bout of sickness.

"Are you okay, Rae?" Bentley asked, his voice a mix of concern and confusion. He knelt beside her, offering a comforting hand on her back as she finished. Raelynn flushed the toilet, then rested her forehead against the cool porcelain, trying to catch her breath.

"I don't know, Bentley," she admitted, her voice shaky. "I've been feeling off for a few days now."

Bentley's mind raced, connecting the dots between Raelynn's recent symptoms and the possibility of what it could mean. As his concern for Raelynn's well-being grew.

"Maybe you should see a doctor," Bentley suggested, his voice gentle but filled with underlying worry.

Raelynn nodded, still catching her breath. "Yeah, maybe I should. Something's not right."

As the day unfolded, Bentley accompanied Raelynn to a local clinic. The air in the waiting room was tense, both lost in their thoughts about the impending doctor's visit. When Raelynn's name was called, they entered the examination room together, the atmosphere charged with anticipation.

The doctor listened attentively as Raelynn described her symptoms – the nausea, the fatigue, the subtle changes she had noticed. Bentley stood by her side, holding her hand, his concern etched on his face.

A short while later, the physician reentered the examination room, politely tapping on the door before entering. His entrance disrupted a fleeting moment of intimacy between Bentley and Raelynn, who were contemplating a quickie in the room.

"Ms. Hart, upon reviewing your blood work, it seems you are approximately eight weeks pregnant."

Raelynn's eyes widened with shock, and Bentley's jaw dropped. The doctor continued speaking, explaining the implications of the news and discussing potential next steps. However, the words became a distant hum as Bentley's mind raced, connecting the dots between Skylar's sudden appearance and now, the unexpected revelation of Raelynn's pregnancy.

The weight of the situation hit Bentley like a ton of bricks. His thoughts spiraled, imagining the web of complications that now entangled their lives. He stole a glance at Raelynn, who sat there, visibly stunned, processing the information. The room felt smaller, and the air grew heavy with the unspoken truth.

As they left the clinic, Bentley tried to find the right words, but his mind was a chaotic mess. Raelynn, too, was silent, the gravity of the situation sinking in. They drove home in a tense silence, both lost in their thoughts.

Later that evening, as Bentley and Raelynn sat in their living room, the weight of the silence between them became unbearable. Bentley finally broke the quiet, his voice hesitant, "Raelynn, we need to talk about this."

Raelynn looked up from where she had been staring at the floor, her eyes filled with a mixture of shock and uncertainty. "Talk about what, Bentley?" she asked, her voice shaky.

Bentley took a deep breath, the gravity of his next words hanging heavily in the air. "About the baby, Raelynn. About us."

Raelynn's gaze flickered from Bentley to the space around them, as if searching for answers in the room. "I... I never expected this, Bentley. I don't even know how to process it."

Bentley nodded, understanding the overwhelming emotions that accompanied such unexpected news. "I get that, Rae. I'm processing it too. But we need to figure out what we're going to do."

Raelynn's eyes met Bentley's, her expression a mix of vulnerability and fear. "Are you asking me if I want to keep the baby?"

Bentley hesitated for a moment, choosing his words carefully. "I'm asking if you've thought about it. If you're sure this is what you want, considering you just signed a record deal that going to put you on the road a lot. I will support you either way, but this changes everything, Raelynn. It makes it more complex."

She sighed angrily, running her fingers through her hair. "I can't believe you right now Bentley. This is supposed to be an exciting and joyful time but instead you're making it anything but."

Raelynn's frustration boiled over, and she stood up abruptly. The tension in the room escalated with each passing second. Bentley, sensing the magnitude of the situation, tried to reach out to her, "Raelynn, I didn't mean to--"

But she cut him off, her voice sharp with anger, "Save it, Bentley. I need some space right now."

Without another word, Raelynn stormed out of their apartment, slamming the door behind her. Bentley sat there, alone in the suffocating silence that hung in the air. He ran his hands through his hair, grappling with the weight of the situation.

Later that evening, Raelynn found herself at Cassidy's doorstep, unable to contain the mounting emotions. Cassidy, sensing her friend's distress, ushered her inside.

"What's going on, Rae?" Cassidy asked, concern etched on her face.

Raelynn took a deep breath, trying to articulate the whirlwind of feelings. "I'm pregnant, Cass. Bentley and I just found out today."

Cassidy's eyes widened in surprise, and she hugged Raelynn tightly. "Oh, Rae, that's wonderful news! Congratulations!"

Raelynn pulled away, her expression serious. "But Cassidy, Bentley's reaction was strange. It's like he's hiding something, and that he's not ready for this. I don't know but it is truly scaring me."

Cassidy's smile faded as she listened, "Rae, there's something I need to tell you."

Cassidy hesitated, gauging Raelynn's reaction before deciding how to proceed. She took a deep breath, her eyes filled with a mix of guilt and concern.

"Rae, I'm about to tell you my biggest kept secret. I know who Skylar's dad is, I've known since day one." Cassidy said with tears forming in her eyes as her voice began to crack.

Raelynn's eyes widened, a mix of confusion and shock crossing her face. She took a step back, processing Cassidy's revelation. "What? Skylar's dad? But I thought... I thought you didn't know."

Cassidy took a deep breath, her shoulders slumping as if the weight of the secret was physically bearing down on her. "I didn't lie when I said it was a one-night stand with someone I didn't know because I didn't know him. I had this image painted in my mind of who I thought he might be like, but I was wrong. So, to avoid that shame I just stuck with I didn't know him even though I knew who it was. Gosh I hate to say this."

"Just say it hun." Raelynn said as she grabbed Cassidy's hands and held them in hers

"Rae, I can't you're going to hate me, and I don't want that." Cassidy said tears free falling.

"Honey, I could never hate you. We've been through too much." Raelynn replied growing concerned.

"You're not going to get over this one." Cassidy said her voice shaky.

"Just say it." Raelynn said as she was growing impatient.

"Cassidy managed to get out while sobbing. "Rae, Bentley is Skylar's dad.

Raelynn quickly yanked her hands back from holding Cassidy's and her eyes grew wide with shock.

"What? This isn't funny Cassidy." Raelynn said angrily.

"I know it's not funny that's why I didn't want to tell you. I was never going to tell you. I'm only telling you because Bentley found out and I don't want you to be mad at him. I told him not to tell you until I told you." Cassidy said still sobbing.

Raelynn just couldn't believe what she was hearing. However, what she was hearing was adding up and making perfect sense to why Bentley had been acting the way he had been acting.

Raelynn was pissed Cassidy had been straightforward with her since the beginning of her pregnancy with Skylar, but she understood. Raelynn understood that it was not her secret to tell. However, it didn't take away the sting of the betrayal especially since Cassidy knew all along that Raelynn was building a romantic relationship with her baby daddy, Skylar's father.

Raelynn's mind whirled as the revelation sank in. Bentley, the man she had fallen in love with and was building a life with, was Skylar's father. The shock, anger, and betrayal brewed within her, creating a storm of emotions. The weight of the secrecy unfolded before her, and the foundation of trust in her relationship with Bentley crumbled.

The room felt stifling as Raelynn grappled with the truth. Cassidy's tearful admission laid bare a web of deception that had entangled their lives for years. Raelynn couldn't fathom how Bentley had kept such a significant part of his life hidden from her.

Unable to contain her emotions, Raelynn paced the room, her anger boiling over. "How could he? How could both of you keep this from me? Do you have any idea what this means for us, for our relationship?" Her voice trembled with a mix of hurt and fury.

Cassidy, still sobbing, tried to approach Raelynn, but she recoiled. "Rae, I never wanted to hurt you. I thought I was protecting you from pain, but I see now that it was a mistake."

"Protecting me? From what, exactly? The truth? I deserve to know the truth, especially when it involves my life and the people I love!" Raelynn snapped back, her frustration escalating.

Cassidy, now sitting on the couch, wiped away tears and nodded solemnly. "I know I messed up, Rae. I should have told you from the beginning, but I was scared. Scared of losing your friendship, of how you would react. I thought I could control the situation, and I made a terrible mistake."

Raelynn, torn between the pain of the revelation and the history she shared with Cassidy, softened a bit. "You should have trusted me, Cass. We've been through so much together. I deserved to know the truth."

Cassidy nodded, her remorse evident. "I understand if you're angry. I messed up, and I'm sorry. But you need to talk to Bentley. He loves you, Rae, and he didn't want to lose you."

Raelynn took a deep breath, her mind still swirling with conflicting emotions. "I need time to process this. I need to talk to Bentley myself, and then we'll figure out where we stand."

Cassidy nodded, understanding the gravity of the situation. "Just know that I never wanted any of this to happen. I care about you, Rae, and I never meant to hurt you."

As Raelynn left Cassidy's apartment, the weight of the truth lingered heavily on her shoulders. She needed to confront Bentley, have an honest conversation about their past, their present, and the uncertain future that now lay before them. The journey back to her house was filled with a mix of anger, sadness, and a burning desire for answers.

33

Facing The Music

"**B**entley Riggs!" Raelynn yelled in frustration, the door swinging open to her home. Startled, Bentley, who had been reclining on the couch lost in his thoughts, swiftly rose to his feet, now confronted by an irate Raelynn.

"When were you planning to tell me that you knocked up my best friend and had a kid with her?" Raelynn blurted out in anger.

"Look Rae, I'm sorry Cassidy wouldn't let me tell you. She said she wanted to do it herself. So, I let her, that was one of stipulations we had in order for me to get to know my son. I wanted to tell you so bad." Bentley replied trying his best efforts to diffuse the situation.

Raelynn's anger lingered, her eyes narrowing as she absorbed Bentley's explanation. "You kept something this significant from me? From your girlfriend? Why didn't you trust me enough to share this?"

Bentley sighed, running a hand through his hair in frustration. "It wasn't about trust, Rae. Cassidy had her reasons, and I had to respect that. I wanted to be a part of Skylar's life, and Cassidy made it clear that was the only way. I didn't like it, but I agreed."

Raelynn paced, the weight of the revelation settling in. "So, all this time, you've been around, pretending like everything's normal, and you never thought it was necessary to clue me in?"

252

"I wanted to tell you. I really did. But every time I tried, Cassidy insisted she'd handle it. I thought it would be better coming from her. Please understand, Rae, I never meant to keep you in the dark," Bentley pleaded.

Raelynn's anger softened into a mix of frustration and hurt. "This is a lot to take in, Bentley. A child, my best friend, and you keeping it from me. I need some time to process all of this. Especially with us expecting a child of our own. "

Bentley nodded, respecting her need for space. "Rae, I understand. I never wanted our relationship to be built on secrets, but I didn't want to jeopardize my chance to be there for Skylar. I hope you can find it in yourself to understand, eventually."

Raelynn turned to face him, her eyes searching his for sincerity. "I need honesty, Bentley. No more secrets. We're expecting a child together, and I need to be sure we're on the same page."

Bentley sighed, realizing the gravity of the situation. "I promise, Rae. No more secrets. I want us to navigate through this together, openly."

Just as the tension in the room began to ease slightly, the shrill ring of Raelynn's phone pierced through the atmosphere. She hastily fished it out of her pocket and answered, a puzzled expression crossing her face as she listened to the voice on the other end.

"Hey Mike, what's going on?" she asked, glancing at Bentley, who looked equally confused.

As Mike, Raelynn's manager, continued to speak, her eyes widened in surprise. "LA? Next Monday? Recording my EP already?" Raelynn's mind raced as she processed the unexpected news.

"Yeah, Raelynn, they want to get started as soon as possible due to the momentum you gained from Cinderella Fest. This could be a game-changer for your career. I know it's short notice, but we need to seize this moment," Mike explained enthusiastically.

The weight of the recent revelations about Skylar and the ongoing turmoil in her relationship with Bentley collided with the sudden career opportunity. Raelynn took a deep breath, trying to navigate the conflicting emotions.

"Bentley, I need a moment alone," she said, holding a hand up to signal him to give her space. Bentley nodded, understanding the gravity of the situation, and stepped away, giving her the privacy, she needed.

As Raelynn listened to Mike's continued excitement over the phone, she couldn't help but feel torn. The professional opportunity was undeniable, but it came at a time when her personal life was in upheaval. She pondered the significance of the decision she was about to make.

After a few minutes, Raelynn ended the call and turned to Bentley, who awaited her decision with a mix of concern and support.

"I don't know what to do, Bentley. This is a huge opportunity for my music career, but everything is so complicated right now," she admitted, her voice tinged with uncertainty.

"You're going to go and record your EP. You have been dreaming of this a very long time, I'm not letting you pass this opportunity up. Me and all our problems will still be here when you get back. Bentley said as he approached Raelynn, wrapping her in a warm embrace kissing her forehead.

Raelynn, still uncertain about the path ahead, found comfort in Bentley's supportive words and embrace. His reassurance brought a sense of stability amidst the chaos. She looked up at him, gratitude in her eyes.

"Thank you, Bentley. I appreciate your understanding. I need to do this; it's a chance of a lifetime," she said, her voice conveying determination.

Bentley smiled, his affection for Raelynn evident. "I know you'll shine, Rae. And when you come back, we'll figure everything out together."

As Raelynn began to consider the logistics of the sudden trip to LA, she realized there was something else she needed to discuss with Bentley. She took a step back, holding his hands in hers.

""There's something else we need to address, Bentley. I know that they aren't going to approve but with all that's happening, I would like to tell my parents. I want them to know about my career opportunities and, well, about us expecting a child," Raelynn said nervously as she wasn't too sure about the idea herself.

Bentley, understanding the importance of involving Raelynn's parents, nodded in agreement. "Rae, it's a big step, but I think it's the right thing to do. Your parents deserve to know about the significant moments in our lives. It'll also bring them into the loop, and we might find some support and guidance."

Raelynn appreciated Bentley's support, though a hint of nervousness still lingered in her eyes. "I hope they understand, Bentley. It's not going to be easy breaking this news to them, especially given the circumstances. They already don't like you and they have never approved of me chasing my musical dreams."

"Well, Rae that's ok. We can deal with them together babe. When do you want them to come?" Bentley said still trying to reassure Raelynn of all her decisions.

Raelynn took a deep breath and let out a mirroring sigh, "I'd like for them to come before I go to LA."

Bentley nodded in agreement, understanding the significance of having Raelynn's parents present before she embarked on her journey to LA. "That sounds like a plan, Rae. We'll face it together, and I'll do my best to make them see the sincerity of our choices. When do you want to arrange for their visit?"

Raelynn looked thoughtful for a moment, considering the logistics. "Dad has a private jet, so they can come whenever. I'll talk to him and see when they're available. It's crucial that we have an honest conversation with them before I leave for LA."

Bentley smiled, appreciating Raelynn's proactive approach. "I'm here to support you, Rae, every step of the way. Let me know if there's anything I can do to help prepare for their visit."

As Raelynn dialed her father's number, Bentley waited with a mixture of anticipation and anxiety. Raelynn spoke with determination, explaining the situation and expressing her desire for her parents to visit before her trip to LA. After a brief conversation, she ended the call and turned to Bentley with a thoughtful expression.

"They agreed to come," she said, a hint of surprise and reluctance in her voice. "Dad said they'll arrange their schedule to be here tomorrow evening. It's going to be intense, Bentley."

Bentley nodded, understanding the gravity of the upcoming meeting. "Wow, that's fast. However, we'll face it together, Rae. It's a step toward transparency, and I'm willing to do whatever it takes to make them understand."

Raelynn smiled appreciatively, grateful for Bentley's unwavering support. "Thank you, Bentley. I know it won't be easy, but it's necessary. I want them to know about everything before I embark on this new chapter of my career."

Bentley gently squeezed her hand. "We've got this, Rae. And after everything settles down, we can focus on your EP and the journey ahead. I believe in you, in us. All we've got to do now is face the music babe."

With a shared sense of determination, Raelynn and Bentley began to prepare for the arrival of Raelynn's parents. The impending visit added another layer of complexity to their already tumultuous situation, but they were committed to facing it head-on.

34

Meeting The Parents

The following evening Raelynn and Bentley sat patiently outside the terminal at RDU airport as they waited for the arrival of her parents in their private jet.

As her parents exited the terminal, they both looked fairly shocked to see Bentley standing alongside their daughter. "Mom, Dad so glad you guys could make." Raelynn said as she gave them both hugs.

Raelynn's father Jim Hart just kept starring at Bentley with a smug look. It was apparent by the look on his face that he wasn't the slightest bit thrilled that Bentley was there. "Raelynn, honey, what is this clown doing here?" Jim asked.

Raelynn was shocked at the reception her dad was giving Bentley. "Dad, stop being rude."

Bentley maintained his composure, despite the evident tension in the air. He extended a hand towards Jim Hart with a polite smile. "Mr. Hart, it's a pleasure to see you again."

Mr. Hart ignored Bentley's gesture as he sucked his teeth in disgust. Bentley however was not surprised as he kept quiet as he began to load the Hart's luggage into the car.

"Mom, this is Bentley Riggs. He is a famous musician. His manager works for Dad." Raelynn said as she introduced Bentley to her mother.

Bentley stuck out his hand to shake hers, but she also rudely rejected his gesture.

"We know who is and we don't like him." Raelynn's mother Olivia Hart said with a snarky attitude.

"You guys' stop being so damn rude. Bentley isn't as bad as the media paints him out to be." Raelynn said as both her parents fake laughed while getting inside the car.

The whole ride back to Raelynn's house was very awkward. It was nothing but silence, not even the radio played as Raelynn both shared glances of "what have we gotten ourselves into."

As they pulled into Raelynn's, Bentley continued to be respectful of her parents even through their rudeness towards him. He opened the door for them to get out the car. He unloaded their luggage and even took it inside the house, so they didn't have to do anything. He even used his manners; yes, ma'am, yes sir, no ma'am, no sir, and thank you. Even through all the nice generosity her parents still wouldn't accept him. They kept giving him the cold shoulder blocking him out like he wasn't even there. Bentley tried everything possible to gain their respect, but nothing was working. He was at a loss on what to possibly do to have them somewhat accept him and not be so rude.

Once Bentley had got Raelynn's parents inside and settled Raelynn grabbed Bentley pulling him aside into the bedroom shutting the door behind them. "Bentley I am so sorry at how they are acting towards you." Raelynn pleaded.

Bentley smiled. "Rae, it's ok. I knew this was going to happen. I'm trying to roll with the punches to make the best out of the worst of it just for you."

"This is why I love you so much." Raelynn said as she reached up to give him a kiss on the lips.

"Rae, I love you too, but we might as well go back in their before they start thinking we have run off or something." Bentley said trying not to laugh through their struggle.

"Do we have too? Can't we just run away?" Raelynn asked sarcastically with a pouty face.

Bentley couldn't contain himself anymore as he let out a chuckle. "No, babe unfortunately we can't, you invited them to tell them you are pregnant, so we have to get back out there." Bentley said as he got behind Raelynn pushing her towards the door as she was dragging her feet.

"But. But I don't wanna." Raelynn cried out. Bentley just laughed as they made their way to the living room with Raelynn's parents.

In the living room Bentley and Raelynn met Jim and Olivia who were sitting on the couch whispering back and forth to one another.

"Hey, what are you guys being so secretive about?" Raelynn asked as she made her way into the living room with Bentley following right behind.

"Oh, nothing honey nothing." Olivia pleaded as she then looked at Bentley with a snarky look.

Bentley finally had enough of trying to play the nice guy. Especially since despite his best efforts he was still met with disdain. He could see the frustration it was causing Raelynn and felt the frustration it was causing him. Bentley decided it finally was time to meet fire with fire.

"Mr. and Mrs. Hart, I'm aware of your unfavorable opinions about me. Your attitudes have only confirmed that. Now, I have tried my best to tolerate your disrespect towards me for your daughter's sake. However, I have had enough. It's stressing your daughter out and her being stressed out is stressing me out." Bentley asserted.

Although his tone was raised and demanding, Bentley still spoke elegantly, and Mr. and Mrs. Hart's faces carried a look of surprise on them. It was almost as if they couldn't fathom the fact Bentley had just raised his voice to them.

"Wow, Bentley the nerve you have…" Jim was saying before Raelynn abruptly cut in.

"Dad, that's enough. He spoke how he and I were both feeling either you can respect that, or you can get out." Raelynn paused for a second as she looked at Bentley with an "I'm sorry" expression on her face. "Bentley, babe just come back later tonight for dinner. Maybe, things will be a little more levelheaded."

Bentley nodded, appreciating Raelynn's attempt to diffuse the tension. "Sure, I'll be back for dinner. Hopefully, we can have a more civil conversation then." With that, he left the room, leaving Raelynn to deal with her disgruntled parents.

As Bentley walked away, he couldn't help but feel a mix of frustration and determination. He had tried to be the bigger person, to win over Raelynn's parents with kindness, but it seemed that approach had reached its limit. Now, he contemplated how he could navigate this delicate situation and make things work not just for himself but for Raelynn as well.

Later that evening after taking some time to cool off, spending time with his son Skylar, Bentley decided it was time to head back to Raelynn's. Bentley wanted to do anything but return to Raelynn's to face her parents. Her parents clearly hated him, and he was starting to hate them too as they were pushing every single one of his buttons.

Bentley got lost in his own thoughts on the drive back to Raelynn's house that he passed the driveway. When he snapped out of his daydream, he had to hit a sharp U-turn. Luckily, he only made it a block away from the house.

However, Mr. Hart was on the front porch when Bentley missed the house and had to hit the U-turn and started laughing. Something else he could try and use to throw in Bentley's face. No sense of direction, non-driving, or the fact he was possibly trying to miss dinner with Raelynn and her parents.

However, none of that would be true except maybe the last one. Bentley did want to miss dinner with Raelynn and her parents. He didn't want to be around them not even the slightest bit but no matter how bad Bentley wanted to miss dinner with Raelynn and her parents he wasn't going to. He was going to suffer through and continue to try and contain his composure through her parents' scare tactics.

Thankfully and luckily for Raelynn, Bentley doesn't scare easy, so her parents' scare tactics didn't work to run him away. However, Raelynn and Bentley's scare tactic of telling her parents that they are dating and expecting a child might run them away, make them accept Bentley, have a heart attack, or all three. Bentley didn't care as long as it was over quickly, so he didn't have to deal with them for too long.

As Bentley made his way inside Raelynn's place, he walked past her dad who was still standing on the porch without saying a word. The tension between the two of them was tense enough to cut through glass.

Bentley made his way through the living room where he spotted Raelynn's mother sitting on the couch with a glass of wine while Raelynn was finishing up dinner. Raelynn didn't talk about it much, but her mother never did any home economics. Raelynn didn't have to tell Bentley either, he could easily pick up on that with her attitude and the way that she carried herself.

"Hey babe, I'm back." Bentley shouted as he came through the door. Mrs. Hart just looked up at Bentley and rolled her eyes as she continued to down her glass of wine.

"Hey, what's up with the pet names? You know we got to tell them we are dating and having a kid all at the same time." Raelynn whispered to Bentley while giving him the eye when he came into the kitchen.

Bentley couldn't believe he had forgot. "I'm sorry, I forgot." Bentley said shockingly as he began to help Raelynn set the table.

"Bentley, can you say grace please." Raelynn asked as they all gathered at the table taking their seats.

Her parents looked at each other with a look of disgust upon their faces. Bentley hadn't said grace in a little over 8 years and was baffled that Raelynn asked. Though he was shocked she asked, he stepped up and owned it.

"God thank you for this food and may you allow it to nourish our bodies with the valuable nutrients that we need to make it through day-to-day activities and God thank you for keeping your hand on Mr. and Mrs. Hart as they traveled to be with us this evening. Amen." Bentley said.

While everyone dug into the pasta to get some on their dish Raelynn broke the awkward silence. "Mom, Dad, me and Bentley have some great news to tell you guys."

Her parent however didn't look like they were going to be thrilled with what Raelynn and Bentley had to say next as the two of them kept exchanging looks of pure disgust.

"Well, what is it dear, you have had us waiting all day long." Mr. Hart said as he took a bite of his pasta.

At that moment Bentley cut in and took control, "Well Mr. and Mrs. Hart me and your daughter are dating. We have been for 2 months going on three now and I love her. She's literally my everything. I know you guys don't like me, it's very apparent but that's okay. Your daughter loves me and that's all that matter to me." Bentley said as he looked over to Raelynn and smiled at her.

Mrs. Hart almost choked on her food as Bentley broke the news. The look of disgust and anger just grew bigger on Mr. Hart's face.

"Oh, is it that so? How long will this last before you get bored and go on to the next breaking my daughter's heart?" Mr. Hart said with a snarky tone.

"Dad!" Raelynn shouted as she was trying to keep a check on the animosity in the room.

"Rae, it's fine. I understand where he's coming from," Bentley said calmly, recognizing the protective instincts in Mr. Hart. "He wants to protect his baby girl at all costs, and I don't blame him; I would do the same thing."

Pausing, Bentley conveyed a sense of sincerity, "With that being said, sir, my past is my past for a reason. Can we please, for the love of God, leave it there? I'm not the same man I was an hour ago, let alone 4 months ago, and the same goes for you; you're not the same. At least, I hope not."

Bentley continued, his gaze unwavering, "I hope there's some acceptance inside you somewhere. But if you must know, your daughter is my end game. Anything she wants, she gets. She speaks, I act. She wanted to keep us on the down low and out of the public eye, and I agreed. Whatever makes Raelynn happy makes me happy. I love her, and that's not going to change."

"You know what, Bentley? You're right," Mr. Hart admitted begrudgingly. "Me and my wife don't like you, but we want our daughter happy, and we can tell she's happy with you. In fact, happier than we have ever seen her."

He continued, a mixture of concern and resignation in his voice, "Every time you come into a room where she is, she lights up and comes to life, so full of energy. That smile on her face is because of you, and that scares the shit out of me because I know you. Yeah, you say you're a changed man, yada-yada, but how do I know that? I don't. I just want to protect my daughter, even if that means from you, but I see I'm fighting a losing battle. The heart wants what the heart wants."

Mr. Hart's tone turned stern, a warning laced in his words, "You hurt her, I will hurt you." Bentley simply nodded, acknowledging the gravity of Mr. Hart's words with a sense of understanding.

After a few moments of letting the atmosphere calm down Raelynn, Raelynn felt that it was time to break the real news to her parents.

"Mom, Dad, that's not the only news I, well, we have to break to you guys…" Raelynn said as she took a slight pause reaching for Bentley's hand "…Mom, Dad, I'm pregnant with Bentley's kid." Raelynn said with a somber expression.

Bentley just squeezed Raelynn's hand tightly as he held it within his as they awaited the unwavering reactions of her parents.

It was a few moments of silence as her parents were trying to process what they had just been told. Mrs. Hart just started to cry. Mr. Hart let his anger get the best of him as he sent his plate flying off the table shattering it into the wall next to him as he stood up from the table and yelled "goddamnit" and stormed off. It was the exact reaction Bentley and Raelynn were both expecting her parents to have.

Later that evening Bentley and Raelynn, were in the kitchen cleaning up the dishes an putting the leftovers away as her dad came waltzing back in. Mr. Hart was still visibly heated as he did not say one word as he walked through the door and plopped on the loveseat right beside Mrs. Hart. Raelynn tried not to let it bother her as she kept with doing the dishes. However, Bentley could tell that it was bothering her.

He knew that she truly was hoping for their reactions to be way different. She didn't expect them to be jumping up and down with joy by any means, but she also didn't expect to be so rude, disgusted, angry, and closed off as they were being.

In that moment Bentley knew that he had to do something. Something he swore he'd never do again. Especially, after how things went down with Michelle. But then again, he did say that he would never fall in love with anyone else after Michelle either but here he was head over heels in love with Raelynn. Bentley was so head over heels in love with her that he had no control over his actions when it came to her.

Bentley was overcome with emotion as he dried his hands, took a deep breath, exhaled, and leaned in to kiss Raelynn before making his way into the living room where Mr. and Mrs. Hart sat with disgusted looks upon their faces.

"Mr. and Mrs. Hart, I understand that you don't like me. I get that, and I respect how you feel towards me," Bentley began, acknowledging the tension. "I have a very regretful past that has given me a bad boy look, which is the farthest thing from who I am. I tried to drown my pain in alcohol and women to avoid dealing with it."

Opening about his painful history, Bentley continued, "Who would want to deal with the pain of being left at the altar by your high school sweetheart at 20 years old? Who would want to deal with the pain of her dying in a car crash not even a week later while you're trying to heal from that blow on what was supposed to be your honeymoon, just to come home and receive another blow that she's gone and there's no mending or fixing that because she's physically gone?"

Reflecting on his journey, Bentley shared, "I swore I'd never fall for another female again. I hated love. I hated the idea of being in love. Then I met your daughter, Raelynn. She has changed my life for the better in the few short months that I've known her. She's made me believe in love again because, whether you believe it or not, I am head over heels in love with your daughter."

Expressing his gratitude towards Raelynn, Bentley continued, "I haven't been this happy since the night of what was supposed to be my wedding, and I owe her thanks for being the light I needed when everything around me was dark."

Addressing the disapproval from Mr. and Mrs. Hart, Bentley asserted, "So, you hating me does not bother me in the slightest. If it makes you feel better, then hate on. What bothers me is how you have disrespected not only me but also your daughter, and for what? Loving me? Having my kid? Your daughter deserves more respect than what you have given her since your arrival, and quite frankly, I'm over the disrespect that she's receiving because it isn't fair to her or me, especially since you don't even know me."

Taking issue with the reliance on tabloids, Bentley argued, "You just know what the tabloids have posted. Guess what? Tabloids lie every single day to get a story worth publishing. Mr. Hart, you should know this. For crying out loud, you are the CEO of a company that manages celebrities from all backgrounds and walks of life. You have seen the damage that tabloids can do with spinning the truth or a blatant lie. Yet, you still choose to believe the tabloids instead of believing the source himself."

Bentley emphasized, "I'm standing right here, and I'm telling you that, yes, I was a party animal who slept with any girl I wanted to, but what they don't tell you is the pain I was running from. They don't tell you that deep down inside I was hurting. They don't tell you that, do they? They tell you what's going to get them their 15 minutes in the spotlight."

While Bentley confronted Raelynn's parents in the living room, Raelynn remained in the kitchen, overhearing their conversation. She was astound at the emotion in Bentley's voice. She also couldn't believe that Bentley had opened up about his past to her parents to show how much he truly loved her.

Raelynn felt a mixture of anger and sadness at her parents' reaction, she was also overwhelmed with happiness knowing that Bentley cared enough about her to stand up to her parents. She had never been with a man that had the courage to do what Bentley did and that was stand up to her father. Hearing Bentley confront her father and mother for their mistreatment of them gave Raelynn a strange mix of emotions.

After what felt like a lifetime of silence, Mr. Hart who was staring blankly at Bentley finally responded. "How dare you stand here in a house that I pay for and tell me and my wife how to act much less how to treat our daughter? Who the hell do you think you are Bentley?" Mr. Hart barked out.

Mr. Hart's blank stare was now gone as it was overtaken by pure anger. His eyes were now dark as night with no emotion in them as his pupils had dilated to that extreme. Even though Mr. Hart was now in full blown rage mode Bentley was unfazed. He stood there with his arms folded staring at Mr. Hart with the sternest look you'd ever seen.

"I, Mr. Hart, am Bentley mother-fucking Riggs. I'm the man who loves your daughter enough to stand up to you and your bullshit antics!" Bentley declared assertively. "If you think for one second that you can intimidate me out of your daughter's life, you are sadly mistaken, sir."

His frustration evident, Bentley continued, "Now, I've tried to respect you, but my patience, Mr. Hart, it's running thin. For the last several hours, I have watched you belittle your daughter to the verge of tears, all because of who she has chosen to love. You've belittled her, you've belittled me, and our relationship, and I have had enough of it."

Accusing Mr. Hart of seeking control, Bentley pointed out, "You're pissed off because this is a situation that is out of your control, and you sir, you thrive off control. Having control is what fuels your sad and miserable ego because what kind of father would treat his daughter the way you have?"

Highlighting Mr. Hart's actions, Bentley expressed his disappointment, "For fuck's sake, you wouldn't even help her get a record deal, and you have all the disposable tools at your fingertips to do so. But guess what? I got her a record deal. Not because I was looking for control, but because I want to see her succeed!"

Accusing Mr. Hart of hindering Raelynn's talent, Bentley continued, "Raelynn has a true God-given talent that you were trying to hinder the world from seeing. Let me guess, it was because you didn't want her to have that financial dependency where she didn't have to rely on you anymore? Yeah, a true jackass of a father." Bentley barked back with unapologetic intensity.

What was supposed to be an exciting evening was on the verge of turning into an exciting warzone if someone didn't intervene but who was going to do that? Mrs. Hart sure as hell wasn't getting into the mix of it. She was sitting there with a baffled look on her face as if she couldn't believe that this was even transpiring. You could visibly tell that she was praying that no punches would be thrown but knew that this needed to happen.

This was two alpha-males trying to out alpha the other, a spat that needed to play out in order to reach common ground.

"Bentley, who are you to tell me how to be a father? You don't have kids. When you do, then you can tell me how to be a parent and how to treat my daughter," Mr. Hart retorted dismissively. "You two have only been pregnant for a hot second, and here you are trying to give me fatherly advice? That's comical."

Making his disdain for Bentley clear, Mr. Hart continued, "Bentley, let me paint this picture very clear for you; I don't like you, and I never will. I don't care if you are dating my daughter; it will not change the way I feel about you. See, I know you, Bentley. I don't need the tabloids to tell me who you are because I know."

Mocking Bentley's background, Mr. Hart stated, "You're just a broke, uneducated hillbilly ass redneck that just so happened to stumble his way into fame and got lucky that it's lasted longer than 15 minutes. Which, by the way, I think you owe me a thank you for because if not for my agent, that fame would have ended just as quickly as it started. If not for me, you'd be back working your balls off at a regular blue-collar job."

Dismissing Bentley's past as a sob story, Mr. Hart continued, "And boo-hoo, so what you got a sad backstory that propelled you to fame. It doesn't change who you are, Bentley. It doesn't change where you came from. No one cares that you got left at the altar, and no one damn sure doesn't care that the same woman that left you at the altar died the following week. So, stop using that as a crutch to gain sympathy. It might have worked on my daughter, and you might have gotten her fooled, but it will not work on me because I can see right through you. To the real you, Bentley."

Without hesitation Bentley went right back at Mr. Hart. "I do have a kid. I have a 5-year-old son that I just found out about. Since I found out about my son there isn't a damn thing in this world, I wouldn't do to help him, or protect him. I damn sure wouldn't treat him the way you have treated you daughter. Yeah, I missed the first 5 years of his life but at the end of the day that's half of my genetic make-up walking around. That little human being is something that I help procreate and because of that I love his life more than I can describe. It does not matter that I just recently met him. That is my son, and I will forever love him."

However, Bentley was not done and before Mr. Hart could get another word out, he barked "Also, if you want to try and hurt me with your words do better than trying to throw my dead fiancé in my face." That really did hurt Bentley, but he was not going to show Mr. Hart that bothered him not the slightest.

As Raelynn eavesdropped on the heated conversation between her father and Bentley, she grappled with a tough decision. Despite valuing her parents' approval, she couldn't deny her deep feelings for Bentley, especially witnessing his stand against her father. Realizing she had to choose between family approval or following her heart, Raelynn took a deep breath, resolved to stand by Bentley and fight for their relationship.

Neither Mr. Hart, Bentley, nor Olivia noticed Raelynn walk into the living room as the arguing was still ensuing.

Oh well would you listen to that Olivia, Bentley has a 5-year-old son that he just found out about and is telling us, me, how to be a good father." Mr. Hart said laughing while looking over at Mrs. Hart. Mrs. Hart just turned her face up and shook her head.

Raelynn couldn't believe that Bentley had told her father that he had a son. She really hoped that Bentley didn't tell her father whom he had fathered the child with. She knew that would start a whole world of new arguments but mainly because Cassidy, didn't want people that did not need to know who Skylar's father was. Mr. Hart definitely did not need to know.

"Who is this child's mother Bentley? Let me guess. A non-educated slut who wanted to be one of your one-night escapades?" Mr. Hart asked while still laughing.

Before Raelynn could cut in to stop Bentley from answering and without stopping to think Bentley blurted out "Cassidy, your daughters best-friend."

At that moment Bentley knew he messed up. He let his emotions arguing with Mr. Hart, do the one thing that he promised Cassidy he wouldn't do; tell anyone he was Skylar's father to avoid them being put in the spotlight.

Raelynn was completely shocked. She could not believe that Bentley let that slip. Mrs. Hart's eyes got wide, and her jaw dropped as she couldn't believe what she had just heard. Mr. Hart had a surprised look come upon his face as he was finally left speechless. Raelynn knew that before anything else got said she needed to step in and put an end to the madness and do damage control.

"Okay you two, that's absolutely and entirely enough! Ben, honey I love you and I appreciate you for standing up to my father. That takes balls of steel, literally. However, I need you to go to the bedroom and cool down, I will be in there shortly." Raelynn shouted at the two of them as sternly as possible while walking over to Bentley to give him a kiss.

Bentley reluctantly turned to walk away as Raelynn began laying into her father. "Dad, yes Bentley is Skylar's father and what you're not going to do is use that knowledge to try and hurt Bentley. You won't be hurting just Bentley, but you'll be hurting Cassidy and Skylar too. Cassidy told Bentley that if he wanted to be a part of Skylar's life that he needed to keep it on a need-to-know basis that he was Skylar's father. Also, yes, I agree with Bentley dad, you and mom have both been extremely rude and I think when the time is right you both need to apologize for your behavior tonight no if's and's or but's."

In the middle of Raelynn going off on her father Bentley stopped in the hallway on the way to the bedroom just to be nosey and listen. He couldn't do nothing but smile as he was so proud that she took a step towards biting back against her father, who wanted to do nothing but control every aspect of her life.

When Raelynn finished hounding her dad, instead of going into the bedroom like Raelynn told him to do, Bentley made his way back out to the living room. He walked right up to Raelynn, grabbing both sides of her face with his hands, looking deep into her eyes and gave her a kiss.

He didn't care that her parents were in the room he was just so proud of her, and he wanted her to know. Raelynn was shocked but she didn't fight it. Him kissing her in-front of her parents who hated him, and their relationship gave it a very hot and sexy rebellious feeling.

Bentley's heart was racing, because yet again his emotions were in the driver's seat steering him in directions, he couldn't even fathom. As the two pulled away from each other, they continued looking deep into each other's eyes as neither of them knew what was about to happen next.

That's when Bentley dropped down to one bended knee pulling out a pretty diamond ring. Raelynn was completely taken off guard as she clasped her face with both her hands in shock. Her parents, Mr. and Mrs. Hart also wore looks of disbelief on their faces.

Bentley himself was also surprised. He couldn't believe he had built up the courage to be down on one knee. Especially since Raelynn and he barely knew each other. Also, after everything that took place with Michelle, he swore he'd never put himself in this position again but here Bentley was breaking his own boundaries.

"What are you doing?" a nervous Raelynn asked while she was looking down at Bentley. She could also tell Bentley was nervous as he had begun to turn red.

With his heart pounding out of his chest, Bentley took a deep breath and locked eyes with Raelynn. "Raelynn," he began with his voice trembling. "I know your parents don't exactly like me, but that doesn't change how I feel about you. These past few months have been the best of my life, and I can't imagine spending a single day without you by my side. You've brought so much light into my world in a short amount of time, and I now know that true love really does exist."

He paused for a moment, taking her hand in his. "I know we have a lot to learn about each other, and there will be challenges along the way, but I want to face them all with you. So, Raelynn, darling, will you marry me?" As he spoke, Mr. and Mrs. Hart looked on with surprised looks on their face.

Raelynn's eyes widened with shock and joy, and she nodded her head before throwing her arms around Bentley's neck. "Yes, yes, a million times yes!" she exclaimed, tears streaming down her face. "I love you so much, Bentley!" Bentley smiled through his own tears, feeling a weight lifted off his shoulders.

The room fell into a stunned silence as Raelynn and Bentley shared this unexpected moment of joy amidst the chaos. Mrs. Hart still had a bewildered expression, while Mr. Hart seemed to be processing the sudden turn of events.

Bentley slid the ring onto Raelynn's finger, and the sparkle of the diamond caught the dim light in the room. Despite the tension that had filled the air earlier, there was now a glimmer of hope and happiness.

Olivia with tears free falling from her eyes was the one to break the silence, "Raelynn, honey. I think your father and I are going to grab our things and get a hotel for the night." Mrs. Hart said with much sadness and disappointment in her voice. "I wish that I could say we were happy for you honey but I feel like you are making a huge mistake and are throwing away your future."

Mr. Hart, still seemingly processing the situation, nodded in agreement. "Yes, we'll leave you two to your... happiness." His tone was curt, and he avoided looking directly at Bentley.

As the couple watched Raelynn's parents gather their things and head towards the door, Raelynn couldn't help but feel a mix of emotions. She was thrilled about the engagement yet saddened by the strained relationship with her parents. Bentley, on the other hand, felt a sense of relief and accomplishment for taking a bold step forward, despite the challenging circumstances.

Once the door closed behind Raelynn's parents, the couple looked at each other with a mixture of joy, uncertainty, and determination. They knew that the road ahead wouldn't be easy, but they were ready to face whatever challenges came their way.

As they embraced each other in the quiet aftermath, Bentley whispered, "I love you, Raelynn. No matter what happens, we'll get through this together."

Raelynn smiled through her tears, feeling a deep connection with Bentley. "I love you too, Bentley."

As they stood there in the empty living room, Raelynn couldn't help but feel a sense of hope and excitement for their future together. Even though her parents didn't approve, she knew that with Bentley by her side, they could conquer anything that came their way.

35

Going Public

Later that night, after all the fireworks had settled down, Bentley and Raelynn laid in bed, with Raelynn's head resting on Bentley's chest. Raelynn gazed at her ring, still in awe of its beauty. She couldn't believe that Bentley had proposed, but she was over the moon with happiness.

"I think we should call your parents," Raelynn said, looking up at Bentley with a smile across her face.

Bentley in return smiled back at Raelynn, "You know what? I think we should." As Bentley reached for his phone to dial his parents' number, he paused. "Actually, I think we should FaceTime them, so they can see your beautiful ring as well as your beautiful face," Bentley suggested.

Raelynn's eyes lit up with excitement "I think that's a great idea!"

As Bentley initiated the video call, Raelynn couldn't help but feel a little nervous, but it was expected as she didn't really know them. As the screen came to life, Bentley's parents appeared on the screen.

"Bentley! Raelynn! What a lovely surprise!" Mrs. Riggs exclaimed. As Bentley held up Raelynn's hand to show them the ring, Mrs. Riggs' eyes immediately locked onto Raelynn's hand.

"Mom, Dad, we have something to tell you," Bentley began as Mrs. Riggs' eyes widened with surprise. "We're engaged!" Raelynn chimed in.

"Oh, my goodness! That ring is absolutely stunning! Congratulations, you two!" Mrs. Riggs shouted joyfully. Bentley grinned widely as Raelynn blushed and thanked Mrs. Riggs.

"That's not the only surprise we have either." Bentley said slyly, looking at Raelynn with a smirk before continuing, "We're pregnant!" Bentley said with excitement in his voice.

You could see the worry and concern spread across Faye and Steve's face as Bentley dropped the news on them. Especially since he just told them about his son Skylar.

Faye and Steve Riggs were initially taken aback by Bentley's unexpected announcement. Their expressions shifted from sheer joy about the engagement to a mix of surprise and concern. Raelynn, glancing nervously at Bentley, braced herself for their reaction.

Mrs. Riggs was the first to break the silence, her eyes widening even more. "Pregnant? Oh my, that's... well, that's quite a double surprise!" she exclaimed, her excitement tempered by the unexpected news.

Bentley, sensing their apprehension, quickly reassured them. "We know it's a lot to take in, but we're thrilled about expanding our family. We wanted to share the joy of both milestones with you," he explained, smiling warmly.

Steve Riggs, though still processing the information, managed a smile. "Congratulations, you two. It's a lot to process, but we're happy for you," he said, his tone reflecting a mix of surprise and acceptance.

As the conversation unfolded, Raelynn and Bentley took the time to address their parents' concerns and share their plans for the future. Slowly, the initial shock turned into understanding, and Faye and Steve expressed their support for the young couple.

As the call came to an end Raelynn couldn't help herself feel a pang of jealousy. She wished her parents were as levelheaded as Bentley's mom and dad. Or at least as half as understanding as Steve and Faye were.

While lying in the still of the night trying to process the emotions of the day, it dawned on Bentley and Raelynn that they couldn't go without telling their best friends.

"I think I should call Cam and tell him about the engagement, and the baby." Bentley said with excitement.

Raelynn agreed, "I think that's a good idea. You call him while I go in the living room to call Cassidy."

As Raelynn got up from the bed, Bentley dialed Cameron's number. After a few rings, Cameron picked up the call. "Hey man, what's up?" Cameron answered.

Bentley took a deep breath, "I just wanted to let you know that I proposed to Raelynn tonight, and she said yes. Also, we are pregnant!"

There was a moment of silence on the other end of the line before Cameron spoke again. "Wow, that's great news, Bentley. Congratulations! Bout time you took my advice and found someone to settled down with."

Bentley smiled, feeling relieved that his best friend was happy for him. However, Bentley could tell there was something on his mind. "What's wrong, Cam?" he asked.

Cameron hesitated before responding, "It's just...I don't know how to feel about all of this. You know, with you and Raelynn getting engaged and everything. It's all happening so fast. But don't get me wrong, I am extremely happy for you man."

Bentley nodded, "I know, man. It's a lot to process. But I love Raelynn and I want to spend the rest of my life with her."

Cameron sighed, "I understand, Bentley. Just please be careful. We don't need a repeat of last time!"

Bentley laughed as he agreed and assured Cameron that this time it was going to be different. It just felt different.

Meanwhile, Raelynn had stepped into the living room and quickly dialed Cassidy's number. After a few rings, Cassidy's voice came through the phone, "Hey girl, what's going on?"

Raelynn could feel her heart beating faster as she exclaimed, "Bentley proposed, and we're getting married!"

There was a moment of silence on the other end before Cassidy's voice responded, "You know Raelynn, I'm still trying to wrap my head around this whole thing with Bentley, but I'm happy for you. And for him, I guess."

Raelynn could sense the hesitation in Cassidy's voice, but she chose to focus on the positive. "Thanks, Cassidy. It means a lot to hear that from you." Raelynn paused for a moment before continuing, "I know this might be hard for you, but I hope we can all move forward and be a family."

Cassidy took a deep breath before replying, "Yeah, you're right. We have a lot to work through, but I'm willing to try for Skylar's sake."

Raelynn smiled, relieved that Cassidy was open to the idea. "Thank you, Cassidy. I really appreciate it."

Cassidy took a deep breath, "So, have you set a date or anything?" she asked, changing the subject.

Raelynn smiled, "No, not yet. We just got engaged tonight. But we're definitely thinking about it."

Cassidy nodded, "Well, let me know if you need any help planning or anything. I'd be happy to help."

Raelynn felt relieved, "Thanks, Cassidy. I really appreciate it."

Bentley caught a glimpse of Raelynn strolling back into the bedroom after their phone calls. "How did it go?" she inquired with a beaming smile.

Bentley returned the gesture, "He was happy for us but admitted he was nervous about us moving so fast."

Raelynn nodded, fully aware that they had received similar responses from everyone they had informed that night.

Despite initially agreeing to take their relationship slow, they were now engaged and expecting a child only a few months into their relationship, making it a reasonable concern.

Raelynn embraced Bentley and informed him that she had called Cassidy and informed her of the news. "Despite everything that's happened in the last few months, Cassidy is trying to be thrilled for us," she said, settling down next to Bentley on the bed before continuing, "I understand her perspective. Five years ago, she had a one-night stand with the man who fathered her child and is now the man her best friend is in love with and expecting a child with as well. So, I totally get it, especially considering all she's done to try and erase you. So, I a hundred percent get it."

Bentley chuckled, "Well, we certainly know how to make things interesting, don't we?"

Raelynn playfully nudged him, "Oh, absolutely. I wouldn't have it any other way."

As they lay there, the playful banter continued, helping to ease the tension that lingered from the earlier conversations. Bentley traced circles on Raelynn's hand with his thumb, lost in thought.

"You know," Bentley began, "I never imagined I'd be here again – engaged and expecting a child with the woman I love. It's surreal."

Raelynn smiled, "Life has a funny way of surprising us. But I'm excited about our future together, Bentley. Even with all the twists and turns."

Bentley leaned in, placing a soft kiss on Raelynn's forehead, "Me too, Rae. And you know what? I think we should have a little celebration, just the two of us."

Raelynn raised an eyebrow, "Oh? What did you have in mind, Mr.”

Bentley grinned, "How about this right here.” Bentley grabbed Raelynn by the waist pulling her closer as he planted a long, deep and fiery passionate kiss on Raelynn's lips. It was so powerful Raelynn moaned in response.

In that moment everything that was an obstacle in Bentley and Raelynn's way seemed to fade away. As Bentley's kiss felt like it lasted an eternity.

As the kiss intensified Raelynn could feel the bulge between Bentley's legs began to grow as she could feel it pressing against her most sensitive part. It was driving her mad, she wanted more as she took control.

Raelynn rolled Bentley onto his back as she hopped on top of him straddling him. The kisses between the two intensifying.

His hands began to caress her hips, pulling her close. She moved her hips back and forth rubbing herself along his length as she ground her moist mound against his rock-hard cock. He slid his hand under her t-shirt grazing the skin of her stomach and chest. Bentley then slid his hand underneath her bra strap, unhooking it as it dangled under her shirt.

His fingers continued to roam her body while his lips tasted every inch of her neck and collarbone.

Raelynn pulled back to catch her breath as she gazed at him. She kissed him tenderly before in one swift move Bentley removed her shirt and bra from over her head tossing them to the floor as he caressed her breast in his hands.

"I want you to make love to me Bentley." Raelynn said with her voice hitched.

Bentley smiled as he aimed to meet her demand. With one swift motion, he rolled her over onto her back positioning himself on top of her. His kisses were the perfect combination of long and slow to keep the fire burning between them.

Soon Bentley's gentle kisses trailed down Raelynn's neck, collarbone, breast, stomach, to her waist where Bentley gently began to pull her legging's along with her panties down. His mouth travelled down further kissing each curve of her thighs all the way to her ankles before stopping briefly.

The moment Bentley looked up at her, his eyes bore into hers, as he slowly peeled her legging off each leg tossing them to the floor. Bentley then began slowly kissing his way back down Raelynn's leg, kissing her ankle, calf, thigh, hip and then finally, Raelynn's most sensitive part.

Raelynn arched her back closing her eyes allowing Bentley to do what he wanted. She sighed softly when he placed his tongue inside her soaking wet core. Her breathing became heavier as he tongued her deeply.

He reached behind him pulling his boxer briefs down as he reached forward placing his fingers between her legs as he entered her warm welcoming core, causing her to moan louder than she intended.

Her fingers laced through his hair as she gave out her own small cries of pleasure. She could feel herself begin to tense up as she began to climax as Bentley's tongue found its target. Her juices lubricated his path as his tongue penetrated deeper.

"Yes, yes, YES! OH GOD BENTLEY!" Raelynn yelled.

"OH FUCK!! YES!!!!" she yelled as she exploded around his face causing him to fall backward.

When she opened her eyes, she saw Bentley looking down at her. He had a lustful look in his eyes as he began licking her juices off his face.

When their eyes met Raelynn smiled as she started grabbing the sheets as she prepared for him to enter her with his long thick shaft.

Bentley, on his knees above Raelynn, he gently stroked his long hard shaft preparing to enter Raelynn.

Raelynn had become impatient as she reached her hand up wrapping it around Bentley's hard cock pulling him closer. She guided the head of his penis to the entrance of her soaking wet vagina, when with a powerful thrust Bentley slid inside slowly stroking in and out of Raelynn's tight warmness.

Raelynn gasped loudly as his thick rod rubbed against her walls bringing pleasure to both of them. His strong arms held her body firmly against him as he increased his pace.

Bentley leaned in kissing her passionately as they moved together, with each thrust they met the other. Their bodies were slick with sweat, Bentley's eyes bore into Raelynn's as she felt herself reaching another orgasm.

Raelynn clenched her muscles around Bentley's penis causing his tip to swell, swelling even more, as he pushed in as far as he could go making Raelynn scream out in pleasure. She tightened her vaginal walls causing him to lose his rhythm as he tried to ease out.

Raelynn continued to tighten her grip around his shaft as she began to orgasm once again.

It didn't take much longer before she felt her clit contract against Bentley's cock as he pumped his load deep within her.

"Fuck I'm gonna cum!" he moaned loudly in Raelynn's ear as he shot his load.

Bentley slowly pulled out sliding his softening member from her willing body, giving her time to adjust to the feeling of emptiness.

He leaned down kissing her deeply as he stared into her eyes letting her know that everything was alright.

They lay there resting together on the bed basking in the afterglow of their passion. They cuddled naked, intertwined holding each other tightly with beams of joy dancing across their faces. The perfect ending to a not so perfect day.

That night, Raelynn found herself unable to sleep, tossing and turning in bed. Meanwhile, Bentley was sound asleep, snoring loudly. Raelynn was over the moon about the recent events in her life – getting engaged, expecting a child, and landing a record deal – but she couldn't shake off the feeling of apprehension about the media attention that would come with her newfound success.

She had asked Bentley to keep their relationship low-key to avoid any unwanted attention from the tabloids. But now, with her music career taking off and her pregnancy and engagement becoming harder to conceal, she felt stuck. How could she hide her pregnancy or her engagement ring from the media? Would she have to abandon their original plan and go public with their relationship?

The thought of being scrutinized by the media made her anxious, and she could already imagine the headlines. "Bentley, the wild party boy, tamed by country star Raelynn!" she muttered under her breath. She didn't want to think about the potentially hurtful headlines that could follow.

Raelynn got up from bed and walked over to the bedroom window, looking out at the city lights. She took a deep breath and tried to calm her racing thoughts. She knew that with success came media attention, but she couldn't help but feel overwhelmed by it all.

She thought about talking to Bentley, but she didn't want to burden him with her worries. He had his own career to focus on and she didn't want to distract him from his goals. As she heard Bentley yawn from behind her, she turned to see that he had woken up and was looking at her with concern. "What's wrong, baby?" he asked softly as he was rubbing his eyes.

Hesitantly, Raelynn opened up to him about her fears and worries, and he listened attentively. That's when Bentley got up from bed walked over to Raelynn and wrapped his arms around her, pulling her close.

Raelynn hesitated for a moment before speaking again. "I'm just worried about the media attention," she restated, looking up at him. "I don't want our relationship to become a media circus. I don't want them to tear us apart."

Bentley sighed and squeezed her tighter. "I know, babe. I hate the media attention too. But we can't let them control our lives. We can't let them dictate how we live or who we love."

Raelynn nodded as she turned to face Bentley burying her face in his chest. "I just don't know if I can handle it all," she whispered.

Bentley lifted her chin up and looked into her eyes. "We'll figure it out together, okay? We'll take it one step at a time. We'll do whatever it takes to protect our love and our family. First step though, we need to call Mike so he can get ahead of this for us and mitigate on how to move forward with going public."

Raelynn smiled and leaned in to kiss him. She felt reassured by his words and his presence. She knew that with Bentley by her side, she could face anything.

Later that morning Bentley and Raelynn decided to give Mike a call so that he could be in the loop on everything. Since, Mike was the manager of them both he needed to be in the loop so he could get a jump start on how to face the media head on with his 'damage control' tactics.

"Hey Mike." Bentley said with his business voice. "Me and Raelynn have some big news to share with you so you can start delegating your time towards running damage control." Bentley continued.

Mike sighed almost as if he was expecting Bentley to hit him with bad news. "Oh boy, what is it?" Mike asked hesitantly.

Bentley smiled as he knew this was the start of bringing his and Raelynn's relationship to life in the media's eyes. Bentley knew Raelynn was nervous about the media's attention and he would by lying to himself if he said he wasn't either. But Bentley had been in the media spotlight for the past six years of his life, so he knew how to better navigate through all the up and downs that the media was going to hurl at them.

That is why he called Mike because Mike was good at public relations as he has had to run damage control several times throughout Bentley's career.

"Well, Mike. Raelynn and I are engaged." Bentley said with such satisfaction. There was a brief pause before Bentley continued "And that's not all. Raelynn and I are also expecting a kid."

Mike laughed as if he were being punked. "Bentley Riggs an engaged man and with a child on the way? Oh, the media is going to love this one for sure." Mike said through his laughter.

"Yeah Mike, see that's what I'm scared of. I'm scared the media is going to love this a bit too much. Raelynn is absolutely terrified right now, especially since she hasn't even gotten in the studio to start working on her EP. So, can you please tactfully handle this for us Mike?" Bentley asked.

Mike was coming out of his laughing spell as he cleared his throat becoming more serious sounding "Bentley, don't you worry bud. I got this. You know I do. Tell Raelynn she has nothing to worry about to just trust me on this. What we're going to do is, we're only going to tell the media that the two of you are engaged right now. We will tell them about the pregnancy when she starts to show and can no longer hide it. I think that is for the best right now."

Bentley agreed as hung up the phone. Bentley looked up at Raelynn and told her "Don't worry darling, Mike has everything under control."

Raelynn let out a deep sigh of relief as she looked at Bentley. "Thank you, Bentley. I don't know what I would do without you."

Bentley smiled and took her hand, giving it a reassuring squeeze. "Hey, we're in this together. We'll get through it, I promise."

Raelynn smiled back at him, feeling grateful for his unwavering support.

36

LA Landing

The following Monday marked the start of Raelynn's professional career as an artist as she waited in the terminal of RDU to board her flight to the infamous LAX.

As Raelynn waited to board her flight, she couldn't escape her racing mind. She couldn't help but wonder why there had been no media coverage on her relationship with Bentley. It had almost been a week since they announced their engagement to the public, yet no media coverage had surfaced.

Raelynn couldn't help but wonder if Mike had truly taken care of everything as promised. Despite Bentley's popularity in the media, she was surprised that there was no buzz surrounding their relationship.

As Raelynn continued to wait for her boarding call, she mindlessly scrolled through her phone, only to finally come across a TMZ article featuring her and Bentley. Her stomach churned with nervousness as she debated whether to open it. Eventually, her curiosity won out and she clicked on the article.

To her surprise and relief, the article was actually quite respectful towards her and Bentley's relationship. They referred to her as an "up-and-coming country star" and praised her for taming America's sexiest playboy. Raelynn couldn't help but feel proud and happy as she read through the article. She let out a chuckle and a small smile as she realized that the media attention might not be as bad as she had feared.

However, that was just one media outlet, and the fans hadn't started chiming in yet and Raelynn was forgetting to take that into consideration.

Now feeling more relaxed, Raelynn made her way to her seat in the first-class section of the plane as they finally called for her to board. She settled into her comfortable seat and took a deep breath as she waited for departure.

As the plane took off, Raelynn closed her eyes, letting out a satisfied sigh and drifted off into a peaceful sleep before the plane even reached its cruising altitude.

Several hours later, Raelynn woke up feeling rejuvenated as the plane started its descent into Los Angeles. Raelynn gazed out the window in amazement at the breathtaking view. The vast expanse of the city was overwhelming, and she couldn't wait to explore every inch of it.

While Raelynn was standing in the baggage claim waiting for her luggage. She overheard a familiar voice talking on the phone in the distant behind her. To her surprise, when she turned around to investigate the voice she had heard, she saw her father deep in conversation on the phone with someone at the baggage claim.

In that moment she didn't know whether to walk over to him and speak or act as if she didn't even see him. She was still angry with her father and how he acted the night that Bentley and she told them they were pregnant. She ultimately didn't want to speak to her father until he apologized but she knew the likely hood of that would be never because of how stubborn he was. With the way she was feeling, she decided to act as if she didn't see her father as she turned back to face the conveyor belt waiting for her luggage.

As Raelynn reached down to grab her luggage her father had made his way over to her. "Hey baby girl." Mr. Hart said as Raelynn felt the hairs on the back of her neck stand up. "What are you doing here in LA?" Mr. Hart continued.

Raelynn wanted to ignore him, but she didn't want to be rude. Aggressively, Raelynn turned around looking her father in the eyes and said "I could ask you the same thing dad. But since you forgot why I am here, it's to record my EP." The anger in Raelynn's body language and facial expressions was very clear to see.

"I'm here for a few days for a business meeting. Trying to get my new client a sponsorship. Which, I've got to run. I'm running late. So, I'll catch you later sweetie, maybe we can get dinner and talk." Mr. Hart said looking down at his watch.

Raelynn was glad that he was running late and had to run because she didn't know if she could indulge in a conversation with her father. At least not at this point in time in her life. Not until he could become more accepting of Bentley and apologized to everyone.

"Good luck sweetie, you're going to kill it, I believe in you." Mr. Hart said as he started to rush off.

His "good luck" comment caught Raelynn off guard as it was the first time in her career that her father had given her a 'pep-talk' and showed signs of support. She wondered if he had said it by accident as he was in rush or if he really meant it.

During the ride to her hotel, Raelynn couldn't stop admiring the city's beauty. The towering skyscrapers, the bustling streets, and the endless palm trees left her in awe. When she arrived at the hotel she immediately checked in, and headed up to her room, which had an amazing view of the city.

Before she headed to the studio Raelynn decided to take a selfie with the view of the city behind her and sent it to Bentley to let him know that she had arrived safely. She didn't want to call him because she didn't want to wake him. She knew that he was more than likely still asleep.

When Raelynn finally made it to the studio, she was greeted by a receptionist who knew who she was right away. "Hey Raelynn, follow me right this way! The producers are waiting for you." as she got up from the front desk and escorted Raelynn down a long hallway to the studio.

Raelynn followed the receptionist down the hallway, feeling a mix of excitement and nerves. She couldn't believe she was actually here, at one of the biggest studios in Los Angeles, about to record her first EP.

As they approached the studio, Raelynn could hear the sound of music and talking coming from inside. The receptionist opened the door, and Raelynn stepped inside to find a group of producers and sound engineers huddled around a mixing board, listening intently to a playback of one of her demos. They turned to greet her as she entered, and Raelynn couldn't help but feel a surge of confidence as she met their eyes.

"Raelynn, great to finally meet you in person," said one of the producers, stepping forward to shake her hand. "We've been listening to your tracks, and we're really excited about what you're bringing to the table."

Raelynn felt a grin spread across her face as the producers began to discuss the direction they wanted to take with her music. They talked about the kind of sound they were looking for, the audience they wanted to reach, and the message they wanted to convey through her lyrics.

Raelynn listened intently, taking in their feedback and suggestions. They even provided her with 20-new tracks with lyrics that they wanted her to record over the week. Their plan was to have her redo her demo songs Mike had provided to them with tweaks to the instrumental and more production behind her voice. They also wanted her to record the songs they provided her with so they could have a variety of songs to choose from to make the EP.

Raelynn took a sit beside one of the producers and started to look over the lyrics for the songs with the instrumentals to each one playing in the background as they navigated her on how they wanted her to approach each individual song. Raelynn began to feel a lot of pressure as she got the feeling that they were trying to change her true sound.

She knew that they knew what was going to sell and what was going to propel her and her bad to superstardom. However, the tracks didn't sound like her or the direction she wanted to take her career. She began to wonder if this is how Bentley felt when he made his first album. Then she remembered Bentley telling her how he was granted full creativity rights in his contract so she knew he wouldn't be able to help her navigate through this stressful situation.

She finally decided to just go with the flow and let the producers do their thing. Afterall, she didn't expect to even make it here. Plus, her contract was only for two years. All she needed to do is do what they said for two years and if she didn't want to continue working with them, she could choose to go a different route.

After sitting with the producers for a couple of hours, the instrumentals started to grow on Raelynn. She was starting to think that this was a sound she could make work. Raelynn liked pop and heavy metal but never thought about mixing that kind of music with country, as she had always chosen to stay the more modern country route.

As they continued conversating about her music, Raelynn had one last question for the producers before stepping into the booth, "I really like that you're trying to give me an authentic sound to make me stand out, it's new and it's growing on me but is it possible for me to make some changes to the lyrics to make them fit me more?"

The producers looked at each other before one of them spoke up, "We're open to hearing your ideas, Raelynn. After all, you are the one singing the songs, and we want it to feel authentic to you even if we are changing your normal sound. Remember change is a good thing here in the music industry. Especially if you are keeping up with the times. Right now, country blended with pop and heavy metal is on the rise and we want you to be one of the first female country artist to make that transition. We've got guys in the country music industry making the transition and they are getting a lot of positive feedback."

Raelynn let out a sigh of relief and smiled, "Thank you, that means a lot. Let's get to work then."

Raelynn emerged from the recording booth, having finished re-recording her songs from the original demo. She settled down next to the producer who had been assisting her and sifted through the lyrics and instrumentals for the next song. One set of lyrics caught her eye, but the instrumental didn't feel right. She found another instrumental from a different song that she thought could complement the lyrics well. She turned to the producer and asked, "Can we mix and match the instrumentals and lyrics to make it work?"

The producer looked at her and gave a small smile, "Of course we can. That's the beauty of making music, it's all about experimentation and finding what works best." He took the instrumental she had chosen and loaded it onto the soundboard.

Raelynn got up and stepped into the booth and begin to record. The instrumental started very dark and melodic, before the heavy drums kicked in taking it to a different stratosphere. As the instrumental played the producers anxiously waited for Raelynn to begin to sing.

They were eager to hear how the instrumental, Raelynn's vocals, and lyrics about a woman seeking revenge after being cheated on by her lover would blend together. As Raelynn began to sing her voice flowed effortlessly over the powerful beat, bringing the lyrics to life. As she sang, she could feel the emotion building inside of her, and it was clear that the new instrumental had brought a whole new dimension to the song.

After the recording was complete, Raelynn stepped out of the booth, feeling a sense of pride and accomplishment.

The producer gave her a nod of approval as he said, "That was amazing. Mixing and matching the instrumentals and lyrics was a great call. I think we have something special here."

Raelynn smiled, feeling validated in her creative vision.

As they listened back to the recording, Raelynn couldn't help but feel amazed at how everything came together so perfectly. The mix of the new instrumental and her vocals was even better than she had hoped for. "I'm glad we took the chance on this," Raelynn said, turning to the producer. "Me too," he replied. "This is going to be a hit." He continued.

As the session drew to a close, Raelynn felt a sense of excitement for the work they had accomplished and anticipation for what was to come. "I can't wait to be back here tomorrow morning," she said to the producer. "So, tomorrow we'll tackle the rest of the tracks with the same approach?" she asked, hoping they could continue to experiment with mixing and matching instrumentals and lyrics.

The producer nodded, "Absolutely. We'll continue to work together to find the perfect sound for each song."

Raelynn smiled, feeling grateful to have found a producer who was willing to push the boundaries and explore new creative directions with her. She was really grateful that he and the rest of the team were pushing her out of her comfort zone instead of letting her put her talents in a box high up on the shelf.

"I just thought about it." Raelynn said shockingly as she clasped her hands to her face. "I haven't asked you your name." Raelynn continued.

The producer chuckled, "It's okay. My name is Jaxon Storm Montgomery. I actually just started here not long ago because I just moved to LA from North Carolina."

Raelynn's eyes widened in surprise as she processed the revelation of the producer's name. "Jaxon Storm Montgomery," she repeated, a mix of curiosity and amusement playing on her face. "Well, Jaxon Storm, it's a pleasure to officially know the mastermind behind these incredible sessions. I had no idea you were the new guy in town."

Jaxon smiled, appreciating Raelynn's genuine enthusiasm. "The pleasure is all mine, Raelynn. I'm thrilled to be working with such a talented artist like yourself. And yeah, LA is a whole different world from North Carolina, but I'm loving the energy here."

As they exchanged a few more words, Raelynn couldn't help but reflect on how fortunate she was to have someone like Jaxon, also from North Carolina, guiding her through this creative process. The fact that he had just moved to LA added an extra layer of excitement to their collaboration – two individuals embarking on a new journey together.

After her session at the studio, Raelynn decided to take a walk around the city and explore her surroundings. She walked down the famous Hollywood Boulevard, taking in all the sights and sounds of the bustling city. As she walked, she couldn't help but feel a sense of excitement for what was to come in the following days. She was finally here, and she was ready to make her dreams a reality and she couldn't wait to call Bentley and tell him about everything!

As the sun began to set, Raelynn made her way back to her hotel room. She pulled out her phone and dialed Bentley's number. He answered on the first ring, "Hey, Raelynn, how did the session go?"

Raelynn couldn't contain her excitement, "It was amazing, Bentley! The producer is so talented he's also from North Carolina, and we've been able to create something truly special. I can't wait for you to hear it."

Bentley was thrilled to hear her enthusiasm, "I'm so happy for you, Raelynn. You deserve this!"

Pausing from discussing her own experiences, Raelynn inquired about life back home. "How are things going back home? Are you spending time with Skylar?" she asked.

Bentley replied, "Things are going well, and yes, I am. I'm actually on my way to pick him up from school now."

As Raelynn was chatting with Bentley, her phone beeped with an incoming call. She glanced at the screen and saw it was her father, Mr. Hart. She hesitated for a moment before answering.

"Hey Ben, Satan is beeping in and he's also here in LA and wants to meet for dinner tonight, so I'll talk to you later. I love you!" Raelynn said before answering her father's incoming call.

Bentley could hear the dreadfulness in her voice as she did not want to answer his call.

"Hey Dad," Raelynn said, trying to keep her voice steady.

"Raelynn, how did today at the studio go?" Mr. Hart's voice came through the line, sounding almost too cheery.

"It went fine," she replied, keeping her tone neutral.

"I'm glad to hear it. Listen, I know things have been tense between us, but I was hoping we could still meet up and have dinner tonight. Just the two of us."

Raelynn felt a surge of anger at the suggestion. After everything he had done to her and Bentley, he expected her to just forgive and forget? But a part of her also felt curious about what he had to say.

She took a deep breath before responding. "I don't know, Dad. I'm still pretty upset with you over what happened."

"I understand that, and I'm sorry. I just want a chance to make things right between us. Please, Raelynn, just give me a chance to talk to you."

Raelynn hesitated for a moment longer before finally agreeing to meet him for dinner. She arranged to meet him at a nearby restaurant in a couple of hours. As she hung up the phone, she couldn't shake the feeling of unease in the pit of her stomach. She wasn't sure if she was ready to talk with her father just yet, but she knew she had to try.

As Raelynn arrived at the restaurant, she spotted her father sitting at a table near the back. He stood up as she approached, a smile on his face.

"Raelynn, I'm glad you chose to meet me," he said, pulling her into a hug. She stiffened at the contact but forced herself to relax.

They sat down and ordered their food, making small talk about life when Raelynn was a kid. Mr. Hart seemed genuine in his attempts to connect with his daughter, but Raelynn couldn't help but feel suspicious of his motives.

As they finished their meal, Mr. Hart cleared his throat and looked at her seriously. "Raelynn, I know I've made mistakes in the past, but I want to make things right between us. And that includes accepting Bentley into our family. I've been doing some thinking and I realize now that I was wrong to treat him the way I did."

Raelynn was surprised at his words but tried not to show it. She nodded slowly, unsure of what to say. "I appreciate that, Dad," she finally said, "but it's going to take more than just words to make things right. Bentley and I both need to see that you're serious about this."

Mr. Hart nodded as he if he understood the weight of her words. "I understand that, and I don't expect you to forgive me right away. But I want you to know that I'm trying to come around to the idea of Bentley. He truly seems like a good guy, and I can see how much he means to you." Mr. Hart said.

As they said their goodbyes, Raelynn couldn't help but feel a glimmer of hope that maybe, just maybe, her father was starting to come around. But as she walked away, she couldn't shake off the feeling that something was still not quite right. She decided to call Bentley and tell him about her evening with her father.

As Raelynn got into her room, she called Bentley and told him about her dinner with her father, he listened intently.

"I don't know, Bentley," Raelynn said hesitantly. "He seemed genuine in wanting to make things right, but I just can't shake the feeling that something's off."

Bentley sighed, "I know it's tough, but maybe it's worth giving him a chance. He might surprise you."

Raelynn thought about Bentley's words for a moment and decided to take his advice. She knew it wouldn't be easy, but maybe it was time to start letting go of her anger and giving her father a chance to make things right.

Trying not to think about it too much Raelynn shifted the topic. "How's everything going with Skylar?" Raelynn asked.

"It's going really great. Every time I look at him, I'm reminded of a little me. I guess that's what happens when he's half of me." Bentley said through a chuckle.

After ending the call, Raelynn felt grateful for having someone like Bentley in her life. He was always there for her, providing unwavering love and support. With a smile on her face, she got into bed, knowing that she had a busy day ahead of her.

37

Homefront

Back home, Bentley was enjoying some much-needed father-son time with Skylar. He had a whole week to spend with Skylar, and he wanted to make the most of it. Bentley knew how important it was to build a strong bond with his son, and he hoped that Skylar would continue to like him. He cherished the moments Cassidy was allowing them to spend together and longed for more time to create lasting memories. Especially, since he had five years of absence to equate for.

Once Bentley hung up the phone with Raelynn, he helped Skylar finish his homework. "So, what do you want to do today, Skylar?" Bentley asked, curious about his son's thoughts.

He had a few activities in mind but wanted to ensure that Skylar would enjoy them, or else he was prepared to switch to a different plan. To his surprise, Skylar had a different idea in mind.

"Honestly, Daddy, I just want to spend more time with you and get to know you better," Skylar replied.

Bentley smiled, happy that his son wanted to build a stronger bond with him and was delighted to spend the day getting to know Skylar better too.

Bentley ruffled Skylar's hair affectionately. "I love that idea, buddy. How about we go for a walk in the park and grab some ice cream?"

Skylar's eyes lit up with excitement. "Yes, please!" he exclaimed.

Bentley grabbed his keys, and they headed out the door, enjoying the warm sunshine and gentle breeze.

After getting their ice cream, they made their way to the park. Spotting a picnic table, they walked over and sat down to enjoy their treats and the lovely weather. Bentley took a bite of his ice cream and then turned to Skylar. "So, buddy, what would you like to know about me? Ask away."

You could see Skylar carefully pondering before replying, "Mom says you can tell a lot about a man from his favorite sports teams. What are your teams?"

Bentley chuckled at Skylar's question. "Your mom told you that, huh? Well, I'm a fan of football and basketball. I love the Carolina Tar Heels for college basketball and football. As for the NFL, I really like the Carolina Panthers. I'm not a big fan of NBA basketball, though, as I think they don't play as hard as college players."

Skylar's eyes lit up with excitement. "Awesome! You're way cooler than mommy. She likes the Cowboys and Duke Blue Devils, but I love the Tar Heels and the Panthers!" he exclaimed, giggling.

That's when Bentley had the idea to take him to a game. "Skylar what do you say we go to a game when the season starts?" Bentley asked.

"Of course!" Skylar exclaimed.

Bentley smiled at Skylar's enthusiastic response. "Great! We'll have a father-son day out at the stadium. It'll be a blast," Bentley replied, excited at the thought of spending more time with his son. "We can get some team merchandise, eat some hot dogs and watch our favorite teams play."

Skylar was visibly overjoyed at the prospect of going to a game with his dad. "Thank you, Daddy! That's the best idea ever!" he exclaimed, giving Bentley a big hug.

"Alright, Sky, do you have any more questions for me?" Bentley asked.

"I do. How did you act when you found you were my dad?" Skylar asked.

Bentley was taken back by his question as it was such a big question for a five-year-old to be asking. Bentley didn't know what to say. He wanted to make sure his answer was as age appropriate as possible.

After a moment of pondering Bentley finally had an answer, he felt Skylar could handle. "Well, son, I was honestly confused. Then as I struggled to accept it, I became scared. I was scared you weren't going to like me. I was scared I wasn't going to be good at this. I was scared your mother wasn't going to allow me to see you. It was so many emotions I felt. Then when I actually got to meet you after knowing you were my son, I instantly loved you as I could see a miniature me standing right before my eyes." Bentley explained.

Skylar listened intently to Bentley's answer, his eyes wide with curiosity. "Wow, that sounds like a lot of emotions to feel all at once," Skylar replied. "But I'm glad you didn't give up and that you came to see me. I love you, Daddy," Skylar said, giving Bentley another hug.

Bentley hugged him back tightly. "I love you too, Skylar. And I'm so grateful that I get to be your dad," he said, feeling a sense of warmth in his heart.

They finished their ice cream and spent the rest of the evening playing catch and enjoying the sunshine.

As they left the park, Bentley couldn't help but feel grateful for the opportunity to be a part of Skylar's life.

As they got home from the park Bentley instructed Skylar to go get in the bath to get ready for his mother to come pick him. Right as Skylar was getting out of the tub there was knock at the door.

"That's probably your mom." Bentley shouted to Skylar as he walked to the door to answer it.

When he opened the door, it was a visibly exhausted Cassidy. Bentley stepped to the side as he let her in. "Skylar is getting out of the tub now." Bentley said to Cassidy as she walked over to the couch and plopped down.

"I'm so tired." Cassidy said with a yawn.

Bentley nodded sympathetically. "I bet you are. You work so hard, Cassidy," he said, walking over to the kitchen to get her a glass of water. "Here, drink this. You look like you could use it," he said, handing her the glass.

Cassidy smiled gratefully and took a sip. "So, how was your day with Skylar?" she asked, curiously.

Bentley smiled and sat down next to Cassidy on the couch. "It was great. We went to get some ice cream, went to the park, and talked about our favorite sports teams. Skylar is a really smart and funny kid. I'm glad to spend time with him," Bentley replied, happy to share his experience with Cassidy.

Cassidy smiled and nodded. "I'm glad you two had a good time. Skylar is always talking about you, you know. He really looks up to you," she said, looking at Bentley with gratitude.

Bentley's heart swelled with pride at the thought of Skylar looking up to him. "I'm happy to hear that. I want to be a good role model for him," he replied, feeling grateful for the opportunity to be a part of Skylar's life.

Cassidy smiled warmly at him. "Believe it or not Bentley you already are. Even if it has been a short time of you being in his life."

As they talked about Skylar and waited for him to finish his bath, Bentley could see that Cassidy was having a hard time staying awake and was beginning to doze off. "Cassidy, why don't you and Skylar stay here tonight? You can take Raelynn's bed and I'll sleep on the couch," Bentley offered.

Cassidy's eyes widened at Bentley's offer. "Are you sure?" she asked hesitantly.

"Of course, I'm sure. You and Skylar are welcome to stay here anytime," Bentley reassured her with a warm smile.

Cassidy sighed just as Skylar emerged from the bathroom, dressed in his pajamas and looking fresh and clean. "Mommy, can we stay here tonight?" he asked.

"Yes, sweetie, we're going to stay here with Bentley tonight," Cassidy replied, giving him a tired smile.

Skylar began to jump up and down with excitement and all Bentley could do was smile at Skylar's excitement as he led them to Raelynn's room to get them settled in for the night. He made sure they had everything they needed and tucked them in, wishing them a good night's sleep.

As he closed the door behind him, he let out a sigh of relief, grateful for the opportunity to help out Cassidy and Skylar. He knew it wasn't easy for Cassidy to balance work and parenthood on her own, and he was glad to be able to provide a helping hand. As Bentley made himself comfortable on the couch for the night, he felt a deep sense of satisfaction knowing that he had been able to assist Cassidy and Skylar.

38

Glitz and Glamour

The next morning back in LA Raelynn jumped out of bed eager to make her way to the studio. She was all set to record the other songs that the producers had requested.

As she walked into the studio, Jaxon Storm who had guided her through everything yesterday greeted her with a coffee in hand. "Good morning, Raelynn! I've got some thrilling news for you today," he exclaimed as Raelynn took the coffee with a smile. "The executive producer loved the song, and he released it to the radio stations this morning," Jaxon said with excitement evident in his tone of voice.

Raelynn could hardly believe what she was hearing. It was like a dream come true, having one of her songs finally play on the radio.

"That's not all either. When we finish here today, they have you scheduled for an interview with a few of the media outlets to help in getting your name out there." Jaxon continued.

Raelynn just smiled the biggest smile as she sat down and the two of them dove right into mixing and matching lyrics and instrumentals.

As the session ended, Raelynn and Jaxon had successfully produced 10 songs, leaving the remaining ones for the next day. Raelynn knew that once they finished recording tomorrow, they would have to go through each song and select only the best for her upcoming EP's Friday release.

"Hey, I don't mean to pry, but I saw the article about you and Bentley being engaged. Have y'all set a date yet?" Jaxon asked as they finished the final song of the day.

Raelynn smiled and responded, "Honestly, we haven't discussed a date yet. Everything happened so fast, and then coming here, we haven't really had a chance to discuss it, but I'd marry that man right here, right now, if I could."

Jaxon smiled as he watched the love for Bentley radiate from Raelynn's eyes. "Well, congrats! I just hope you don't pay any mind to the trolls trolling because I saw some pretty hateful comments under some of those articles."

Raelynn's smile quickly faded as she grew concerned. When she had read the article, it was all positive vibes. What could people be saying that was so hateful? As she put the finishing touches on the last song of the day, she couldn't shake off what Jaxon had said.

When Raelynn left the studio, she pulled out her phone and began browsing through the comments on the article. As she walked back to the hotel, she read through a few of them and was appalled.

There were so many negative comments that it started to make her feel insecure about her relationship with Bentley. Two comments, in particular, stood out to her: one claiming that she was only with him to ride his coattails into fame, and the other insinuating that her father wouldn't help her achieve fame and attention, so she found a vulnerable Bentley to use instead.

Raelynn's heart sank as she read the hurtful words. She knew that there would always be people who would try to bring her down but seeing it in writing made it feel all the more real. She couldn't believe that people would say such things about her and Bentley, whom she loved with all her heart.

As she reached her hotel room, Raelynn sat on the bed and continued scrolling through the comments. But the more she read, the more upset she became. She couldn't let these comments affect her relationship with Bentley, but she couldn't help feeling self-conscious and vulnerable.

Just then, her phone rang. It was Bentley. "Hey, babe. How was the studio session today?" he asked.

Raelynn tried to sound upbeat as she responded, but Bentley could tell that something was wrong. "What's going on, Raelynn?" he asked gently.

Tears welled up in Raelynn's eyes as she told Bentley about the hurtful comments she had read. Bentley listened patiently and then said, "Raelynn, don't listen to those people. They don't know us or our love. We know the truth, and that's all that matters. I love you, and I can't wait to marry you someday."

Raelynn felt a wave of relief wash over her. She knew that Bentley was right. She couldn't let the negativity of others affect her relationship with him. With renewed strength, Raelynn wiped away her tears and smiled. "I love you too, Bentley," she said. "And you're right. We know the truth, and that's all that matters."

Bentley finished his phone call just as a groggy Cassidy entered the kitchen. "Coffee, I need coffee," she muttered while rummaging through the cabinets. He joined her and helped her locate the coffee.

"How'd you sleep?" Bentley asked, handing her the bag of coffee.

"Amazing. I haven't slept that well in a long time," Cassidy replied with a relieved sigh.

Bentley grinned, happy to hear that Cassidy had rested well. "I just spoke with Raelynn," he continued. "I told her you guys stayed over last night, and she's grateful that I'm taking care of y'all." Bentley chuckled before adding, "But really, I'm the one who's grateful. I appreciate you trusting me to get to know my son. Spending time with him has been great."

Cassidy smiled, but then confessed, "Bentley, I'm still finding it hard to trust you. But for Skylar's sake, I'm trying. And having you around has been nice. I'm starting to get used to it, honestly." She finished making her coffee and headed to the living room to watch the news before waking Skylar up for school.

As Cassidy finished her coffee, she checked the time and it was time to wake Skylar for school. She rose from the couch, leaving her coffee mug on the kitchen counter, as she made her way to wake Skylar. "Skylar, wake up sweetie. It's time for school," Cassidy gently shook him awake.

Skylar groaned and rubbed his eyes, but eventually sat up and stretched. "Good morning, mom," he mumbled.

Cassidy smiled at him, "Good morning, sleepyhead. Did you sleep well?"

"Yeah, I did," Skylar replied with a smile. Cassidy helped him get dressed and made him breakfast while he got ready for school.

As they finished breakfast, Bentley emerged from the spare bedroom, now tidied up. "Morning Skylar." Bentley said with a smile.

Skylar smiled back, still feeling a bit groggy from waking up so early. "Morning, Bentley," he replied, rubbing his eyes. "Did you sleep well?" Bentley asked, pouring himself a cup of coffee.

"Yeah, I guess so," Skylar said with a shrug. "I'm just tired of waking up early for school."

Bentley nodded understandingly. "I used to hate getting up early for school too," he said. "But it's important to get a good education, so it's worth it."

Skylar nodded in agreement as he finished his breakfast.

As Skylar was finishing brushing his teeth to get ready for school, Cassidy and Bentley worked together to clean up the kitchen. Once they finished, they settled on the couch. "So, what are your plans for today?" Cassidy asked, taking a sip of her coffee.

"I thought I might take a walk, explore the neighborhood a bit. How about you?" Bentley asked.

Cassidy nodded in agreement, "That sounds nice. It's a beautiful day outside. And I just must get Skylar to school, run some errands, and then I'll be at the diner for the rest of the evening. Speaking of which, I didn't bring any extra clothes for work. This is awful. Let me go figure out what to do with this head as I try to freshen up a bit."

As Cassidy got up to attend to her situation, Skylar emerged from the bathroom, ready for school. "Hey sweetie, give mommy a second to get ready and I'll be ready to leave, ok." Cassidy said as she hurried into the bathroom.

A few minutes later, Cassidy returned from getting ready, her hair now in a ponytail. "Okay, let's go get you to school," she said, looking down at Skylar who was waiting on the couch for her return. As they were leaving Bentley got up and walked them to the door.

"Have a good day at school, Skylar. And Cassidy, don't worry about the clothes, I can swing by the diner and drop off a fresh outfit for you later," he offered.

Cassidy smiled gratefully, "Thank you, Bentley. You really are a lifesaver." As they walked out the door, Bentley watched them go, feeling a sense of happiness and contentment wash over him.

Bentley took a deep breath of the fresh morning air before closing the door behind him. He decided to start his walk by heading towards the park a few blocks away. As he strolled through the neighborhood, he couldn't help but feel a sense of peace and calmness. The sun was shining, the birds were chirping, and the trees were swaying gently in the breeze. Bentley took his time, enjoying the sights and sounds around him. He even stopped to pet a friendly neighborhood dog who came up to him wagging its tail.

As he reached the park, Bentley found a bench to sit on to take in the scenery. The park was bustling with activity, yet it was still a peaceful retreat from the city's hustle and bustle. That's when Bentley found the creative urge to start jotting down lines for potential new lyrics to put in his new rap songs. Something Bentley had been secretly struggling to do.

As Bentley was taking in the scenery and jotting down lines his phone began to ring, it was Raelynn. When he answered the phone at first, he thought it was pocket dial because he could hear a lot of commotion going on in Raelynn's background.

"Hey Bentley, can you hear me okay?" Raelynn said. "I'm sorry if it's noisy, I'm currently in hair and makeup getting ready for this interview. I wanted to let you know so you could watch it and give me some feedback afterwards. Would you do that for me, please? I could use your pointers if I mess up."

Bentley smiled at the excitement in Raelynn's voice, "Of course, I'd love to watch the interview and give you some feedback. Just send me the details and I'll make sure to tune in."

Raelynn thanked him and quickly gave him the details of the interview before saying goodbye and hanging up. Bentley couldn't help but feel proud of Raelynn and all that she was accomplishing with her career.

He made a mental note to make sure to watch the interview and give her the best feedback possible.

After completing his walk, Bentley headed over to Cassidy's apartment to pick up a fresh outfit for her to drop off at the diner. As he made his way, he couldn't stop thinking about Raelynn and her upcoming interview. He felt a sense of eagerness and anticipation for her success and was looking forward to seeing her shine like a star on the big screen. This sparked an idea for him and Skylar to bond over; they could watch Raelynn's interview together.

Once at Cassidy's Bentley quickly grabbed the outfit and headed out the door, making his way to the diner. As he walked into the diner, Bentley couldn't help but feel a sense of pride as he saw Cassidy working hard behind the counter.

He handed her the bag of clothes and she smiled gratefully. "Thank you so much, Bentley. Again, you really are a lifesaver," she said, echoing her earlier sentiment.

"No problem at all. How's it going here?" he asked, taking a seat at the counter.

"It's been busy, but nothing I can't handle," Cassidy replied, wiping down the counter.

Bentley nodded, watching as Cassidy efficiently served customers and made small talk with them. He admired her work ethic and dedication to her job.

As the lunch rush began to wind down, Bentley asked, "Hey, do you mind if Skylar and you stay over again tonight? Raelynn has an interview that airs tonight, and I'd love to watch it with you guys. I think it would be a great bonding experience for all of us."

Cassidy smiled, "Of course not, that sounds like a great idea." As she rushed off to clean tables before the next wave of customers.

As Bentley went to exit the diner, Cassidy quickly rushed back to him, "Hey Ben, before you go, I almost forgot to tell you. The doctor called me earlier today about Skylar. Skylar isn't going to need the bone marrow transplant thankfully."

Bentley's eyes widened with a mix of relief and gratitude. "That's incredible news, Cassidy!" His voice carried a genuine sense of happiness.

Cassidy nodded, her smile widening. "Yeah, the doctor said test indicated that it's something he should naturally outgrow with time. We just need to keep an eye on him and schedule regular check-ups, but it looks like he's going to be okay."

Bentley couldn't help but feel a weight lift off his shoulders. "I'm so glad to hear that. Skylar is a trooper, and I'm sure he'll handle everything like a champ."

Cassidy chuckled, "He takes after his mama, I suppose." She then grew more serious. "Thanks again, Bentley, for everything. You've been such a great support, especially during these challenging times."

Bentley placed a hand on her shoulder. "It's the least I can do. Skylar is family, and so are you. Now, let's focus on celebrating this good news and looking forward to Raelynn's interview tonight."

With that, Bentley left the diner, a renewed sense of joy in his step. As he made his way back home, he couldn't help but reflect on how life had a way of surprising you with both challenges and unexpected moments of happiness. The evening promised to be a special one, with Raelynn's interview bringing them together for a night of shared joy and support.

39

Lights, Camera, Action

Later that evening, Bentley and Skylar found themselves cozily nestled on the couch, eagerly anticipating Raelynn's upcoming interview. They were also awaiting Cassidy's arrival from work, knowing that she planned to spend the night again, Cassidy had to make a quick stop at home to pick up clothes for herself and Skylar.

As the interview began to air and Raelynn appeared on TV Bentley was breath taken as she looked like an absolute rockstar. She looked beautiful as ever in that long black skin-tight dress. She was also wearing the confidence of a seasoned veteran.

"Wow!" Bentley muttered under his breath.

Skylar still heard it as he began to chuckle at his father's reaction to seeing Raelynn on the screen. Bentley just gave Skylar a playful 'get out of here' nudge in response.

"Welcome to the 'Katelynn After Hours Show,' Raelynn! You look stunning today," Katelynn greeted Raelynn as she walked onto the set.

"Thank you so much," Raelynn replied with a smile.

"So, Raelynn, you've been making headlines recently with your engagement to Bentley and the release of your new single. Can you tell us a bit about yourself and how you got into music?" Katelynn asked, her enthusiasm evident in her voice.

"Well, I'm a 28-years-young, a Nashville native, and my father runs a talent agency representing athletes, movie stars, and artists - everyone except myself. I've loved country music ever since I received my first guitar at the age of seven. Also, as you all saw yesterday, I'm the woman engaged to the sexy Mr. Bentley Riggs" Raelynn shared.

Katelynn nodded in approval as she quickly changed the topic, "Let's talk about your new single. Where did you draw inspiration from?"

Raelynn took a deep breath before answering, "Honestly, Katelynn, the single is not what I envisioned. When I got here to record this EP, I had my mindset on sticking with my same old style. So, for this song I want to give thanks to my producers for seeing my full potential and not allowing me to keep myself in a box high up on the shelf. They really pushed me and convinced me to step outside out of my comfort zone. They encouraged me saying this was my chance to stand out, be different, and build a name for myself. So, that's what I did, I rolled with the teams envision instead of mine and my bands that's how this masterpiece was born. Honestly, I surprised myself because it is amazing." Raelynn explained.

Impressed, Katelynn asked, "So, how much creative control did you have over the EP?"

"I had about 50% creativity. The producers provided the instrumentals and lyrics they wanted me to use, but I had the freedom to mix and match them in a way that felt authentic to me. I also had a say in how everything was mixed, so it's definitely my stamp on the project," Raelynn explained.

As Bentley and Skylar were deep into Raelynn's interview, Cassidy arrived, rushing into the room, panting slightly, "Hey guys, sorry I'm late," she apologized as she put her bag down. "How's it going? How's Raelynn's interview?" she asked, walking towards the TV screen.

Bentley and Skylar turned to her with amazement in their eyes, "It's going great, you have to see her, she's killing it," Bentley said with excitement.

Cassidy's eyes widened as she saw Raelynn on the screen, looking stunning as ever. "Wow, she looks amazing," she said, before sitting down beside Bentley and Skylar. T hey all watched the rest of the interview in silence, completely consumed by Raelynn's story and her new single.

"Okay, Miss Raelynn, before you get ready to perform your new single tonight, I have two more questions for you," Katelynn said, getting straight to the point. "As talented as you are, why isn't your dad supporting you and having his company represent you?"

Raelynn took a deep breath before answering. "Well, my father has never wanted me to pursue music. Neither him nor my mother. They've seen the fame and money ruin people in this line of work, and they didn't want that for me. So, I set out on my own and pursued my music career without his help. I was doing fine by myself until I met Bentley, and I never thought I'd be here, but I'm thankful. Truly, I am."

Katelynn then asked the big question that everyone was dying to know. "Okay, Miss Raelynn, we, the people, have got to know. How did you meet Mr. Bentley Riggs, and how did you tame him into proposing to you in just a few short months? Also, do you guys have a date set yet?"

Raelynn couldn't help but laugh. "Well, I met Bentley about eight years ago in Cancun at a dive bar singing Karaoke. Eight years later, present day, I ran into him again while I was performing at his best friend's club. He spent the whole night trying to run game, and I kept shutting him down. When I went back up on stage to perform, I had this feeling come over me out of nowhere, and I called him up on stage, and the rest has been history. And no, we don't have a date yet. So much has happened since he proposed with my career, that we just haven't had a chance to figure out a date. But if I could, I would marry that man right here, right now."

Katelynn raised her eyebrows in surprise at Raelynn's answer. "Wow, so he was persistent, huh?" she commented.

Raelynn chuckled and nodded. "Yes, he definitely was. But I'm glad he was, or else I wouldn't be here now," she replied with a smile.

Bentley watched intently as Raelynn answered the questions with poise and grace, knowing she had worked so hard to prepare for this moment. Skylar and Cassidy were equally captivated, listening intently to every word Raelynn said.

After the interview ended, Bentley turned to Skylar and asked, "What did you think, buddy?"

Skylar responded with wide eyes, "She was amazing, Dad!"

Cassidy joined in, adding, "Yeah, she really killed it!" As she locked eyes with Bentley for the first time without hostility, Cassidy felt a gut-wrenching feeling.

In that moment, she finally understood why Raelynn was so in love with Bentley. He was charming, soft-spoken, kindhearted, and had the deepest blue eyes that anyone could truly get lost in. It also made her realize why she fell for him six years ago.

Despite the feeling, Cassidy knew she had to ignore it and not act upon it again because the consequences that would follow would be much greater this time.

Bentley caught Cassidy staring at him, her gaze lingering for a moment longer than usual. He tried to ignore it, as he excused himself with a stretch, "Alright, I need to go to the restroom before she comes back on air to perform her new song."

Meanwhile, Cassidy sat there trying to control her racing heart and push away the unexpected rush of emotions that had surfaced for Bentley.

As she watched Bentley leave the room, Cassidy knew she had to regain control of her feelings. She clenched her fists, trying to focus herself. She couldn't let her past romantic feelings for Bentley affect her behavior now, especially with Raelynn in the picture.

She reminded herself of the potential consequences of acting on her feelings. She couldn't risk jeopardizing her friendship with Raelynn, who had been her rock for the past five years, helping her raise Skylar when she had no one else to turn to.

Cassidy knew she had to keep her emotions in check, no matter how difficult it may be. She had to put her friendship with Raelynn above anything else. Raelynn's unwavering support and love meant too much to Cassidy to risk losing it over unresolved feelings for Bentley.

As Cassidy was on the brink of drifting into her own thoughts, Raelynn made her way back to the screen, prepared to showcase her new song.

Simultaneously, Bentley had made his return to his living room seat. As Raelynn's performance began her voice soon filled the room captivating everyone's attention. As Bentley watched Raelynn's performance, Cassidy couldn't help but to stare at him.

Bentley was in such awe as he was amazed by Raelynn's on-screen presence. He also was loving the new style producers were trying to take her music. The country mixed with heavy metal really matched Raelynn's rebellious personality.

As Bentley, Cassidy, and Skylar watched Raeylnn's performance, Cassidy felt a pang of jealousy, but she pushed it aside and tried to focus on the positive. She knew that Raelynn was perfect for Bentley and that they were meant to be together.

As Raelynn's performance came to an end, Cassidy's internal struggle with her feelings for Bentley continued to gnaw at her. She quickly let out a forced yawn, trying to mask her unease. "Oh boy, I am tired. I think I am going to go to bed," Cassidy said, making her way to Raelynn's bedroom.

She wasn't actually tired; she just needed some space from Bentley, given the turmoil of emotions she was experiencing towards him. Cassidy hoped that distancing herself from him would help quell the growing turmoil inside her.

She closed the bedroom door behind her, taking a deep breath, trying to calm her racing heart. She knew she needed to sort out her feelings before they became too overwhelming to handle. Cassidy sat on the bed, lost in her thoughts, as she tried to make sense of the tangled mess of emotions; some she had been avoiding for years. She knew she couldn't keep ignoring them forever.

With a heavy sigh, Cassidy decided that it was time to confront her feelings and face the consequences, whatever they may be. She decided to have an honest conversation with Bentley and put an end to the turmoil once and for all. She knew it wouldn't be easy, but she couldn't let her feelings for Bentley continue to affect her mental state and potentially harm her relationship with Raelynn.

Cassidy took a deep breath, preparing herself for the conversation ahead, and made her way back to the living room where Bentley was still sitting. She knew it was time to confront her feelings and find a resolution, one way or another.

As she approached Bentley, she could feel her heart pounding in her chest, but she was determined to finally address the elephant in the room. She was glad Skylar had fallen sound asleep on the couch because she didn't want to strike his suspicions if they asked him to leave the room or if they went into another room. So, she knew it was time to be brave and face her feelings head-on.

She took a deep breath, and with a steady voice, she spoke up, "Bentley, we need to talk."

Bentley looked up at her with surprise in his eyes, and Cassidy knew that the moment of truth had finally arrived. She was ready to lay her cards on the table and find a resolution, no matter how difficult it might be. She braced herself for what might come next, knowing that it was time to face her feelings and put an end to the internal struggle that had been haunting her for years.

"Bentley, I know this may not be right of me, but please hear me out. I have feelings for you that never went away, despite my efforts to ignore them for the past five years. I have pretended to hate you, and when you reappeared in my life without even remembering me, I was able to keep up the charade. I pretended to hate you, and I was good at it. But then you found out Skylar was yours, and that's when everything changed for me. I knew I couldn't pretend to hate you anymore. But how can you pretend not to have feelings for someone, especially when that someone is engaged to your best friend and is having a child with them? I don't know, Bentley. I've been trying to cope with all these emotions and feelings, and shit, but then last night happened. Your act of kindness in letting me crash here, bringing me my clothes when I needed them, and spending time together as a family tonight, the three of us. Then when our eyes locked, all these emotions came rushing back to me. I feel so guilty because I see how you and Raelynn adore each other, and it hurts me. I know it's wrong of me to say, but I wish it were me instead. I just needed to get this off my chest to feel better." Cassidy sounded frustrated as she struggled to find the words to express her feelings.

As Cassidy poured her heart out to Bentley, he listened closely, his expression a mix of surprise and confusion. He had never expected Cassidy to confess feelings for him, especially considering their tumultuous history the past few weeks and his current relationship with Raelynn. He could see the pain and guilt in Cassidy's eyes as she spoke, and it tugged at his heartstrings.

After Cassidy finished speaking, there was a brief moment of silence. Bentley took a deep breath, trying to process everything Cassidy had just said. He could feel a mix of emotions stirring within him as well. He had a soft spot for Cassidy, despite their issues, and he couldn't deny that there had been moments when he had wondered what could have been if their circumstances were different. But he was strongly committed to Raelynn.

"Bentley, I know this is a lot to take in, and I don't expect anything from you," Cassidy said softly, tears glistening in her eyes. "I just needed to be honest with you and put an end to this internal struggle that has been consuming me for years. I understand if you don't have anything to say."

Bentley looked at Cassidy, his heart torn between his loyalty to Raelynn and his empathy towards Cassidy. He reached out and placed a hand on Cassidy's shoulder, offering her a reassuring squeeze. "I appreciate your honesty, Cassidy," Bentley said softly. "But I am committed to Raelynn and our future together. My priority is with her, Skylar and the baby."

Cassidy nodded, her tears falling freely now. She knew deep down that Bentley's commitment to Raelynn was unwavering, but she had needed to get her feelings off her chest and face the truth.

"I understand," Cassidy said, her voice choked with emotion. "I just needed to be honest with you and myself. I don't want to jeopardize your relationship with Raelynn or our friendship."

Bentley nodded, understanding the weight of Cassidy's words. He wanted to support her as a friend, but he also needed to be clear about his boundaries. "We can still be friends, because at the end of the day Cassidy we still have to co-parent" Bentley said gently. "But we need to be mindful of our feelings and respect each other's boundaries."

Cassidy nodded, wiping away her tears. She appreciated Bentley's understanding and respected his commitment to Raelynn. "Thank you for listening," Cassidy said, her voice steadier now. "I needed to get this off my chest, and I appreciate your understanding."

"Anytime, Cassidy," Bentley said. "I'm always here for you and Skylar."

With that, Cassidy and Bentley shared a silent understanding. They knew that their conversation was not the end of their story, but rather a new chapter that would require careful navigation. They both needed time to process their emotions and find a way to move forward without letting their feelings for each other interfere with their co-parenting abilities. It wouldn't be easy, but they were determined to handle it with maturity and respect.

As Cassidy left the living room and retreated to Raelynn's bedroom, Bentley remained in the living room, lost in his thoughts. He knew that Cassidy's confession would change things between them, and he needed to be mindful of his actions going forward. He loved Raelynn deeply and was committed to building a future with her, but he couldn't deny the complex situation he shared with Cassidy.

40

Blurred Lines

That following Saturday morning, the tension was still high between Cassidy and Bentley as Cassidy tried her best efforts to keep her distance. Skylar was beginning to pick up on the tension between them. That's when he made the demand that the three of them go to the park to play catch. He wanted to make things feel less awkward.

When they arrived at the park, Skylar eagerly ran off to play catch, his infectious laughter filling the air. Bentley couldn't help but smile at his son's enthusiasm and joined him in a game of catch, trying to put aside the tension he felt with Cassidy.

Cassidy watched them play from a distance, her heart aching with a mix of emotions. She couldn't deny the love Bentley had for Skylar and seeing them bond only made her feelings for Bentley resurface even stronger. She tried to focus on playing catch with Skylar, but her mind was   preoccupied.
As they played catch, Bentley never even noticed the guy with the camera. The man had been following Bentley, Skylar, and Cassidy the entire way from their house to the park, taking pictures of Bentley and Cassidy holding Skylar's hands, as well as capturing shots of them playing catch.

He was capturing candid moments that Bentley was trying to share with his son in privacy. Bentley always noticed the paparazzi, but today he was distracted by so many other things; mainly Cassidy. When Bentley thought he saw something, the man with the camera quickly left, satisfied with enough "dirt" to go about his day.

While enjoying the moment with Cassidy and Skylar, Bentley caught himself thinking about Cassidy as he kept taking long glances at her sitting on the park bench, while she was watching him and Skylar playing catch. He had never had the thoughts about Cassidy that he was having.

Yeah, he had thought about what if things were different when he first found out that Skylar was his son because he had always imagined raising his kids in a two-parent home. But never had he ever had dirty thoughts about her. Were they lustful thoughts or were they signs that he too was developing feelings for her as well?

All Bentley knew was that it was wrong. He was engaged, engaged to Cassidy's best friend at that, and they had a baby on the way. It was wrong because he also loved Raelynn very much and wanted a future with her.

As Bentley tried to push away the confusing thoughts and feelings that were bubbling up inside him, he focused on playing catch with Skylar, trying to distract himself.

However, every time he glanced at Cassidy, he couldn't deny the attraction he felt towards her. Her presence was intoxicating, and he found himself drawn to her in a way that he hadn't anticipated. He tried to shake off the thoughts, reminding himself that he was engaged to Raelynn and that Cassidy was her best friend. It was all wrong, and he couldn't let these feelings take control of him.

Cassidy, on the other hand, was also struggling with her emotions. She had poured her heart out to Bentley, and although she felt relieved to have finally expressed her feelings, she knew that pursuing anything with him would be complicated and potentially hurtful to Raelynn. She tried to push aside her feelings for Bentley but being near him and seeing the way he interacted with Skylar only served to reignite the spark she had tried to extinguish for years.

As they continued to play catch, Bentley couldn't ignore the chemistry between them. The tension and attraction were palpable, and he found himself stealing glances at Cassidy whenever he could.

Cassidy, too, was finding it increasingly difficult to keep her distance, as memories of their past relationship and the unresolved feelings she had for Bentley came rushing back. She tried to remind herself of the consequences and the potential harm it could cause to her friendship with Raelynn, but her heart was torn. Especially, with her imagination being the enemy.

In her imagination, Cassidy wanted nothing more than to just grab Bentley and kiss him. She wanted to rip his shirt off and kiss all over his torso as her hands trailed down Bentley's chest, feeling his muscles beneath her fingertips as she worked her way below his waist to feel the hardness of his penis in her hand. She imagined herself pressing her lips to his skin, leaving a trail of soft, lingering kisses along his collarbone, his chest, and his abs. Her mind was filled with vivid images of Bentley's reaction to her touch, the way his breath would catch, and his eyes would darken with desire. She imagined his hands in her hair, pulling her closer, urging her to explore every inch of his body with her lips and tongue.

Cassidy's heart raced with anticipation as she imagined Bentley's responses to her advances. She could almost taste the saltiness of his skin, feel the warmth of his body pressed against hers. Her body tingled with arousal as she imagined the passionate encounter that would ensue, fueled by their mutual attraction and longing for each other.

Lost in her daydream, Cassidy's lips parted slightly as she let out a soft, longing sigh. She shook her head, coming back to the present moment, realizing that Bentley was still playing catch with Skylar in front of her, oblivious to her innermost desires. Blushing, Cassidy quickly composed herself, tucking her wild imagination away. She knew it was wrong, but she couldn't help but to imagine, besides what was the harm in fantasying over something that would never happen anyways.

As the day at the park came to an end, Bentley and Cassidy exchanged awkward glances, both feeling the tension that had been building up between them. As they arrived back at Raelynn's place, Bentley excused himself to the bedroom, needing some time alone to process his emotions, as Cassidy went into the spare room.

Later that evening, after putting Skylar to bed, Bentley and Cassidy found themselves alone in the living room. They couldn't ignore their feelings any longer as the air in the living room was thick with tension as Bentley and Cassidy sat on opposite ends of the couch, avoiding each other's gaze.

Both were struggling with their desires, the forbidden attraction they felt towards each other, and the guilt that came with it.

Bentley's heart was pounding in his chest as he stole a glance at Cassidy. He couldn't deny the pull he felt towards her, he knew it was wrong, but the chemistry between them was undeniable.

Cassidy's breathing hitched as she met Bentley's gaze. Her body was on fire with longing, and she could see the same desire reflected in Bentley's eyes. She wanted him, and the temptation was overwhelming. Her mind was clouded with thoughts of what could be, and she found herself leaning towards him, her lips parting slightly.

Bentley's resolve faltered as Cassidy moved closer to him, her scent intoxicating him. He reached out to touch her, his fingers brushing against her soft skin. Cassidy's eyes closed as she leaned into his touch, her body responding to his with eagerness.

Bentley's hand moved up to cup her cheek, his thumb caressing her lips. Their lips met in a searing kiss, their pent-up emotions exploding into a frenzy of passion. They pulled each other closer, their mouths locked in a desperate embrace.

As the kisses got deeper, longer and more passionate Bentley pulled Cassidy on top of him.

As Cassidy straddled Bentley, she began to rock her body back and forth grinding her pelvis with his. She could feel the tension building up in his penis as he became aroused.

Bentley's hands roamed over Cassidy's body caressing her breast and her ass, igniting a fire within them both.

Just as things were escalating, Bentley abruptly pulled away, his breathing heavy, and guilt washing over him like a tidal wave. He pushed Cassidy gently off him breaking their intense connection.

"We can't do this," Bentley breathed, his voice strained.

Cassidy's eyes were filled with a mix of desire and disappointment as well as embarrassment. She knew Bentley was right, but it didn't make the longing any less intense. She nodded, tears glistening in her eyes. "You're right," Cassidy whispered, trying to steady her breathing. "I'm sorry."

Bentley got up from the couch, needing to put some distance between them. He ran a hand through his hair, trying to calm his racing heart. "We can't let this happen again," Bentley said firmly, trying to remain empathic. "We need to stop this before it goes any further."

Cassidy nodded, tears welling up in her eyes. She knew he was right, but it didn't make it any easier to accept. She had to put an end to this forbidden attraction, no matter how difficult it was.

With heavy hearts and bodies still charged with longing, Bentley stepped back, putting more distance between them. He took a deep breath, trying to steady himself.

Cassidy did the same, wiping away her tears. They both knew it was time to end this before it went any further, before they risked hurting themselves and others even more.

They stood in silence for a moment, the air heavy with unspoken emotions. Bentley then turned and walked away, leaving Cassidy standing in the living room, feeling a mix of longing and heartbreak.

She knew she had to find a way to move on, to let go of this forbidden attraction, no matter how much it hurt. As Bentley disappeared from her view, Cassidy sank down onto the couch, burying her face in her hands. She cried, letting out the pent-up emotions that had been building inside her for so long. She knew it wouldn't be easy, but she had to find a way to move forward and put an end to this forbidden love, no matter how much her heart ached.

Bentley, as he walked away, felt a mix of relief and sadness. He knew he had made the right decision, but it didn't make it any less painful. He needed to focus on his responsibilities and his commitment to Raelynn and being a father to Skylar. He couldn't let his desires cloud his judgment. It was time to put an end to this forbidden chapter in his life, and he vowed to himself that he would do whatever it took to make things right, starting with telling Raelynn what had happened.

41

Taking Responsibility

As the week in LA ended, Raelynn felt the confidence radiating with inside her. She was thrilled to have the opportunity to explore Los Angeles with Owen, Elijah, Levi and Jake as they worked alongside Jaxon and the rest of the producers on their EP.

Raelynn poured her heart and soul into her work at the studio, getting the chance to collaborate with some of the industry's top producers and songwriters, and the experience was nothing short of magical. She felt grateful for the opportunity to do what she loved and to share her music with the world. Overall, it was a successful and memorable trip, and Raelynn felt grateful for the opportunity, but she was more than ready to be back home to Bentley's loving arms.

As Raelynn's flight touched the tarmac in RDU she grew anxious to feel that Carolina air hit her skin, as well as Bentley's warm welcoming hug.

Raelynn walked out of the airport terminal and breathed in the familiar scent of home. She looked around, taking in the sights of the airport, the people rushing to catch their flights, and the taxis waiting to take them to their destinations. She started to feel a bit 'homesick' as she thought about the memories she had made in LA, but she knew deep down that her heart belonged in North Carolina.

As she stepped outside, she saw Bentley standing by the car, a bouquet of her favorite flowers in his hand. He smiled at her as their eyes met, and Raelynn ran towards him, her arms open wide.

They embraced tightly, holding onto each other as if they hadn't seen each other in years.

"I missed you so much," Bentley whispered into her ear, his voice filled with love and longing.

Raelynn smiled as tears welled up in her eyes, feeling overwhelmed with emotion. "I missed you too," she replied, burying her face into his chest.

As they made the drive back to Raelynn's house, she couldn't contain her excitement as she was telling Bentley all about her week in LA. She told him about the album, how they wanted her to do it, the producers that she worked with, all the celebrities that she got to meet, and all the sights she got to see when exploring.

Bentley listened closely taking in every word with a smile on his face as he watched Raelynn's eyes light up with enthusiasm. He was happy to see her so excited and passionate about her music. "I'm so proud of you, Rae," he said, reaching over to take her hand in his. "You worked hard for this and it's paying off."

Raelynn blushed at Bentley's praise, feeling grateful for his unwavering support. "I couldn't have done it without you," she said, leaning over to give him a quick kiss on the cheek. "You have believed in me since the moment you met me, even when I've doubted myself."

Bentley chuckled, "I knew you had it in you, Rae. You're destined for greatness."

Raelynn smiled, feeling grateful to have someone like Bentley by her side. "I'm just glad to be back home with you," she said, snuggling into his side as they pulled into her driveway. "I missed you so much."

Bentley wrapped his arm around her, pulling her closer. "I missed you too, Rae," he said, pressing a kiss to the top of her head. "Welcome back home."

As Bentley helped Raelynn grab her things from the car and get inside, he couldn't help but to feel the guilt crashing down on him starring at the door knowing what happened on the other side. He knew he needed to tell Raelynn what had transpired between him and Cassidy, but he was afraid too. Raelynn was on such a high from her trip and he knew his news would only crush her and that was the last thing he wanted to do but he knew that he had to be up front and honest.

As they reached the front door and Raelynn fumbled with her keys to get the door unlocked, Bentley felt that it was best to tell her right then. As Bentley sat her belonging down leaning them up against the house, Raelynn could sense something was wrong as she looked up at him. She could see the somber expression that he was wearing. "Bentley, is everything ok?" Raelynn asked growing concerned.

Bentley sighed a deep breath before looking up and locking eyes with Raelynn. It was hard for him to look her in the eyes with what he had done but telling her the truth was even harder. "Raelynn, I think it's best that I don't go in." Bentley said.

Raelynn looked at him confused, "Why?" she asked even more concerned.

Bentley could feel his heart beating in his throat as tears began to form in his eyes, he knew there was no holding it in anymore. "Rae, you know I love you more than anything in this world and I never would intentionally do anything to hurt you."

Raelynn started to grow worried as she could see the guilt and sadness in Bentley's eyes as tears began to fall down his face. "I want to spend the rest of my life with you, that I know for sure. But for that to happen we must have trust and right now I am not deserving of your trust." Bentley continued.

Raelynn feared what was about to come next as Bentley continued confessing to her. "While you were away, I had an amazing time getting the opportunity to bond with Skylar and Cassidy. It was the greatest feeling ever getting to know my son and my son's mother…"

Before Bentley could finish Raelynn cut in "No, please tell me no." with pure heartbreak in her voice.

Bentley hated that he could physically see her heart destroying right in front of him and it was at the cost of his doing. "Raelynn, please just let me finish. I've got to get this off my chest. While spending time with Cassidy feelings got heavy, vision got hazy, and mistakes that I can't take back or erase were made. We kissed and it got very heated, but I did stop before it went further than it should have never already gone. I'm sorry Raelynn, I truly am. It was a moment where my clarity was blinded." Bentley said as he was choking on his word and tears streaming down his face.

Raelynn was in shock as she could feel the betrayal and the heartbreak began to sink in. In that moment the world seemed to stop turning as she processed what Bentley had just confessed to her. She couldn't believe what she was hearing. After a few moments of silence, Raelynn hauled off and smacked a crying Bentley across the face as she began to scream at him.

"How could you do this to me, Bentley?" Raelynn cried out, feeling betrayed and hurt. "I trusted you with everything, and you went and did this behind my back? I'd probably be more forgiving right now if this was with a random female, but you did this with my best friend, one that you have a history with. I mean fuck Bentley you have a kid with her."

Bentley looked at her with her handprint across his face, his eyes filled with regret and shame. "I don't know, Rae," he said, his voice trembling. "I don't know what came over me. I was just so confused and lost in the moment. I never meant to hurt you."

Raelynn shook her head, feeling lost and broken. "I don't know if I can forgive you for this, Bentley. You broke more than my heart but my trust as well."

Bentley took a step forward, reaching out to try and comfort her even though he didn't know whether he should or not. "Please, Raelynn. Let me make it up to you. I'll do anything to prove my love to you and earn back your trust."

Raelynn pulled away from him, feeling hurt and betrayed. "Bentley, I think it's best that you just leave and go stay at your parents. I can't stand to look at you right now. So, just go. I need some time, most importantly I need some space."

Bentley nodded, feeling defeated but understanding. "I'll give you all the time and space you need, Raelynn. I just want you to know that I love you and I'll do whatever it takes to make this right."

As Raelynn entered her house, she slammed the door shut leaving her belongings on the porch. She also left Bentley outside to contemplate his mistakes.

Inside the house, Raelynn collapsed against the door she had just slammed shut in Bentley's face and began to sob uncontrollably. She began to think that her father and been right about Bentley all this time because how could he betray her like that. How could Cassidy betray her like that?

The more Raelynn's thoughts began to spiral the angrier she became as she pulled her phone out of her pocket and began to call Cassidy.

Bentley could hear her sobs from the other side of the door, and it broke his heart knowing he had caused her so much pain. He wanted nothing more than to hold her and comfort her, but he knew he had to give her space to process everything. So instead, he stood outside the door, tears streaming down his own face, feeling the weight of his mistakes.

Raelynn waited impatiently for Cassidy to answer the phone, her anger and hurt building with each passing moment.

Finally, Cassidy picked up the phone, "Hey." She said as you Raelynn could hear the dreadfulness in her voice.

"How could you do this to me, Cassidy? How could you betray me like this?" Raelynn yelled into the phone, her voice shaking with emotion.

Cassidy's voice began to crackle on the other end of the line, "I'm so sorry, Raelynn. It was a mistake; it shouldn't have happened."

Raelynn's anger boiled over, "A mistake? You kissed my fiancé, Cassidy! How could you even think that was okay? Like ok yeah you hooked up in college and have Skylar together but now he is my fiancé. Something way more than a college party one night stand. What the absolute fuck Cassidy!"

Cassidy started to cry as Raelynn's words pierced through the phone, "I'm sorry, I wasn't thinking clearly. I never meant to hurt you, Raelynn. It just happened. Seeing him interact with Skylar I had a moment of weakness and thought just for a second what if Skylar could have both his parents together. I never meant for this to happen Rae. He loves you; I love you. It was just a moment of weakness that we can't take back we can only choose how to move forward"

Raelynn didn't want to hear it, "I don't want to hear your excuses. You knew how much Bentley means to me, and you still went ahead and did this but that's ok. I'm calling off the engagement. You can have his sorry ass. You trifling bitch!" Raelynn yelled as she hung up the phone.

Bentley stood outside the door as he listened to the interaction between Raelynn and Cassidy, still feeling the weight of his mistake. He couldn't believe what had just happened. He had never wanted to hurt Raelynn, and he couldn't believe he had betrayed her like this. He knew he had to talk to her and explain everything.

He took a deep breath and knocked on the door. "Raelynn, please let me in. I need to talk to you," he said, his voice cracking with emotion.

Raelynn heard Bentley's voice, but she didn't want to face him right now. She was too hurt and angry. She didn't want to listen to his excuses or apologies. "Go away, Bentley. I don't want to see you right now," she yelled back, her voice shaking with anger and pain.

Bentley knew he had to give Raelynn space to process everything, but he couldn't just walk away. He sat down on the steps outside the door, his head in his hands, and began to cry. He couldn't believe he had ruined everything with Raelynn. He loved her more than anything in the world, and now he was on the verge of losing her.

As the tears streamed down his face, he knew he had to make things right. He couldn't just give up on Raelynn. He had to fight for her and show her that he loved her more than anything and show her that he was serious about their relationship. He took a deep breath and wiped away his tears as he walked away. He was determined to make things right with Raelynn.

Bentley arrived at his parents' house where he was greeted by his mother and father. His parents both could see that something was wrong, as even Stevie Wonder could see that Bentley had been crying.

"Everything ok Ben?" Mrs. Riggs asked.

Bentley didn't want to hear a lecture from his parents right now, but he knew they would keep nagging if he didn't disclose what was on his mind. As he was telling his parents what had happened his mother slapped him across the back of the head "You're such a fool!" she barked at him.

His father just shook his head in disbelief.

"I know mom, I really fucked up!" Bentley said starring at the floor, his voice cracking.

Mrs. Riggs could see Bentley was hurting as she wrapped him in a warm embrace consoling him.

Bentley felt a wave of relief wash over him as he leaned into his mother's embrace. He knew he had made a terrible mistake, and he deserved to be reprimanded for it, but he also needed comfort and understanding.

His father placed a hand on his shoulder, "Son, you need to fix this. You need to make things right with Raelynn."

Bentley nodded in agreement, "I know, Dad. I'll do whatever it takes to make things right with her."

His parents both looked at him with concerning looks as Mrs. Riggs rubbed his back, "We'll support you, Ben. Whatever you need, we're here for you." Bentley nodded, grateful for his parents' love and support.

42

Heartbreak is Inspiration

Alone in his childhood room, surrounded by posters featuring his favorite bands, rappers, and sports teams, Bentley finally found the inspiration he had been secretly struggling to find.

With his laptop and microphone at hand, he delved into crafting lyrics for a new album, drawing from ideas he had jotted down in the park a few days prior. As he immersed himself in the creative process, a sudden realization struck him – he wanted this album to serve as a love letter to Raelynn and a tribute to Skylar and as well as his unborn child.

In the midst of his brainstorming Bentley also decided on the album name, 'The Power of Music.'

Bentley envisioned narrating the story of how music had led him to Raelynn and guided him into the joys of fatherhood. Given that their lives were deeply intertwined with music.

Bentley was a firm believer in the old saying, "when words fail to speak, music does," and that was his aim to make amends with Raelynn.

As a part of this project Bentley intended to keep the entire album project a secret from Raelynn to create and element of surprise. Bentley also intended to create a remix of his hit song 'Cinderella.' This song had ignited a special chemistry between him and Raelynn during their rendition at Electric.

Bentley envisioned transforming that memorable performance into a studio masterpiece, with Raelynn's voice playing a crucial role. However, he was lost on how to make that happen while keeping this album and its entirety a secret.

Late into the night, he poured his heart and soul into the lyrics and beats, driven by a sense of purpose and direction that had been absent for a long time.

Determined to make this album his most personal yet, Bentley decided to strip away the trappings of a fancy studio. He chose to go back to basics, recording the album in the comfort of his own home, harking back to the days before he had access to professional studio equipment. In doing so, he aimed to convey the true essence and significance of the album to his fans.

As Bentley continued working tirelessly through the night, he lost track of time, completely absorbed in the creative process. The room echoed with the sound of his voice as he laid down tracks and fine-tuned lyrics, pouring his emotions into every note.

Amidst the solitude of his room, Cameron, who Bentley forget he had invited over, knocked softly on the door before entering. Bentley looked up from his laptop, exhaustion evident in his eyes, yet determination burning brightly.

Cameron, taking a seat beside Bentley, observed the intense focus on his friend's face. "Bentley, you look like you've been through a lot. What's going on?"

Bentley sighed, his shoulders slumping. "It's Raelynn, man. We're going through a rough patch. I messed up, Cam. I cheated on her with Cassidy."

Cameron's expression shifted, a mix of understanding and concern. "Bentley, that's heavy. But you've got to face it. You need to make things right with Raelynn. You can't let a mistake define your entire relationship."

Bentley nodded, appreciating Cameron's honesty. "I know, Cam. I'm trying. That's partly why I'm pouring everything into this album. It's my way of apologizing, by expressing what I can't put into words."

Cameron leaned in, offering a supportive pat on Bentley's back. "You've got this, man. Relationships are tough but love and dedication can overcome a lot. Just be genuine with Raelynn, let her see the real you."

Encouraged by Cameron's words, Bentley decided to open up further. "I want this album to be a surprise for her. I'm calling it 'The Power of Music.' It's about how music brought us together and led me to Skylar. It's also a letter to our unborn child. I even want to remix 'Cinderella' and make it special, with Raelynn involved."

Cameron's eyes widened in amazement. "That's a beautiful idea, Bentley. She'll appreciate the effort and sincerity. And who knows, this might be the bridge to healing."

As Bentley continued sharing his plans, Cameron became a sounding board for his thoughts and a pillar of support. Eventually, Bentley played a snippet of the album for Cameron, who was genuinely blown away by the raw emotion and authenticity embedded in the music.

"Bentley, this is fucking incredible. The pure rawness of it, man. This is the best thing you've ever recorded. Raelynn will definitely feel this, I'm sure of it," Cameron exclaimed, a genuine smile forming on his face.

Bentley, grateful for Cameron's support, took a deep breath. "Thanks, Cam. Means a lot coming from you. But there's something else. I want Raelynn to be part of this remix for 'Cinderella,' but with her mad at me. I have no idea how to approach her about it, especially when I'm trying to keep this entire project a secret."

Cameron nodded thoughtfully. "Alright, man. First things first, you've got to mend things with Raelynn. Apologize sincerely and give her the time she needs. Don't rush it. Once you've made some progress on that front, then you can figure out how to get her on the remix secretly. Timing is crucial here."

Bentley sighed, understanding the complexity of the situation. "You're right, Cam. I just hope she can forgive me. I don't want the project to be tainted by the mess I've created."

Cameron reassured him, "She will, Bentley. Just be patient. Now, about getting her on the remix, I have an idea. Since the rendition y'all performed at the club went viral, tell her the label is requesting that the two of you make a studio version."

Bentley's eyes lit up at Cameron's suggestion. "That's a brilliant idea, Cam! It's a perfect cover since we just went public with our engagement. I can tell her it's a special request from the label, and it's an opportunity to take our careers to the next level."

Cameron grinned, pleased with Bentley's enthusiasm. "Exactly, Bentley. It adds a layer of authenticity, and she won't suspect a thing. Also, it gives you a chance to still work together in case she hasn't forgiven you."

Bentley nodded, feeling a renewed sense of optimism. "You're right, Cam. This way, I can focus professionally on the music without putting additional pressure on our relationship. I'll tell her that the label sees the potential in our partnership and wants to capitalize on it."

Cameron patted Bentley on the back. "And who knows, maybe the power of music will be the catalyst for healing, especially once she sees the dedication you're putting into this project. Keep the focus on the music, my friend."

As Bentley and Cameron continued discussing their plans, the door to Bentley's childhood room slowly creaked open. Bentley's parents, Mr. and Mrs. Riggs, entered quietly, their eyes filled with curiosity. They had heard fragments of the conversation and couldn't help but be drawn in by the intense atmosphere.

Mr. Riggs, with a warm smile, greeted them. "What's all this excitement about, boys?"

Bentley looked up, momentarily surprised, then smiled at his parents. "Hey, Mom, Dad. Sorry, I forgot to mention Cameron was coming over."

Mrs. Riggs waved off the apology. "No need to apologize, dear. We're just curious to know what has both of you so engrossed."

Bentley, feeling a surge of excitement, decided to share his secret project with his parents. "Well, I've been working on a new album, and it's something special. I'm calling it 'The Power of Music.'"

Mrs. Riggs's eyes lit up with intrigue. "That sounds wonderful, Bentley. What's the inspiration behind it?"

Bentley took a moment to collect his thoughts, then began to pour his heart out. He explained the journey of his relationship with Raelynn, the joys of fatherhood, and the deep connection they shared through music. As he spoke, Bentley's parents listened attentively, captivated by the raw emotion in their son's voice.

"I want this album to be a love letter to Raelynn, a tribute to Skylar and our unborn child," Bentley continued. "But there's more. I'm also planning to surprise Raelynn by recording a remix to 'Cinderella,' it's the song we performed together at Electric. I want that rendition we performed together on this album. It's part of my apology to her."

Cameron chimed in, providing additional context for Bentley's parents. "Bentley's plan is to tell Raelynn that the label is requesting a studio version of their rendition since that performance did go viral and the fact, they just went public with their engagement."

Mr. Riggs, clearly moved by the sincerity of Bentley's words, placed a hand on his son's shoulder. "Bentley, that's a beautiful way to express your feelings and make amends. Music has a way of healing wounds, and I'm sure Raelynn will appreciate the effort."

Mrs. Riggs wiped a tear from her eye, her voice filled with emotion. "It's like a love story told through music. I can't wait to hear it, Bentley."

Encouraged by his parents' support, Bentley decided to give them a sneak peek of the album. He played a few snippets, each filled with raw emotion and the essence of his journey. As the music filled the room, both Mr. and Mrs. Riggs were moved to tears, visibly overwhelmed by the depth of their son's artistry.

Mrs. Riggs hugged Bentley tightly. "Oh, Bentley, this is breathtaking. Your talent has grown, and this album is going to be something truly special."

Mr. Riggs, visibly moved, added, "You've poured your heart into this, son. I'm proud of the man you've become. And I believe in the power of music to mend what's broken."

"Well, this album is going to be a personal bust no matter how well it may perform on the charts if Raelynn doesn't forgive me, and I end up losing her." Bentley said as he looked down at the laptop making a few changes.

Mrs. Riggs, sensing the weight in Bentley's words, gently cupped his face and spoke with a comforting tone, "Bentley, love has a remarkable way of finding its way back. Your sincerity and the emotions poured into this music will speak volumes. Just give it time, and be patient with both yourself and Raelynn."

Mr. Riggs added, "Your journey with Raelynn has been intertwined with music since the very beginning. Let this album be the soundtrack of your love story, a testament to the strength of your bond. And remember, healing takes time."

Cameron, chiming in with a reassuring smile, said, "And who knows, Bentley? Maybe this album will be the bridge that brings you two closer together. The power of music can work wonders."

With newfound encouragement from his parents and Cameron, Bentley took a deep breath, determined to face the challenges ahead. As the night wore on, they continued discussing the album, tweaking lyrics, and fine-tuning melodies. The room echoed with a mix of emotions, from vulnerability to hope, as Bentley navigated the delicate path of healing through his art.

43

Fireworks

The following morning, Bentley was abruptly awakened by the blaring sound of his alarm clock. Still half-asleep and annoyed by the persistent ringing, he fumbled to hit the snooze button but accidentally knocked his phone to the floor, compelling him to get out of bed.

As Bentley hastily searched for his phone, tracing the irritating alarm's sound, he realized that Raelynn had an OBGYN visit scheduled for today. This explained why his alarm was set; they were supposed to hear the baby's heartbeat for the first time.

Despite conflicting feelings, Bentley wanted to be there for the appointment. He grappled with the dilemma of wanting to express his care for Raelynn and the baby, yet not wanting her to feel overwhelmed or ambushed.

In the end, Bentley made the decision to attend the appointment. His desire to support Raelynn during this crucial moment outweighed the uncertainties between them. He wanted to share the experience of hearing their child's heartbeat for the first time with the woman he loved, despite the challenges that lay ahead.

Despite feeling like a zombie due to lack of sleep, Bentley arrived at the doctor's office where he waited in the parking lot, shielding his tired and sensitive eyes from the bright sun with his aviators. Surprisingly

Bentley arrived well before Raelynn, who was usually on time for everything.

After a short while, Raelynn pulled into the parking lot, and Bentley approached her. The moment Raelynn laid eyes on him, a disgusted expression instantly appeared on her face. Bentley could still discern the pain and betrayal in her eyes, and her body language stiffened at the sight of him.

Unresponsive to Bentley's presence, Raelynn sharply questioned, "What are you doing here, Bentley? I told you I didn't want to see you!"

Acknowledging her need for space, Bentley responded, "I know you said you needed your space, and I'm going to give it to you. But I couldn't bear to miss hearing our baby's heartbeat for the first time today. I missed that experience with Skylar, and I refuse to miss it with this one." Bentley's words were tinged with irritation.

Although Raelynn wasn't thrilled about Bentley's presence, a part of her was secretly glad he showed up. Despite her hurt and anger, she reluctantly conceded, "Fine, Bentley. Have it your way," huffing under her breath, crossing her arms, and turning her face away from Bentley as they made their way inside the building.

While Raelynn completed her check-in for the appointment, Bentley sought out a quiet corner at the back of the office, settling in and grabbing a People's magazine from the table to pass the time. Bentley, still sporting his aviator shades, casually skimmed through the magazine.

"You're inside, take the glasses off. You look like an idiot," Raelynn remarked with evident disgust as she took a seat beside him.

In response, Bentley mimicked her under his breath, refusing to remove his shades.

As Bentley continued flipping through the magazine, an alarming photo caught his attention, prompting him to rapidly scramble back to the page. When he reached the page and saw the picture, his eyes widened, and a surge of anger rushed through his body. As he yanked the glasses off his face.

"Finally!" Raelynn muttered under her breath as she had no idea of the anger boiling inside Bentley.

The photo depicted Bentley, Cassidy, and Skylar holding hands on their walk to the park. It was attached to an article that bore the caption: "Exclusive: Does Rap Star Bentley Have a Secret Love Child?"

As Bentley scanned through the article, he could feel the anger boiling inside of him. "Fuck! I'm going to kill somebody!" Bentley shouted in the waiting room startling all the patients waiting to be seen. Raelynn quickly turned to confront Bentley for his outburst when she could finally see the dark circles under his eyes as well as the anger fuming all over him. "Bentley!" She shouted before lowering her voice to regular speaking volume. "Is everything ok?"

"No everything is not fucking ok, not at all!" Bentley shouted as he shoved the article in Raelynn's face.

As Raelynn read the article and saw the pictures are eyes grew big as she knew what this meant for Bentley. It meant that things with Cassidy were about to get even more complicated. She also knew that Cassidy was going to blame her for leaking the article out of spite.

"Oh my god." Raelynn muttered under her breath as she clasped her hand over her mouth in shock. "Bentley, when she sees this, she's going to think I had something to do with it. I promise you I didn't. Yes, I may be mad at you both, but I'm not mad enough to jeopardize anything between y'all when it comes to co-parenting Skylar." Raelynn said trying make sure Bentley knew she had nothing to do with it.

"Rae, I know you had nothing to do with. An article of this magnitude doesn't get published overnight; this takes some serious digging. Someone tipped them off and I bet I know who." Bentley said as there was then a slight pause. "Your father did this Rae." Bentley said as he looked into her eyes.

Raelynn's eyes widened in shock as Bentley accused her father of being behind the leaked article. Especially, when Bentley had just recently told her to give her father a chance. She couldn't believe it, but at the same time, she knew her father's history of meddling in her personal life.

Raelynn took a deep breath and shook her head. "I can't believe he would stoop this low," she said, her voice filled with disappointment and frustration.

Bentley clenched his fists, feeling the anger continuing to build inside him. He knew that Raelynn's father disapproved of their relationship, and this seemed like one of his attempts to sabotage them.

"I should have known," he muttered, his jaw tight with anger. "This is just another way for him to try and drive that wedge between us. Like I have needed any help with that."

Raelynn reached her hand out and placed it on Bentley shoulder to calm him down. Though she was still angry with him and Cassidy for their betrayal she knew Bentley needed her more than ever.

"Bentley, I'm still upset about what happened with Cassidy. I understand there were unresolved feelings, guilt, and sympathy involved, with the situation dealing with Skylar. I'm willing to forgive, but we need to take it slow. I love you, and I'm here for you. We'll navigate through this together; I promise not to let you suffer." Raelynn said as she leaned over to kiss Bentley on the cheek who was still fuming with anger.

Bentley took a deep breath and nodded in understanding, trying to control his emotions. "You're right," he said, looking into Raelynn's eyes. "I'm truly sorry I hurt you! That's the last thing I wanted to do. Baby… I love you and I need you in my life. I will do whatever it takes to make things right but first I have got to deal with this, and Cassidy and I need you to be ok with that. Actually, I'm going to need your help with that. I really need us to work through our debacle a lot quicker than anticipated. I've got a feeling things are about to get really ugly."

Just then, the doctor entered the waiting room calling Raelynn to the back, interrupting their conversation. He apologized for the delay and proceeded to lead them into the exam room where he began to perform the ultrasound, showing them their baby's healthy heartbeat. Bentley and Raelynn looked at the screen, their hearts swelling with love and excitement. In that moment, they both knew that they had to be strong for their baby and each other, despite the challenges they were facing.

After the appointment, Bentley and Raelynn left the OBGYN's office together. Bentley couldn't shake off the anger completely, but he was determined to handle the situation in a more strategic and composed manner.

As they walked to their cars, Bentley held Raelynn's hand tightly. "Thank you for being there for me," he said softly, looking into her eyes. "I know things are complicated, but I really appreciate you for wanting to be here for me."

Raelynn smiled warmly at Bentley, feeling a sense of relief like after all everything was going to be ok between them. "Of course, Bentley," she said. "We're in this together, no matter what challenges come our way. We'll figure it out." There was a slight pause before Raelynn continued "Hey, Bentley come over to the house when we leave here."

Bentley nodded, feeling a renewed sense of determination. He leaned in and gave Raelynn a gentle kiss on the cheek before leaving.

As Bentley drove to Raelynn's house, he couldn't help but replay the events of the day in his mind. The article and the pictures of him, Cassidy, and Skylar had stirred up a mix of emotions within him - anger, frustration, and worry about how Cassidy would react. He knew that Cassidy might think Raelynn had something to do with the article being leaked, but Bentley knew Raelynn had nothing to do with it.

Just as he was about to lose himself in his emotions his phone began to ring; it was Cassidy. Bentley immediately felt his stomach drop as his heart began to race. He was dreading the inevitable.

Bentley took a deep breath and answered the call from Cassidy. Her voice sounded tense, and Bentley braced himself for what was to come.

Cassidy wasted no time as she confronted Bentley about the article and it's pictures. She was clearly upset, and Bentley could feel her anger through the phone.

"Bentley what was the one rule I had when you entered Skylar's life?" Cassidy asked in a seriously angry tone.

"That you didn't want you or Skylar in the spotlight." Bentley said softly.

"Ok. Then explain to me why the fuck there is an article with our faces plastered in it for the world to see about us." Cassidy said as her tone grew angrier.

Bentley let out a huge sigh as he truly didn't know how to explain it because he, himself didn't know how this had happened. "Cassidy, I have no idea. I can assure you that I had nothing to do with it. Why would I jeopardize a relationship with my son when I'm trying to get to know him? However, I feel like Raelynn's father had something to do with this. Raelynn said he was in LA last week same time she was for a business meeting, well TMZ headquarters is also in LA and this article was released by a TMZ owned outlet." Bentley explained, hoping that Cassidy would be more receiving.

Instead, he could hear the anger grow in Cassidy's voice. "Oh, so Raelynn did this to get back at us because she's pissed at us. I get it. Because how else would her father know Skylar was your son to begin with if she hadn't told him." Cassidy barked as there was a brief pause.

Bentley didn't know how to respond because Cassidy now wasn't angry at him but with Raelynn, and he knew if he told the truth about how Mr. Hart knew Skylar was his son, he would be jeopardizing his relationship with his son. Bentley knew he had to tell the truth no matter how much it was going to hurt him. He knew he couldn't let Raelynn bare that blame when she was truly innocent in all of this.

Bentley took a deep breath before responding "Cass, I can assure you it wasn't Raelynn. This was solely her father. The night me and Raelynn got engaged me and her father got into an argument and in the heat of the argument I accidentally slipped up and told him that Skylar was my son." Bentley said regretfully.

"Oh, so, everything does come back to you! Everything boils down to you Bentley! I gave you fair warning that you wouldn't be allowed to see your son and get to know him if you jeopardized his safety or mine by putting him in the spotlight and what did you do? You went and put him in the spotlight anyway, intentionally, unintentionally, it doesn't matter Bentley. You will not be seeing Skylar anymore! I gave you a fair warning and you blew it. Completely blew it!" Cassidy barked as her voice began to crack with emotion.

Bentley's heart sank as Cassidy's words sank in. Losing the chance to get to know his son was devastating to him, and he realized the gravity of his mistake. "Cassidy, please, I'm sorry. I never wanted this to happen. I understand if you need time, but please don't cut me out of Skylar's life completely. I love him, and I want to be there for him, I want him to know his baby brother or baby sister, " Bentley pleaded, his voice filled with desperation as tears began to form in his eyes.

Cassidy didn't respond for a moment, and Bentley could hear her breathing heavily on the other end of the line. He knew she was struggling with her emotions, just as he was.

"I can't trust you anymore, Bentley, I can't trust that you are capable of being able to keep him out the spotlight" Cassidy finally said, her voice filled with sadness. "Skylar's safety and privacy are my top priority, and I can't risk it anymore. I have to protect him."

There was a long silence on the phone, as Bentley and Cassidy were struggling with their emotions, not knowing what else to say. Finally, Cassidy spoke again, her voice softer this time. "I don't know if I can forgive you, Bentley," Cassidy said, her voice trembling. "But I hope that one day we can find a way to co-parent Skylar without any more drama or publicity. He deserves a normal life."

Bentley nodded again, feeling a mix of sadness and relief. He didn't know what the future held, but he was willing to do whatever it took to make things right with Cassidy and be there for his son in any way possible.

"I'll do whatever it takes, Cassidy," Bentley said earnestly. "I'll respect your wishes and stay out of Skylar's life for now. Just know that I'll always be here if you need me, and I'll do everything I can to make things right."

Cassidy didn't respond for a moment, and Bentley held his breath, hoping that she would be willing to work things out in the future.

Finally, Cassidy let out a sigh. "Okay, Bentley," Cassidy said softly. "I'll let you know when I'm ready to talk again. For now, please give us some space."

Bentley nodded, even though Cassidy couldn't see him. He knew it was the least he could do, and he would respect her wishes. With a heavy heart and tears streaming down his face, he hung up the phone he felt a mix of emotions swirling inside him.

When Bentley pulled into the driveway Raelynn, who was paitiently waiting for him could clearly see that something was wrong as Bentley just sat in the car, his face red from where he had been crying. Raelynn walked over to the driver side of the car and tapped on the glass and waited for Bentley to roll down the window.

Bentley took a deep breath and rolled down the window, revealing his tear-streaked face. Raelynn's heart sank as she saw the anguish in Bentley's eyes.

"Bentley, what happened?" Raelynn asked with concern, placing a hand on his arm.

Bentley took a moment to compose himself before speaking. "Cassidy found out about the article and the pictures. She's furious, and she blames me for putting Skylar in the spotlight risking their privacy and safety. She's decided that I won't be allowed to see Skylar anymore."

Raelynn's eyes widened in shock. She couldn't believe what she was hearing. "But that's not fair! It wasn't your fault, Bentley. You didn't intentionally put Skylar in the spotlight."

Bentley nodded, grateful for Raelynn's support. "I know, Raelynn. But Cassidy is really upset right now. She's determined to protect Skylar at all costs even if that means keeping him away from me."

Raelynn's heart ached for Bentley. She knew how much he had enjoyed getting to know Skylar and building a relationship with him.

"I should have been more careful about keeping Skylar's existence a secret. But we can't change what has already happened. Right now, I need to figure out how to fix things with Cassidy and make sure I can still be a part of Skylar's life. I need to call Mike and see if he can do some digging to see who leaked this to TMZ to be 100% sure that it was your dad."

Raelynn nodded, understanding Bentley's determination. "Yes, please do call Mike! He really does seem to work wonders!"

Bentley gave Raelynn a grateful smile. "Thank you, Raelynn. I really appreciate your support right now." He then took a deep breath and got out of the car, walking towards Raelynn's front door.

<h1 style="text-align:center">44</h1>

Heartbreaking Betrayal

Feeling a sense of urgency in resolving the situation. Bentley quickly dialed Mike's number and explained the situation to him, asking if he could investigate who leaked the information about Skylar to TMZ.

While Bentley was on the phone with Mike, Raelynn couldn't help but worry about the repercussions of the article and the pictures. She knew Cassidy's concerns about Skylar's privacy and safety were valid, but she also understood Bentley's desire to be a part of his son's life. She paced back and forth in her living room, her mind racing with thoughts about how she could help Bentley.

After a few minutes on the phone, Bentley hung up and turned to Raelynn with a determined expression. "Mike said he will do his best to find out who leaked the information. I really hope that I'm right and it was your father because I can't lose Skylar, Raelynn. He means everything to me."

Raelynn nodded in agreement. "I understand, Bentley. You need to do whatever you can to make things right and I'm here by your side to help. Which means I need to go call Cassidy and talk things through about what happened between you two. I'm still angry about that but that is aside the point right now, this is more important than petty relationship drama."

Bentley gave Raelynn a grateful nod. "Thank you, Raelynn."

He knew that Raelynn calling Cassidy would be a crucial step in resolving the situation. He understood Cassidy's concerns as a mother, but he also wanted to make sure he could be a part of Skylar's life as his father. Bentley decided to wait in Raelynn's living room, anxiously tapping his fingers on the coffee table as he waited for Raelynn to finish her call.

Raelynn quickly dialed Cassidy's number and anxiously waited for her to pick up. When Cassidy finally answered, Raelynn could hear the tension in her voice. "What do you want, Raelynn?" Cassidy asked shortly.

Raelynn took a deep breath, trying to remain calm. "I want to apologize about last night for calling you a bitch. It was wrong even if it was in the heat of the moment. We've been best friends since we were little kids and we've always been able to get through our difference with guys. You and Bentley, I get it Cass, I truly do. You have unreconciled feelings, he developed feelings through the guilt that he feels and the love you both share for Skylar. It's all new to both of you, hell all of us and we're all trying to navigate through this together, so I get it. Just because I get it doesn't mean it takes away the hurt and the feeling of betrayal though because I very much still feel that. I just refuse to let that come between us especially when there's something bigger than that occurring."

"That means a lot to me right now Rae because I could really use my best friend right now! Also, I'm truly sorry for doing that to you." Cassidy said with sadness in her voice.

Raelynn pretended that she didn't know what was wrong with Cassidy, but she knew. "What's wrong Cass?" Raelynn asked.

Cassidy took a moment before responding, "Well, a lot is wrong Rae. I made out with your fiancé for starters almost costing me my best friend who has been more like a sister to me than anything. Um, I don't know if you saw but there was an article posted about me, Ben, and Skylar and as a result I told Ben he couldn't see Skylar anymore because his safety and privacy meant more to me than their father-son bond." Cassidy sighed on the other end of the line. "He put my son's safety at risk, Raelynn. I can't just let that slide."

Raelynn understood Cassidy's concerns, but she also knew Bentley's intentions were not malicious. "Yeah, I saw the article that's reason why

I wanted to call. I wanted to apologize and forgive you and see how you were holding up. Bentley is devastated. He had already started spiraling when he saw the article and then you called and told him he couldn't see Skylar anymore, he completely lost it. This isn't all his fault you know?"

Cassidy let out a deep breath on the other end of the line. "I know, Raelynn," she said softly. "I'm just scared for Skylar. He's my son, and I have to prioritize his safety above everything else."

Raelynn nodded, even though Cassidy couldn't see her. "I understand, Cassidy. But Bentley is also Skylar's father, and he loves him too. He didn't mean for this to happen, and he's devastated right now. He wants to make things right."

Cassidy sighed again, torn between her love for Skylar and her feelings towards Bentley. "I know he didn't mean for this to happen, but it did. And now we have to deal with the consequences."

Raelynn took a deep breath, trying to find the right words to say. "Cassidy, I know this is difficult, but we need to come together and find a solution. Skylar needs both of his parents in his life, and Bentley wants to be there for him. Can we sit down and talk this through? Maybe we can come up with a plan that ensures Skylar's safety while also allowing Bentley to be involved."

Cassidy was quiet for a moment before responding. "I don't know, Raelynn. This is all so overwhelming. I just want to protect my son." Raelynn could hear the vulnerability in Cassidy's voice, and her heart went out to her. "Yeah, I think we need to talk," Cassidy said softly. "I don't want to keep Skylar away from Bentley forever, but I need to make sure he understands the importance of protecting Skylar's privacy and safety."

Raelynn nodded, even though Cassidy couldn't see her. "I'll talk to Bentley and let him know that you're willing to talk," Raelynn said. "I think it's important for all of us to be on the same page and work together for Skylar's sake."

Cassidy agreed, and they ended the call with a shared understanding that they needed to have a conversation with Bentley to resolve the situation.

As Raelynn walked back into the living room to fill Bentley in on her conversation with Cassidy, she could see Bentley fuming with anger again.

While she was on the phone with Cassidy, Mike had called Bentley back to let him know of his findings.

"Rae, baby I could kill your dad right! I just got off the phone with Mike and he just confirmed what we already knew. God, I was hoping I was wrong. Mike said that your father paid five-million-dollars to TMZ for them to leak the story." Bentley said angrily.

Raelynn's heart sank as she listened to Bentley's words. The betrayal from her father cut deep, and she could see the pain in Bentley's eyes. She reached out and placed a comforting hand on his shoulder. "I can't believe he would do something like that," Raelynn said, her voice filled with anger and sadness. "I'm so sorry, Bentley."

Bentley nodded; his jaw clenched tightly. "Yeah, it's a lot to take in," he said through gritted teeth. "But I won't let him ruin things for us. We'll figure this out, Rae."

Raelynn squeezed his shoulder gently, offering him a reassuring smile. "We will," she said. "We'll get through this together."

Bentley took a deep breath, trying to calm himself down. "So, what did Cassidy say?" he asked, shifting his focus to the conversation with Cassidy.

Raelynn filled Bentley in on her conversation with Cassidy, explaining that Cassidy was willing to talk and find a solution that prioritized Skylar's safety while also allowing Bentley to be involved in his life.

Bentley listened attentively, and Raelynn could see a glimmer of hope in his eyes. "That's a step in the right direction," Bentley said. "I want to be there for Skylar, Rae. I love him so much, and I'll do whatever it takes to make sure he's safe and happy."

Raelynn smiled at Bentley's words, knowing how much he cared for Skylar. "I know you do, Bentley," she said. "And I believe Cassidy wants the same. Let's all sit down and have a conversation, try to work things out."

Bentley nodded; his expression determined. "Yeah, let's do that," he said.

Later that night Bentley and Raelynn joined Cassidy at her apartment to discuss a plan for Skylar's involvement in Bentley's life while ensuring privacy and safety. Cassidy proposed a temporary plan involving limited visitation, strict guidelines for privacy, and secure communication. Bentley, appreciative of Cassidy's thoughtfulness, agreed to the plan. They discussed logistics and finalized details.

Afterward, Cassidy took the opportunity to apologize to Bentley and Raelynn for the recent turmoil. She acknowledged her mistake, expressing regret and commitment to making things right. Bentley thanked her for the apology, emphasizing his love for Raelynn. Raelynn, while accepting the apology, set clear boundaries and warned against any recurrence. The atmosphere remained emotional as they addressed the challenges ahead, prioritizing Skylar's well-being. Despite the difficulties, they were determined to move forward, rebuild trust, and create a positive environment for Skylar.

Later that night, back at home, Raelynn found herself grappling with the whirlwind of events that unfolded within the 24 hours of her return from LA. It was a staggering amount of drama, enough to make the average person throw in the towel. However, Raelynn was anything but average, and she was resolute in her determination to confront the issues head-on, starting with her father.

Seated in her living room, Raelynn decided to reach out to her mother, Olivia, unable to contain her frustration and anger any longer. She needed to vent and inform her mother about the betrayal orchestrated by Mr. Hart, her father, in an attempt to sabotage her relationship with Bentley.

With a few rings, Olivia answered the phone, and Raelynn dove straight into the details. Olivia was taken aback and stunned by her husband's actions. While she knew Jim harbored dislike for Bentley and wished to keep him away from their daughter, the extent to which he had gone to disrupt their relationship was beyond belief.

Raelynn underscored that the repercussions extended beyond herself and Bentley, affecting Cassidy, who Jim had treated like a daughter, and Skylar, whom he considered his grandson. It was a bitter pill for Olivia to swallow, realizing Jim had taken such drastic measures to damage their family dynamics. She assured Raelynn that she would have a serious talk with him.

"Mom, I don't even want him at the wedding at this point," Raelynn expressed, her frustration palpable in her words.

"He doesn't deserve to have any part of mine or Bentley's lives. He is toxic and poisonous, and he has no place in our world anymore."

Olivia couldn't argue with Raelynn's assessment, and the conversation ended with Olivia promising Raelynn that she would handle Jim's behavior accordingly.

45

Playing Cupid

The next morning, Raelynn nestled close to Bentley, her head resting on his chest. As he awoke to find her gazing at him, he planted a tender kiss on her forehead. "Good morning, beautiful," he greeted, and Raelynn responded with a smile.

"Good morning, you sleepyhead," Raelynn playfully teased, hoping to maintain a light mood. She didn't want Bentley to dwell on the sabotage her father had caused the previous day by leaking the story of Skylar's existence to the media.

Despite a restful night's sleep, Raelynn and Bentley felt lingering exhaustion from navigating the drama that resembled a minefield the day before. They yearned for a better day, one where the news favored them. Bathed in the morning sunlight, their playful banter persisted, eventually taking a more serious turn.

Discussing their wedding, Raelynn expressed a desire to marry Bentley sooner rather than later, emphasizing a preference for a small, intimate ceremony. They also addressed the absence of her father due to his recent antics, with Raelynn expressing the wish for Bentley's parents to walk her down the aisle—a departure from societal norms.

Bentley's eyes reflected love and admiration as he agreed, relishing the idea of a simple wedding. In a sweet moment, they affirmed their commitment to each other.

As their banter continued, Raelynn excitedly sat up in bed, looking down at Bentley as if about to share the best news ever. "Oh my God, Bentley. Last night, I had the weirdest dream. You and I played cupid, and we successfully hooked up Cassidy and Cameron," Raelynn revealed. Pausing to let her words settle into the atmosphere, observing Bentley's reaction before continuing, "Honestly, I think we should make it happen."

Bentley chuckled through a confused expression, trying to read Raelynn's intentions. "Oh. You're not joking. You're serious," he said, his eyes widening with realization.

"As a heart attack," Raelynn affirmed with seriousness.

Bentley, still processing Raelynn's proposition, couldn't help but laugh nervously. "You're suggesting we play matchmaker in real life based on a dream?" he asked incredulously.

Raelynn, undeterred, nodded with determination. "Absolutely! I mean, think about it. Cameron already knows about Skylar, and you know he would be a good role model to have around your son. It's fate giving us a sign. Plus, Cassidy and Cameron would make such a cute couple," she insisted, a playful glint in her eyes.

Bentley, now fully grasping the sincerity of Raelynn's suggestion, couldn't help but smile at her enthusiasm. "Alright, let's entertain this idea. How do you propose we set them up?" he asked, intrigued by the unconventional notion.

Raelynn leaned in, her eyes sparkling with mischief. "I was thinking a casual get-together, something low-key where they can spend time together without feeling pressured. Maybe a game night here at the house?"

Bentley considered the plan, appreciating the simplicity. "Sounds reasonable. We'll need to be subtle though. I don't want them catching on too quickly," he mused, already envisioning the playful scheme taking shape.

Raelynn grinned, pleased that Bentley was willing to entertain her matchmaking idea. "Exactly! Subtlety is key. We don't want them to feel like they're being set up," she agreed. "We'll make it seem like a spontaneous gathering, just friends hanging out. And then, who knows? Cupid might work his magic."

Bentley chuckled at the playful optimism in Raelynn's eyes. "Alright, let's play matchmaker then. But we should also be prepared for the possibility that it might not work out as smoothly as in your dream," he cautioned.

"Of course," Raelynn replied, her excitement undeterred. "But hey, it's worth a shot. Cassidy and Cameron are both amazing people. It could be the start of something beautiful."

As they continued to brainstorm the details of their plan, Raelynn couldn't help but feel a sense of joy. It was a welcome distraction from the chaos surrounding Skylar's revelation to the public and her father's actions. Playing cupid seemed like a lighthearted adventure that could bring happiness not only to Cassidy and Cameron but also to their own lives.

Raelynn stopped all her brainstorming ideas when she heard the TV in the background echo the words, "Emerging country sensation Raelynn is making waves with her latest EP, currently holding the top spot, on Apple Music's country chart. If this is a glimpse of her future, it seems she's on track for a thriving career in the music industry." Raelynn quickly rushed to to the living room to rewind the channel to catch the full report. She thought maybe her mind was playing tricks on her.

As Raelynn listened to the report play again, Raelynn let out a scream of excitement. "Bentley! Did you hear that!" Raelynn shouted in excitement as tears were starting to uncontrollably fall from her eyes.

Bentley, drawn by Raelynn's enthusiastic shout, quickly joined her in the living room. "What's going on?" he asked, his eyes widening as he saw the tears of joy streaming down Raelynn's face.

"They just reported on the news that my EP is at the top of the country charts on Apple Music! Can you believe it?" Raelynn exclaimed, her voice a mix of excitement and disbelief.

Bentley's face lit up with genuine happiness for her. "Raelynn, that's fucking killer dude! I'm so proud of you." He pulled her into a tight embrace, sharing in her joy.

At that moment, Bentley recognized his window of opportunity open wide. It was his golden chance to discreetly feature Raelynn on his upcoming album.

"Here's something even more unbelievable, Rae. The label contacted me earlier and shared that, following our engagement announcement to the media, they see an opportunity to leverage the buzz. They want us to record a studio version of the 'Cinderella' rendition we performed at Electric," Bentley revealed, sensing the universe aligning in his favor.

Raelynn's eyes widened in surprise, her tears of joy transitioning into a mix of astonishment and excitement. "Are you serious, Bentley?" she exclaimed, still processing the unexpected turn of events.

Bentley grinned, holding her at arm's length to meet her gaze. "Dead serious. They believe it could be a massive hit, especially with the buzz around our engagement. It's a golden opportunity for both of us," he explained, his voice filled with enthusiasm. "They also want us to record it like I did the original version. From the comfort of my own bedroom." Bentley continued.

Raelynn's eyes sparkled with a combination of disbelief and delight. "Recording it from your bedroom? We could do that right now," she exclaimed, imagining the unique intimacy that recording in a familiar space could bring to their rendition.

Bentley adored her enthusiasm as he began to pull out all his recording equipment. He was eager to get this song recorded and mastered because it was the final piece to the masterpiece he had been working on.

Inside Raelynn's makeshift recording studio once again where all the musical magic truly began between the two of them, Bentley realized this was a full circle moment as he set up his equipment. Raelynn, still caught in the whirlwind of emotions from the news about her EP and the unexpected recording opportunity, eagerly joined him in preparing for the session.

As they huddled around the microphone, Bentley pressed play and the familiar instrumental for' Cinderella' played through both headphones.

The air was saturated with the captivating melody, prompting Raelynn to shut her eyes and lose herself in the music. Bentley effortlessly delivered his verses over the beat, a skill he had honed over numerous performances. Yet, in a bid to distinguish this rendition and elevate it from the original, he opted for a fresh approach to his flow.

His adjusted rhythm seamlessly melded with Raelynn's vocals in the chorus. Which, to ensure this version stood out, Bentley granted her complete freedom to revamp, rephrase, or modify the chorus and bridge as she saw fit, allowing her to put her unique stamp on the song.

As Raelynn commenced singing, her voice reverberated throughout the room, weaving through the harmonies of their shared history.

The chemistry between Bentley and Raelynn was palpable, as their voices intertwined in a dance of emotions. The lyrics of 'Cinderella' took on new life, each word infused with the authenticity of their love story. Bentley watched Raelynn with a profound appreciation, marveling at how their connection translated into a musical masterpiece.

In the midst of the recording, Raelynn took creative liberties with the chorus, adding subtle nuances that reflected her individuality. Bentley, impressed by her artistic interpretation, couldn't help but smile as the song evolved into a collaborative expression of their journey.

As they reached the final notes, the room resonated with the lingering echoes of the music. Bentley stopped the recording, and a serene silence enveloped the space. Raelynn looked at him with a mixture of joy and satisfaction, knowing they had created something truly special.

Bentley reached over to stop the playback, and the room returned to its natural quiet. "Raelynn, that was incredible. Your touch on the chorus added a whole new dimension. Me changing the rap lyrics? This song is now uniquely ours, almost completely different from the original" Bentley remarked, his eyes reflecting admiration.

Raelynn blushed, humbled by the compliment. "It felt natural, Bentley. This song is a piece of us, and I wanted to make sure it resonated with our story."

With the recording completed, Bentley began the process of mixing and mastering. Raelynn sat beside him, her hand intertwined with his, as they fine-tuned the details to perfection. The song, now a harmonious blend of their voices and emotions, was ready to be shared with the world.

As the final version played, Bentley and Raelynn listened, immersed in the magic they had created together. The room filled with the rich sound of their rendition, and it dawned on them that this song would forever be etched in the soundtrack of their lives.

Bentley turned to Raelynn, a spark of excitement in his eyes. "This is it, Rae. Our song, our story, ready to be heard by the world. And I couldn't be happier that it's with you."

Raelynn leaned in, pressing a gentle kiss on Bentley's lips. "I'm so grateful to share this journey with you. Our music, our love—it's an adventure I wouldn't trade for anything."

In the midst of their musical triumph, Bentley and Raelynn decided to take a break and indulge in a well-deserved moment of celebration. They sat together, basking in the afterglow of their creative collaboration.

It was during this moment of joy that Raelynn turned to Bentley with a mischievous glint in her eyes. "You know what we need to do next, right?"

Bentley raised an eyebrow, intrigued. "What's on your mind?"

A playful smile spread across Raelynn's face. "Game night silly. Let's send the invites to Cassidy and Cameron for this coming weekend. It'll be the perfect setting for them to spend time together without feeling pressured."

Bentley chuckled, realizing that Raelynn was seamlessly transitioning from their musical venture to playing cupid. "You're right. Let's do it so fate can do the rest."

Excitement bubbled between them as they began to plan the details of their upcoming game night. It was a welcome diversion from the challenges they had faced, a chance to spread joy and create new memories.

46

Game Night

It was Friday night, and the moment of truth had arrived to test the success of Raelynn's master plan. She and Bentley eagerly awaited Cassidy and Cameron's arrival for game night, curious to see if Cassidy and Cameron would form the connection Raelynn had envisioned.

The atmosphere in Raelynn and Bentley's home was filled with a mix of excitement and nervous anticipation. They had set up a cozy game night setting, complete with board games, snacks, and soft background music. As the doorbell rang, signaling the arrival of Cassidy and Cameron, Raelynn exchanged an enthusiastic glance with Bentley.

"Here we go," Bentley whispered, a playful grin on his face.

Raelynn opened the door, greeted by the smiles of Cassidy and Cameron, as they exchanged glances of confusion with each other. "Welcome! So glad you could make it," she said with obvious enthusiasm, ushering them inside.

Cassidy and Cameron stepped into the warm ambiance of Raelynn's home, their eyes scanning the inviting setup for game night. Bentley greeted them with a welcoming smile, embracing the role of the charismatic host.

"Thanks for coming, guys. We've been looking forward to this," Bentley said, exuding a welcoming energy.

"This is going to be a blast. Thanks for having me over," Cassidy responded, sharing a brief smile with Bentley.

As they settled into the living room, Bentley took the opportunity to introduce Cassidy and Cameron formally. "Cassidy, this is Cameron, my weirdo of a best friend and somewhat business partner. Cameron, this is Cassidy, Raelynn's best friend, and Skylar's mom," Bentley said with a giant smile.

"Wait. You're the woman that made me an uncle with the most awesome nephew ever." Cameron said with amusement, while point at Cassidy taking in the realization of who she was.

Cassidy chuckled at Cameron's remark, a warm blush creeping up her cheeks. "Guilty as charged," she replied with a playful grin. "And you must be the uncle who spoils Skylar rotten."

Cameron nodded proudly. "Absolutely! Skylar's the coolest kid in town, and I make sure he knows it." The ice seemed to break between them as laughter filled the room.

Raelynn, observing the interaction, exchanged a satisfied look with Bentley. It seemed like her intuition about Cassidy and Cameron's potential connection wasn't off the mark. As the night progressed, the alcoholic drinks began to flow smoothly, and the atmosphere became even more relaxed. The clinking of glasses and the occasional burst of laughter filled the air as they moved on to the next phase of their game night.

As the ambiance shifted to a more relaxed tone, Bentley, determined to fulfill Raelyn's master plan, suggested a personal and adult-oriented drinking game. This unconventional game delved into the depths of everyone's secrets, leaving no topic off limits. It became a unique opportunity for each participant to open up.

Raelynn, the only sober one due to her pregnancy, found joy in observing her plan unfold. The dynamics of the game revealed a spectrum of emotions and connections among the participants, adding an unexpected layer to the evening.

As the game progressed, the questions became more intimate, revealing personal anecdotes, dreams, and even embarrassing stories.

Cassidy and Cameron, along with Raelynn and Bentley, found themselves sharing laughter, vulnerabilities, and a growing sense of camaraderie.

Cassidy, already known for her wit and humor, surprised everyone with a touching story about her journey as a single mother and the challenges she had overcome. Cameron, in turn, shared a heartfelt moment about the importance of family and the impact Skylar had on his life in just a few short weeks.

The atmosphere in the room became charged with a blend of shared experiences and newfound connections. Bentley, glancing at Raelynn, couldn't help but feel a sense of accomplishment. The game, intended to be a lighthearted diversion, had evolved into a catalyst for genuine connections.

As the night wore on, Bentley suggested another change of pace. "Let's switch gears and play a few rounds of 'Never Have I Ever.' It's a classic that never fails to bring out some interesting revelations," he proposed, a mischievous twinkle in his eyes.

"I'll go first," Cameron shouted as he proceeded. "Never have I ever, slept with Bentley," fighting back his laughter.

Raelynn and Cassidy immediately cut their eyes at him, as Cassidy playfully smacked at him.

Bentley, caught off guard, couldn't help but burst into laughter. "Well, I can't argue with that one," he admitted, sharing an amused look with Cameron. Raelynn and Cassidy joined in the laughter, the unexpected revelation lightening the atmosphere.

Cassidy kept the momentum going by following Cameron's daring move. "Alright then, let's continue with the surprises. Never have I ever gone on a blind date," she declared, casting a knowing look at Bentley and Raelynn.

Raelynn, taking a sip of her non-alcoholic drink, raised an eyebrow playfully. "Does game night count as a blind date?" she teased, earning a round of laughter from the group.

Cameron, seizing the opportunity, added his own twist to the game. "Never have I ever been set up on a date by my best friend playing cupid," he declared, looking directly at Bentley.

Bentley chuckled, raising his glass. "Guilty as charged. Raelynn, baby, we've been caught," he quipped, causing everyone to laugh.

The clock ticked past midnight, and Raelynn decided to shake things up. "Since y'all busted us and our little plan, what do you say we up the ante and play a little truth or dare?" she suggested, a mischievous glint in her eyes.

Cassidy and Cameron exchanged amused glances, intrigued by the prospect of a new twist to the evening. "Sounds like a game-changer. I'm in," Cassidy said with a playful smile.

Cameron, always up for a challenge, grinned. "Bring it on, Rae. Let's see what truths and dares you have up your sleeve."

"Before we start, how about we move this party to the backyard? I've got some fairy lights set up, and it's the perfect setting for some star-gazing," Bentley proposed, his eyes gleaming with enthusiasm.

The group agreed to Bentley's suggestion, and they made their way to the backyard, where the soft glow of fairy lights adorned the surroundings. The night air was crisp, and the stars overhead added a touch of magic to the setting. They settled into comfortable chairs arranged in a circle, ready for the next phase of the evening.

Raelynn, eager to continue the momentum, turned to Cameron. "Alright, Cameron, truth or dare?"

Cameron, never one to back down, flashed a confident smile. "Dare, of course."

Raelynn, with a mischievous gleam in her eyes, pondered for a moment. "I dare you to tell Cassidy your first impression of her."

Cameron chuckled, his eyes meeting Cassidy's. "Oh, this should be interesting. So, when I met Cassidy… tonight… I thought she was a combination of fierce and mysterious. You know, the kind of person you're intrigued by and want to get to know better."

Cassidy smiled a wide smile. "Well, I guess I've always had that effect on people."

Bentley, with a playful grin, opted for truth. "Hit me with your best shot, Rae."

Raelynn, after a moment of contemplation, asked, "What's your biggest fear?"

Bentley smiled, "Oh that's super easy. My biggest fear is losing you." As he leaned in planting a quick kiss on her lips.

As the game continued, Bentley turned the spotlight back on Raelynn. "Your turn, my love. Truth or dare?"

Raelynn, deciding to play it safe, chose truth. "Ask away."

Bentley, with a twinkle in his eyes, asked, "What's the most embarrassing thing you've caught me doing?"

Raelynn smirked, reminiscing about a particular incident. "Remember that time you tried to dance to impress me, but you tripped over your own feet and knocked over a vase? It was endearing, though."

Bentley chuckled, acknowledging the memory. "Yeah, not my finest moment."

With a playful atmosphere prevailing, it was finally Cameron's turn again and Raelynn knew Cameron would choose dare. So she had a trick up her sleeve.

"Truth or dare Cam?" Raelynn asked with a mischievous grin.

"You already know, give me that dare." Cameron exclaimed.

Raelynn decided to introduce a daring element to the game. "Okay, here's the ultimate challenge. Cameron, I dare you to share a kiss with Cassidy."

Cameron and Cassidy exchanged surprised glances, a hint of blush coloring their cheeks. The group watched with anticipation as Cameron, ever the daredevil, flashed a confident smile and leaned in towards Cassidy.

As their lips met, the atmosphere seemed to hold its breath for a moment. The kiss, albeit prompted by a dare, held a spark of unexpected connection. When they pulled away, there was a shared sense of amusement and a newfound awareness lingering in the air.

Bentley, breaking the silence, erupted into laughter. "Well, I must say, that's one way to spice up game night!"

Cassidy, her playful demeanor intact, grinned at Cameron. "Who would've thought truth or dare could take such an interesting turn?"

Cameron, wearing a charming grin, complimented Raelynn, "I've got to give it to you, Raelynn, you really know how to keep things lively. And Cassidy... wow. You're an exceptional kisser." He playfully raised his hands in a praying gesture, bowing his head towards Cassidy.

Cassidy, in response, blushed with a shy smile.

As the night progressed, the bond between Cassidy and Cameron deepened, and Raelynn and Bentley exchanged knowing looks, satisfied with the success of their plan. Raelynn felt a sense of contentment seeing the connection unfold as she and Bentley discreetly slipped back inside, leaving Cassidy and Cameron alone in the backyard beneath the moonlight.

Back inside, Raelynn and Bentley shared a quiet celebration, their plan to bring their friends together proving to be a success. Bentley grinned at Raelynn. "I'd say our game night was a hit."

Raelynn nodded, a satisfied smile playing on her lips. "Looks like the stars aligned for more than just stargazing tonight."

The following morning, Bentley and Raelynn eagerly gazed into the backyard, astonished by the success of their mischievous scheme. Cassidy and Cameron lay there in the open, snuggled up in the nude, blissfully asleep.

"Imagine when the sprinkler system goes off and catches them unaware," Bentley chuckled, leaning down to give Raelynn a kiss.

Raelynn, her eyes gleaming with excitement, giggled mischievously at the thought of the impending prank. "I can't wait to see their reaction when the sprinklers hit them, and I'm definitely not turning it off," she whispered to Bentley.

As Cassidy and Cameron slept peacefully, oblivious to the impending mischief, Raelynn and Bentley, watching from the kitchen window, saw the sprinklers go off. Cassidy's high-pitched scream filled the air as she tried to shield herself, while Cameron, amidst the chaos of water spray, fumbled to find his pants. Raelynn and Bentley burst into laughter, tears streaming down their faces at the priceless scene. Cassidy and Cameron, sputtering and shivering, managed to put on their clothes, looking around to understand what triggered the sprinklers.

Barely containing their giggles, Raelynn and Bentley stepped into the backyard with grins on their faces. "Gotcha!" Raelynn exclaimed, reveling in the mischief.

"You two are troublemakers!" Cassidy said, shaking her head but with a playful glint in her eyes.

Bentley, grinning, took Raelynn's hand. "Guilty as charged," he said with a wink. "But we couldn't resist."

Cameron chuckled, wrapping an arm around Cassidy. "Well, you definitely got us," he said, still amused. "That was quite the wake-up call."

Smirking, Bentley teased, "So, how was last night? I assume it went well, considering we found you naked and afraid," he chuckled.

Cassidy blushed, and Cameron playfully rolled his eyes, their connection from the previous night still evident. "Yeah, it went great," Cassidy replied with a shy grin, and Cameron nodded in agreement. Bentley and Raelynn felt satisfied that their matchmaking plan had worked so well.

Raelynn nudged Bentley playfully. "Looks like our plan worked perfectly," she said with a wink. "I'm glad you two had a good time."

The satisfaction of successfully bringing their friends together lingered in the air. Bentley and Raelynn were pleased to see the genuine connection that had blossomed during the course of the night. As Cassidy and Cameron shared shy smiles, it was evident that game night had not only been a hit but had also sparked something special between the two.

As the sun continued to rise, Raelynn and Bentley basked in the warmth of the morning, knowing that their master plan had not only closed the chapter of an unforgettable game night but had opened a new and exciting one for their friends the way they had hoped.

47

Wedding Planning

The following week ushered in more opportunities for Bentley to bond with Skylar, dedicating more time to get to know his son. This was part of the orchestrated plan by Bentley and Raelynn to bring Cassidy and Cameron together, and indeed, they were spending significant time in each other's company.

As they spent significant time together, Bentley simultaneously poured his efforts into finalizing his album. He engaged in continuous collaboration with his sound engineer, exchanging files of song edits. His free moments, when not with Skylar, were consumed by the meticulous mastering of the album. Perfection was his goal, and he was dedicated to making that happen.

Meanwhile, Raelynn took on the responsibility of wedding planning for the week. Handling all the details alone, she found the process to be increasingly stressful. Despite the challenges, she understood and accepted Bentley's prior commitments to his label and fatherly duties, realizing that these took precedence over wedding planning. Additionally, she considered Bentley's potential disengagement due to the emotional aftermath of his previous wedding, where he had been left at the altar.

Determined to craft a memorable and beautiful wedding, Raelynn embarked on the task of selecting the perfect date. Considering their mutual desire for a prompt celebration, she carefully pinpointed a date that harmonized with both their schedules and the availability of five potential venues. The challenge was considerable, given the urgency of planning for a rapidly approaching wedding. Placing certain plans in a chokehold as she wrestled with inevitable time restraints. Nevertheless, she triumphed in securing a date and now had to make the choice on one of the five potential venues to commemorate their marriage just a month away—a timeframe that would soon hold deep sentimental significance for both Bentley and herself.

Having successfully chosen a date, Raelynn dove into the intricate process of selecting the perfect venue for their wedding. Knowing that the venue would set the tone for the entire celebration, she considered various factors such as size, style, and location.

With five potential venues in contention, Raelynn faced the daunting task of making a selection that would capture the essence of their love story and provide a memorable backdrop for their special day. Each venue came with its unique charm, amenities, and ambiance, making the decision even more challenging.

After carefully considering the size, style, and location of each potential venue, Raelynn decided to embark on a journey to visit each one personally. She wanted to immerse herself in the atmosphere of each location to ensure it resonated with the vision she had for her and Bentley's special day.

At the top of her list was 'Amazing Graze,' an authentic dairy barn wedding venue tucked away in the countryside. This picturesque setting boasted rolling hills, abundant greenery, and a rustic barn for the reception. Raelynn envisioned the natural beauty of the surroundings harmonizing with the romantic tale of their love. While exploring the venue, she couldn't help but notice a sizable cross window positioned behind the altar in the dairy barn. The image of exchanging vows with Bentley, bathed in sunlight streaming through the cross window, already painted a vivid picture in her mind.

The second option was the 'The Hudson Manor Estate', a venue known for its elegance and sophistication. Nestled by a serene lake, the manor exuded timeless beauty with its crystal chandeliers, grand ballrooms, and panoramic views of the water. Raelynn imagined a classic and refined wedding, with a touch of glamour that reflected Bentley's artistic persona. The lakeside setting added a touch of tranquility to the grandeur of the celebration.

Raelynn meticulously planned her visits to the remaining three venues, ensuring each one received the attention it deserved. The third option on her list was 'Azalea Gardens,' a botanical wonderland that promised a fairytale setting for their union. Lush greenery, vibrant flowers, and winding paths created a magical atmosphere. Raelynn envisioned a whimsical celebration surrounded by nature's beauty, with Bentley by her side amid the blooming flowers and enchanting landscapes.

Raelynn moved on to the fourth option on her list, 'Rooftop TwentyTwo,' a breathtaking rooftop venue in the heart of Charlotte. Perched atop a high-rise building, this venue offered panoramic views of the city skyline, creating a modern and chic atmosphere. The thought of exchanging vows under the open sky, surrounded by the city lights, resonated with Raelynn's vision of a contemporary and stylish wedding. The venue's sleek design and urban charm appealed to her sense of aesthetics, and she could already envision the cityscape becoming a backdrop to their love story.

Raelynn's last choice was the 'Berry Hill Resort,' a transformed historic mansion now serving as an opulent venue within a resort setting. Tucked away in the midst of nature, Berry Hill Resort presented a captivating backdrop for any occasion, featuring a verdant circle of lush green grass as its central highlight. The timeless allure of the mansion's classical facade added a touch of enchantment, making it an ideal setting for their ceremony.

With visits to all five potential venues completed, Raelynn found herself faced with the challenging decision of selecting the one that would serve as the canvas for the beginning of their journey as a married couple. Each venue had its own unique charm, and Raelynn's meticulous planning had provided her with a deep understanding of what each had to offer.

As she reflected on the options, Raelynn considered not only the aesthetics of the venues but also how well they aligned with the vision she and Bentley shared for their special day. The choice would be a significant one, setting the tone for the entire celebration and creating lasting memories for both of them.

Amid their busy schedules, Raelynn carved out moments to discuss important updates with Bentley. She sought his input, making sure the venue selection aligned with their shared vision. Raelynn described each venue meticulously, accompanying her descriptions with detailed pictures.

"Honey, I'm torn between The Hudson Manor and Amazing Graze," Bentley confessed, rubbing his temples, as Raelynn showed him pictures of the venues. The stress from finalizing his album radiating off him.

"I feel the same way. There's something about that giant cross window that just speaks to me," Raelynn expressed with frustration about choosing the venue.

Bentley responded, "Well, choose the one you want. It's your day, and I want it to be magical for you. Don't stress about my input. Any venue you pick will be magical for me because I'm marrying you." Leaning in, Bentley placed a kiss on Raelynn's lips, holding her legs stretched out across his, as the relaxed on the couch.

"I think I'm leaning towards 'Amazing Graze.' The rustic charm, the cross window, and the countryside setting—it feels like us, you know?" Raelynn expressed, seeking Bentley's opinion once again.

Bentley nodded thoughtfully, "I agree. It has a special touch, and I can already picture us there. Let's go with 'Amazing Graze.' It's perfect."

With the decision made, Raelynn felt a sense of relief, although the planning was far from over. She still had to work through the guest list, although short, still tedious. She had to decide on flower arrangements, a wedding dress, bridesmaid dresses and grooms attire, along with catering.

Raelynn delved into the next phase of wedding planning with enthusiasm and meticulous attention to detail. The first on her list was selecting the perfect flowers to adorn their chosen venue, 'Amazing Graze,' and complement the rustic charm of the dairy barn setting.

For the ceremony, Raelynn envisioned a breathtaking floral arrangement framing the cross window behind the altar. After careful consideration, she decided on a combination of lush greenery, delicate white roses, and hints of soft lavender. The greenery would symbolize growth and new beginnings, while the white roses represented purity and the lavender added a touch of romance. Raelynn imagined the floral display creating a natural and elegant backdrop as she and Bentley exchanged their vows.

Moving on to the reception area, she envisioned long wooden tables adorned with rustic centerpieces. Raelynn opted for a mix of wildflowers, including daisies, sunflowers, and baby's breath. The vibrant colors and untamed beauty of the wildflowers would enhance the pastoral atmosphere of the barn, creating a warm and inviting space for their guests.

With the floral arrangements decided, Raelynn turned her attention to the attire. She wanted the colors and designs to reflect the natural beauty of their chosen venue. For her wedding dress, Raelynn envisioned a gown that echoed the rustic elegance of 'Amazing Graze.' She chose a flowing A-line dress with delicate lace detailing, reminiscent of wildflowers. The dress featured a sweetheart neckline and a subtle train that added a touch of classic romance.

As for Bentley's attire, Raelynn aimed for a look that harmonized with the rustic setting. She envisioned him in a tailored charcoal gray suit paired with a crisp white shirt and a lavender bowtie to complement the floral theme. Bentley, always the artistic soul, embraced Raelynn's vision, eager to look his best on their special day.

For the bridesmaids, Raelynn selected dresses in a soft lavender hue. The flowing chiffon dresses featured a bohemian style, tying in with the natural and whimsical atmosphere she envisioned. The groomsmen would complement Bentley in charcoal gray suits with lavender ties, creating a cohesive and stylish bridal party.

As Raelynn finalized the attire choices, she turned her attention to catering. Embracing the rustic theme, she opted for a farm-to-table menu featuring local, seasonal ingredients. The menu included hearty dishes inspired by the countryside, ensuring a culinary experience that would delight their guests' taste buds.

With each decision, Raelynn carefully considered how it would contribute to the overall ambiance of their wedding day. Bentley, though still engrossed in his album, made time to support Raelynn in the planning process. Together, they navigated the intricate details of wedding preparation, ensuring that every element would come together seamlessly to create a day filled with love, beauty, and cherished memories.

48

Tragedy Strikes

A week before their wedding, Raelynn and Bentley found themselves immersed in final preparations. While Raelynn worked on wedding details, Bentley, feeling the pressure, focused on putting the finishing touches on his album. His goal was to present it to Raelynn as a special wedding gift.

Amidst discussions about the reception playlist, Raelynn's phone interrupted the moment with her mother's frantic call. Olivia, on the other end, was hysterically crying, sending shivers down Bentley's spine.

"Rae, baby, he's gone," Olivia managed to convey amid tears. Raelynn, struggling to comprehend through the sobs, urged her mother to slow down. Olivia took a deep breath before revealing the devastating truth – Raelynn's father had passed away.

Raelynn, initially in disbelief, clutched her face in shock. As Olivia explained the tragic plane crash, Raelynn's heart began to break, and tears welled in her eyes. "No. You're lying, Mom," Raelynn responded, her voice cracking.

Olivia, more composed now, confirmed the heartbreaking news. The realization started sinking in for Raelynn as tears streamed down her face. Bentley, beside her, sensed her anguish but remained unaware of the details.

"Mom, stop. This isn't funny," Raelynn pleaded, her voice filled with disbelief and cracks. Unable to bear the uncertainty, she rushed to the living room to turn on the news. The headline confirmed her worst fears – "Mr. Hart, CEO of Hart Management, dies in a private plane crash in the Tennessee Mountains."

Raelynn broke down, dropping the phone and collapsing to her knees. Bentley, entering the room and seeing the news headline, immediately understood the gravity of the situation. He rushed to Raelynn's side, consoling her as best he could.

As the reality of her father's sudden death sank in, Raelynn's world crumbled around her. Despite their recent estrangement, the thought of never seeing him again overwhelmed her. She cried uncontrollably, feeling lost and alone in her pain. Bentley held her tightly, his heart breaking for her, providing comfort during this difficult moment.

In the midst of Raelynn's inconsolable grief, Bentley remained a steadfast source of support. Holding her close, he whispered words of comfort and reassurance, realizing that words alone couldn't ease the profound pain she was experiencing.

As the news continued to unfold on the television screen, Raelynn's mind became a tumultuous sea of memories and emotions. Flashbacks of cherished moments with her father clashed with the harsh reality of his sudden absence. Bentley, though not the biggest fan of Raelynn's father, empathized with the depth of her sorrow.

Time seemed to stand still as Raelynn grappled with the overwhelming waves of grief. The wedding preparations, once filled with excitement and anticipation, now felt like a distant and insignificant concern. Bentley recognized the need for space and allowed Raelynn to navigate her emotions, offering silent support as she processed the shock and loss.

Later that night, Raelynn continued to shed tears, grappling with the sudden loss of her father. As Bentley observed her emotional unraveling and felt helpless in easing her pain, his own heart ached.

"Rae, I believe we should consider canceling the wedding. You need to be in Nashville with your family," Bentley suggested, his voice heavy with solemnity.

Looking up at him with eyes brimming with tears, Raelynn asserted, "That's the last thing we're doing! I'll fly to Nashville to be with my family, and then I'll fly back here to marry the man of my dreams this weekend. But you're coming with me to Nashville."

Bentley nodded in understanding, recognizing the importance of Raelynn being with her family during such a challenging time. He assured her that he would stand by her side every step of the way. Quickly, Raelynn made arrangements to fly to Nashville the next morning, determined to navigate the difficult journey, of funeral planning with Bentley by her side.

The following morning, Raelynn and Bentley boarded a flight to Nashville, their hearts heavy with grief and uncertainty. The plane journey felt surreal, as if suspended in a world where joy and sorrow coexisted. Raelynn stared out of the window, lost in her thoughts, while Bentley sat beside her, a silent pillar of strength.

Upon landing in Nashville, they were enveloped by the somber atmosphere of mourning. Raelynn's family, though devastated by the loss, found solace in her presence. Bentley seamlessly blended into the role of a supportive partner, offering comfort and assistance where needed.

In the days that followed, Raelynn and her family navigated the challenging task of arranging her father's funeral. Bentley, though an unliked outsider to the family dynamics, respectfully contributed and ensured that Raelynn had the space to grieve while handling the practical aspects of the funeral arrangements.

The day of her father's funeral dawned, and Raelynn experienced a mix of sorrow and numbness as she stood beside her father's casket, surrounded by grieving family and friends. As the funeral service commenced, Raelynn felt nervous anticipation, knowing she was about to address her father's closest acquaintances, both familiar and unfamiliar faces.

When the time came for Raelynn to deliver the eulogy, a mournful hymn filled the air as she stood at the pulpit, facing the somber assembly gathered to honor her father. A wave of regret and sorrow washed over her, acknowledging the estrangement that had characterized her relationship with her father at the time of his sudden passing.

Her voice trembled with emotion as she began to speak, pouring out her love for her father and expressing profound remorse for the unresolved differences between them. "My father was a good man," Raelynn shared, tears streaming down her face. "His love for my mother and us kids was unparalleled. Yet, I stand before you today with shame, regretting that due to our disagreements, my father and I weren't on speaking terms when he left this world. It's a regret that will linger with me for the rest of my life."

In her heartfelt address, Raelynn urged the congregation to let go of grudges, emphasizing the unpredictability and brevity of life. "If you love them, forgive them," she implored, resonating with those present. "Our time is precious, and holding onto grudges might lead to a future filled with regret."

As Raelynn continued to share cherished memories of her father, she summoned the strength to speak directly to him. "To my father, I love you, and I'll miss you deeply. Most importantly, Dad, I forgive you," she declared, her voice raw with emotion. "I forgive you for our disagreements, for any hurt we may have caused each other. Though I wish I could have said this when you were still here, I hope you can hear me now and understand how much I truly love you."

With these words, a palpable sense of healing and forgiveness permeated the room. Raelynn's family and friends gathered around, offering words of comfort and support. Bentley, standing steadfastly by her side, provided unwavering support as the funeral service concluded with a final hymn and a moment of silence. Raelynn bid her last goodbyes to her father, placing a single rose on his casket as a symbol of love and forgiveness. Leaning on Bentley for support, they exited the church together.

Following the service, everyone gathered at Raelynn's parents' house, creating a space filled with both sorrow and warmth to commemorate Jim. Laughter and tears intermingled as friends and family shared anecdotes and memories, honoring Jim's life and legacy. Raelynn found solace in discovering the profound impact her father had on the lives of those around him.

As the day progressed, the somber ambiance from the funeral began to subside. Raelynn, Olivia, and her siblings were left to confront the stark reality of Jim's absence. Raelynn knew she needed to discuss her upcoming wedding with her mother, but the weight of the recent funeral made her hesitant to bring it up.

"Mom, I love you, but Bentley and I need to return to Raleigh. We still have some final wedding preparations to handle before this weekend," Raelynn conveyed tentatively, pausing with a sense of guilt for mentioning her wedding amid the somber atmosphere.

Olivia turned to Raelynn with a brief smile. "No, honey, it's okay. Your wedding is a source of joy, and we shouldn't let this tragedy overshadow your happiness. Your father may not have been a fan of Bentley, but he would want you to be happy, too, sweetheart," Olivia reassured, reaching out to hold Raelynn's hands.

Emotions overwhelmed Raelynn, tears welling up in her eyes. "I am excited, but it just feels wrong to be," she confessed. "Anyway, what I was going to say is that if you can't make it to the wedding, Bentley and I will truly understand.

Olivia smiled again, offering a glimmer of hope. "Honey, I will try my best to make it because I don't want to miss my daughter getting married. But it will depend on how I'm feeling once everything calms down here," she explained.

Grateful for her mother's understanding, Raelynn and Bentley prepared to leave. Olivia called out to Bentley, injecting a hint of skepticism into her voice. "Hey Bentley! You better treat my princess and my grandbaby right now! You know Jim didn't like you, and I'm still coming around to you. I just hope you prove us wrong and love her like you can't live without her!"

Bentley turned back, smiling and reassured her. "Mrs. Hart, I love your daughter more than anything in this world. There isn't a thing I wouldn't do to protect her. So, trust me, ma'am, she's in good hands."

Olivia's skepticism softened, witnessing the sincerity in Bentley's eyes. She nodded, tears welling in her own eyes. "Thank you, Bentley. I appreciate your sincerity," she said, her voice choked with emotion. Raelynn embraced her mother tightly, and Bentley offered his condolences once more before they departed for Raleigh. To everyone's surprise, Olivia pulled Bentley into a hug too.

As Raelynn and Bentley made their way back to Raleigh, the atmosphere was heavy with both grief and the anticipation of an impending wedding. The plane ride seemed to encapsulate the contrasting emotions they were experiencing, and Bentley kept a supportive arm around Raelynn, silently acknowledging the rollercoaster they were on.

Once they landed, the couple returned to their home, now adorned with the decorations that had been set up for their joyful celebration. However, the air felt different, and the house echoed with the lingering sorrow from the recent events. Bentley decided to give Raelynn some space to be with her thoughts, understanding the magnitude of the emotions she was grappling with.

As the day unfolded, Raelynn and Bentley tackled the remaining wedding preparations, the excitement subdued by the recent loss. They went through the motions, addressing the final details with a mix of determination and melancholy. The wedding playlist, once a topic of joyful discussion, now carried a bittersweet weight.

In the midst of these preparations, Bentley received a call from his sound engineer, notifying him that the final mixed-down version of his album, "The Power of Music," was ready. Bentley felt a surge of pride and excitement, knowing that this gift would be a token of his love for Raelynn amid the somber circumstances.

However, he decided to stick to his initial plan and wait until their wedding day to share the album with her. The music, which had been a solace for him during challenging times, would now serve as a source of comfort and healing for both of them.

As the wedding preparations progressed, Raelynn gazed at Bentley, appreciating his unwavering support, and inquired, "Ben, we haven't discussed this yet because everything has happened so quick, but after we exchange vows, where do we plan to move? Are we staying here, or is the plan to relocate to Miami in your enormous mansion?"

Bentley paused, his mind momentarily shifting from the wedding preparations to the future they were about to embark on together. He took Raelynn's hands in his, a solemn expression on his face as he considered her question.

"It doesn't matter, Rae. I'm content with whatever you decide because as long as I have you, we can stay here in Raleigh or move to my place in Miami. Hell, we can even relocate to Europe if that's what you want."

Raelynn smiled, grateful for Bentley's flexibility and understanding. However, as she looked into the future, she couldn't shake off the responsibilities and uncertainties that awaited her. The recent turn of events had brought her face-to-face with the unpredictability of life, and she felt the need to address some practical matters.

"Bentley," she began, her tone gentle yet serious, "there's something else we need to talk about. I've been thinking about our future, and given the recent changes in my life, I believe it's crucial that we consider certain aspects to protect both of us."

Bentley furrowed his brow, sensing the shift in the conversation. "Of course, Rae. What's on your mind?"

Raelynn took a deep breath before broaching the sensitive topic. "I think we should discuss putting a prenuptial agreement in place."

Bentley's eyes widened slightly, surprised by the suggestion. He remained silent, allowing Raelynn to explain her reasoning.

"I'm about to receive a significant amount of money from my father's life insurance, and there's a high likelihood that I'll inherit his business, Hart Management," she elaborated. "I've also just started my music career, and I want to protect both of us in case anything unexpected happens. This isn't about lack of trust; it's about being practical and ensuring that we both have a secure future."

Bentley nodded thoughtfully, understanding the gravity of Raelynn's situation. "Rae, I appreciate your honesty, and I understand where you're coming from. I've always believed in being open and transparent with each other. If a prenup is what you feel is necessary, then I'm willing to discuss it and work together to make sure it's fair for both of us."

Relieved by Bentley's understanding, Raelynn continued, "This is not about doubting our love or commitment. It's about facing the reality of life, especially considering the unique circumstances surrounding my family's wealth and business. I want us to be on the same page and protect each other's interests."

Bentley nodded in agreement, showing his support for Raelynn's decision. "Rae, I completely understand where you're coming from. It's important for us to have these discussions and plan for our future, especially given the circumstances. I trust you, and I want us to do what's best for both of us."

Raelynn smiled gratefully at Bentley's understanding. "Thank you for being so understanding, Ben. I know this isn't the most romantic topic, but I believe it's necessary for us to have these conversations and make sure we're both protected."

Bentley reached out to gently cup Raelynn's face in his hands. "Rae, our love is strong, and I have no doubts about our commitment to each other. This prenup is just a formality to ensure that we're both taken care of, no matter what happens in the future."

Raelynn leaned into Bentley's touch, feeling reassured by his words. "I'm glad we're on the same page, Ben. I want us to build a future together, and part of that means being responsible and planning for all possibilities."

Bentley nodded, a soft smile playing on his lips. "Absolutely, Rae. We're a team, and we'll face whatever comes our way together. Now, about the prenup, do you already have a draft prepared, or do we need to start from scratch?"

Raelynn nodded, her expression serious. "Actually, the legal team at Harts Management has already drafted a prenup based on my father's estate and the potential inheritance of the business. I can have them send it over to you if you'd like to review it before we make any decisions. And of course, if there are any changes you want to make, we can discuss them together.

Bentley nodded in agreement. "That sounds like a good plan, Rae. I'll review the draft and let you know if there's anything I think we need to adjust. But more importantly, I want you to know that I'm fully committed to you, regardless of what's in the prenup. Our love is what matters most to me."

Raelynn's eyes glistened with gratitude as she wrapped her arms around Bentley, feeling overwhelmed by his love and support. "Thank you, Ben. I love you more than words can express, and I'm so grateful to have you by my side through everything."

Bentley held her close, pressing a gentle kiss to her forehead. "I love you too, Rae. And I promise to always stand by you, no matter what life throws our way."

As they held each other in a comforting embrace, Raelynn felt a sense of peace knowing that they were facing the future together, with love, honesty, and a shared commitment to building a life filled with happiness and security.

49

Bentley & Raelynn Riggs

The day of the wedding, Bentley found himself awake unusually early due to his nerves. Despite feeling a sense of déjà vu, he was more certain about this marriage than he had been on his last wedding day.

Unable to sleep, Bentley decided to arrive at the venue early. He wanted to witness the magic as the vendors brought Raelynn's dream to life at the 'Amazing Graze.' Although he didn't know much about the venue other than its proximity to Raleigh and the presence of a giant cross window at the back of the altar, he was eager to discover what had captured Raelynn's attention.

As Bentley stepped onto the grounds of the 'Amazing Graze,' he was instantly captivated by the rustic charm that surrounded him. The authentic dairy barn wedding venue boasted rolling hills, abundant greenery, and a rustic barn that exuded a timeless appeal. The air carried the sweet scent of wildflowers, and the countryside setting added a touch of serenity to the atmosphere.

The venue's centerpiece was the majestic cross window behind the altar, which immediately drew Bentley's attention. It stood tall and elegant, casting a warm glow as the morning sun streamed through its intricate design. The pastoral setting seemed almost surreal, creating a picturesque backdrop that promised to elevate the beauty of Raelynn's envisioned ceremony.

With each step, Bentley admired the craftsmanship of the barn and the thoughtfulness that went into preserving its rustic authenticity. Weathered wooden beams adorned the interior, and the ambiance carried a sense of history and tradition. The charm of 'Amazing Graze' was undeniable, and Bentley couldn't help but appreciate Raelynn's choice.

As the vendors meticulously set up for the ceremony, Bentley observed the transformation of the space into a haven of natural elegance. The lush greenery, delicate white roses, and hints of soft lavender adorned the altar, framing the cross window in a breathtaking display. Bentley could envision Raelynn standing there, surrounded by the symbolism of growth, purity, and romance as she exchanged vows.

Moving to the reception area, Bentley marveled at the long wooden tables adorned with rustic centerpieces. The mix of wildflowers – daisies, sunflowers, and baby's breath – created a vibrant burst of color and untamed beauty. The pastoral charm of the barn seamlessly blended with the warm hues of the flowers, transforming the space into a welcoming haven for their guests.

Bentley couldn't help but smile as he imagined the joy that would fill the air, knowing that every detail had been carefully chosen to reflect Raelynn's vision. The 'Amazing Graze' was turning into a place where their love story would unfold, surrounded by the beauty of nature and the authenticity of a venue that spoke to the depth of their connection.

With the sun climbing higher in the sky, Bentley took a moment to absorb the serenity of the surroundings. The rolling hills, the vibrant wildflowers, and the rustic elegance of the barn created a picturesque scene that perfectly encapsulated the essence of their wedding day. Bentley felt a sense of peace, knowing that this venue, chosen by Raelynn with such care, would witness the beginning of their shared journey.

As the morning carried over in afternoon it was finally the scheduled time for the wedding party to make their arrival to the venue to start getting ready.

As morning transitioned to afternoon, the eagerly awaited time for the wedding party's arrival had finally come. The wedding coordinator led Bentley to the men's dressing room, where he and his groomsmen would await their cues throughout the day.

Raelynn and Cassidy were among the first members of the wedding party, besides Bentley, who had been there for a couple of hours already, mentally preparing himself. As the wedding coordinator escorted Raelynn and Cassidy to the women's dressing area, Raelynn's attention was drawn to a white box adorned with a bow.

While exploring the venue and savoring the ambiance created by the vendors, Bentley seized the perfect moment to leave Raelynn her wedding gift. As Raelynn picked up the box, she noticed the tag beneath it that read "To my love." Recognizing Bentley's handwriting, she eagerly opened the box, finding a handwritten letter from Bentley along with his new album, which he had secretly worked on to share with her.

As Raelynn unfolded the note, it began:

"Raelynn, I love you to the moon and can't wait to spend forever with you. I know this is all happening so fast, our love, your music, your father, and now throwing not one but two kids in the mix. You are a rockstar. You are my rockstar, and I am so lucky to call you mine. For weeks now, I have been secretly working to bring to life my fourth studio album that I was struggling to write until you. Thanks to the love and excitement you have brought into my life, not only did I find out I had a kid, but I also found out that we are also expecting a child. I also found my creative edge again, and I wanted to share my appreciation for you with you and the world. When I started writing this album, I wanted it stripped away of all the fancy studio mixing boards and edits. I wanted this album to be raw. I wanted it to be felt, every single emotion. I also wanted it to tell a story, the story of us. That's how the album got its name 'The Power of Music.' This album is my love letter to you, my son Skylar, and our unborn child. I can't imagine life without either of you, and I want the world to know that. I want the world to know that Party Boy Bentley is no more. I love you forever and a day."

Raelynn, overwhelmed with emotion, clutched the letter and album to her chest. Bentley's words resonated deeply within her. She felt an indescribable mix of love, gratitude, and anticipation for the future.

Overwhelmed by a rush of emotions, Raelynn seized Cassidy's hand, urging her into the dressing area. The two of them hurriedly searched for a CD player, driven by Raelynn's desire to experience the album before the chaos of everyone demanding her attention unfolded. She also wanted to savor it before the makeup session commenced.

Cassidy located a CD player, and Raelynn swiftly approached it. With a sense of eagerness, she opened the CD player and gently unveiled the album. The cover, adorned with a simple yet profound design, conveyed Bentley's heartfelt intentions. The title, "The Power of Music," struck a chord with Raelynn, encapsulating the essence of their shared love and the transformative impact of music in their lives.

As the first notes of the album filled the room, Raelynn and Cassidy found themselves immersed in Bentley's musical journey. The raw, unfiltered sound resonated with the emotions he had poured into each composition. The songs unfolded like chapters, weaving a narrative that mirrored the highs and lows of their relationship.

As the music played, Raelynn closed her eyes, allowing the melodies to wash over her. The lyrics, intertwined with Bentley's soulful voice, told the story of their love—from the moment they met to the challenges they faced and the joyous milestones they celebrated together. Each track unfolded like a page in a love story, capturing the essence of their shared experiences.

Cassidy, too, was captivated by the album, recognizing the genuine emotion behind each song. The harmonies and acoustic arrangements created an intimate atmosphere, as if Bentley was singing directly to them. The powerful lyrics resonated with Raelynn, reaffirming the depth of Bentley's love and commitment.

As the final notes of the album played, Raelynn opened her eyes, her heart brimming with emotions. The combination of Bentley's handwritten letter and the heartfelt album created a profound moment of connection between them.

At last, the moment arrived for the wedding to commence. Bentley and Cameron proceeded to the altar to stand beside the minister. Bentley's nerves intensified, unexpectedly triggered by a PTSD flashback from his previous wedding day to Michelle. He struggled to push aside the haunting memories.

As they stood together at the altar, Cameron observed the turmoil brewing within Bentley. Placing his hands on Bentley's shoulders, Cameron offered a comforting massage. "Calm down, Bentley. Everything will be alright. Take deep breaths," Cameron whispered reassuringly.

Bentley, feeling the weight of Cameron's supportive touch, took a series of deep breaths to steady his nerves. The haunting memories began to dissipate as he focused on the present moment—the breathtaking venue, the love that surrounded him, and the promise of a new chapter with Raelynn.

He reminded himself that Raelynn wouldn't have made him sign an agreed upon prenup if she wasn't serious about marrying him.

As Bentley grounded himself in the present, he felt a renewed sense of determination to embrace the love and commitment he shared with Raelynn. The haunting echoes of his past marriage slowly faded into the background, replaced by the anticipation of a beautiful future with the woman he loved.

At last, the chosen song for Raelynn's aisle walk began to play, filling the air with music. The audience rose, turning their attention towards her entrance. Bentley's eyes filled with tears as he caught sight of Raelynn and Skylar at the top of the aisle. Raelynn looked stunning in her wedding gown, adorned with intricate lace details and a flowing train that added an elegant touch. Bentley felt overwhelmed with emotions, struck by Raelynn's beauty and the love he felt for her.

It wasn't just Raelynn who captured Bentley's heart; Skylar, his son, stood proudly by her side, holding her hand and looking incredibly handsome in his tiny tuxedo. Bentley felt immense affection for Skylar, recognizing the important role he played in their lives. Gratitude and joy filled Bentley's heart as he realized he was about to marry the woman of his dreams.

As Raelynn and Skylar stood before Bentley, he knelt down to give Skylar a hug and a forehead kiss, expressing his appreciation for the courage Skylar showed in walking Raelynn down the aisle. Bentley then stood up, addressing both Raelynn and the audience.

"As you all know, today is supposed to be an extremely happy day for Raelynn and me as we start a new journey together," Bentley began, his voice filled with emotion. "However, today we can't help but feel a sense of sadness as there is an emptiness in our hearts. For those who don't know, Raelynn's father, Mr. Hart, perished in a plane accident this past Saturday."

Bentley took a deep breath, his eyes scanning the audience. "Now, Mr. Hart didn't like me much, but I love his daughter, and his absence is greatly felt today," Bentley continued. "As you can see up front, there are two empty seats, one in honor of Mr. Hart and the other for Raelynn's mother, who couldn't make the trip as she is still grieving."

Bentley paused for a moment, looking at Raelynn with a reassuring smile. "Baby, I know you wish your dad was here, and it breaks my heart that I can't fix that for you," Bentley said, his voice choked with emotion. "But what I can do is this." Bentley pointed back to the top of the aisle, and there stood Olivia, Raelynn's mother, all smiles as she looked down at her daughter and Bentley.

Raelynn was overcome with emotions, unable to believe that her mother had made the trip. The last she had heard was that her mother wouldn't be able to make it.

As Olivia approached Bentley and Raelynn, she embraced them both in a deep, warm hug. Tears filled the eyes of everyone in attendance as they cheered, touched by the powerful display of love and support. Bentley held Raelynn and Olivia close, feeling grateful that Raelynn's mother was able to be there on this special day, despite the pain of their recent loss.

As Olivia gracefully took her seat, Bentley and Raelynn intertwined their hands and gazes, attentively absorbing the minister's words as the wedding ceremony continued.

The minister, acknowledging the couple's decision to craft their own vows, inquired, "Which of you would like to go first?" Without hesitation, Raelynn volunteered.

"Bentley, today I stand before you in absolute awe of the remarkable man and father you've become to Skylar. It's challenging to articulate the profound love you've brought into my life. Since the moment we crossed paths, I sensed something extraordinary about you, and I am profoundly grateful that destiny led us together, not once, but twice because I would be utterly lost without you. Your unwavering support during my moments of doubt, fear, and especially following my father's untimely passing has been a blessing beyond measure. In the presence of our cherished ones, I pledge these vows to you. I promise to love you with every fiber of my being, to stand as your equal partner in all facets of life. I vow to nurture your dreams, to remain steadfast at your side through every triumph and trial, and to serve as your constant source of love and encouragement. I pledge to listen with an open heart, to communicate honestly and openly, and to face any challenges that arise hand-in-hand. I promise to share in both the laughter and tears that life brings, to be patient, understanding, and forgiving, acknowledging our shared humanity and the inherent imperfections therein. Together, we will craft a home imbued with love, warmth, and solace—a sanctuary where we can flourish individually and together, allowing our love to continuously blossom. I vow to shower you with love and appreciation each day, to remain faithful and steadfast, prioritizing our bond above all else. Together, we'll navigate life's journey, hand-in-hand, tackling every adventure and obstacle as a united front. Bentley, you've captured my heart in a way no one else ever could. You are my rock, my confidant, my true love. I am profoundly grateful to call you my husband, and I promise to love you fiercely and unconditionally for all eternity," Raelynn declared, her voice quivering with emotion.

Bentley smiled fighting back the tears. "Damn I should have gone first because how the hell am I supposed to follow that up?" Bentley joked.

Everyone, including Raelynn laughed as Bentley took a deep breath before beginning his own vows to Raelynn.

"Raelynn, today, as I stand here, I am in awe of the love we share, and I am honored to be able to call you my partner, my confidante, and my best friend. From the moment I met you, my heart knew that you were someone extraordinary, and my love for you has grown deeper with each passing day. See you came into my life when I was lost and broken and needing direction. You have been my direction. You have been my light that I needed when everything around me was dark and grey. You have healed this heart of mine and made me believe in love again. You are my lighthouse, my anchor. As we begin this journey of marriage, I make these vows to you. I promise to love you with all that I am, to honor and cherish you, and to always put you and our relationship as my top priority. I promise to support your dreams, to encourage your passions, and to stand by your side through all the ups and downs that life may bring. I promise to be your rock, your comfort, and your safe haven in times of need, and to share in your joys and sorrows. I promise to always be there to listen to you with an open heart, to hold your hand through life's challenges, and to celebrate your victories with uncontainable joy. I promise to be patient, understanding, and forgiving, and to always strive to be the best version of myself for you and for us. I promise to be loyal, faithful, and devoted to our love, and to work tirelessly to keep our love alive and thriving. With you, Raelynn, I have found my home, my heart, and my soulmate. Today and every day, I choose you to be my partner in life, and I promise to love you unconditionally, now and forever. I love you with all my heart, and I am honored to be yours for all eternity." Bentley expressed emotionally with his voice shaking.

Everyone in attendance was moved by their vows as they could feel the love the two shared for each other.

"Well, why should we wait any longer. Bentley do you take Raelynn Hart to be your wife?" the minister asked.

Bentley smiled and without hesitation said, "I do!"

"Raelynn, do you take Bentley to be your husband?" the minister asked looking at Raelynn.

Raelynn hesitated as she smiled and looked back at Cassidy, "I don't know do I?" Raelynn said jokingly before saying "I do!"

Everyone laughed as the newlyweds' locked lips for their first kiss as husband and wife.

"I now pronounce to you for the very first time Mr. Bentley and Mrs. Raelynn Riggs!" the minister shouted as everyone cheered and again the newlyweds locked lips exchanging a kiss to display their love.

The sound of applause filled the air as Bentley and Raelynn shared their first kiss as husband and wife, sealing their vows with a moment of pure, unbridled joy. As they pulled away, their eyes met, sparkling with love and happiness.

Hand in hand, they turned to face their guests, their hearts overflowing with gratitude for the love and support surrounding them. Friends and family erupted into cheers and applause, celebrating the union of two souls destined to be together.

As the sun began to set, casting a warm glow over the 'Amazing Graze,' Bentley and Raelynn embraced, savoring the magic of their wedding day. In that moment, surrounded by loved ones and the beauty of nature, they knew that their love story was just beginning.

With laughter, music, and the promise of a lifetime of love ahead, Bentley and Raelynn danced under the stars, their hearts united in a bond that would withstand the test of time. As they twirled and swayed to the rhythm of their love, they whispered vows of forever, grateful for the journey that had led them to this moment of pure, unadulterated bliss.

And as the night faded into dawn, Bentley and Raelynn embarked on their new adventure hand in hand, ready to face whatever the future held together. For in each other's arms, they had found their home, their sanctuary, and their happily ever after.

And so, their love story continued, a testament to the enduring power of love, music, and the unwavering belief that true love conquers all. As they walked into the future together, Bentley and Raelynn knew that with love as their guide, they could weather any storm and bask in the sunshine of endless possibilities.